SWEET SEDUCTION

"Damn it, woman, don't ever sneak up on a man like that." Aaron lowered his knife and reached out to grab her hand.

"I—I just wanted to touch you," she sobbed.

"What for?" His hands were on her shoulders, his smoky eyes filled with desire.

"I thought you wanted me as I—" Blushing furiously, she bent her head in shame, then burst out, "I want so desperately to hold you."

"Oh, Rumor, my sweet, my own . . ." His lips came down on hers in a bruising kiss as he explored her mouth and crushed her against his chest, making her breathless and panicky.

She bit his lip. Drat the man! She would not be taken by a clumsy oaf of an American patriot. She'd teach him a thing or two.

With a cry of rage, he was on his feet, blood seeping from his mouth.

Looking at him with a sweet smile, Rumor said quietly, "Your undue haste flatters me, Mr. Fleming, but please allow me to remove my clothes before you ravish me. . . ."

PASSION'S DISGUISE

RITA BALKEY

ZEBRA BOOKS

KENSINGTON PUBLISHING CORP.

ZEBRA BOOKS

are published by

Kensington Publishing Corp.
475 Park Avenue South
New York, NY 10016

First printing: September, 1988

Printed in the United States of America

This one's for Meredith Cary
Ever faithful, ever true

Prologue

With an artful movement of her slender arms, the delicately lovely young girl in the gauzy silken gown lifted the dagger high above her head, her flower-petal hands encircling the encrusted silvery sheath. Holding it there, head thrown back, she cried out, "O happy dagger! This I do for thee, sweet Romeo!"

Juliet's melodic voice echoed in the darkened theater, soaring rich and clear above the screeching of the rooftop weathercock, whirling madly in a strong North Atlantic wind. Undaunted, Rumor Seton, the seasoned Jamaican actress who was playing Juliet, welcomed the unholy racket. The fearsome banshee wailing sent shivers down every spine, forming a perfect accompaniment to the timeless Shakespearean tragedy being enacted on the makeshift stage.

She counted mentally to ten. The silence beyond the footlights was total. Even the wooden cock on the rooftree had ceased its wailing, as if holding its breath. The universe, it seemed, was waiting for the lovestruck maid to plunge the dagger into her sweet bosom and join her beloved Romeo in death.

7

A feeling of glorious triumph swelled Rumor's heart. The play had gone well. Her acting skill and fresh young beauty had once again ensnared her audience in a web of enchantment. Eighteen-year-old Rumor knew she was good. And getting better all the time. The critics thought so, too. "The Jamaican minx is a perfect Juliet, a cunning, bewitching, luminous mix of purity and naive eroticism," one had written of her.

The tension in the theater pulsed like a living thing. Lowering the dagger, inch by agonizing inch, Rumor plunged it into her heart, making a quarter turn with her supple body so that the audience could not see the stage weapon fold up. With a long, drawn-out half-sigh, half-sob designed to break the heart of any who heard it, she fell upon the prostrate body of her dead lover, holding her hands to her gown to keep it from riding up and uncovering her milk-white thighs.

She would lie there for two full minutes. Those were David's orders. He had told her, "Give them time to pull themselves together, the weeping women must wipe their eyes and cheeks, the men must blow their noses." Besides being manager, David was Rumor's stepfather, and her guardian since her mother's death last year in Jamaica.

"Oh, my God!" a woman sobbed aloud. There was an epidemic of coughing, a spate of nose blowing, even a sneeze or two, usually faked, David chuckled to himself, to give the spectator an excuse to draw out a hanky from a pocket to wipe his tears.

As David expected, there was no applause. There could be none. The American Rebels in their high and mightiness had prohibited all theatricals within the colonies. "Stage dramas and comedies are time-consuming, money-wasting, sinful," the posted edict had proclaimed.

The message had been clear and blunt. All citizens of these newly independent United States of America must bend every energy to winning the righteous battle against the tyrannical English king. In the grim months and years ahead, David mused, there would be no room for pleasure.

But despite the ban, many New Yorkers were eager enough for diversion to sneak into contraband performances, like this one. For three weeks past, David and the Seton Company had been secretly flouting the direct order of the new Continental Congress by presenting scenes from Shakespeare's plays in the windowless loft of a weathered sugar house on a lonely stretch of New York waterfront. To his great relief, there had been no trouble from the authorities. People going in and out the narrow door raised no suspicion. To the passersby, they were obviously transacting business — buying sugar, flour, spices from abroad.

But the sound of a hundred hands clapping, the echo of wild "bravos" would surely fetch the magistrates. Or, David thought bitterly, those damnable Sons of Liberty, those rascally Rebel scum. Disguised as naked Mohawk Indians, replete with scalplocks and war paint, a band of rabid patriots had been enforcing their own brand of punishment, terrorizing any who defied the edicts of the revolutionary government.

In the first weeks of their colonial tour, David had worried every night about being attacked by the Sons of Liberty. The young hellions had driven off every actor and actress from the northern colonies, even to the point of putting them, bag and baggage, on a ship for Jamaica, the sunny West Indian island from which most of them had come.

But in a few moments, when the curtain fell, David Seton's worries would be over. A British fleet the size of the vanquished Spanish Armada fairly choked the harbor, and by dawn the red-coated Royal Army would be marching six abreast through the city. "Rule Britannia" would sound from drum and fife, and deadly bayonets would flash and glitter in the morning sun. The city would be free at last of the tyrannical Rebels.

As Rumor lay on the stage, she reflected that tomorrow night she would once again hear the delicious thunder of applause. She would take the twenty curtain calls that were her due. God, how she had missed all that in the months they had been in these puritanical provinces.

Maybe, if they worked fast enough, they could even perform tomorrow in a decent theater. There were several fine ones in this city, which had flourished before the bluenoses took over.

One of Romeo's silver jacket buttons was digging into her soft cheek. She winced, but dared not move. Juliet was supposed to be quite dead. Rumor stuck a sharp-nailed finger into Romeo's neck above his stiff medieval collar, hissing through tight lips, "Move your chest."

Nothing happened. Romeo was actually a wickedly handsome lad named Percy, and he was fast asleep, having drunk too much wine, as always, at dinner.

From where she lay, Rumor could see big Caesar's black face grinning broadly at her from behind the curtain. His hands clutched the rope, ready to pull, and his full lips were moving in a sibilant whisper. "The dagger, the dagger."

Quickly she opened her hand and allowed the silver blade to fall onto the stage, signaling to the audience that Juliet's spirit had left her body, to join that of her dead Romeo. A long, collective ripple passed over the audience. It was a sound like the rustling of autumn leaves and never failed to raise goose bumps on Rumor's entire body.

Caesar grinned again, winking one dark brown eye at her. "Well done!" His evident relief was almost comical.

Despite the imminent British occupation of the city, David and Caesar had been anxious about a Rebel attack on the sugar house. A group of twenty savage Indians were in the audience, leaning against the walls on three sides, all decked out as for a ceremony — feathered headdresses, war paint on their hawkish faces and muscular bodies. Tomahawks dangled menacingly from the band above their breechclouts.

From time to time, as she moved about the stage, Rumor could see the gleam of their shaven heads, and the single tuft of hair on the crown which marked them as belonging to the Mohawk tribe.

Before curtaintime, Caesar had walked into the theater to check the audience. He had come backstage with a puzzled frown. "Those Indians are too quiet, and I saw one with blue eyes, I swear. I think they're the Sons of Liberty."

David had snorted. "Nonsense. I've seen any number of blue-eyed Indians. They're not so rare as you think. Besides, nothing's been heard of the Sons for weeks. Doubtless, they've all run off like rats before the British, just like their booby in chief George Washington."

Rumor had ventured, "The savages have been here for three nights running. They seem very civilized. If they wanted to attack us, they would have done so by now. Don't you think so, Calpurnia?"

11

She had turned to Caesar's buxom wife, who had rolled her ebony eyes back in her head, as if terror-stricken. "No, I don't, Miss Rumor Seton. I drew a two of spades this afternoon, when I laid out the cards. We'll all lose our scalps tonight." Her wide black nostrils had flared. "You'd better start saying any prayers your mama taught you."

The woman had cast a baleful eye on David Seton, as he donned tight satin breeches for his part as Romeo's friend, Mercutio. "We should've all gone straight back to Jamaica when that proclamation came out. Now it's too late."

There had been a titter from the half-drunk Percy. "There's a Jamaica-bound packet at the dock a few hundred yards away. We could be on it within the hour." He had shivered, hugging his body. "They tell me that New York winters would freeze the backside off a polar bear."

Now Rumor's back began to ache from her prone position. Surely two minutes had passed. She looked again at Caesar but he was staring glassy-eyed out over her head into the theater. His black face had turned an ashen gray as if he'd seen the devil himself rise up from hell.

Frightened, Rumor lifted her head to peer into the audience. What she saw was not the devil, but a tidal wave of savages surging onto the stage, leaping nimbly over the candle footlights, tomahawks raised high. As they ran, a bloodcurdling whoop issued from their wide-open mouths. It was a noise like a thousand twirling weathercocks.

Rumor froze, as her very blood turned to ice. She was only half aware that Percy had vanished and that the savages had knocked over the stage candles, setting the dusty curtains afire. Instantly the oiled paper backdrops roared into flame with a whoosh.

On her knees, head up, she was paralyzed with fright. It was all nightmares rolled into one. So this is how she was to die, she thought wildly, burnt to a crisp, hideously, in utmost agony, writhing like a witch, or a virgin of old sacrificed to a pagan god.

Virgin! A wild thought consumed her. She was a virgin. She was to be the human sacrifice for this pagan holocaust. Only eighteen, she would die without ever knowing the love of a man.

Unable to bear the sight of the voracious fire, Rumor bent her head into her hands, her hip-long honey-brown hair falling about her like a shroud. She prayed, "Now I lay me —"

In her torment, she imagined that a strong, loving arm went round her waist, lifting her up. Another arm cradled her knees. Was she in heaven, then being carried to her dear dead mama by an angel?

But she soon realized her savior was no angel. He was very solid, very human, very warm. The arms that held her close were thick and taut and firm as iron bands around a rum barrel. A rough male hand pressed her face against a neck that reeked of strong, masculine sweat, singed hair, and something else she could not place.

Paint! War paint! She knew that smell. The actors had used some vivid Indian pigments brought them by a trader.

She was being carried out of the fire by one of the savages who had attacked them. Her initial flash of pure terror was quickly replaced by a feeling of wondrous gratitude that in turn yielded almost instantly to a curious tingly feeling in her lower torso.

As the Mohawk strode masterfully out of the burning theater and through the screaming crowd, holding his hapless victim close, Rumor felt a sudden jolt of pleasure shake the center of her being. A

13

warmth crept into the secret place between her thighs. A rush of blood into her veins brought a kind of heat she knew had nothing to do with the fire.

Could this be passion, she thought, amazed. This searing touch of flesh on flesh, this bittersweet yearning to feel a man's skin against your own, to hold on and never let go? Even if the man was a mindless, cruel savage who would use her as a stallion does the mare? Hard and cruel and completely without pity?

No one in the world but her mama and her nurse Calpurnia had ever held her close like this. Rumor Seton had never kissed a man except on stage. Mama had warned her of the evils of passion. "Don't let any man get under your skin," she used to say.

Now Rumor finally understood what her Mama had meant. Helplessly, she thought, if he takes me to his wigwam and makes me slave to his unbridled, primitive passions, will I have strength to fight him off?

Outside, the cool night air rudely brought her to her senses, and when the Indian dumped her like a sack of dried corn on the cobbles outside the sugar house, all passion left her. Obviously, the savage did not share her momentary lust.

Without a word, her brawny savior moved into the shadows beyond a bonfire which crackled in the middle of the street.

Scrambling up, Rumor darted after him to thank him for her life, but was caught and hauled back by another Indian who shouted to the others, "Ho, lads, who will be the first to taste the little Jamaican piece?"

One of the men at the fire called back. "Later,

14

Jake. After we have some fun with her fancy man, we'll help you entertain the girl."

Wildly, she gazed around as best she could, for the second Indian held her fast from behind with two cruel hands on her upper arms. Circling the bonfire, Mohawks were stirring the bubbling contents of a huge iron cauldron, set on a tripod over the fire.

They were singing a rabid song she'd heard before. "Huzza, huzza, huzza, in freedom we live, and in freedom we die."

With numbing shock Rumor realized that the painted warriors were not Mohawks at all, but were really the Sons of Liberty! With a gasp, she peered at the place where her rescuer had disappeared. Nothing could be seen but thick black smoke and flames.

Perhaps he had gone back into the inferno to rescue any who might be trapped. David, Caesar, Calpurnia might still be in there, being burned alive. The tinder dry sugar house was completely enveloped in flames.

Frantically Rumor whipped her head around again, straining against her captor, searching for her loved ones. A goodly crowd was now assembled on the cobblestones as drunken patrons poured out of nearby taverns to join the theater audience and dockside stragglers.

The noise was deafening, the crowd looked threatening. She could be thrown to the ground and raped in front of their very eyes, and no one would move to save her.

Raising her rich stage voice to its highest and most piercing, she called out, "David, where are you? I'm here, I'm safe. Da—aa—vi-i-d!"

Her agonizing call ended on a sob, as her captor

tightened his grip. "David is it? Well now, missy, somethin' tells me you're gonna see your precious David sooner than you think."

As he talked, the man thrust one hand down into her bosom to cup her rounded breast. Feverishly, he began to knead the soft, tender flesh.

Rumor winced at the pain, but what was happening at the fire drove all sense of modesty or the very real threat to her virtue from her mind. Some poor wretch was being dragged by two men toward the tar pot. He was stark naked, from gray head to spindly legs.

"David!" Rumor lunged forward but was forced back by her captor.

Although David Seton was only fifty now, he had always seemed older, being thin and frail. As he drew close to where Rumor was being held outside the sugar house, he fixed suffering blue eyes on hers.

"Save yourself, Rumor, for I cannot. Run, run like hell!"

They were daubing tar on his writhing body when he called out again. "Caesar got away. As for Calpurnia, I don't know. I fear for her—"

A woman in the crowd called out, "My God, they're going to dip the poor man in boiling tar! Someone go for the British soldiers. I saw an entire brigade on the dock, ready to march."

But no one moved—all were engrossed in the gruesome spectacle of an old man being tortured to death by a troop of stalwart Sons of Liberty.

These so-called Rebel patriots are truly savages, Rumor raged inwardly. A hatred fiercer than she had ever imagined began to fill her heart. Rumor's captor now had both hands on her breasts, and was kneading vigorously. His panting breath was hot on the back of her neck. An enormous erection was pushing into her buttocks. With a desperate rush of strength born of rage and terror, she pulled away from him, sending him sprawling with a curse.

Shrieking like a demented thing, she threw herself on the cobbles by the fire, curling her arms around David's legs.

"Mercy, in the name of God, have mercy. Do not do this vile thing. He is my father, and has never harmed a living soul."

"He's an actor, ain't he," a loud voice jeered. "He shoulda took himself back to Jamaica with the rest of the sinful lot."

Regaining his feet, her captor pulled her from David with such violence that she fell perilously close to the fire. Her long hair began to burn. Instantly, another man came forth, stamping out the burning locks, and drew her up into his arms. Almost absently, he thrust out a long foot and kicked her captor in the groin. The man doubled up in agony, clutching his genitals.

"Begone, Jacob," growled a soft, southern American voice, "before I have you dumped into that boiling tar yourself. There'll be no rapine while I'm a Son of Liberty."

Gratefully, Rumor gazed into the hawklike face looming above her in the orangey firelight. For the second time that night, the tall Mohawk had rescued her. Their eyes met and locked. His were a smoky blue and for a long moment the horror surrounding them vanished, and she found herself caught up in a hypnotic gaze. She thought she saw tenderness there also, so she whispered urgently, "Please, can't you save my father?"

He shook his head, from which he had removed the feathered headband. But the thick, colorful war paint still covered every inch of his face. She was struck by the strength of the longish nose, the sweep of brow, the jutting chin.

"It's too late," he snapped, then, added more gently, "I couldn't stop it anyway, if I tried. They'd have my hide. Even if he really *is* your father—" He emitted a raspy little laugh. "Which I very much doubt, Mistress Seton. It's odd that you call him by his Christian name. Why not Father, or even Papa, as a daughter should."

"David took the place of the father I never had," she responded heatedly, "we were friends as well. I adored him, as did Mama—" She stopped as a shout went up. The crowd was throwing feathers at poor David, who was now completely covered with glistening tar. She could hear him gasping and spluttering for breath, as the feathers crept into his nose and mouth.

"He's dying, I must go to him," she moaned.

But all her struggles to free herself only made him tighten his ironlike grip. "You fool," he grated, "if they get hold of you again, they'll rape you to death. In these colonies, an actress is considered something lower than a prostitute, and only slightly higher than a pig."

She gaped into his face, but his blue eyes were fixed on the grisly scene by the tar pot. A dreamy smile was playing about the Mohawk's lips as he watched David's tormentors hoisting him up on a rail. The devils then lined up on both sides of the tarred man, preparing to march him through the streets, like a trophy of war.

The old man's head had fallen on his chest, and they were having trouble getting him to sit on the narrow rail. His tarry body kept sliding off, and his hands hung limply at his sides, his head lolling drunkenly from side to side.

Unable to bear the pitiful sight, Rumor dug her face into the shaven chest of her rescuer, sobbing hysterically.

"Merciful God," she prayed, "let him die, quickly."

"Your prayer is answered," her captor mumbled. Then, raising his voice to a thunderous shout he said, "For the love of heaven, put the man down. He's dead."

Rumor lifted her head from his neck to stare at him. The dreamy expression once more came into the smoky eyes, as he murmured, "Good night, sweet prince, and flights of angels sing thee to thy rest!"

Amazingly, incredibly, the Rebel was quoting from Shakespeare's *Hamlet*. Then before she could speak, he started loping through the crowd, across the cobbles, weaving in and out of the narrow, burning streets. A number of fire wagons were busily pumping water from the bay into tanks in a desperate, but futile attempt to put out the rapidly spreading fire.

He moved easily, rhythmically, with the grace of a natural athlete. His heart was thudding hammerlike under her cheek. A tiny red tattoo in the shape of a turtle encircled his left nipple. He must be a sailor, she mused. Or was he actually an Indian? Many native Americans had been educated by the missionaries, David had told her, and could read, write, and speak respectable English. Quite possibly, some could even quote from Shakespeare.

Emotionally drained, not caring if her savior were Indian, English, American, or even Eskimo, Rumor lay within the circle of the man's powerful arms. David's horrible death did not seem real as yet. She would think about it later. It had been that way when Mama died. The mind and heart can bear only

19

so much pain before it closes down, like a trapdoor on a raging beast.

Drowsily, she contemplated the rippling muscles of the man's broad chest, which she now saw bristled with spiky new hairs. So he was *not* an Indian. Indians were naturally hairless on the chest. She wondered, idly, what color his hair would be when grown out again. Imagine, a grown-up, educated man like this one pretending to be an Indian! Like little boys at play.

That tingly warmth was creeping into her loins again, a delicious, mindless, abandoned feeling which she welcomed. It meant life.

Everyone she had ever loved was dead. Mama had died last year from a fever. Now sweet David was dead. Her dear childhood nurse Calpurnia had been her only true friend. And her guardian and friend Casear—was it possible that his huge strong body was now a heap of ashes?

In the midst of all this death, Rumor craved the life she felt in the arms of this Son of Liberty. But Mama had always warned, "Passion for a man is deadlier than a witch's potion. It dulls your senses, confuses your brain, and bewitches you, so that you will gladly sell your soul for him."

Mama spoke from bitter experience. Madeleine d'Estivet had fled her native France to escape a forced marriage. She had fallen promptly, madly in love with a ne'er-do-well of a gambler right on the dock at New Orleans as she stood, confused, her carpetbag in her hands. Beaumont Carter got her pregnant, wasted her fortune, and abandoned her. "Just like a melodrama," Mama used to say, grimacing.

But not all men were like that, Rumor had always hoped. This man, this fraudulent savage, who

20

moved so swiftly through burning city streets was her knight in shining armor. Had he not saved her? Twice? Yet he had stood by, smiling, quoting Shakespeare, while her sweet David was dying horribly.

A sudden, startling thought made her go rigid. *Rumor Seton, you are a fool, an utter nincompoop. He saved you from the others so that he could ravish you himself in some secret lair.*

Her head came up sharply to strike his chin. "Murderer, ravisher," she yelled. "I swear before God to kill you for the wicked deeds you've done tonight."

Pushing with both hands on his chest, she kicked and squirmed with all her might to free herself from his arms. But his grip remained firm. Recalling his treatment of the would-be rapist, she shoved her knee into his groin, at the same time biting him in the neck with her sharp white teeth.

She heard a smothered oath, and the hand under her knees let go as he clutched his genitals. Nimbly, she slid out of his arms and started running down the street, but he soon caught up with her. She felt herself being pulled violently around to stare once more into the painted face.

"Damn you, woman," he gritted, in a voice filled with pain, "you are a witch, I swear."

"I'll kill you with my own two hands," she spluttered, even as she reeled toward him. "This is my vow."

Without warning, he hauled back a sinewy arm, delivering a stunning blow upon her chin.

As she felt the darkness closing in, the bloodred figure of a turtle filled Rumor's blurring eyes.

Chapter One

Aaron Fleming gazed moodily out the third-story window of a tall brick house in New York City, whose blackened ruins were gradually emerging into a dismally muggy autumn dawn. A third of the wooden buildings had been destroyed in the blaze that had started at the old sugar house. God only knows, he thought guiltily, how many poor souls had been roasted in their beds, how many more deprived of shelter for the coming winter.

The fire was a tragic accident. You could hardly fault the Sons of Liberty for the careless placing of those footlight candles. Anyone—an actor who walked too far to the edge, or even a drunken front-row spectator—could have started the conflagration at any time.

To his credit, Aaron had argued strenuously against attacking the contraband theater. But to no avail. The New York unit of the Sons of Liberty wanted one last stab before the British occupied the city at what they called the "lewd" displays put on nightly by the Seton Company.

Aaron had yielded, finally, to the majority, his love for the theater coloring his better judgment. Firing the old building meant that he would get to see the play. *Romeo and Juliet* was one of his favorites.

But then, Aaron loved all of Shakespeare's dramas. Ever since boyhood, when his mother had taken him to Williamsburg to view the productions at the splendid brick theater in the Virginia capital, he had loved the stage. Shakespeare's plays, both comedies and tragedies, had been presented regularly by Jamaican companies.

That part of last night's adventure had been a joy, hearing those beautiful, inmortal words again, watching the poignant drama of star-crossed lovers unfold before his eyes. Cajoling the others to string it out three whole days and nights had taken all his powers of persuasion. There was always the chance that the British, already massing in the harbor, would occupy the city before the attack and make the whole enterprise useless. Aaron wasn't worried about the Lobsterbacks attacking the Sons. Most of them were straight from England and would run like hell from anything with feathers on its head.

Damnation, though, it had been a lark until the accidental fire and the tarring to death of the company manager. But the man deserved it. Men had been punished for less than he had done. Not only had Seton flouted the express command of the Continental Congress against theatricals, but with the help of his Jamaican connections, had been smuggling forbidden British tea into the city for months, making a tidy profit at it, too, if reports were true.

Aaron reached a long white-gloved finger beneath his thickly powdered wig to scratch his shaven head. Much as he enjoyed dressing up like a wild Indian and scaring the bejeebers out of lawbreakers, he hated the itch which accompanied the returning hair.

His chest was also on fire. But it was far from

24

easy to get at that part of his anatomy, smothered as it was by layers of dandified garments.

The tall, totally masculine Virginian was forced to dress up as a macaroni when he assumed his alter ego as Sir Oliver Mowbray, keeper of the royal brothel and counterspy extraordinaire, a masquerade Aaron thoroughly detested.

Sourly, he stared fixedly out the window. A squadron of British soliders were marching up the street below. They stepped smartly to the music of bagpipe and drums. In their crimson coats and white breeches, they were a reassuring sight to the war-weary citizens of America's biggest town.

Judging from the sound of the cheers and huzzas resounding from the people lined up on the stoops and roadsides, the Redcoats were as welcome as flowers in May.

The soldiers passed on, and Adam turned his attention to the nearby steeple thrusting into the now bright sky. Thanks to a fortuitous turn of wind, the conflagration had not reached this far north, and St. Paul's Chapel had been spared. The handsome Georgian house in which he stood had also escaped with every brick in place.

The untidy clutter of shacks and hovels surrounding the church was known as Holy Ground. It teemed with life. This makeshift village housed the sprawling dens of iniquity which would from today, the first day of the British occupation, serve the king's officers and men with the traditional wine, women, and song. The Rebels before them had been served in the same hovels with gusto, if not always with refinement. Harlots, barkeeps, and musicians know no politics, Aaron mused wryly.

A sudden, painful throbbing, centering on a wound in his neck, brought a wince to his craggy

25

features. Gingerly, he touched the sore place. It was hot, inflamed. He'd have to get a tincture on it before it festered. People would start asking questions. A bite on the neck would be difficult to explain. Sir Oliver Mowbray was known as a man who had no use for women, and what other creature, save a teething infant, would plant its teeth into a man's neck?

Playing the dandy was a masquerade prepared with exquisite care by Aaron Fleming. General George Washington had given a few choice bits of sage advice to Aaron. He had also ordered his secretary to forge a letter. The general's secretary was a wonder with the quill.

When, supposedly fresh from England, Aaron had reported to General Sir William Howe, the commander of British forces in America, he carried a letter, reputedly from King George himself, which told a sad tale of a young man made into a eunuch by an unfortunate fall from a horse.

"To overcome his tragedy, my wife's cousin has become a dandy," the letter had said, "but is intelligent and capable. He has been living in France, but wishes to be with his countrymen. Find some useful task for him to do in the colonies."

Delighted, Howe had placed Sir Oliver in charge of the brothel, then at the Staten Island headquarters. "No task is more important to the winning of the war," the British commander in chief had told Lord Mowbray, whom, whatever else he was, demanded respect as the queen's cousin.

"Men must have their pleasures." He had flashed a lewd grin. "Women of that sort oft tend to be a bit wild."

The counterfeit dandy had fooled everyone. General Howe was happy to have found a man for his harlots and General Washington was happy with his top spy.

For the past year Aaron had played a brilliant role. He had delivered reports of Rebel movements to British General Sir William Howe, and as Aaron Fleming, buckskin patriot, he informed General Washington about the British.

There was a small but crucial difference between the two assignments. The information to Howe was false.

Now he would be chatelain in charge of the brothel at Holy Ground.

Aaron was vainly proud of his brilliant playacting as an effeminate macaroni. He had always loved the theater, but that was before he fell in love.

His mind dwelt on the lovely bitch who had left her mark on his neck. For three nights as he had watched her on the stage, his eyes had feasted on her beauty, and his lust had raged inside him. Lust? No, he admitted grudgingly, this was more than what a man felt when he wanted to mount a slut from Holy Ground. Unfortunately, Aaron Fleming was deeply, passionately, irrevocably in love with a woman who was unworthy of him.

Rumor Seton was a consummate actress who would surely break the heart of any man fool enough to think she could be true. A strumpet who no doubt spread her legs for any whose palm was crossed with sufficient money. A man might just as well bed down with a rattlesnake.

He had already endured agonies for love. For the past three nights as he stood in the crowded and stuffy theater, he had sweated like a randy stallion in that greasy war paint, while a cunning, bewitching Juliet on the stage had stolen his heart and soul, and body, too, if his constant state of arousal were any

27

indication.

In the darkened sugar house, beneath the loose, heavy deerskin breechclout, his rebellious loins were given full rein. But in his now snug-fitting satin breeches, a telltale bulge would be ludicrous, and downright disastrous.

There it goes again, he groaned inwardly, as he felt the dismaying movement between his legs. The mere thought of Rumor Seton had stirred his desire. Alarmed, he turned to glance into the tall mirror on the wall. It had taken him a full hour in his locked bedroom, to scrub off the war paint and another hour to dress for his first day as chatelain for the king's brothel.

With trepidation his glance slid to his green silk breeches, flowered in silver and gold. The place between his thighs seemed to him as round and full as a small Virginia smoked ham. He had to get rid of it, before anyone else noticed it.

The austere face of his commander General Washington appeared in his thoughts. "Major Fleming," he had said in his soft Virginia voice, "a successful spy must above all keep shy of females. Even the most casual encounter can be your undoing."

His telltale bulge gone at last, Adam turned to view the woman on the four-poster bed. It had been laughably simple to sneak her into the house. In the clamor and confusion of the British takeover, a tall Indian with a limp woman in his arms had not aroused suspicion. Many were carrying the sick and elderly from the fire. The officer in charge of the Georgian brick, which was part of Holy Ground, was in a frenzy sorting out the hordes of women seeking refuge in the brothel.

Feasting on the beauty of his prize for a few precious moments longer, Aaron moved with prac-

28

ticed ease into his persona as Sir Oliver. As a fop, he now assessed her absently. She was a piece of merchandise, no more. He had trained himself to banish all feeling from his eyes, so that they presented at all times a vapid, vacant look. After many hours of practice he had managed to set his strong, masculine face into a supercilious, impersonal smirk.

A bar of sun from the window fell upon the wealth of Rumor's brown hair, gilding it with threads of gold. The delicate face showed a perfection one saw occasionally in old paintings of Aphrodite. The ugly bruise left by his blow to her chin only served to enhance the alabaster sheen of her skin.

Her flesh was so truly luminous that only a Shakespeare could find words to describe it properly. Aaron clenched his gloved hands to keep from reaching out to touch it. Her head was turned to one side, and the long, lovely line of neck and shoulder brought a maddening pressure to his chest.

Quickly, he shifted his gaze. The tar-stained Juliet gown was pulled up on one side, revealing a stretch of milky thigh. At the top, her rosy nipple peeked out like a shy rosebud from the disheveled neckline. There were bruises on her breast from that animal Jacob, who had tried to rape her.

One day, no matter how long he had to wait, Aaron Fleming would possess her.

It was high time she woke. The day was getting on. She must be bathed and dressed for the journey to Sir William's headquarters on Staten Island.

"Yes, oh my yes, yes, *yes*," he said in a loud, affected high-pitched voice he had worked hard to perfect. "You'll do very well for General Howe. Very well indeed!"

She stirred, turned, buried her face in the pillow.

He coughed raspily.

Sitting up, she gazed at him a moment with clouded brown eyes. Then, holding her head between her hands, she sank back on the pillow, moaning.

Her head was probably on fire, he thought, from the blow he had delivered. He squashed the flicker of regret that he had hit her so hard. He could not afford to feel anything for the tempting wench.

He waited, deliberately silent, imagining her shock when she fully regained her senses. Enlightening her on where she was and what would happen to her promised to be great sport.

Struggling up again, her vision seemed to clear. Seeing the tall man gaping at her, she blanched, and with a hasty movement of her arms, she yanked the counterpane up to hide her exposed bosom. Then, her smooth cheeks took on a blush like a ripe strawberry.

Enchanting, he thought, but he said, "Your modesty is commendable, Miss Seton." His high-bridged nose lifted in disdain. "But please be assured that your female body, naked or covered, is of complete indifference to me."

Her eyes widened, losing their fuzziness. She sniffed, wrinkling her own somewhat smaller nose. "What is that vile odor? And who are you?"

Little men with hammers were moving around in her head, pounding, pounding. Moving nothing but her wide-spaced brown eyes, she examined the room. Handsomely furnished in gleaming dark mahogany, thickly carpeted, tall windows curtained in burgundy damask. Bric-a-brac in porcelain and silver stood about. Obviously the establishment of a gentleman, a very rich gentleman at that.

He was a vision of sartorial splendor—the latest

30

from London no doubt — in his ruffled linen shirt with gold-embroidered gorget at the neck and frock-coat of palest blue satin with the new fashionable deep pockets. Lace blossomed from his wrists, and the heels on his blue satin shoes were three inches high.

The man was at least six four, Rumor reflected, amazed. The fancy high-heeled shoes would make him a towering figure in any gathering. His wig was in the ridiculous macaroni style, sharply raked in front and rising to an absurdly high toupet on top of his head.

Questions danced on Rumor's tongue, but one of Calpurnia's multitude of aphorisms jiggled into her head. "With people you know nothing about, just keep your mouth shut and let them do the talking."

Snatches of an erotic dream nagged at the corners of her consciousness. The man had a garishly painted face, with the nose of an eagle, the slitted eyes of a panther, and a muscular body, with a tiny red turtle around his nipple. In the dream, she lay on a bed of forest leaves, and huge trees arched overhead, shutting out the sky, shutting out the world. He had kissed her on the lips, his arms had lifted her warm body to his, and then . . .

Beyond that, she could not go. How could she even imagine what came next? Rumor had only a nebulous idea of what transpired when a man and woman made love. Every time she tried to think about it, her entire body was covered with shivers of delight and terror.

Aside from the headache and an ache in her chin where the brute of a Son of Liberty had hit her last night, she seemed to be intact.

But how the devil did she get here? Could it be the Red Turtle's house? No matter, this reeking macaroni would shortly inform her, though she could hardly imagine how he could be connected with the handsome savior who had snatched her from a fiery death. She waited, hoping he wouldn't drag it out too long. She was ravenous, and a hearty breakfast would put her completely to rights. Then, she'd have to get David's body and give it a Christian burial.

Ignoring her insult of the cloying perfume which he applied liberally each morning, Sir Oliver laid one languid arm on the carved marble mantel. With maddening slowness, he dipped into his vest pocket and drew out a gem-encrusted snuffbox. Snapping it open, he took a large pinch between thumb and forefinger.

As her headache subsided, Rumor studied the man. He was a genuine peacock, even had a velvety black beauty spot pasted on his cheek. An honest-to-God dandy. She knew his kind. Obviously a man so in love with himself he had no eyes for women. Any other man would not be gazing at her with such vapid contempt. Rumor was far from vain, but she was fully aware of her beauty and the effect it had on a real man.

The dandy sneezed copiously into a lace-trimmed hanky. Fussily, he pushed it back into his sleeve.

"God bless," she said absently.

He threw her a surprised look. Then abruptly he began to speak, mincingly, emphasizing every word. "You have the very great honor, my dear woman, to be in the care of Sir Oliver Mowbray, a lord of the realm, major in His Majesty's army, cousin to his gracious Majesty's beloved consort, Charlotte."

"Lord!" Rumor cut in sarcastically. "I thought there was no aristocracy in the new United States of America."

Moving toward the bed, he drew himself up

proudly to his full six four. His powdered brows lifted to his powdered wig and his stiff lips bent in a disdainful curl. "What is this America of which you speak? England reigns supreme in New York City, as in every inch of the thirteen American colonies."

Waves of relief washed over her. Miraculously, she had fallen into Loyalist hands. Instantly regretting her pert rudeness, she simpered, "I humbly beg your pardon, Lord Mowbray. I, too, am a loyal subject of His Majesty, King George, and am ready to serve him in all possible ways."

A pleased look crossed his powdered face.

Good, Rumor exulted. She would cultivate the man. Such a high-born personage could be of help to her in revenging David's death. Perhaps he could manage to find out if her beloved Caesar and Calpurnia had escaped the fire.

"Bravo!" He smiled, though frostily. "Well said, indeed."

But despite his warm words, his eyes bored into hers with such an icy look that she cringed. Had she said something wrong? Drat the man!

A burst of laughter from downstairs brought her head up in alarm. Doors slammed, footsteps sounded on the stairs. In the corridor outside the room, a man cursed, a woman shrieked. A scuffle appeared to be taking place right outside the door.

"Are there others here?" Suddenly fearful, Rumor huddled into the counterpane,

"I am given the third floor for my quarters," he began, but stopped as a sharp knock on the door brought a scowl to his face. "I am not to be disturbed," he yelled.

A thin female voice came through the paneled wood. "Sir Oliver, your presence is required in the kitchen. The young captain can't deal with the enormous crowd of applicants."

"Entrez!"

Stepping into the room, a young girl with a cheerful, heavily freckled face stared boldly at Rumor from beneath her ruffled servant's cap. "The cap'n's a mere lad, Sir Oliver, I doubt he's ever been in a brothel himself." She giggled. "I trust you get my meanin', sir."

Taking out his hanky, the dandy wearily wiped his face. "I'll come directly."

The girl cocked her head toward Rumor. "Will I be takin' this one downstairs, too? The surgeon will have to examine her 'fore we send 'er over to the huts." She rolled her eyes. "There's such a clamor for more harlots."

"No," he said sharply. "This one is not for Holy Ground. She goes to General Howe. He will have his personal surgeon examine the doxy for disease."

The girl smiled toothily at Rumor. "My, ain't ye the lucky one! Sir William be treatin' his ladies like they be highborn like hisself."

"Hold your tongue, Alice." Sir Oliver snapped. "Have a breakfast brought up for the lady and send a soldier up here." He glanced at Rumor. "Two of them. Can't have her running off, after all the trouble I've been to."

Pausing for one last sneeze into his hanky, the man added dryly, "I don't think Miss Rumor Seton of Jamaica is as eager for our hospitality as the rabble in the kitchen."

The servant departed, slamming the door behind her. Stunned by the conversation, Rumor had thrown the bulky counterpane aside, sliding off the enormous feather mattress. But the massive four-poster was so high, she sprawled in a heap on the carpet. Scrambling to a sitting position, she flung both arms around a needlepointed footstool.

"Am I to understand that I am in a brothel?"

Nodding, he suppressed his mirth at the comical astonishment on her pretty face. Her rosy lips hung wide open, revealing rows of tiny white teeth and a pink tongue.

Pursing his lips, he snorted, "Perhaps you would prefer to be in the lusty clutches of the savage Mohawk who sold you to me?"

He began to pace back and forth in the room, his high-pitched voice rising angrily as words poured forth. *"Merde!* Count your blessings, woman. It's better than you deserve. If I had my way, you would be dispatched without further ado to the hovels in Holy Ground where you would be fresh meat to our hungry enlisted men."

"Holy Ground?" Her fine brows came together, puzzled. "Is that a church?"

He snickered. The usually vapid Sir Oliver was having trouble controlling his expression. "That's the soubriquet applied to the village that huddles around St. Paul's Chapel." He strode toward the tall window. "Come, see for yourself."

Rumor made no reply, huddling against the footstool as if it were a log in a stormy sea. Her face was upturned, and in her wide-eyed expression, he read little fear. Only a strong bravado. Sir Oliver braced himself, half expecting her to fly at him like a squawking hen whose nest has been invaded. Recalling her temper of last night, his hand unconsciously flew to his throbbing neck. Catching himself before he touched the tender bite, and perhaps gave himself away, he ended up scratching his chin thoughtfully.

A smile was tugging desperately at the corners of his lips, but clenching his teeth, he managed to keep his lips together. God, but she looked good enough to eat, sitting there, spraddle-legged, every line of her exquisite female body shouting defiance.

His heart caught as he detected a glaze of tears in the luminous brown eyes. He had once had a mare that color. Obviously a battle was being waged within her. Would she fight, would she succumb? Would she weep? He sensed that the child that still lingered within her was struggling with the emerging woman. She was, after all, very young.

At last the woman won. Thrusting out her chin and bringing her shoulders erect, she raised her head high and flung back her hair with both hands. The bewitching brown eyes took on a distinctly mulish look.

Inside Aaron Fleming's heart a hearty "bravo" could be heard. He hoped General Howe was man enough to handle her, and cursed the fate that kept him from enjoying her himself. But one day he would. Aaron liked the idea of looking forward to taming her as he had that mare so long ago.

"So you bought me from the Indian like a piece of goods?" she asked coolly. "And will you sell me to General Howe in turn?"

Her brain was working furiously. She was in luck. Howe would help her. No highborn gentleman would take any woman by force. The king's highest man on the American continent would soon rectify this horrible mistake and see that this dandified boob got his comeuppance for daring to treat her like a harlot.

Rising up with as much dignity as she could muster in her torn gown, she said bitingly, "Kindly see that I am taken to Sir William Howe immediately."

"*Certainement!*" Sir Oliver bowed his head to hide the smile that had burst out despite his iron will. "Once you are suitably clothed."

Two soldiers entered to guard the general's prize, and Sir Oliver departed to dress for the journey. He hoped the general would take to the little witch. Having her here at Holy Ground would be a living hell for Aaron Fleming. Despite his self-control, his manhood was once more tingling as if someone had sprinkled pepper on the damn thing.

The whole affair had worked out nicely. He was due to report to Howe today in any case. Hundreds of Rebel stragglers and deserters had remained in the city as Washington's forces had retreated. Sir Oliver would have plenty of fabricated news for his British commander.

Then on to Harlem Heights and the other general with news of Howe and the British movements.

Precisely an hour later, Rumor gazed at her transformed image in the tall mirror. Two burly men had brought a small bathtub into the room, with soap and towels and six buckets of cool water. Rumor had put herself into Alice's capable hands and was forced to admit that the result was more than satisfactory. She was truly a lady of fashion, dressed much more elaborately than was her taste.

"The gen'ral likes his ladies dressed to the nines," Alice had assured her.

The billowing hooped skirt of watered silk in a rich teal blue was embroidered with tiny roses and rows of Brussels lace. The velvet bodice was so tight Rumor could scarcely breathe. When she had cried out at the cruel lacing, Alice had scolded, "The gen'ral be fond of big breasts, miss, kind o' spillin' over, if you please. Yours be nice, miss, but we need to push 'em up, up, up."

The ruched neckline did not entirely clear the rosy

areolas around the nipples, but Alice assured her that this was the way all the fine Loyalist ladies walked around. The girl had winked. "With their goods on display."

Bright satin ribbons wound in and out of Rumor's cascading hair, and a few curls at her temple and cheeks added a touch of wantonness. Paste and powder had covered the bruise on her chin, aided by two round beauty patches. She wore no jewelry. She would be showered with gems and trinkets, Alice informed her, "if'n you proves yourself, miss."

Still bothered by the exposed areolas, Rumor tried shoving the soft flesh down into the bodice, but succeeded only in bruising herself. Sighing, she let nature take its course. Nothing must mar her first impression on the British commander. All men, whether highborn or base, were putty in a beautiful woman's hands, Calpurnia was always telling her.

Rumor found herself regretting her lack of actual experience with men. She would be constrained to employ all the wiles learned from her many roles as seductress. She had done a fair Cleopatra once. Rumor was prepared to go to almost any lengths to gain her freedom. Well, almost any. She wasn't sure she was ready to sacrifice her virginity to a lecherous old man.

Challenged, she began to look forward to the encounter with Sir William Howe, and when a liveried footman came to fetch her to the waiting carriage, she stepped into the bright autumn day, with glowing cheeks and sparkling eyes. The footman's admiring glance restored her confidence, which that supercilious Sir Oliver had almost managed to destroy. Thank heaven she was out of his charge, at least.

Now the nightmare could end at last. Not even the

38

gaping crowd gathered on the street could shake her restored spirits. As the footman helped her into the shining red-and-gold two-horse chaise, Rumor shut her ears to the bawdy catcalls. "That's the actress what got burned out last night. They say she was saved by a wild Indian."

A quick reply was added. "Prob'ly took his fill on 'er 'fore he sold 'er to Sir Oliver."

"She be safe now with the fop, tha's for certain."

Then there was an answering cackle. "A slut like that'un might e'en get the fop's pants down."

Her feigned coolness abandoning her, Rumor's cheeks were burning as she sank back on the leather seat in the darkness of the heavily curtained coach. Would she never be free of vile gossip? It wasn't fair. She had done nothing wrong. Perhaps it would be wise to ask the general to send her home to Jamaica, where she was known and respected as a decent woman. But first, David must be buried and Calpurnia and Caesar found. And there was her vow of vengeance . . .

"Mon Dieu," came a high-pitched whiney voice from the gloom of the coach which had started rumbling down the cobbled street at breakneck speed. "The Loyalist rabble is no better than the Rebel scum."

In her embarrassment, Rumor had not noticed that Sir Oliver was already seated in the coach. His cloying scent nearly choked her in the closed vehicle. She tugged at the window curtain, parting it for air.

Heavily, hurtingly, his hand thrust out to come down on her arm. "I wouldn't do that, unless you want a rotten egg in your face."

"Why are you here!" she asked, dismayed that she had not escaped him after all.

"Why, I could trust no one but myself with such a

39

precious quarry." She felt rather than saw the smirk on his face. "Your wiles are far too potent, I fear, for a susceptible underling, no matter how loyal he may be."

Sniffing, she refused to gratify him with a reply.

"Get some sleep," he said. "You'll want to look fresh and rested for the general."

As her eyes became accustomed to the gloom, she saw that he, too, had changed his garments, becoming, though it didn't seem possible, even more resplendent. A brightly flowered brocade frock coat covered him from neck to ankle, and his satin pumps had been exchanged for gleaming leather boots.

Resting his powdered head on the high seat back, Sir Oliver settled himself to sleep. After a few minutes, his deep, regular breathing assured Rumor that he was fast asleep. She waited a while longer, listening to the bustle of the city beyond the curtains.

He began to snore, softly, then a bit louder. Cautiously, she lifted the curtain edge a crack, peering outside. The streets were a beehive. Troops marched in formation, children and dogs running alongside; pigs rooted for garbage in the filthy gutters. They were approaching the waterfront area, Rumor realized, for the masts of tall ships were in view.

Shortly, the carriage reached the docks, and Rumor saw two women fishing from the wharf through her peephole. They looked carefree, happy, as they chatted. The shrill sound of their womanly laughter fell upon her ears.

The carriage stopped with a jolt. The driver and footman descended to clear debris from the roadway. Fearfully, Rumor stole a glance at Sir Oliver, but after a restless turning, he seemed to sleep as sound as ever.

Her brain worked furiously. Women would shield her from men who would enslave her. Women always stuck together. Could she trust this General Howe to deal with her honestly, compassionately?

Quickly, without another thought, Rumor pushed her arm through the curtain, reaching for the outside handle of the door. Like a thunderbolt, she felt a gloved hand encircle her neck, knocking the breath out of her. He whipped her round to face him. "Zounds, woman, would you had brains to match your beauty!"

The coach had started up again with such a jolt that she was hurled against him, and for the second time in as many days Rumor found herself being held fast by a very strong, virile man. His frock coat had fallen open, and she could feel the muscles moving beneath the ruffled linen of his shirt. There was an aura of masculinity about him that belied what he seemed to be. Startled, she thought last night she had been held fast by an Indian who was also not what he had seemed.

The perfumed dandy held Rumor close against him with a grip of steel until the coach was well under way once more. Then, drawing back, he took both her small hands in one of his big ones. With the other he reached behind her to pull the curtain fast again.

His eyes were slits in the dark. He's like a panther, she mused with a tinge of excitement as her gaze locked with his. A sense of great power held in check permeated the stifling carriage. But curiously, she had no fear of him. Rather, she had an almost irresistible desire to pull his silly powdered head down to hers and kiss him squarely, soundly, on his wide, sensuous, mouth.

On his part, Sir Oliver seemed incapable of

speech. His handsome face was working, as if from an inner struggle, and his long nose was actually twitching.

She giggled. The sound seemed to touch off a hidden spark in the man, and for a wild moment she thought she saw a softening in the steel-blue eyes. But it was followed by a flash of pure anguish.

"You poor man," she whispered contritely. "I am a peck of trouble to you, and it's not your fault, either, is it? You're as helpless as I."

She swayed toward him almost drunkenly, but then the carriage stopped again, and the footman was opening the door.

They got into a sloop bristling with cannon and British sailors with rifles on their shoulders. Weaving swiftly in and out of the myriad craft in the harbor, the sloop crossed the bay from Manhattan Island to Staten. The sunny day had unaccountably turned stormy, and the rain was coming down in sheets by the time they were lowered into an open skiff to take them to the shore.

She began to shiver from the cold and wet. Sir Oliver drew a flask from his inner pocket and forced it to her lips. The brandy went down smooth and burning, and as a welcome warmth coursed through her chilled blood, Rumor glanced up to the silent man at her side.

"You'll be greatly relieved, Lord Mowbray, will you not, to be shed of me at last," she said almost tenderly and after a moment, added, feeling a genuine warmth toward the poor man, "I wish to thank you for your tender concern." Her words came out a little wobbly. She had swallowed more brandy than was her wont.

"You seem overconfident of your reception by General Howe," he challenged. "Perhaps he will not want you."

"I will win him over," she twinkled pertly. "I must."

The man with a divided soul stared for a long time at the approaching shore, where men were bustling about, unwinding ropes, ready to receive the sloop. The rain had let up for a moment, and in the light of a pale, watery moon, his face was solemn.

But when he spoke again, his voice was mocking. "You are an actress, are you not, my girl, accustomed to pretending to be other than you are." Then he said in a milder tone, "He will like you, never fear. The general is known as a man with a sharp nose for good horse flesh and for women of quality."

An ironic laugh erupted in Aaron Fleming's gut, but the screeching gulls who whitened the sky above their heads drowned out any sound.

Chapter Two

A red-coated sentry escorted Rumor and Sir Oliver into the spacious stone farmhouse that General Howe had commandeered for his headquarters. An open military cart had transported them from the dock along a rutted road between long avenues of tents. The heartening effect of Sir Oliver's brandy had dissipated long ago. The rain had started up again, and by the time they reached the door, Rumor's velvet cloak and beribboned hair were soaked. She was bedraggled, cold, and hungry. The general would take one look at her and pack her off to an almshouse, she thought, miserably.

It was fully dark now, and every window of the three-story gabled home blazed like a Christmas pudding. Clamorous sounds of revelry—gay music, loud laughter, female shrieks, and accompanying manly shouts—spread throughout the countryside.

"The men are celebrating the British occupation of New York," Sir Oliver mumbled. "Philadelphia will be next to fall. And then—" He shrugged, chuckling mirthlessly, "The filthy revolutionaries will be dealt with as they deserve. Every tree on the eastern shore will sport a hanging Rebel."

Just inside the door, the sentry said, "The general

will see Sir Oliver at once." He nodded to Rumor. "Wait here please, miss."

Her duenna, as she had begun to think of the lanky macaroni, hastened after the soldier down a long central corridor. Rumor was left alone in a large, square hearth room swarming with British officers. Some played cards on tables, some sat on the wide pine-board floor drinking brandy, others lounged against the white plastered walls, conversing idly. Several sat at a long table, busily scratching away with quills on sheets of foolscap.

But at her entrance, one and all fixed bold eyes upon her, staring in delighted amazement. Even the scribblers held their feathered quills aloft as they considered the novelty of a beautiful young woman in their midst.

Bracing herself for the predictably lewd remarks, Rumor lifted her face toward a painting of a landscape over the carved stone mantel, taking herself on the wings of imagination into another world. She prayed to be summoned before the men grew troublesome. Some were very drunk.

The clamor of many voices ceased abruptly, as though a command had been issued.

"Heigh ho, looks like the fop has snagged a winner this time." A tall officer with a pile of gold braid on his shoulders spoke into the silence. He ambled up to Rumor. "I'd wager a month's pay that you'll be the minx to finally kick Liz Loring out of the old man's bed."

Planting himself squarely in her line of vision, he forced Rumor to meet his gaze. Extending a gloved hand, the officer gingerly touched a sodden hair ribbon which had fallen over her brow. "By jove, you do look more like a half-drowned chicken than a courtesan, though. Hope the general is hot enough to dry you out before you catch your death."

His tone was soft, respectful, and the merriment in his black eyes brought a smile to Rumor's mouth. He meant no harm. Men always made jest about these matters.

The roomful of his cohorts laughed uproariously at the officer's wit, and when the sentry returned for her, cries of "Good luck" followed her out of the room.

General Sir William Howe was a bulky man with an olive complexion, a broad, self-indulgent face, a flaring, bulbous nose, and thick, sulky lips. A thickly powered wig was pushed half off his graying hair and his gleaming blue-and-white military coat hung on a hook behind him. A huge linen cloth was tucked about the neck of his ruffled shirt as he gorged from a little table placed in front of him.

She stood there a moment before he looked up, a thick chunk of roast beef impaled on his body knife. Thrusting the meat into his mouth, he sank back in the capacious burgundy leather armchair, chewing, staring.

Sir Oliver sprawled languidly in another armchair, his gloved hands caressing a goblet of dark red wine.

Several wooden chairs stood about, but although she had begun to feel dizzy from lack of food and the excessive heat emanating from a crackling fire, Rumor dared not sit. Nor was she asked to.

She met the general's slit-eyed appraisal with aplomb, staring back unblinkingly, appraising him as he studied her. Everything about him shouted "rake," and she felt waves of repulsion churning in her stomach.

He snapped his fingers, and a wooden-faced orderly poured his commander a snifter full of golden brandy. Lifting his drink, the general twirled it round and round between his pudgy fingers. "Turn round, girl, take off your cloak."

"I regret that we got so wet," Sir Oliver murmured apologetically from his chair, "but I assure you the wench is pure gold beneath the sodden garments."

Scowling, Howe motioned the fop to silence. "That remains to be seen." He glanced sharply at the dandy.

Rumor's bodice had gotten wet in front from the unbuttoned cloak, and she became painfully conscious of her nipples showing darkly through the thin silk. For a terrified moment, she feared that she would be asked to strip naked in front of the two men so that both could see the "pure gold." She began to sweat from nervousness and the heat of the room.

"You may stop twirling," the general ordered. Heaving a great sigh which lifted his belly in and out, he mumbled to Sir Oliver, "By jove, Mowbray, you'll get a bonus for this."

Sir William's voice had become low, hoarse, and somewhat breathy. He sat up, flicked his tongue over a fat underlip, and fiddled with his breeches. For another terrified moment, Rumor thought he was going to undress and ravish her here and now.

"Fetch Mrs. Loring."

The orderly scuttled out of the room.

"My housekeeper will put you to bed, and prepare you for my indulgence later in the evening," Sir William said to Rumor.

Smiling broadly, he winked at the dandy. "From the look of her, she'll be fast asleep when I come to her, but I'll enjoy waking her up. The young ones are so soft and tender when they've just been sleeping."

Rigid with shock and indignation, Rumor hurled

herself at the general's feet, angrily thrusting aside the little table. Meat and potatoes scattered on the wooden floor in an unsavory mess. The brandy sifter rolled under the table, the amber liquid making wet trails on the floor.

"Sir, you mistake me for something I am not," she stated, lifting up her head proudly. "I am a professional actress, not a harlot. I will not be used in this way. As a loyal subject of the English king, I demand that I be treated honorably."

Rearing up like a caged lion, Sir William's face turned brick-red with fury. "You will be treated for what you are, wench. A captive of the royal army." He clenched his fist as if to strike her.

Quickly, Sir Oliver bounded from his chair to calm the waters. Taking Rumor by her upper arms, the dandy raised her up gingerly, as if she were afflicted with the pox. Quickly releasing his hands, he said, "Best take care, girl. Men and women have been flogged for impudence much less severe than you have displayed to the general."

"I would sooner die than go to this man's bed." Spitting out the words, she flung out an arm toward the officer.

But the enraged old man had left the room, shouting, "Mrs. Loring! Where is that infernal woman? Mrs. Lo-o-ring! Liz!"

Holding his scented hanky to his nose, Sir Oliver stared with disdain at the food scattered on the floor. Impulsively, Rumor put both hands on his jutting chin, cupping it and twisting his head around so that his gaze was forced to hers. The rain had washed the powder off his face, and his flesh was warm and vibrant beneath her fingers. Once again, as in the chaise, she was struck by the feeling of unleashed power in the man.

"If you have any soul within you, fop, plead my case," she murmured brokenly. "I have been kidnapped, sold into slavery, I am about to be ravished. Have you no pity? Have you not a sister or other dear one who might one day find herself in such degrading circumstances?"

She heard an indrawn breath, and his nostrils contracted sharply. The masklike face seemed to crumple around the edges, and the blue eyes took on the same glittering anguish she had spotted in the carriage when he had held her close. Rumor was struck with a feeling of déjà vu, a penetrating kind of second sense which told her that she had seen this face before. Maybe in a dream . . .

But instantly, the softening was gone, the eyes resumed their irritating, vapid look. The stone wall that surrounded this very strange man was firmly back in place higher than ever, and seemingly impenetrable.

He addressed her through stiff lips. "You're acting like an idiot. You're not going to the gallows, nor even being consigned to a dungeon for the rest of your natural life."

Pausing to extract his snuff box from his pocket, he continued flatly "General Howe is a kind and generous patron. Once you have served him well, like his mistress Elizabeth Loring, you will be rich enough to buy a house, a coach and four, and who knows —" the dandy thrust a pinch of snuff into his patrician nostrils, finishing in a richly condescending tone — "a titled husband, as well. One, of course, who is willing to settle for used goods."

"Used goods indeed! And what would you know about any kind of female goods, used or spanking new?"

Rumor turned as a hearty female voice sounded

from the open door. Instantly she was enfolded in a pair of motherly arms and pressed against a full bosom smelling of summer flowers.

"Merciful God, you look like a drowned sparrow," continued the woman whom Rumor assumed to be Mrs. Loring. Her buxom form was swathed in a lacy satin negligee through which her generous charms were amply visible.

As she steered her out of the room and past Sir Oliver, who was sneezing violently from an overdose of snuff, Elisabeth Loring spat out, "Men! Animals, one and all. I don't know a single, solitary one of them who's worth the powder to blow him to hell and back."

Feverishly, like a lost child who's just been found by its mother, Rumor clung to the kindly woman. They were met on the third-floor landing by a servant girl named Janet and in no time, the exhausted Rumor was stripped naked, and her lithe body dried briskly with fresh linen until her flesh glowed and tingled. Slipping a soft cottony nightshift over the girl's still damp head, the capable Janet pushed her into an enormous bed which smelled of Mrs. Loring's richly floral scent.

Propped up on two feather pillows, Rumor stared up at the underside of a dainty, flocked dimity canopy on which had been fastened a large fabric painting of a naked man and woman making love. It was very lifelike, and Rumor felt a blush cover her face.

Mrs. Loring bustled about the richly furnished bedroom, picking up cast-off garments from the floor, stuffing them into the narrow drawers of an ornately carved highboy. Her movements were quick and efficient, yet completely feminine. So like her own dear dead mama, Rumor reflected with a pang.

The maid returned and handed Rumor a glass of

cordial, which she eagerly gulped down in two swallows. She'd had nothing to eat since breakfast, and the sweet, thick, fruity liquid instantly set her senses reeling. Drowsily, she watched through slitted eyes as Janet helped her mistress dress for the celebration already underway in the rest of the big house.

"I'm afraid I've taken your bed," Rumor murmured thickly. The satin sheets were warm and caressing against her skin. Absently, she rubbed the red welts left by the boned corset.

The woman laughed merrily. "I won't be needing a bed tonight, dearie. The general and I had our tumble earlier today. He demands that I play gracious hostess at his victory party."

Walking to the window, Liz looked out. "In Howe's camp, parties don't end until the sun's well up over the bay." She sighed pensively. "I rarely see the sun."

Stepping out of her negligee, Liz Loring stood naked before the window, gazing out at a pale moon. Janet was at the armoire, awaiting instructions. "The crimson brocade, I think, Janet," her mistress said without turning, "I want to look like a queen tonight."

While Janet drew out the gown and assembled the rest of the undergarments to complement it, Rumor studied the woman at the window. Over thirty, she was well preserved. Her figure was plump but firm; generous hips swelled from a remarkably narrow waist. Large, full breasts with long, enticing nipples thrust out proudly below erect shoulders. The long column of her neck was like polished white ivory. A luxurious pile of golden hair adorned her small head. A goddess. Little wonder the general was enchanted with her.

"Why then, does he need to ravish virgins?" She

had not realized she had spoken aloud until Mrs. Loring whipped round to face the bed.

"He is a man of voracious appetites, my girl." The woman chuckled. "In truth, his occasional 'tasting' of sweet young fillies spares me from nightly bed duty."

Pursing her rouged lips, the older woman cocked a skeptical brow. "Why, pet, surely you do not expect anyone to believe that a beautiful actress like yourself is actually a virgin!"

"But I am, I am," Rumor retorted with exasperation.

"Child, child, don't take on so. If in truth you are as innocent as you say, why 'tis high time you were deflowered." She giggled, "The girls tell me the general is marvelously gentle. You won't feel but a tiny prick."

Tossing the covers aside with an angry gesture, Rumor spread her legs apart, knees up. "Come, see for yourself, madam."

But instantly, she crumpled back onto the bed, her words ending on a sob. Suddenly all the anguish of the past twenty-four hours, since that fateful moment when the Sons of Liberty had set fire to the Sugar House, descended on her, engulfing her in despair. She could hardly breathe for thinking about it. The safe, sure world she had known had vanished in a sea of flames. She longed for Jamaica, she longed for her mother, for Calpurnia, for David, for big black Caesar with his wide, wonderful smile.

Shrugging into a taffeta sacque, General Howe's mistress sat down at the dressing table as Janet prepared to brush and arrange the thick golden hair. But upon hearing wrenching sobs from the bed, Mrs. Loring hurried to Rumor with a cry. Rising from the pillow, Rumor threw her arms around the creamy shoulders, holding tight as if she never wanted to let go.

As she held the weeping girl, Liz carefully extracted the ribbons from the honey-brown hair. Then, riffling her fingers through the tangled mess, she spread the long strands out fanwise. "My daughter has hair like yours, exactly this warm brown color," she said. "Amazing."

Drawing back, Rumor fixed brimming eyes on the older woman. "Would you allow your daughter's maidenhead to be ripped out by a man she despises?"

The woman rose up, red-faced, obviously shocked at the bold question. "My darling daughter is nothing like you, miss. She is but sixteen, a child. She plays the pianoforte, speaks French, has been carefully schooled to become the wife of a highborn man of property."

Once more in control of her emotions, Rumor replied coolly. "Madam, I am scarce eighteen, and have been gently reared, also. I can play the spinet, speak French, and Spanish, too. I can write a fine hand, and am capable of engaging in witty conversation with people of quality."

Shaking her fist angrily at the woman, she exploded. "My mother, madam, no more than you, did not raise her only daughter to be a whore."

Lost in thought, Mrs. Loring had been pacing around the room as Rumor ranted. Returning to the bed, she fixed astonished blue eyes on the girl's pale face. The enormous brown eyes were guileless as a fawn's; a blinding purity shone up like a beacon. She imagined the sweet form of her own daughter, safe at school in England, in this bed, awaiting this one's fate.

Liz lowered her own blue eyes in shame. If the girl

were lying, then in truth she was a consummate actress. Too fine to be wasted on the crudities of William Howe and his restless cock. She bit her pretty underlip. But how to save the girl?

Strategy was called for. She stared at the violets on the wallpaper, thinking hard.

After a moment, Liz's blue eyes cleared, and taking Rumor's trembling hands into her own, she spoke with fervor. "You will never be pinned to the mattress by General Howe, or anyone else in the British Army, darling. None, I swear, save the man you marry."

"Madam," Janet pleaded. "It grows very late."

Chuckling with satisfaction, the general's mistress returned to the dressing table. Rumor met the woman's eyes in the mirror. "If only I could believe you—"

"I am known among the officers as the Sultana," Liz boasted. "Even the general is afraid of me once I set upon a course." Sobering, she added, wryly, "Besides, I am just a tiny bit afraid of *you*, my child. Beauty you have to spare, but so have many others I've slipped into his bed. But—" she wrinkled her creamy brow—"I see a certain quality about you, an elusive, intriguing kind of sexuality that I never had, nor could ever cultivate. What is your parentage?"

"My mother was of a fine French family, d'Estivet. Old nobility. My father was American of English descent. His family have a plantation in Virginia, but I don't know exactly where." Rumor's voice grew faint. The emotional scene had wearied her.

"Hmm, interesting."

The older woman was slipping into the brocade gown without benefit of corset, the whalebones to support the bosom having been sewed into the jeweled bodice. Her voice came muffled from under the billowing gown as it covered her head. "You might look into it, my dear. Perhaps you are heiress to a huge fortune."

Liz prattled on as Janet buttoned her into the ravishing gown. "Marvelous things happen in this America. Now don't talk anymore, child, get some rest. I will arrange everything. Trust me."

Turning to her maid, she said, "Janet, fetch Miss Seton some more hot broth and perhaps a cake or two. The lovely ones with raisins and nuts. She will need sustenance for an early-morning journey."

Opening her fan with a snap, she winked at Rumor. "You leave the general to me."

Liz Loring swept regally out of the room, resplendent in jewels and feathers. Her infectious laugh was heard throughout the house as she joined the party.

Left alone, Rumor settled back onto the pillows, her mind and heart at peace. The spasm of weeping had left her drained, as though she had taken one of Calpurnia's purges. She had managed to escape that lecherous old rake. What good fortune to have encountered Mrs. Loring. Could she trust the woman? She smiled to herself, trying to imagine the kind of story the flamboyant Liz would tell the general to keep him from enjoying his new toy.

Once out of Howe's clutches, though, she would be alone. Completely, totally, for the first time in her eighteen years on earth. Taking the ends of her long hair in her hands, Rumor drew it round her like a protective cloak.

She must take care never to be victimized again. Long discipline in theater work had taught the young actress the value of planning. Mentally, Rumor ticked off the steps she would take to regain a semblance of respectability.

First, she would get some money. Acting was all she knew. Surely the British would promptly restore the colonial theater which the bluenosed Americans had abolished. She would apply immediately to the authorities in New York.

Second, when this ill-advised colonial rebellion was over—and from all indications, that happy day would occur in spring at the latest—she would journey to Virginia and find her father's family.

"The plantation is known as Albemarle," Mama had told her just before she died. "It's on the Pamunkey River. Your father was banished from his home, but he spoke of it many times, longingly. They will cherish you as his only offspring, I am certain."

But Rumor Seton would not go as a beggar. If she could not become rich by acting, she would marry that rich, older man Mama always talked about. One whom she could not possibly love in a passionate, hurting way.

Third . . . Rumor's mind went blank. Sleepily, she stretched, yawned. Deciding that she had planned enough for one night, she settled down to sleep. Music sounded from below, together with the clink of glasses and laughter. High and Mighty Lord Mowbray was down there. She hoped that the silly fop was enjoying himself with the officers and their doxies. She hoped there were plenty of mirrors in the house for him to admire himself in. To think she had actually pitied the scoundrel for his deficiencies.

Anger surged afresh within her. The man was nothing but a toady, a servile flatterer who would sell his own sister, or even his mother, if she were pretty enough, for thirty pieces of silver. A real Judas. Enjoy your ill-gotten gains, you snake, she fumed inwardly, as she added the name of Sir Oliver

Mowbray to the list of people she would wreak vengeance on one day. In her mind, she wrote his name directly under that of the Red Turtle.

Her thinking done, Rumor snuggled into the scented sheets. She felt safe, secure, protected. It was the same kind of feeling she'd had in the arms of that treacherous Red Turtle. Odd, but she had felt the same way in the chaise today, when the dandy had held her close.

A garishly painted hawklike face began to weave in and out of her tired brain as she hovered between sleep and waking. Then, curiously, like a puppet on a string, it was whisked aside, and another face surfaced. This one also had the proud, supercilious hauteur of an eagle on a mountaintop, surveying the world beneath with calculated disdain. Amazingly, try as she might to banish it, the powdered, smirking visage of Sir Oliver Mowbray intruded on her dream.

After a while, the two faces seemed to merge, executing a kind of mad dance in her brain. She should have taken some broth, that cordial was stronger than it looked, she thought, but when the maid returned with the steaming broth, she found her charge fast asleep. Chuckling, Janet bent to remove the thick hair from the lovely face so that the poor thing could breathe.

The morning was crisp and sparkling after the rain, and the tall, buckskin-clad man astride the sorrel mare sniffed with relish. His smoky blue eyes drank in the gold and scarlet beauty of the forest that covered the upper reaches of Manhattan Island.

A stone tomahawk swung from the rope which held up Aaron Fleming's breeches, a long Kentucky rifle was lashed to his saddlebag. Inside the leather bag were flint, powder, a piece of beef jerky, a skin of brandy, and a bunch of tow to clean his rifle if he should need to fire it.

Aaron sincerely hoped that wouldn't be necessary. Much as he enjoyed an honest fight, he had no hankering to meet up with one of the British patrols that honeycombed the wilderness between New York City and Harlem Heights, where General Washington was encamped.

The young man's garb was designed to make him appear no different from any other backwoodsman who roamed these parts, scouting for game and the fat rainbow trout that abounded in the many streams. The butternut hue of his long shirt and breeches blended into the browning hills, and the snug-fitting beaver pelt hat was pulled down low over his brow, the furry tail bouncing jauntily behind as he rode.

He reflected on the evening's work. He'd delivered the Jamaican baggage—good riddence to her—and had given General Howe an earful of American troop movements he had gleaned, so he said, from the hundreds of Rebel deserters and camp followers who had poured into the newly British Holy Ground.

"The Americans are ready to wave the white flag," he'd said flatly to a delighted Howe. "I doubt there's any army left—" he'd laughed—"aside from the booby in chief and a few faithful retainers."

The old lecher had actually giggled, being halfway to roaring drunk at the time. "Egad, what great news, man. I'll move against him tomorrow. We'll flush 'em out like the rats they are."

Politely but firmly refusing the invitation to stay and enjoy the victory party, Sir Oliver had taken quick refreshment and recrossed the bay. There was absolutely no danger that Howe would order an attack on Harlem Heights tomorrow, or any other day soon. Why waste men and ammunition on an army that was soon to give up the ghost? Best wait until the cocky commander in chief came to him on his knees. Cleaner that way, and cheaper. No glory in vanquishing a mouse with an elephant.

Besides, Aaron mused dryly, attacking at dawn would spoil the rutting bastard's frolic with his newest female toy awaiting him upstairs in the farmhouse. Perhaps, now, this very moment, Sir William was enjoying that sweet loveliness.

Cursing, Aaron banished the revolting scene from his mind. The chit was a grown woman, she was an actress who flaunted herself before one and all. She would be fine. Her kind always managed to survive.

As to her claim to virginity, it was clearly a case of desperation fostering a gigantic lie. Why the hell would she object to being favored by a general, he wondered angrily. She could do no better for herself unless she sailed to England and jumped into bed with old King George himself.

Aaron turned his thoughts to how he had made good his escape to General Washington's camp.

He'd picked up the mare as usual at a certain stable where a coin or two in his palm assured the stable boy's silence. At a remote place a few miles into the woods just north of New York City, well hidden from the rutted trail, there was a blasted willow arching over a stream with a beaver dam, where Sir Oliver was accustomed to transforming himself into Aaron Fleming. Reaching the secluded place, he had shed the dandified garments, slipping into crude homespun. But not before a vigorous swim in the stream among the startled beavers had

59

rid his body of the hated raspberry scent.

A jay scolded from a nearby branch and a squirrel gathering nuts chattered at him from the fallen oak in whose decayed interior the man had thrust the skin-wrapped bundle of macaroni clothing.

Ordinarily, Aaron looked forward to these outings. He loved the forest. It was the only place he could feel free to be himself. But the war intruded even here. Not far from this very spot they had hanged a young colonial by the name of Nathan Hale, yesterday at dawn, with drums rolling.

Tomorrow or the next day Aaron Fleming alias Sir Oliver Mowbray could well have a rope around his own neck. He snorted. Such an event would bring to an untimely end his dream of possessing Rumor Seton.

It was a foolish hope, this newfound love of his. But then, life is filled with foolish dreams. One day, damnit, if it was the last thing he ever did, he would hold her in his arms, and love her with all his heart and soul and body. Even after Howe and God knows how many more had finished with her. He had never understood why it was so hell-fired important for a woman to be a virgin. It was but a bit of tissue, designed by nature to be broken.

Blast, there it was again, the maddening tightness below the belt, the burning knot in the pit of his gut. As Aaron's desire resurged to torment him, a wild thought intruded. Why not return, steal the girl? Maybe take one of his Son of Liberty pals along? It would be a lark, perhaps the last one, now that the British were everywhere. In the midst of Howe's victory party, who would notice? And if the general were in the saddle at the time with his Jamaican prize so much the better.

The tall Virginian indulged his fantasy for a long,

delicious moment before common sense reared its head. "No, damn it," he said angrily. "No woman is worth risking my neck for."

Or betraying my country for, he added mentally, for sure as death and taxes, his masquerade would come to an untimely end. He could hardly make passionate love to the girl as Sir Oliver the macaroni, and to reveal himself as Aaron Fleming would lead inevitably to unveiling himself as the Indian who had stood by while David Seton had been tarred and murdered.

Gradually, as he rode along beneath the cover of the forest, a fierce anger grew inside him. What unholy right had the woman to enslave him? She had made him want her in a way that he had sworn never to want a woman. Aaron had been his own man since he'd run away from home at fourteen. No one on God's green earth was going to change that, certainly not a female who was half his size.

In a somewhat grumpy mood, Aaron rode into the American encampment which sprawled untidily on a broadsided hillock overlooking the Hudson River. A forest of tents was relieved by a few hastily constructed log huts. It was dusk, and the smoky haze of supper fires cloaked the miserable sight. Men roamed about, digging trenches or drilling in haphazard fashion. Few uniforms were in evidence, most recruits being clad as he was in buckskin or the popular farmers' overalls.

Their movements were slow, dispirited. Aaron's heart sank into his boots. The brand-new republic's forces were even more ragtag than he had reported to Howe. Mentally, he compared them to the smartly stepping redcoats he had left behind in New York.

As he entered the headquarters hut, stooping into the low doorway, a very tall man glanced up from a

61

rough-hewn table on which he had been writing. At the sight of Aaron, his austere face broke into a smile, and throwing down his quill, he came forward eagerly, his hands outstretched. He took both Aaron's hands into his own and spoke with great warmth. "My son, you're a sight for these tired old eyes!"

The two men stood a moment, grinning foolishly at each other, their eyes saying what their tongues could not. Aaron was not a religious man, but he believed with all his heart that George Washington had been sent by Divine Providence to bring his people into freedom as a nation.

At fifty-four, the man was magnificent. Six four, wide shouldered, deep chested, he held himself as erect as an Indian. The lightly powdered brown hair was drawn back in a neat queue. The general detested wigs, and wore them only for the most formal state occasions. He was immaculate as always in his regimental uniform of sky-blue coat, golden epaulets, and buff-colored breeches.

The mere sight of the man walking among his troops was enough to restore confidence, and as Aaron gazed into the steel-blue eyes he found his own heart strengthening.

Releasing his hearty handclasp, the general sat down in a brocaded wing chair that looked incongruous in the rude hut. Stretching out his black-booted legs, he motioned Aaron into its mate. The orderly who had admitted Aaron into the inner sanctum entered again with the general's favorite Madeira.

Drinking from pewter mugs, they emptied the decanter as Aaron talked without interruption. The commander nodded now and then, his craggy face breaking into a frown or smile as the news warranted.

"Howe has no intention of moving his staff into New York," Aaron said. "I have informed him that you cannot possibly attack the city, that you are dug in here at Harlem Heights for the winter."

"Good." The general smiled. "And how is the old lecher?"

Aaron laughed. "Occupied with his usual sport, sir. He spends more time on the mattress than on the battlefield, I fear."

"His dalliance between the sheets may well lose the war for his king." The older man made a steeple of his hands. "Let's only hope he doesn't change his ways."

"Small chance of that." Grimacing, Aaron clutched his pewter mug with both hands, attempting to keep all emotion from his voice as he spoke of Rumor. "He has a new plaything. A Jamaican actress whom I saved from the burning sugar house."

"Ahh, yes, the fire. A tragedy, and so needless." Washington's voice was heated. "I've never approved of the shenanigans of those rascally Sons of Liberty. Law and order must undergrid our new republic."

"Well, the dramatic troupe was breaking the law—"

Shrugging, Aaron fell silent. His old friend pretended to be ignorant of Aaron's membership in the vigilante group, and Aaron went along with the game.

"Tell me boy," the general said, "how are you, on the whole?" His blue eyes held concern.

Leaning forward, Aaron blurted out, "Sir, I beg of you, relieve me of this irksome Sir Oliver Mowbray. I want to fight like a man, surely you have other informants."

The general raised a staying hand. "But none that

63

I trust so wholly as you, my son." His eyes twinkled at the younger man. "Has your masquerade not proven a spectacular success?"

Aaron nodded miserably. "Sir, I am no longer the boy of fourteen you snatched from the Indians. I am a man with a man's needs and wants."

Quietly, the other man replied, no longer smiling, "None knows better than I that you are every inch the man, Aaron Fleming. My word, you *have* grown like a young tree."

The orderly reentered just then, and with an "excuse me a moment, Aaron," the general conferred with the soldier concerning the repast to be served him and his guest.

Closing his eyes to snatch a minute of much-needed rest, Aaron leaned his head on the back of the chair and for the first time in years relived in memory his first meeting with George Washington.

As a boy of sixteen, Aaron had run off to the West from a Potomac River plantation which had been gambled out from under him by a dissolute stepfather. His gentle mother had died shortly after of shame and neglect.

Two days from home, men who had befriended him had stolen his horse and clothing and money, leaving him literally naked in the wilderness. Falling in with a band of outlaw Indian braves, Aaron had spent two years with them, and was burnt with the red turtle token of their tribe.

One morning, while stalking a deer alone, he had been surprised by a group of royal army officers. A tall, handsome Virginian named Colonel Washington was in charge.

An immediate and permanent friendship had sprung up between the boy and man. The quiet, dignified, but affectionate squire of Mt. Vernon had become the father Aaron had never known. For this man, and this man alone, had Aaron Fleming assumed the degrading masquerade that had become a thorn in his flesh.

The orderly left, and the general refilled the young man's mug, resuming the conversation. "Have you fallen in love, then?" He cocked a sandy brow. "Is love the reason you wish to be freed from your dual role?" His handsome face broke into a wide grin. "Ah, love. So Cupid has felled you with his tender arrows."

Aaron nodded mutely, with bowed head. He could not lie to the man who had saved his life in the forest of Kentucky so many years ago and who had been both friend and father to him since.

"Is the lady perhaps this Rumor Seton whom you have so generously handed over to General Howe?"

"How—how did you know?" Mortified, Aaron felt the traitorous hot blood rush into his face and neck above the homespun shirt. Unable to hide the onslaught of emotions that had seized him at the mention of his secret love's name, Aaron lifted blazing eyes to his adopted father's twinkling gaze.

General Washington laid a hand on Aaron's broad shoulder. "It was the way you spoke her name," he said gently. "Like a caress."

"She has bewitched me. I—I need time."

Resuming his seat, Washington said lightly, "Tell me about her. It helps to talk about it."

As Aaron eagerly described the luminous Juliet who had bewitched him, his adopted father leaned his tired head back on the chair, an expectant smile erasing the tiredness from the noble face.

"My dear wife and I went many times to the showings at Williamsburg, before the puritanical Yankee contingent in Congress decided to deny the

65

rest of us that special pleasure. I have seen the masterful David Seton render Shakespeare. And I remember well the girl's mother, Madeline Seton. In fact, I have probably also been treated to a performance by your Rumor as a child."

Meat and bread and fruit from the general's farm at Mount Vernon were brought in, and over supper and more Madeira, the two Virginians spoke of home. Mount Vernon and Aaron's Golden Hill were a few miles from each other in the Tidewater region of Virginia. Aaron had been promised that if he served faithfully and well as Sir Oliver Mowbray, George Washington himself would see that Aaron's family home was restored to him.

"If you are to be squire of Golden Hill when we have won our freedom, you must get yourself a good wife," Washington said in fatherly tone, "one preferably with a bit of property." He grinned. "A plump young widow, perhaps, like my own dear Martha."

"Um-mm," Aaron mumbled through a mouthful of food.

"One, I might add, who won't lead you a merry chase." Washington coughed behind his napkin. "As that pretty little actress surely would."

Jerking his head up from his plate, Aaron put on a show of great surprise. "Why, sir, I thought you understood. What I feel for Rumor Seton is a passion of the moment. She is not fit to grace the halls of my mother's ancestral home."

"Hm." It was the general's turn to be noncommittal. He had listened, rendered advice. The rest was up to fate, and the whims of the gods.

Later, as the Rebel commander's favorite spy lay on the packed earth floor of a nearby hut snatching a few hour's sleep in a saddle blanket, he dreamt of Golden Hill. Despite his vehement denials to the

66

general, Aaron's visions of his mother's home were filled with Rumor Seton. Rumor walking on the green that swept down to the river, Rumor presiding graciously at the dinner table, the cut-glass chandelier turning her brown hair to gold, Rumor at the harpsichord . . .

As he sank deeper into sleep, the iron control that kept him sane in waking hours was lost in the labyrinths of a dream, and Aaron saw Rumor's white, seductive body stretched out on his mother's golden oak four-poster. She was naked, and as he entered the room, she sat up expectantly, holding out her arms to him. Her brown eyes were luminous with desire.

"Come," she coaxed in her marvelously throaty voice, "love me, Aaron. take me, I am yours forever."

Chapter Three

Rumor sat on an uncushioned wooden bench, bent over a silk stocking stretched on a wooden darning egg. Her back ached like the very devil and a sharp, nagging pain was knifing in a zigzag pattern from her shoulder to her waist.

Letting the stocking fall into her lap she lifted her head, and putting both hands to her back, massaged vigorously with all her fingers. The pain eased somewhat, and she sighed audibly with relief. Oh how she wished for Calpurnia's strong, agile fingers now.

Her loud, complaining sigh caught the sharp ear of Lady Olympia Spenser, in whose house Rumor now resided. From across the long room, the woman's high soprano voice sounded clearly. "Rumor, you are lollygagging again!"

The voice of her ladyship overpowered the noise of whirring spinning wheels, clacking looms, and clicking knitting needles.

Flushing with embarrassment, Rumor pulled her hands from her back, and picking up the stocking, set diligently back to work. For over an hour she'd been trying without success to pull together a large jagged hole in the heel of Sir Lionel Spenser's stocking. Sir Lionel was Lady Olympia's brother, and the titular head of the large brick mansion perched high on a pretty green hill overlooking the Hudson River in a fashionable part of New York City.

Like his house, Sir Lionel's garments were the finest to be had—shimmering China silk, with an elaborate white clock design all over. Lord Spenser was on active duty with the British Army, and was due home on furlough at any time.

Rumor dreaded his homecoming. His sister had made it plain that Rumor's remaining in the house depended entirely upon her brother's approval. What if he didn't like her, and ordered her to leave? She might well find herself back in that dreadful Holy Ground. She would sooner die. Her very life depended on winning the favor of Sir Lionel Spenser. And once, she was safely in his good graces, she could begin the search for Caesar and Calpurnia.

Lady Olympia's voice droned on. "Everything must be in perfect order when my brother arrives. That includes his garments." She paused. Every ear in the crowded room stood at attention. "Sir Lionel is very particular about his stockings."

Hoity-toity, Rumor fumed inwardly. The man is probably a dandy of a clothes horse like Sir Oliver. Damn the woman. The fortyish spinster had treated the Jamaican girl like a servant since the morning Mrs. Loring's driver had set her on the doorstep with a message "to take care of the minx until such time as she is summoned by Sir William Howe."

While grateful for her narrow escape from the British general's bed, Rumor found her situation galling and humiliating. She was given gray sacklike homespun to wear, wooden clogs instead of proper shoes, and forced to bind up her long brown hair and stuff it into a white cap, starched and ruffled. Not

69

so much as a single strand of Rumor's shining tresses was allowed to slip beneath the cap.

"You'll have to earn your keep in this house, young woman," Lady Olympia had snapped, even as Mrs. Loring's chaise was driving away down the long driveway. Tall and forbidding in gray bombazine, the woman had loomed over the trembling Rumor like a battleship. Her graying hair was pulled back so tightly from her narrow face that her hazel eyes, which could have been lovely if she ever smiled, were forced into evil-looking slits.

When informed by Rumor that she had no household skills, that she had been trained to act, not to sew and scrub and wash, and furthermore that she had never used a spinning wheel, except occasionally in a play where she "pretended" to spin, the woman's scanty brows had flown to meet the edge of her own white cap.

Olympia's voice had risen to a near shriek. "There will be no playacting here, my girl"—she had paused meaningfully—"nor any of the other occupations you are notorious for."

Remembering that she was in no position to argue, or to even take offense at the slur on her character, Rumor had merely tightened her lips.

"Battle-axe Olympia," the servants called their mistress behind her back. What Rumor called the woman to herself, she did not disclose to anyone.

After Rumor had failed miserably at various household tasks, she had received three hours of not so patient instruction from Olympia, then put to work with a lapful of Sir Lionel's black silk stockings.

About ten women were seated in the common room, on this sunny September morn, all but Rumor

70

being neighbors who gathered here daily for companionship while working. But there was little chatter when Olympia was present. When their hostess left the room to tend to other household duties, the tongues were loosened and shrill voices rang with gossip and female chitchat concerning servants, children, and the like.

Nobody talked to Rumor, though. She was a stranger, a strumpet, "Howe's woman." Olympia had spread it about that she was unwillingly keeping Rumor in her home at the commander's express order. After the first curious glances, the Jamaican girl was left strictly alone.

Now, bored to distraction, Rumor glanced out the wide-open window at the sloping greensward behind the house. An avenue of tall maple trees flamed in full autumn glory all the way down to the river. How she longed to run down the leaf-strewn path to the marshy banks and splash in the shallows. To lift up her skirt, throw off her shoes and stockings, to feel the cool wet on her bare flesh and to hear Calpurnia reprimanding her for her recklessness would be the nearest thing to heaven.

Rumor sighed, and a girl of ten who was fashioning silken flowers from strips of castoff gowns in a basket looked up to stare at her. Her pale face broke into a quick smile, then, as she caught her mother's stern glace, bent once more to her task listlessly. The child should be outdoors in the fresh air and sun, Rumor thought. At ten, though she had been on the stage each night acting with her parents, Rumor had spent her days frolicking in her mother's Jamaican garden, or swimming in the warm waters of the bay. She had been free as a summer butterfly. When this stupid war was over she would be free again. She would simply have to bear with the old biddy's persecution and with the loneliness of snobbery as best she could.

"This silly revolution won't last long," Liz Loring had promised, "the Rebels are already on the run."

"Then what?" Rumor had asked Sir Oliver when she had repeated what Liz had told her.

"If you're sensible you'll go back home to Jamaica," Sir Oliver had told her the first time he dropped in to pay a call on her at Spenser House. He had even offered to make all arrangements, war or no war. He seemed unduly anxious to be rid of her, as if he found her very presence hateful.

Much as Rumor longed for the sunny isle of her birth, she was adamant in her determination to stay in the colonies. "I will not leave until I find my stepfather's murderer and see him punished," she had retorted. Neither would she leave without Caesar and Calpurnia.

The fop had become very angry then, the handsome face visibly reddening beneath the thick layer of powder.

"The Sons of Liberty, whom you intend to punish, were in disguise, and were more than a few," he'd expostulated. "You'll spend a lifetime hunting them down, and never be really certain—"

"Ah, my dear Lord Mowbray, there's but one I seek. He bears a totem on his chest. A red turtle." She had giggled. "And very likely the marks of my teeth on his neck."

"And just supposing, though it is highly unlikely, that you find the man you seek?"

"I will kill him."

His blue eyes had narrowed haughtily. "As a class, women are fools, but you, my dear Miss Seton, take the prize for utter idiocy."

Now, days later, as if summoned by her thoughts, she heard his voice. There was no mistaking that high, whiny, affected speech. A group of visitors had just arrived for a midday dinner to be held on the spacious side piazza. Olympia was a superb hostess, and Spenser House was the hub of social life among the upper echelon of New York society. The three parlors and two dining room teemed with daily visitors, most of them British officers and their ladies.

Not a day passed, it seemed, that the tall, bewigged aristocrat was not at Spenser House. He was extremely popular among the gentry, even the ladies, despite his lack of romantic interest in any of them. Obviously, his duties as chatelain of the brothel at Holy Ground were extremely undemanding. Or perhaps, Rumor mused, he found that managing the harlots was distasteful to him.

The talk at Spenser House often waxed loud and argumentative, especially around the punch bowl. Though not even in the room, Rumor could plainly hear talk of troop movements, battles past and forthcoming, the relative merits of this general or that one. There was, apparently, no fear of Rebel spies among the company or servants.

As if on signal, the women in the common room ceased their toil, and began to gather up their goods. The daily session was over and the big room emptied out quickly, the spinning wheels became silent, the looms ceased their rhythmic banging. Rumor would partake of a simple dinner in the kitchen with the housemaids, then resume her work on Sir Lionel's stockings in her narrow attic room. Rising from her bench, she stretched her arms high into the air. Then a shadow on the window caused her to turn.

Sir Oliver Mowbray stood immediately outside, his large frame covering the opening. His back was toward her, and his hands were clasped behind his neck. The proud head was flung back, the strong legs in their satin breeches spread wide apart as he contemplated the vista of trees, grass, and river.

Once again, she was struck by the power of his figure, which belied his effeminate personality. At the same time, as he stood there alone against the sky, he seemed infinitely sad and vulnerable. She was but a few steps from the window. She could reach out and touch him.

Unconsciously, her arm lifted up, extended toward the gaudy red-and-orange satin-covered back. She would speak to him. She had never thanked him properly for collecting David Seton's body and giving it a decent, Christian burial and for making inquiries about Caesar and Calpurnia.

Her head bowed low in grief, Rumor had stood at Sir Oliver's side as the simple pine coffin was lowered into the freshly dug grave and the hired parson had offered prayers for the dead. But on that sad day, when she'd lifted up her head to thank him, he was gone, his chaise already rolling out of the cemetery.

Suddenly turning, he stared at her now through the open window of the common room, as if she were a stranger met accidentally on the street.

He spoke, "There was an avenue of maples, much like this, at Golden Hill." His tone was soft, unguarded. The deep-blue eyes were wide open, and filled with a curious yearning light. He paused, as if waiting for her response.

"Golden Hill?" she echoed. "Is that your family

estate?"

He nodded, and fell silent; the blue eyes seemed to dream. Then shaking his bewigged head as if to rid it of unwanted thoughts, he reached into his pocket for his snuff box. Taking a pinch, he held it between his fingers, his eyes cast down, studying the shreds of tobacco intently, as if finding in them solace for his melancholy.

"Ah no," he laughed abruptly. "Golden Hill is a hunting lodge my family has in Scotland. I spent summers there as a lad. Except for the maples, I scarcely remember the place."

He's lying, she thought swiftly. The man is hiding something. This Golden Hill is close to his heart and memory. When he lifted his eyes to meet her glance once more, his eyes had filmed over. The veil was back.

"I've never thanked you properly for burying my stepfather," she said. "It was most kind of you—"

Interrupting her, he put a hand on her shoulder through the window opening. "The funeral was not my doing. Orders from General Howe."

Rudely, Lady Olympia's imperious voice cut in, shattering the gentle mood. "Ah there you are, you naughty man." Linking an arm in Sir Oliver's, the woman pulled him toward the piazza, where the dinner party was already underway.

Catching sight of Rumor in the window, she frowned. "You best get to your own meal, girl, before Cook gives it to the dogs."

One blowy day in the first week of October, Rumor rose at dawn, and after breakfasting with the kitchen help, repaired to the common room to take up the task of sewing tiny china buttons on Olympia's new ball gown. There were thirty of the slippery things, running all the way down the back. The garment was the ugliest thing she had ever seen—yellow and dark purple in alternate stripes, with a busy design of cabbage roses down the front and sides. A muddy brown lace smothered the edges of neck and sleeves and hem.

The woman should wear rose or petal green, she thought. Soft, flattering hues, in a gown of simple design. Though far from pretty, with a long nose and too prominent chin, Olympia possessed a kind of austere high English handsomeness that could be easily enhanced with proper costuming.

Rumor was alone in the common room, the town ladies being occupied with a war benefit bazaar to which she had not been invited. Hours passed. It began to rain, a slicing autumn downpour. The wall sconces shed little light, the mistress being one to save on candles. Squinting, Rumor continued to sew, trying desperately to avoid pricking her finger on the needle and staining the rustling taffeta with her blood.

"You're to dust the music room immediately." Nell the parlormaid stood in the doorway. "You're to use the lemon polish on every stick of furniture."

"But there's still three buttons—"

"The master's coming home tonight," Nell panted, running into the corridor. "There's to be a big party, and the house must be sparkling from top to bottom."

Sighing, Rumor folded the gown back into its dustbag, and sped to Olympia's third-floor bedroom to hang it carefully in the armoire. The gown would be needed for tonight's party. She had to find time somehow to finish the work. Fear took a tormenting hold on her heart. What if Sir Lionel took an instant dislike to her?

"If the Spensers throw you out," Liz Loring had warned, "you will find yourself back in Holy Ground." This day might well be her last at Spenser House.

A sound of rolling drums outside brought her to the window. Rebel prisoners were being marched in sorry parade to the gallows on a nearby hill. All had ropes around their necks and were seated in their own pine coffins. These were the diehards. All who swore allegiance to King George were granted pardon, provided they did not try to leave New York.

Little good it had done her to declare her loyalty to the throne of Britain, Rumor reflected wryly. Despite her protests that she loved England, she had almost been imprisoned in a brothel. Were it not for the kind Liz Loring, she would be even now serving the lusts of General Howe and his officers.

She shuddered. The gently reared Jamaican girl had only vague notions of what the word "lust" meant. She had seen a stallion and a mare together, a few coupling dogs. On the stage she had played the role of temptress and woman of the world. But on the stage, the man and woman talked, they rarely kissed and they never, never went to bed together.

Banishing the fearful images, Rumor sped to the music room, cloth and polish in hand, and began to sing a merry tune in the Jamaican patois. She refused to be depressed. She would simply charm Sir Lionel as she had done so many others. Even the truculent woman-hating Sir Oliver, who had heartlessly sold her to an old rake, was softening. Today, gazing at the maples, he had seemed almost human.

As she sat at the fine rosewood pianoforte cleaning the keys, Rumor began to play. She was a skilled musician. After teaching her child the basics, Mama had engaged a teacher for her, a young man from the finest European circles, who was spending a year in Jamaica to restore his health. In a few years Rumor had commanded a considerable repertoir of classical music, as well as folk tunes. She often filled in at the theater when no orchestra was available.

Now, dreaming, lost in memories of her childhood home and her departed loved ones, Rumor began to play a passionate sonata by the amazing Austrian youth, Wolfgang Mozart. The lilting notes fell from her fingers like water from a fountain. Time and dusting vanished from her mind.

As she brought the piece to a finish with a brilliant arpeggio, she heard the sound of clapping. Startled, she looked up into a pair of the sweetest and merriest gray eyes she had ever seen. The eyes, and the thatch of curly blond hair that topped them, belonged to a tall young man scarce a few years older than herself. A weather-stained red-and-white British officer's uniform hung on his thin, gangly figure. He seemed to her a boy playing at being soldier.

"Upon my word," he exclaimed, "I've never heard such wonderful sounds emanating from this instrument. Pray, continue, please." He placed a gloved hand on her shoulder. "I beg you."

Though as cultured as his sister's, Lord Spenser's voice was soft and gentle. There was no doubt as to his identity; a large portrait of him hung in the dining room.

Rumor gaped. She was still in the dreamland of her music. But then, as she spied the tall, stern shape of Lady Spenser at the door, the hot blood rose to her face, and bolting from the piano bench, she darted across the room toward the door to rush past Lady Spenser.

"Not so fast, my young beauty," the officer exclaimed, thrusting out a long arm to grab her by the wrist. "I must needs be told how a woman in servant gray happens to play my pianoforte so wondrously."

Rumor stood frozen, filled with fear. But as he bent an infectious smile upon her, she relaxed, parting her own full lips in an answering smile. "I am not a servant, sir, but an actress. A native of Jamaica, whom bad fortune has stranded here in the Colonies."

He whistled, his gray eyes lightening with interest. "But what luck, you must be none other then the famous—" his eyes twinkled, "—or should I say *infamous* Rumor Seton!"

"You have the advantage of me, sir," she said, warming to the repartee.

Bowing deeply, without releasing his firm grip on her arm, he replied with mock solemnity, "I am Sir Thomas Lionel Spenser, and am, I might add, your most humble and devoted servant."

"Lionel!" Olympia swept into the room. She was in street attire, her reticule on her arm, having just returned from the market. Her plain face was a thundercloud of disapproval. "The girl is a minx, a strumpet, whom I have been constrained to shelter under my roof."

The woman came forward, eyes flashing venom as she noted her brother's flushed features. "I see that she has already worked her invidious charms on you."

Sir Lionel smiled. "Truer word was ne'er spoken,

79

Sister." Releasing Rumor, he embraced Olympia, kissing her roundly on the mouth.

She drew back, spluttering but pleased. "Why was I not informed of your arrival? You were not expected until this evening."

"I made better time than anticipated," he replied, keeping his eyes on Rumor, who stood quietly to one side. "Wanting to see the garden, I entered through the side porch."

Winningly, he smiled at Rumor. "Hearing the wonderful music, I ran immediately to the music room, discovering there this enchanting young woman doing magical things to the pianoforte."

Olympia turned. "Get to your sewing, girl. My gown must be ready by six."

"Sewing!" the young man fairly exploded.

Reaching out once again to Rumor, Sir Lionel took both her slender hands between his own, running his thumb over the pinpricks suffered in needlework and the rough places made by scrubbing with strong soap. "I'm thinking, sister dear, that these little hands were made for diviner tasks than pushing a needle."

"Please, sir," Rumor pleaded, with a wild glance at Olympia's outraged face and narrowed nostrils.

"Of course, forgive me." Sir Lionel's handsome face broke into a conspiratorial smile. Two cunning dimples creased his smoothly shaven cheeks.

As she fled back to her attic room Rumor's heart bounced for joy. Sir Lionel Spenser liked her. Tremendously. He had made it very obvious. Let Olympia do her worst. She was safe.

An hour later, when she delivered the purple gown to Lady Spenser with every button in place, Rumor found her nemesis at the vanity table. Her personal maid hovered over her, massaging a thick white emollient over the narrow face. The oily smell pervaded the room.

Wrinkle cream, Rumor thought, thinking that an occasional smile would enhance the woman's appearance more than all the cosmetics in the Colonies.

"Lay the gown on the bed," Olympia snapped.

Rumor did so, noting that a second gown lay in a heap over the footboard. It was a bilious green and even more hideous, if that were possible, than the purple creation the mistress intended to wear.

"That one is for you," Olympia said testily. "My brother insists that you attend the reception tonight, and that you perform for the company on the pianoforte."

Grimacing with anger, she met Rumor's eyes in the vanity mirror. "Against my wishes, I might add." She pursed her thin lips beneath the cream. "Ordinarily my brother has a sensible head on his shoulders, but you seem to have cast some kind of witchlike spell on him." She grunted. "Some sort of Jamaican voodoo, I imagine."

Ignoring the slur on her character and native land, Rumor lifted up the gown, holding it at arm's length. It was even worse than she had guessed. One of Olympia's castoffs, it was ready for the workbasket in the common room. The color had faded and streaked into varying shades of green. There was a large tear under each armpit, several in the billowing skirt. Dusty-looking pink and yellow rosettes with rhinestone centers, half of which were missing, marched forlornly up and down the front closing as well as the back.

It was apparent that Lady Olympia Spenser would

have her unwanted guest appear as unattractive as possible.

Rumor swallowed hard before venturing, "I—I may wish to alter it—"

"Do what you want with it, no matter" came from Olympia in a muffled grunt from beneath the steaming towel applied by the maid to the cream-slathered face.

Back in her room Rumor's heart raced. The party was at eight, the town clock had just struck six. She had two hours to bathe, rest, and do something with that impossible gown. Reaching for the scissors in her workbasket, her fingers flew. First, the rosettes fell victim, one by one, settling into a heap on the wooden floor. Then she speedily patched up the holes in the fabric with large, basting stitches. Slipping it over her head, she noted happily that the bodice that had been designed for Olympia's flat bosom was snug on her own fuller endowments. The shadowy defile between her youthful breasts was shamelessly alluring.

Rumor grinned at herself in the mirror. The tempting roundness above the neckline would no doubt catch the eye of Sir Lionel. All is fair in love and war, Mama used to say. She must charm him into tolerating her as guest in his house, and keeping her out of General Howe's bed or anyone else's for that matter.

But her initial elation soon faded. The stomacher was too low for Rumor's high waist. And without the rosettes, the streaked dye was only more obvious. She looked like what she was—a war orphan pretending to be a highborn lady. She'd be a laughing stock.

As the clock struck seven, tears of frustration

pushed behind her eyes. Darting to the window, she thrust aside the Indian gauze curtain and stared out into the thin, driving rain. After a while, she became conscious of the fabric bunched up in her fist. Inspiration struck. There were yards and yards of curtain.

Moments later, she stood before the pier glass, draping the curtain over the gown. It would do. A few stitches at the shoulder, a scissors to the hem . . .

At half past eight, Rumor Seton walked airily into the music room. The place swarmed with people. The news that Howe's Jamaican doxy would not only appear but render her skills on the pianoforte had lured the company from the lavish buffet table in the main dining room.

Lord Lionel Spenser came toward her, his face alight, his arms outstretched. "I declare, Miss Seton, you are a vision. You could be a Greek goddess. Aphrodite herself come to bide awhile with mortals."

"Exactly what I intended, sir," she murmured, as he drew her to the instrument that she had polished so diligently that afternoon. The rosewood shimmered like glass in the reflected light of the candlelabra.

If this is a dream, let me never awaken, she prayed. Head high, she glanced boldly into the crowd. The men were smiling, the women looked sober. Lady Spenser stood by the mantel, rigid with disapproval.

Save for the shabby gown hidden by the curtain, Rumor's costume was a replica of one she had worn as Helen of Troy in a Seton Company drama of the Trojan War. The fulsome gauze was caught at the waist by a length of gold braid she had found in the castoff basket. A band of the same gold caught back her brown hair, which hung loose about her shoulders, rippling down her back in long, shining strands. Daringly, she had cut the sleeves from the castoff gown, exposing her arms in all their warm, clear-honeyed loveliness.

Rumor sat down at the pianoforte, Sir Lionel standing devotedly at her side. The room fell silent, waiting. A candle sputtered. Her bravado deserted her at the end, she fingered the keys nervously. But after a shaky beginning, she lost all sense of where she was, and became lost in the music. Warming up with a Bach prelude, she moved without pause into the Mozart that had so enchanted Sir Lionel this afternoon.

Finally, she dared to play a wild piece by that new Italian, the mad Scarlatti, her slim body rocking back and forth on the bench in rhythm with an evocative Spanish dance arrangement.

When she'd finished, there was a hushed pause before the room exploded with applause. Cries of "brava, brava," and "more, more" resounded. Sir Lionel lifted her by both hands to face the audience. Rumor bowed graciously several times, imagining herself back in the theater. Tears of happiness filled her brown eyes as the men and women clamored for more.

"Later, later," their host cried. "First we must all partake of the buffet."

As she turned back to Sir Lionel, Rumor spied a flash of brilliant tangerine almost hidden in the portiere at the doorway. It was Sir Oliver Mowbray, in his customary fashionable attire, and as he caught her eye, he bowed, so deeply that his powdered head touched his knee. Then, silently, he vanished into the shadowy corridor. Chameleonlike, Rumor mused absently.

A beaming Sir Lionel leaned forward to plant a kiss on Rumor's lightly sweating brow. His gray eyes were luminous with worship.

People moved toward the door, chattering. "The man is besotted," Rumor heard a loud whisper. "Mayhap we will see a new Lady Spenser ere long."

The young officer had been married briefly when just twenty, Rumor had learned from one of the maids. Sadly, his wife had died giving birth to a son who had also died. Lord Spenser was considered the most eligible bachelor in New York, with estates in England, as well as a coat of arms stretching back to the fourteenth century. Although constantly besieged by eager mothers with marriageable daughters, after five years he was still very much unattached.

Olympia swooped from the mantel to grab her brother by the arm and steer him rapidly out of the room. Immediately, Rumor felt a pair of plump arms enfolding her in a tight embrace. The familiar fragrance of a summer garden surrounded her as Liz Loring hissed into her ear, "Well done, m'dear, you've exceeded my wildest hopes."

"Liz — I mean, Mrs. Loring . . ."

"Liz, please," General Howe's dimpled doxy said.

"I'm so happy to see you," Rumor exclaimed with feeling. The woman was radiant in cherry silk, her blond hair shining like a harvest moon. "It's been so lonely here."

The older woman cocked a penciled brow. "Until now, darling. From the way Lord Spenser was ogling you, I'll wager you'll not have a single lonely hour from this day forward."

Rumor blushed. "He adores my music."

"Posh, it's you he's fallen for." She giggled. "If looks could burn, this fine mansion would be ablaze." She rolled her expressive eyes toward the elaborately carved plaster ceiling.

The two women followed the dinner guests into the dining room, filled two Sèvres china plates with pressed duckling, broiled sturgeon, and an assortment of rich cakes. Ignoring overtures by several men for her and her companion to take dinner with them, Liz pushed Rumor into a tiny sitting room and closed the door.

Seated side by side on a sofa, she began. "Now, I want you to listen, girl, to what I have to say."

Rumor nodded, chewing on a piece of succulent duckling. She'd eaten nothing since breakfast and was famished.

"The general intends to revive the theater in New York, and I have proposed that he ask you to be in charge."

"But how marvelous, how can I thank you—"

"Be still, we haven't much time. Your ardent swain is apt to break the door down at any moment." There had been several loud knocks on the door since they had entered.

Liz pursed her rouged lips. "But none of the theater business can happen until after the wedding. As a married woman, you'll have the needed respectability." She frowned. "Besides, I doubt that society will accept a Jamaican minx."

Unable to contain herself, Rumor bolted up, holding her plate in trembling hands. The woman was rambling on like a lunatic. "What wedding?"

Liz looked surprised. "Why yours, of course, to Lord Lionel Spenser. Now sit down and set that plate on the chess table there before you spill it on the carpet."

Rumor sat down, stunned, holding onto her plate as if it were a lifeline. "But—but I've known him less than a day. How can you even think that he—that I—"

Liz waved a dismissing hand. "My dear, naive girl, it's the only sensible thing for you to do. If your mother were alive, she would say the same. If you continue in your spinsterhood, you will continue to be ostracized by society. Furthermore, and most important to you, perhaps, you will assuredly not be permitted to partake of theatricals. Any woman who appears on stage in the Colonies must do so under the protection of marriage. An unmarried girl necessarily attracts scandal." She laughed. "The general most definitely wishes to avoid trouble in his new theater."

Rumor sat rigid, white-faced. "But it's all so cold-blooded, so calculating." She faced the painted face of the woman who had saved her from a life of lechery. "What if I cannot love him?"

"You must." Clasping the girl's cold hand in hers, Liz murmured, "A girl in your straitened circumstances cannot marry for love. Besides, he is of a sweet, even temperament, and is mad about you." A tiny frown creased Liz's smooth brow. "A mite pompous at times, given to making pretty speeches, but—" Liz leaned forward earnestly, "Could you not learn to love him? A little? Love can grow, I promise you."

Rumor's eyes widened in thought. Plucking a bright candied cherry from atop a little cake, she rolled it around in her mouth. Learning to love the charming, attentive, rich, young officer would be like learning to play a role for the stage. Many times

she had become so caught up in a dramatic character, it had become more real to her than her own
life. When she had played Juliet for weeks on end,
she had lived the part, had gone around in a romantic haze. Calpurnia had despaired of her mistress's
sanity at the time. Thinking of Calpurnia created a
weight in her chest.

But Liz's motherly voice droned on, breaking
through Rumor's reverie. "Could you not, my dear?
Believe me when I say, you will not find another his
like in all the Colonies. But you must move fast,
without delay, ere some other ensnare him."

The two women sat, hands clasped, for a long
time. Clashing emotions filled Rumor's heart. The
idea was outlandish, of course, but also eminently
sensible.

"Imagine me," she breathed, swallowing the
cherry at long last, "Lady Rumor Spenser." She was
filled with awe.

Liz Loring smiled. "Bravo, my child." Then, her
hearty laugh rang out. "Best of all, you'll force that
bitch Olympia to give up the title she has arrogantly
taken upon herself since the death of her brother's
wife."

"That settles the matter," Rumor agreed, breaking
out into a bubbly laugh.

A loud and very angry masculine voice yelled
from the corridor. "If you do not open this door at
once, Elisabeth Loring, I will have you arrested and
hung at sunrise."

It was Sir Lionel Spenser, resembling not at all the
even-tempered gentleman the general's mistress had
extolled so earnestly to Rumor.

Though long past midnight, the four men at the baccarat table in Lord Spenser's gaming room showed no signs of retiring. Sir Oliver Mowbray wiped his brow and took another gulp of his brandy. Setting another gold sovereign to the pile already on the table, he replied to a question put to him by a young captain sitting across.

"Am I weary, you ask? Should I not take to my bed?" He snorted. "Why, lad, the game is just now warming up." He chuckled nastily. "Come on, young man, shuffle and deal."

His companions exchanged worried glances. The invariably circumspect and sometimes jolly dandy seemed to be ill. The haughty features were beet-red, and numerous snifters of brandy had brought a sweat which made rivers in the thick layer of rouge and powder on his face. What's more, the ordinarily thrifty dandy was so intent on betting large sums that the friendly game had ceased to be sport and had become a pitched battle.

A rare passion lit up the vapid blue eyes. Brows lifted. Had the man who seemed impervious to female charm succumbed at last? How delicious, if it be true.

But much as they egged him on with innuendoes, the chatelain of Holy Ground revealed nothing. He merely stretched his long, tangerine-clad legs under the table and grumbled at their questioning.

"My indisposition is merely the resurgence of an old stomach complaint. Nothing more."

A vision of a girl at the pianoforte, her loveliness made ethereal by candlelight, slithered like a rattlesnake through Sir Oliver's tortured brain. Goaded rather than hampered by the disturbing image, the dandy ended the evening with a jackpot of four hundred sixty-seven pounds sterling.

As a misty dawn hovered over New York City, Aaron stumbled into his bedroom at Holy Ground. Viciously, he tore off the hated tangerine breeches, and hurled the scented bouffant wig out the window, to the astonishment and delight of a ragpicker pushing his cart through the deserted street below.

The man waved, "Thanks, gov'ner," and Sir Oliver burst into a hearty laugh.

The counterfeit dandy fell upon the bed, setting his bag of winnings on his bare haunches. He cradled it with his hands, thinking that General Washington would be as overjoyed at receiving the loot for his beleagured army as the ragpicker was with the hated wig.

The agony in Aaron's heart softened. He heaved a sigh of resignation. It was clear as day that Lionel Spenser was already captivated by the Jamaican wench's charm.

Rumor would soon become Lady Spenser, and be forever lost to him and their wasn't a damn thing he could do about it.

Chapter Four

One week to the day that Sir Lionel Spenser had first set eyes on Miss Rumor Seton at the pianoforte, he begged her to become his wife. The young officer pleaded for an immediate ceremony before he had to report back to his regiment. Though his ardor had been obvious from the start, his proposal had come more swiftly than she had ever expected. Another more conventional man might have simply asked her to be his paramour.

Modestly, however, Rumor begged for time. "I must prepare myself for the awesome responsibilities awaiting me as the new Lady Spenser," she explained.

There was also the matter of decorum, Olympia shrewdly pointed out. What would society think of such headlong haste?

"Nothing but the worst," she replied to her own question. "They will think my brother ravished the orphaned actress and got her with child."

A Christmas wedding would allow a decent time to publish the banns in church, to have a proper trousseau prepared, she maintained.

The older woman reminded her impulsive younger brother that nothing whatever was known of the girl's background. A few months leeway would permit Olympia to thoroughly investigate Rumor Seton's pedigree.

"Love is blind," the spinster said darkly to her brother. "You must be absolutely certain that the mother of your children is worthy of the honor."

"The devil with all of that," Lionel exploded. "I don't give a tinker's damn who her parents are. My darling is a thoroughbred. I love her beyond reason and will have her and no other. If I should die in battle, I want Rumor to inherit my name and all my wealth."

"Poppycock," his sister answered, thoroughly out of sorts with her brother's melodramatics. "You are not enacting a role on the stage. This is real life."

Olympia Spenser cared very much whom her brother married. That magpie Liz Loring was bruiting it about all over town that her protegée Miss Seton was descended from a notable French family on her mother's side.

"The d'Estivets are connected to the Bourbons, whose progency have sat on every throne in Europe," Liz had sworn.

The paternal family tree was even more illustrious, according to Mrs. Loring. Anyone of consequence was aware that there had been Setons at court since the time of the great Elizabeth.

Pleased with her now rosy future, and fearful of endangering it, Rumor was loath to inform the helpful Liz that Seton was her adoptive father's name and that the man who had conceived her in Madeleine d'Estivet's womb went by the name of Beaumont Carter.

Lionel kissed his fiancée farewell one balmy Indian summer day in late October under the marble portico of Spenser House. Rumor stood with Olympia, watching the young major board the chaise that would carry him swiftly to his post.

Wiping the tears from her eyes, Rumor exclaimed, "Is he not the most handsome officer in the entire British Army? I am so proud."

"Hm," Olympia grunted. "Best pray he returns to us in one piece. The fighting is fiercer than anyone ever anticipated."

Rumor bristled, and turned on the other woman heatedly. "Pray, future sister, do not even think of such terrible things. The war will be over by Christmas."

The older woman raised a supercilious brow. "How would a ninny like you know of such things?"

Rumor had learned to deal with the woman's nasty temper as well as with her condescending air. She considered the Jamaican girl far beneath herself in social status.

"General Howe himself has declared that this rebellion cannot last more than a few more months. Mrs. Loring says so, and she is very close to the general," she responded evenly.

"Close!" Hooting, Olympia turned with a purposeful air toward the house. "That is not the word I would use to describe the relationship." She planted a heavy hand on Rumor's shoulder. "Come, girl, time for another fitting. We must not keep the seamstresses waiting whilst we dally here."

With a last look at the cloud of dust raised by Lionel's chaise, Rumor followed her future sister-in-law inside. She sympathized with the spinster. It was probably very difficult for her to surrender power over a wealthy household to a mere chit of a stage actress who seemingly came out of nowhere to steal her brother from her. When she and Lionel were married, she would be mistress here, and Olympia

93

would be relegated to the background.

Despite her problems with Lionel's sister, Rumor seemed genuinely happy. She went about in a dream-like state, causing one and all to exclaim, "Why, the girl is as much in love as poor Lionel. This is a match truly made in heaven."

Since that night in the little parlor when Liz Loring had cajoled her into a marriage of conven-ience rather than passion, Rumor had been playing a role. She was Juliet, she was Cleopatra, she was Ophelia to Lionel's Hamlet. What was love, after all, but a game which those involved persuaded themselves was real? Life itself was a cruel game played by cruel and indifferent gods, David often said. The dice were rolling in her favor now, she must not hesitate. Her path was clear.

Mama would be happy. Madeleine d'Estivet's only daughter had found a rich and powerful man who was mad about her, and who demanded no undying passion in return.

Dreamily, Rumor thought about the night he had proposed. They'd been in the music room, where she had been playing for him. Dreamy, seductive music. He had been standing at the tall window, his hand parting the curtain, gazing out at a huge, orangey harvest moon.

As the last rhapsodic chords died away, he had turned, was silent a moment, then drew in a long, deep, torturous breath. Rushing forward, he had pulled her from the bench with such force that she had cried out.

He had held her tightly against him. "Marry me, darling, please. If you refuse me, I will surely perish from a broken heart."

He'd kissed her, hard, parting her lips with a pas-sion she had not known the otherwise gentle man possessed. The hardness of his erection had pressed into the softness between her thighs. His face had become bright red and sweaty, and his breath had come in short, convulsive gasps.

Returning his kiss with maidenly coolness, she had murmured, "I am so confused. I cannot—I do not know if I can return your love with equal fervor."

His arms tightening, he had tilted back his head and gazed deeply into her eyes. "I will teach you to love me, sweet Rumor. Vile gossip about your virtue has reached me, but I know that you are a virgin, sweetheart. Your coolness betrays you. You have never known a man when he is—"

He had stopped, chuckling. "You cannot possibly conceive of the kind of bodily pleasures you will feel in that enormous bridal bed upstairs."

Thrusting his long leg between her thighs, parting them a little, he had added, "A naked man and woman can make such beautiful music together."

"I look forward to your instructions," she had responded primly. She had felt a deep happy calm within her being. It had all happened exactly as Mama had said it should.

But when the seamstresses fitted the silky undergarments of her trousseau upon her vibrant young form, and she felt a kind of rising anticipation in her blood, Rumor began to wonder. When Lionel kissed her, she felt only a comforting kind of sweet and mindless acceptance. It was the same feeling she used to get when her stepfather David would hold her close and comfort her after a childhood scrape.

At night, when she lay abed, gazing out the moonlit gable window, in that nebulous twilight state between sleep and waking, other feelings assailed her. More violent feelings, such as she had felt that fiery night in September when a sweating savage had held her against his brawny turtle-painted chest. The tingle in her loins and the tightening in her breasts had sprung up at his touch.

She had needed no instructions then. The surging white-hot passion had come, unbidden. Wild, untrammeled passion brings only misery, Mama had said. But what joy might come before, she thought wistfully as she drifted off to sleep.

Scarce a mile into the city from the rarefied atmosphere of Spenser House, Sir Oliver Mowbray stormed into a small, unpainted hovel in the section surrounding St. Paul's Church, known as Holy Ground. His rakish wig was askew, his sculptured, elegant face was set in anger. This was the third time in the past week that he had been summoned to resolve a problem with the harlots.

"Well, hie ho, my lovely, look who's come to call. And so soon after the last time, too." A tall, high-breasted woman lay sprawled on a rumpled bed that took up most of a tiny cluttered parlor. Two deep scratches on her cheek and a purpling bruise that had completely closed one eye marred her once pretty face.

Scuttling out of bed, the slut fell to her knees in mock obeisance. Curling two hands around the brothel manager's gleaming leather boot, she cried, "Oh, yer eminence, save me from this life of toil and slavery. I'll do anythin' yer manly heart desires. Anythin' atal'!"

Lasciviously, she licked her lips with a pink tongue and burst into a bawdy laugh. Moving her hands from his boots to his crotch, she began to knead his manhood beneath his garments.

Recoiling in disgust from the lewd woman, Sir Oliver kicked her plump behind, hard, so that she sprawled faceup on the filthy floor. "Stop that, Maryann. You know it will do no good. I have no desire for women."

He gazed down at her, trying to hide his genuine compassion. Maryann was a young Irish girl whose entire family—parents and six brothers and sisters—had perished in the September fire that had ravaged the city. After nearly being raped to death by incoming British soldiers, she had sought shelter at Holy Ground.

"You've been fighting again, I'm told," he said sternly. "I warned you the last time that you will be punished if you cannot keep the peace."

She cringed. Punishment at Holy Ground consisted of withholding food for days. But rallying, she jerked her head toward the next room. " 'Tis that bitch, Helen. The trollop marched right in here, bold as brass, and stole my young lieutenant right out'n me bed, whilst I be relievin' meself on the commode in the closet."

Sir Oliver suppressed a laugh. The competition over desirable and well-heeled officers was a continuing source of friction. There was really no solution. A few weeks in the huts, being mounted by a series of lusty, drunken men made even the gentlest into animals.

Damnation, what to do with the girl? If only he could find her a place in a respectable New York house. Perhaps Rumor would hire her as a scullery maid.

But as quickly as the thought arose, he banished it. His precarious situation as counterspy required that he fulfill his duties to the letter. As keeper of the harlots for General Howe, he must do exactly that. Keep them here for the soldiers pleasure, not send them away.

Maryann's Irish beauty had made her very popular. She was sturdy, too, had been known to entertain upward of twenty men in a twenty-four-hour day.

As always, the fleeting thought of Rumor caused a minor disturbance in the satin-covered crotch. He was not aware of the slight hardening until Maryann sat up, staring. "Holy Mither, if'n yer cock ain't risin' right out'n yer breeches," she shrieked, lapsing into gutter Irish.

Stiffening in fright, Sir Oliver whipped round toward the door. Damn, he'd catch it one of these days. He dashed out into the tiny yard, the girl's taunting voice following him like a pesky fly. "Ye mought be foolin' the high and mighty gentry with that outfit o' yourn, yer eminence, but ye can't fool a whore like me. Ye be no more a eunuch than me ass."

"Come back, come back, lemme show ye a foin time," she cackled, lounging in the doorway, watching him leap madly onto his horse.

Goddamn it all to hell, fumed the fraudulent eunuch, viciously digging his boots into his startled mare's belly. That was close. One of these days a cunning harlot would be his undoing. Officers and others of high estate frequented Holy Ground. Even tonight, as she lay beneath a pumping captain or colonel, the silly girl might betray his secret. He imagined the scene. "Why, Captain, I know a secret that be worth a bit o' gold—"

The prodded beast bolted into the crowded street, scattering a multitude of vendors carts and carriages to the leaf-choked gutters.

"The sluts've gotten to 'im again, bejesus," chuckled an old appleseller, as she fled to safety in a doorway.

But the man who rode so madly through New York seemed oblivious of his surroundings. His brain was teeming. If he had a grain of the sense God gave him, he'd lead his mount right into the forest and straight on to General Washington, camped somewhere along the Delaware. The war was heating up, for certain, a good hand with a rifle would be of far more use to the American cause than a beruffled, sweet-smelling dandy who couldn't even keep his manhood in control.

But oddly, as he skirted the northern edge of the city and the wilderness beyond came into view, he turned the reins toward a towering brick mansion atop a green hill. He would stop at Spenser House for refreshment, for he had not paid his compliments to Miss Olympia for some days. She would be missing her brother now that he had returned to duty. It was best to keep up appearance, until he could persuade Washington to relieve him of this insufferable masquerade.

But it was not toward Olympia Spenser's waving hand that he turned his steps after surrendering his mount to the stable boy. Trilling notes from the pianoforte halted him halfway across the greensward. It was a siren call he could not resist. Ignoring the older woman's calls, he darted onto the side porch and into the cozy place where his love sat enveloped in music.

He would explain to Olympia later. The spinster was clay in his hands.

Looking up as he entered, Rumor stopped short. She rose to her feet, held out both hands in greeting. "We have not seen you for a long week or two, Sir Oliver. I pray you've not been ill."

Nimbly avoiding the muslin-clad outstretched arms, Sir Oliver planted his tall form, feet apart, in the center of the small room, filling it like a colossus.

God, she was beautiful! Steeling himself against the tenderness rising within him, he said coldly, "Save your witching charms for others, strumpet. You may have use of them soon."

His blue eyes became like glass as he bent over her menacingly. "I have come to warn you that if you persist in your intention to marry my naive young friend, Lionel Spenser, you will rue the day."

"Wha-at?"

Her bewilderment was almost comical. Then, composing herself, she snapped, "Your power over me is long past, sir. I can no longer be bought and sold like chattel. I now am under the protection of a kind and decent man who loves me dearly."

"Love!" He spat out the word. "For such as you, the word is a mockery."

Burning, scathing words danced upon her tongue. How dare the man presume to order her life! She clutched her throat with both hands to keep from spilling out invective upon this mockery of a man who reviled her in such manner. She gaped, wide-eyed with contempt, at the dandy. That ridiculous high wig, the high-heeled shoes, the bilious green weskit and breeches were clownlike. He was a complete and utter fool, nothing more.

Suddenly, her heart filled up with pity. His attacks on her were mere ventings of his frustrated passions. She and Liz Loring had talked about it. How monstrously sad, she thought, to be doomed to a life without passion, to never know the joys of a woman's love.

"Please leave me, Lord Mowbray," she said in a

small voice. "I wish to return to my music. My future husband wishes me to increase my repertoir before his return from battle." Briefly glancing at the man, she added, "Lionel is a lover of beauty in any form. I intend to erase the horrors of battle for him any way I can."

Sitting down on the bench, she began to play a loud and boisterous Scarlatti dance, sliding back and forth on the polished bench with such vigor that a few rebellious strands of brown hair tumbled out of her topknot.

Feeling a hand on her head, she whipped round with sudden fear. Was the man attacking her? Was his determination to stop her marriage driving him to murder?

But as her eyes met his and locked, he merely said, "There was a bug in your hair. I have removed it." With a curl of his sensuous lips, he rubbed two fingers together, as if squashing the insect.

"Thank you," she said weakly.

The man was truly astonishing, filled with surprising turns of mood. Silently, she watched him go through the curtained doorway and turn into the corridor toward the front of the house. As he stood in profile, she saw that his tight breeches were bulging in an unseemly way between his legs, just below the lacy hem of the weskit.

But how mad, she thought. The man was a eunuch. Impotent. So everyone said. Running her fingers along the keys, she became lost in speculation. Who really knows? What proof was there, after all? Or—but how mad—perhaps he was one of those who preferred lovers of their own sex?

Could he—she gasped audibly at the thought—perhaps have a secret yearning for Lionel? That would explain, at least, his violent aversion to their

101

marriage.

Liz Loring had also warned that men "like that" could be very dangerous. "When you are Lady Spenser," she had advised, "I suggest that you discourage Lord Mowbray's frequent visits to your house."

The sound of female laughter drew Sir Oliver into the little sitting room where he found not only his hostess, but Mrs. Elisabeth Loring. Despite her scandalous situation with General Howe, Liz Loring was welcomed everywhere in New York society. Even churchgoing strait-laced spinsters like Olympia Spenser showered her with invitations. One simply did not snub a woman whose influence with the British commander was legendary.

Liz and Olympia were seated side by side on a settee, and were partaking of tea and cakes. Their laughter ceased as he entered.

"Well, my dear man, at last you honor us with your company," Olympia said huffily as he sat down in a leather chair and accepted a cup of tea from the maid. "I never guessed that you were such a music lover."

Quaffing his tea in a single gulp, the dandy set it down on the saucer with a clatter. "The minx must go before Lionel returns. She will bring nothing but scandal on this noble house."

His tone was low, tense, and his powdered face was set in anger. Mrs. Loring gaped at him with some surprise. "Why do you think so, sir?" She met his eyes over her cup.

"The reasons should be obvious to a woman of the world like yourself," he replied equably. "She is an actress, has led a dissolute life both here and in Jamaica. Her lineage is questionable, she may even be illegitimate."

Liz Loring bristled. "You are mistaken, sir. Rumor's family is quite distinguished. On her mother's side she is—"

Olympia broke in, beaming at Sir Oliver. "At last I seem to have an ally in my campaign to stop this disastrous union."

Getting to her feet, she took a gilt-edged leather-bound volume from the drawer of a little table. Standing between her two guests, she held the book to her scanty bosom.

"Between these covers lies the glorious history of the Spensers. Every name inscribed therein is without blemish. There has never been the tiniest stain on our escutcheon, not a hint of—" She stopped, her plain face suffused with emotion. "Miss Rumor Seton is a strumpet and will never marry my brother."

Turning to Liz Loring, she said sharply, "We have only Rumor's word on her family background. She may be lying. Actresses are notorious liars—their very lives are spent in playing roles."

Slowly drawing on her white kid gloves, Mrs. Loring rose to leave. "Much as I would like to stay and chew on this delicious topic, I must be off to rejoin the general."

"And where is Sir William at the moment?" Sir Oliver inquired lightly.

"In Newport, Rhode Island. With the fleet. We will probably sail for England within the week."

"But the war is not yet over—"

"Sir William considers his presence in the Colonies no longer essential. He feels that trusted junior officers can wipe out any remnants of American resistance that remain."

Liz Loring rolled her eyes heavenward, and tucked

a stray blond curl into her feathered hat. "I am overjoyed to be returning to England. I have a daughter there, you know, in school."

The heart of Aaron Fleming beating beneath the satin weskit of Sir Oliver Mowbray began to race. Howe had been reported with his troops on the left bank of the Delaware, at Trenton.

He glanced covertly at Mrs. Loring. Could he trust her? Had she, like the harlot, penetrated his disguise? This casual remark might well be a trick to catch him up. Howe might well be hundreds of miles from Newport, right here on the Delaware, baying like a hound at Washington's scattered troops.

She did not have the air of a woman about to embark on a long ocean voyage. Much too calm. He kept his eyes downcast, least he betray his anxiety. But the woman was oblivious to his agitation; she was staring at her hostess with indisguised hostility.

"Take care, Olympia Spenser, that your campaign against his fiancée does not alienate your brother. If I recall correctly, he has the power to cut you off without a penny."

Lady Spenser gasped, but Liz Loring shot her a withering look from wide blue eyes. "The general has always been fond of Rumor. He will not take kindly to her being ill-used."

When she had gone, Sir Oliver sniffed, "Pay no heed to her threats, dear lady. General Howe would be delighted to have the Jamaican vixen back in his bed." He winked. "A pleasure, I might add, which his loving Liz so cleverly denied him."

Then, taking the gilded book from Olympia's hands, he set it on the table. Placing one gloved hand upon it, as upon a Bible, he intoned, "I vow that together we shall undo this scheming adventuress."

Olympia looked relieved. "Oh, dear friend, I am in sore need of a strong man's help."

Sir Oliver beamed. "You have it. Now tell me what you have done."

Dismissing the maid, Olympia related to Sir Oliver in low, conspiratorial tones that she had despatched a courier to Virginia, another to Jamaica. "To unearth the truth about this Rumor Seton," she declared.

"What news have you?" he prodded, leaning forward intently.

"None," she mourned and sighed. "I fear that both men have disappeared, taking my money with them."

Sir Oliver shook his head. "Not surprising. Men who take such work tend to be scoundrels. Send two more, or even four, after them. Separately, of course. Out of six investigators, one at least is sure to be honest."

"And one can check up on the other," she said brightly, tugging at her lacy cap. "Travel to Jamaica is so hazardous these war days. Many ships have been lost to the British."

"Forget about Jamaica. Her father was Virginia born, she claims, but ended up in Louisiana a penniless gambler. There is undoubtedly a scandal there."

Promising to hire the needed detectives for her, and assuring her that she need worry no more about the delicate matter, the dandy took his leave of the distraught Olympia.

A pox on the woman, he fumed as he galloped toward the town. Why did he let himself get entangled in her affairs? He had meant only to indicate his dislike of the coming marriage, not to play detective. To be honest, though, he would be happy to keep Lionel Spenser out of Rumor's bed.

The news of Howe imparted by his doxy was startling. He should be riding posthaste to General Washington with the report. Whether the Redcoat chief wished to be thought in Newport, or somewhere else, could be vital at this crucial time in the war. Instead, he must take precious hours to scour the taverns of downtown New York, rousting up four men he could trust. Some cash would also be needed to speed them on their way.

It was near midnight before Sir Oliver had accomplished his task to his satisfaction and was pointing his mount toward Harlem Woods and the beaver dam where he would transform himself into Aaron Fleming.

What was left of the Rebel Army was huddled on the far side of the Delaware opposite Trenton. Crossing the river would be dangerous; he might well be caught and hanged by sunrise. He swallowed hard, imaging the tightening of the hemp on his throat.

He urged his mare to greater and greater speed through the dark woods and over shallow streams into Jersey. Once close to his destination, the thoughts of the young Virginian dwelt on more pleasant imaginings.

For the first time since he had fallen headlong in love with Rumor at the sugar house, Aaron dared to imagine a happy ending. Perhaps this skullduggery with the detectives had a silver lining. If Rumor's family were uncovered, they would want to stop the wedding. It was obvious. Why had he not thought of it before?

Her father was dead, she had told him, but surely there was a grandfather, aunts, uncles, cousins. Aaron was Virginia born and bred himself. Families down there stuck together. Blood meant everything.

Rumor's newfound family would surely step in

106

and stop—or at least postpone—her hasty nuptials to Lionel Spenser. They were surely true-blooded Americans, English haters no doubt. One and all, they would be horrified at the thought of one of their own marrying into decadent nobility and settling in England under the tyrant's rule.

By that time, the revolution would be at an end and he would press his suit. As a true Virginian, friend and neighbor of the great George Washington, he would not, could not, be denied.

Caught up in his fancies, Aaron reached into the pocket of his buckskin shirt and pulled out a bit of folded cloth. Unwrapping it as he rode, he gazed rapturously at the single lock of honey-brown hair catching the light of the moon.

He chuckled, then threw back his head in a hearty laugh. A bug, he'd told her, had settled in her hair. The sweet little fool never felt the tiny snip of the knife as she had sat at the piano this afternoon.

Chapter Five

It was a wedding that would long be remembered in the annals of New York City society. The crème de la crème of British aristocracy was there. Olympia had snagged two dukes, three earls, and any number of lesser nobility. All connected to the British Army, of course, and all in splendid red-and-white uniforms with more gold braid than anyone had seen in an entire lifetime.

Their commander in chief, General Sir William Howe, was very much in evidence. Although Olympia had not issued her an invitation, that brassy doxy, Liz Loring, hung upon her paramour's arm. She looked gorgeous in royal blue and pink, topped by an enormous feathered hat. All said she looked like a Gainsborough painting come to life.

Sir William had agreed to give away the fatherless bride.

"Mon dieu, the man is nothing if not a good loser," Sir Oliver Mowbray had quipped to Olympia.

In truth, the tall brick house on the hill was so full of royal officers that Sir Oliver Mowbray was also heard to observe that "this would be a good night for Washington to attack. The dreaded Redcoats are all at Rumor Seton's wedding."

"Attack? With what?" Sir Lionel exclaimed. "George Washington has barely two thousand men at most left in his sorry Rebel army, and most of them half-starved and in rags."

The bridegroom shot a glance to the window where a sleety rain made staccato sounds. "Attack? In this weather? Not likely, my good man."

"Any fool knows that the rebellion is over," opined another. "Yet the colonial general hangs on like a demented dog with a dry bone. Little wonder they call him the booby in chief."

"Yet there are those who call him an old fox," Sir Oliver murmured, half under his breath. "With a very large bag of tricks and a maddening way of evading King George's hounds."

The tall chatelain of Holy Ground towered over a group of men playing darts in the Spenser gaming room. Finding the young bridegroom near hysteria from the agony of awaiting the ceremony at six, Sir Oliver had collared Sir Lionel and led him downstairs into the basement.

The hogshead of Jamaican rum in the corner emptied out fast, as draught after draught was drawn by the liveried servant. The master of the house was already so drunk he could hardly hold the dart.

"Best lay off the drink there, mate," joked a naval officer. "Else there will be no mounting the beautiful bride tonight."

Sir Lionel hooted. "No matter. The lovely Rumor will be mine forever. There will be tomorrow, and tomorrow and tomorrow—"

Hurling a red-tipped dart dead center to the target, Sir Oliver grimaced. His blood was afire with rum and peach brandy, and beneath the powdered wig his head was spinning like a top.

Still, the raw pain in his chest continued to pulse and burn and chew. He felt as if he had swallowed a snarling wilderness varmint alive. Nothing could stop the wedding now. Short of an earthquake or a tidal wave.

The investigation into Rumor's Virginia connections had come to nothing. Two of the couriers had fallen victim to robbers; one had been killed. The other two had not reported back at all.

His love was lost to him. He heard a clock strike five. In an hour she would belong to another. If he were half a man, he would kidnap her, run off with her into the night.

That she did not—could not—love Lionel Spenser with passion was of little comfort to him. Few women actually married for love, yet still remained faithful and true.

If only he could reveal his true identity. But his country needed him as Sir Oliver now more than ever. He alone of the wedding crowd was aware that the Rebels, far from giving up, would launch a major attack tomorrow, on Christmas Day, when the Redcoats and their hired German Hessians were sleeping off their rowdy celebrations.

Upstairs, Spenser House was resplendent. Rich green holly graced every mantel, pine wreaths hung in the tall Georgian windows. There was even a Christmas tree, gaily decked in the German style, filling a corner of the vast tiled foyer.

Lady Olympia moved serenely among her guests in a panniered dress of pale gray jaconet, her scanty hair curled and frizzed about her plain face. If she seemed unusually agitated, if at odd moments she seemed remote and thoughtful, her company laid it to the sadness of losing her only brother to a fresh young upstart of a girl.

At precisely half past four, however, the hostess was summoned to the back of the house where a visitor in travel-stained garments awaited her in the kitchen. Olympia shooed him into the vast pantry, away from the servants, and closed the door behind them.

"Well," she hissed, "what have you discovered?"

Grinning tiredly, he handed her a skin-wrapped tube containing a printed handbill. The parchment was streaked and almost torn to shreds, but unrolling it carefully on the wooden cutting table, Olympia held a candle over it. It was an advertisement, printed on the broadside paper in large black letters.

Beaumont Carter of Albemarle Plantation on the Pamunkey River of Virginia will give fifty pounds sterling to any person with knowledge of the whereabouts of a maid named Rumor Seton. Said maid is daughter to Mr. Carter and is lost to him since birth. Mr. Carter is desperate to restore her to his bosom.

Impatiently, Olympia darted to the door. "Well, where is this Carter? Bring him in."

The courier shook his head. "Ironically, Beaumont Carter himself is missing. Albermarle Plantation is deserted. I waited for days, nobody came."

Handing him a purseful of coins, and ordering the cook to feed him and give him a bed for the night, Olympia scurried to the gaming room. In the absence of the girl's father, the handbill should be enough to stop her brother's headlong plunge into matrimony.

"Why the devil should I stop the wedding?" roared Sir Lionel when confronted by his sister with the document. "After I deflower the gal good and

111

proper and have a few romps in the big bed upstairs, my bride and I will travel to Virginia to meet my new in-laws."

"There may be problems," declared Sir Oliver, gazing at the broadside with jubilation he struggled valiantly to hide. "What if this Beaumont Carter is not agreeable to the marriage?"

"There may even be a hidden scandal," Olympia prodded with an angry toss of her frizzy head. "Why has he not seen his daughter since she was born? Perhaps there is an impediment of a legal nature."

Clutching his arm, she continued feverishly. "I beg you, Brother, come with me. Together we will announce to the company that there has been a last-minute hindrance."

"No, confound it, I will have her."

A surfeit of drink had turned the naturally mild-tempered and malleable Sir Lionel Spenser into a raging bull. There was no deterring him, and when the strains of wedding music sounded from above, and a harried Mrs. Loring appeared to announce that the bride was on the landing with General Howe, the drunken groom made for the steps.

Olympia and Sir Oliver exchanged defeated glances. The game had been lost.

Distraught, Olympia shrieked and put both hands to her head, but Sir Oliver put a hand on Mrs. Loring's arm. "Give us five minutes to revive a tipsy bridegroom."

While the woman raced to halt the bridal procession, Sir Oliver and his cronies snatched the groom from the stairs. Ignoring his outraged screams, they dipped Lionel's rum-flushed face into a basin of ice-cold water fetched from the ice house. After three dunkings and a general straightening of his dazzling dress uniform, Lord Spenser was ready to be married.

The bride was a vision in brocaded white silk with an overlay of sheerest gauze set with tiny pink rosebuds. Frothy lace ruffles hung from the elbows of the tightly fitted sleeves. Her honey-brown hair was arranged over a high cushion in front, with large sausage curls on either side.

A triple row of pearls encircled her lovely neck, tied behind with a satin ribbon. They were the Spenser pearls, and Olympia stifled a gasp of dismay and regret at seeing them on the girl she hated.

A sigh of general admiration rippled through the assembled guests as Rumor stepped solemnly to the music on the arm of a beaming General Howe. She felt like an overdressed doll, a puppet being pulled about on invisible strings. As she moved stiffly toward the bank of flowers where the pastor awaited with her Lionel, a soul-numbing weariness threatened to envelop her. Since dawn, she had been closeted with her maids and hairdresser, being fitted, pummeled, and generally hauled about.

Worse to tell, as evening drew on, the doubts that had been plaguing her for days assailed her mercilessly. All the romantic dreams of her girlhood came back to haunt her. Lionel's face was dear and kind, but it bore no resemblance to the face that appeared in her erotic fantasies. His lithe, slender form was far from the muscular giant with whom she indulged upon occasion in imagined lovemaking.

To cap it all, she had had a dream of disaster two nights ago. She dreamt that she was in a dark cave, unable to breathe. When she tried to scream, she could make no sound.

Calpurnia had told her that when one dreams under a full moon, the opposite will occur. There had been a full moon in the sky all week. Though she ignored the dream, she could not forget it. Perhaps it carried a deep, hidden message.

Why was she taking this terrible, irrevocable step? Sir Lionel Spenser was a stranger. She hardly knew him, he had gone off to war a few weeks after they had met.

Oh, Mama, her heart cried out, as she laid her cold hands in the warm ones of her bridegroom. Oh, Mama, help me.

Her smooth, beautiful face showed none of the inner turmoil, however, and together with a somewhat dazed Lionel she answered the fateful questions put to them by the cleric.

More than a trifle breathless, Sir Oliver scrambled into the room and sidled into place behind the small string orchestra. The high, raked front of his toupet was askew, and the enormous silver buttons on the front of his brocaded waistcoat glistened with water.

Beside him, Liz Loring snickered under cover of the music. "Been swimming, Lord Mowbray?"

He grimaced, straightening his wig. "Lionel managed to soak me whilst we were dunking him."

The ceremony concluded, and the dandy moved with Mrs. Loring into the dining room to greet the newly married pair. Sir Oliver whispered into the woman's ear, "The general did not sail for England, as you promised, Mrs. Loring. Must I take you for a liar who dispenses fraudulent information?"

"Change of mind," she simpered. "The king thought his departure premature."

They took their places in the reception line, and all eyes, including theirs, fixed upon the brand-new Lady Spenser. Liz poked Sir Oliver in the ribs. "You look at Rumor like a sick calf, my friend. I do believe General Howe is not the only one who does not always mean what he says."

"Even a eunuch can savor beauty," he laughed, lifting a glass of claret to his mouth with such haste that several drops of the purplish wine splattered on his already wet coat. Luckily, General Howe appeared to claim his mistress for dinner, and with a murmured "I must change," the fop quickly made his escape.

But to avoid suspicion, he could not take his leave without greeting the happy pair. There would be talk, and much speculation at his too abrupt departure. Lord Mowbray was known as one who never left a party until the last cat was hung.

Bowing deeply before Rumor as she stood with her husband at the head of the receiving line, he muttered for her ears only. "Does your thirst for vengeance still consume your heart, Lady Spenser?"

Her brown eyes grew thoughtful, and she curled an arm about her husband at her side. "I have an ally now to aid me in my search for David Seton's killer."

As he turned and made his way through the throng toward the side porch and the stables, Sir Oliver felt that all heads were turning in his direction, that all eyes were mocking him.

"Your little masquerade is over, traitor," the faces seem to say. A puppet show was being presented in the music room for the children of the guests. Passing in the corridor, he heard the shrill voice of the puppeteer: "You will be caught and hung at sunrise from the nearest tree, you villain."

The sleety rain had turned to snow. Lights from the house made bars of gold on the smooth white greensward. The man who ran like the wind through the rising drifts was oblivious to all but the need to flee.

But as he mounted the mare and rode toward

Harlem Woods and the clothes of Aaron Fleming, he flung off his wig. This time there would be no argument. His commander in chief was bound to see the danger. The jig was up for America's top counterspy. When George Washington attacked tomorrow, Aaron Fleming would be carrying a rifle.

The thrill of the coming battle set the young Virginian's blood ablaze. Aaron never felt the deepening cold as he headed toward the forest.

On the second floor of the splendid house of which she was now the mistress, Rumor lay atop the silken sheet in the historic Spenser bed. Its carved and fluted pillars rose almost to the ceiling, but the mattress was old and swaybacked so that she snuggled into the caved-in middle.

A fire crackled in the grate, shedding a warm crimson glow over the fine old furniture and the pair of Hogarth engravings on the wall.

A peignoir of sheerest Indian gauze covered her slender body. The wedding guests had departed early, fearing the snowy streets. The maids had gone to bed. Olympia had darted in to say good night and wish blessings on the bridal night.

Her sister-in-law had also handed her a torn broadside, wrapped up tightly in a piece of doeskin. After reading the printed message, Rumor had glanced up, at first amazed, then angry.

"My father is dead," she stated flatly. "This advertisement is a hoax, a trick."

"For what reason?" Olympia countered. "Are you such a prize that a stranger would want to claim you as his daughter?"

"I don't know," she'd replied dully. Too weary to continue the dialogue, she turned her head as if to sleep.

"We will see," Olympia fumed, storming out the door. "Lionel will certainly want to investigate the matter."

Dazed, numbed with fatigue, Rumor set the document on the bedside table. She would think about it later. Whoever was looking for her might have evil purposes in mind. If her real father wanted to find her, it should be easy enough to do without advertising. She had hardly kept her whereabouts a secret.

Sighing, she thought of the many, many times she had longed for a father's protection. Now that it seemed it could be possible, it was too late. Sir Lionel was her protector now.

Hearing footsteps outside in the corridor, she hastily snuffed the candle on the table. Now that the time had come for her to yield up her cherished virginity, she found herself suddenly terrified.

"Lionel will be gentle, I am convinced," Liz Loring had consoled her before departing with the general. Then she had giggled. "I doubt, however, that he will be able to perform tonight. The drink, you know—"

Not quite certain of the woman's meaning, Rumor had nodded with a tiny knowing smirk. She'd had no experience with men in bed, drunk or not.

His muttered words preceded her husband into the room. "Blast, light the candle, will you? I'm half blind, as it is."

"The firelight is bright enough, my darling, and, besides, it's more romantic," she crooned, wanting somehow to laugh. Then, as he stumbled toward the bed, hands out as though playing blind man's bluff, she cried, "Come to me, my darling, I am eager to receive you."

She would be a good wife and true, whatever

117

happened, Lovemaking was a game, Liz had said, so why not enjoy it?

Lionel was in a satiny dressing gown, his valet having undressed him. In a vain attempt to cloak the smell of rum and brandy, the man had doused his master with a musky cologne. As Lionel fell upon the bed beside her, Rumor stifled her repugnance at the pungent scent, and turning swiftly, threw her arms about his upper body.

Without a word, he reared up and mounted her, fumbling with his robe and reaching under the silk negligee with hot fingers. He forced her legs apart. His erection was enormous, and he began immediately to pump up and down with vigor, as if embarking on a race.

She cried out with sudden pain as his swollen manhood dug into the tender flesh of her upper thigh, inches away from the center of the hairy triangle where it was supposed to be.

Her bridegroom was obviously still very drunk. "Be gentle with him, and he will return the favor," Liz had instructed.

Resisting an impulse to bolt up and throw him to the floor, Rumor crooned into his ear, "Husband, you will waste your seed if you do not improve your aim."

Rousing from his semistupor, Lionel abruptly ceased his wild pumping. Rearing back, he gazed deep into her eyes. "Help me, Rumor. I swear I'm too drunk to find the place I seek. Surely a woman of your vast experience—"

Rolling over with a kind of obscene giggle, he went on, "Come on now, show me how."

So he too doubted her virginity. What now, she thought. Must she take the lead in this silly game?

Lionel appeared to be asleep beside her, his nose

tucked into her underarm. Why not let him be? When he awoke, they could start afresh. Gratefully closing her own eyes, Rumor promptly fell fast asleep.

She awoke to the feel of teeth and tongue on her right nipple. Her negligee was open, falling around her waist, and Lionel lay atop her, naked. Feverishly, he went from one breast to the other, chewing on the nipples whilst kneading the soft flesh with his hands.

Rumor felt arousal in her lower body, a kind of pleasant stirring in the belly. She had felt this way in the Red Turtle's arms, that fiery night he had carried her from the burning sugar house.

Leaning her head back into the pillows, she arched her body, luxuriating in the feel of his mouth on her nipples. His hands began to wander, stroking, stroking, making tiny little circles around her breasts, in her navel, in the dark, hidden regions between her thighs.

It was going to be all right, she exulted, as sensation after thrilling sensation rippled through her veins wherever he touched.

Rumor was afire, the center of her womanhood was moist and ready for him. Languidly, she spread her legs wide apart. "Please, Lionel, enter me, I want you now."

Suddenly, his body lifted from hers, and he straddled her, sitting on her hips, his swollen manhood thrust out.

"No, my sweet minx, not yet," he said hoarsely.

Inching his tall body forward, he thrust himself toward her face. "I want something more from you. Go on. There's a good girl."

Astonishment and repulsion filled her mind. "Wha-at?" she shrieked, and sitting up, thrust him

119

from her body with all the power she could muster.

Falling backward, he muttered, "She-devil, I'll punish you for that."

She was on her feet, standing by the bed. Bounding up, he joined her, cruel hands on her shoulders. The fire had died down, but the moon was bright through the window. His eyes had narrowed, and his kindly face was set in anger.

"You are my wife, and will do everything I command," he said in low tones.

She bowed her head. "I cannot do the . . . thing . . . you ask." Lifting up, she gazed directly into his eyes. "I love you dearly, Lionel, but I am a virgin. I have not ever—"

A loud laugh erupted from his mouth. "Don't lie to me, Rumor. You have been on the stage, you have been available to many men."

She shook her head. "No, dear husband. My maidenhead is as intact as the day I was born."

Her words had the ring of such sincerity that Lionel drew her to him at last, fondly, tenderly. "Forgive me, sweet, it is the drink still within me that makes me such a beast."

"Come," she whispered against his chest. "Take me back to bed, and make me a woman. Then, one day I will do anything you desire to give you pleasure."

She lay back on the bed, and drew him back on top of her. His organ was no longer erect. Guiding her hands to his flaccid member, she stroked him, gently.

As he lay beside her, his arms flung upward on the pillow, he became aroused again, and as she continued to stroke him, he began to pant and utter little grunts of arousal.

"It is time to enter me again," she whispered,

releasing her hands.

"Damnit," he yelled, "don't stop, don't stop!"

In seconds, his fulfillment came, and the seed she had hoped to receive into her womb spilled out upon the satin sheets of the historic Spenser bed.

"I've never entered a woman," he muttered. "Disease, you know."

Thereupon Lord Spenser fell fast asleep again.

Rumor lay wide-awake a long time, thinking. It wasn't fair. Her husband had had his pleasure. Her own aroused passions churned within her, dying a slow and painful death. So this is marriage, she thought bitterly. Where was her own fulfillment, the ecstasy she had so looked forward to? She would have to talk to Liz the next time she saw her.

Dawn was streaking the sky above New York, before Rumor finally found oblivion in sleep.

At precisely midnight on Christmas Day, the "old fox" George Washington of Virginia made an audacious move. He ordered his remnant of an army to pile into boats with all their arms and artillery and cross the Delaware River in wintry darkness.

The plan was bold and filled with danger. The normally placid stream which divided Jersey from Pennsylvania was swollen to a flood, and dark masses of floating ice loomed everywhere.

A stunned British army was taken in broad daylight. Crying "Victory or Death," the Americans cut down the Redcoats, who were blissfully sleeping off a night of carousing on Christmas Eve.

Reporting to his commander barely seconds before the last boat was launched, Aaron gave the man no time to deny his plea to join the fighting. Washington was riding among his men, exhorting them in his deep and solemn voice, "to keep by your officers, keep your heads, victory is ours."

Laughing, he waved Aaron into the last boat. Shouldering his long Kentucky rifle, Aaron said good-bye forever to Sir Oliver Mowbray.

One week later, Aaron sprawled on the floor of a comfortable farmhouse in the highlands of New Jersey. Days of mopping up, of rousting out small bands of British and their hired Hessians had kept him at a fevered battle pitch. He himself had accounted for fifty Hessian prisoners, who had been taken to Philadelphia to be marched through the streets.

The face of the war had been changed. Aaron longed to see the look on General Howe's face at the news of Trenton's capture. It might even get the old goat out of Mrs. Loring's bed.

The revived American Army would not harass the British as before, chasing them through the Jersey flats, back and forth across the Delaware. The ragtag Continentals had cornered the British rats.

"Hail the conquering hero!"

Lifting his head, Aaron stared at a tall, slim figure in a blue-and-white uniform just coming through the door. His name was Charles de Borre, and he was one of a group of Frenchmen who had sailed across the Atlantic to fight alongside the Americans in their battle against tyranny.

"There is talk that you will get a medal pinned to your chest," the man went on in his lilting French accent.

Aaron grunted. "I'm thinking our new country has better uses for its gold." Getting to his knees and facing the fire, he picked up a burning coal with the iron tongs and lit the long wooden pipe in his mouth.

"Care to smoke?" he addressed the Frenchman, who had stretched his lanky form on a sofa. As always, de Borre was flawlessly attired in the colorful blue of his regiment. Gold lace adorned his collar and sleeves, and snowy plumes waved from a tricornered hat.

The man wrinkled his aquiline nose. "I cannot bear the filthy weed."

Aaron laughed. He liked the Frenchie. He had been in the boat with Aaron on the perilous Delaware River crossing. In fact, despite his dandified appearance, Monsieur de Borre had proven to be a superb boatman and had steered them through the treacherous shallows near the banks.

Other men soon joined them, many smoking companionably with Aaron. Real tobacco—not the weeds in common use since the war—was obtained through mysterious channels from Virginia.

Food was brought in by an orderly—succulent slices of ham, legs of roast turkey, puddings, and other sweets. The Hessians from whom they had taken the house had left a larder full to bursting.

Wine and beer flowed endlessly from cellar kegs. Talk flowed just as freely. One of the men had seen the list of British officers killed and captured. "Sir Lionel Spenser is among the fallen," he reported. He shook his head. "And him with a new bride, too."

Controlling his emotions with difficulty, Aaron spoke casually. "Are you certain? I would have thought him on his honeymoon, for he was married on Christmas Eve."

"My bunkmate saw him dead." The man shot a quick glance at Aaron. "Why are you so interested? Did you know the man or his family?"

"More likely he was acquainted with the bride," hooted another. "I hear she was an actress in New

123

York."

"A bloody good one too, so I hear," Aaron laughed, throwing an arm across his face to hide the sudden rush of blood.

"Be done with this gossip," de Borre chimed in. "Let us talk of strategy. What has our honored general up his sleeve for tomorrow?"

Aaron sunk back to the floor, smoking quietly. His blood was singing. Rumor a widow. Death had given him a boon. But there was no way he could court her now. Mourning demanded at least a year of celibacy and wearing black. Moreover, he could hardly leave his post. Washington had given strict orders that no furloughs would be granted for months to come. Under no circumstances. A man whose mother and father had both died in an accident could not even attend the funeral in Vermont.

Aaron longed to comfort Rumor in her time of sorrow. She had been genuinely fond of Lionel. She would need a man's strength to guide her now and protect her from Olympia's vicious schemes.

But there was her father awaiting her in Virginia. Beaumont Carter was surely at his daughter's side by now.

In the summer, when this last fierce campaign had run its course, he would travel to New York. Until then, he had a war to win.

Chapter Six

On a brilliantly warm day in February, Lady Rumor Spenser stood at her parlor window, gazing mindlessly out at the long, curving driveway. Liz Loring was coming for tea, and she tingled with anticipation. She had not seen the vivacious and motherly woman since her wedding night.

A soft breeze blew in from the bay, and she breathed in long and deep. Despite the woman's protests that unhealthy vapors would blow in from the gutters, which were used as sewers by the populace, Rumor had ordered the housekeeper to throw all the windows wide open. It was a false spring, she knew. Winter would come again with bitter cold and snow.

It had been snowing hard on New Year's Day when they had laid Lionel's bloodied body to rest in a marble vault, the ground being too frozen to bury him. Olympia was all for keeping her dead brother in the house, but the authorities forbade it.

The stunned young widow and her nearly prostrate sister-in-law had come back to Spenser House, which still bore the gay finery of the Christmas wedding. Olympia had gone straightway to bed, and

Rumor had proceeded to reorganize her life.

Upon the surprise attack by the Rebels, Lionel had been recalled to battle early Christmas morning. The next day, twenty-four hours later, he had died.

Rumor had been a wife scarce two days. A wife? In name only, she thought ruefully. She was now a widow, very rich and influential. It was too much to absorb all at once.

Custom decreed that she go about in black. "Weeds," they called the drab clothing she was bound to wear. She must not leave the house, she must not entertain, she must not laugh, she must not sing, she must not play the pianoforte.

So pronounced Olympia from her sickbed.

Her usually stalwart health deserting her, the spinster had remained prone in her massive bed, the bedroom curtains drawn. A slight sniffle developed at the funeral had turned into pneumonia. One stormy night the doctor had declared her near expiring, but owing largely to Rumor's constant care, she survived the crisis, but seemed to have lost the verve and vitality that had been her mainstay.

Fretfully, Rumor plucked at the fringed woolen ribbons dangling from her stiff black housecap. She began to sweat beneath the woolen frock which fell in heavy folds about her slender form.

Wildly, impulsively, she tore off the cap, and feverishly tugging at the hairpins in her bun of hair, shook out the long brown strands about her shoulders. The wonderful sense of freedom intoxicating her, she ran up the long staircase and into her bedroom.

Back in the parlor just in time to hear the carriage wheels upon the gravel, she flung open the wide front door to admit a fur-draped Mrs. Loring.

Her friend's face froze in astonishment. "Rumor!

What the devil can you be thinking of? That sprigged muslin is charming on you, but it's much too soon to doff your widow's weeds."

A girlish smile lit up Rumor's pale face. "Not too soon for a widow whose wifehood lasted but two short days."

Liz threw back her head in a hearty laugh as the maid relieved her of her silver fox pelisse. "Well said, m'dear. I must say I never thought of it quite that way. How very clever of you."

"Sh-h," Rumor cautioned, drawing her guest into the parlor, where tea had been laid in front of the fire. "We must not awaken my sister-in-law. I've given her a double dose of her sleeping potion, so that I could have a few undisturbed hours with you."

She rolled her eyes up to the ceiling. "Olympia's been gravely ill and she's out of danger, thank God, but she's been a trial. She'll have no one tending her but me, and orders me about like a servant, even from her bed—" She flashed an impish grin. "I suppose my wearing this bright frock today is a kind of rebellious gesture."

Embracing Rumor warmly, Liz held her close for a long time. "I understand and sympathize my dear, but you now have a position to maintain. You are no longer Rumor Seton, actress, but Lady Rumor Spenser, a leader of society."

The women sat down close together on the blue damask sofa and Rumor poured a cup of tea for herself and her friend. Stirring cream and sugar into her tea, she ran her thumb on the plump, carved heron adorning the handle of the silver spoon.

"I have so much, more than I ever dreamed," she commented, gazing round the richly decorated room. "Why am I so unhappy, Liz?"

Liz stood a long swallow of tea. "Genuine Ceylon

brew. Hard to get these war years." Sighing, she gazed thoughtfully at Rumor. "Is there any word from the man who says he is your father?"

Rumor shook her head. "We have dispatched two letters, but have seen nothing in return. No letters, no messages by courier. It's all very strange."

Nibbling thoughtfully at a raisin cake, she continued. "I am more than ever convinced that the handbill is a hoax, a trick of some sort. Now that I am wealthy and possess a title, any sort of scoundrel can claim to be my parent."

She shrugged. "I have never set eyes on Beaumont Carter, and wouldn't know him if he stepped through the door this very minute."

"Perhaps you might travel to Virginia—when the weather clears of course. Even if this claimant should prove false, you will want to view your ancestral acres."

"Ye-es," Rumor replied slowly. "But somehow the urge to find my family is not as strong as it once was. In any event, nothing can be done until Olympia is well and on her feet again"—she tugged ruefully at her flowered skirt—"and despite my impulsiveness of today, I shall have to go back into mourning. Olympia says I must not show my face in public for another six months at least."

"Olympia, Olympia," Liz Loring exploded in a near shout. "Is she your keeper then? Have you traded a husband for an overseer?" Taking Rumor's hand in hers, she gazed intently into the brown eyes. "You are free, my girl, to do as you wish."

Jumping up, Rumor ran into the next room, a little library, returning in seconds with a sheaf of papers in her hand. "Well, then, Mrs. Loring, I wish to begin to revive the theater in New York, as General Howe himself decreed last fall. Here are two

128

plays, *The Jealous Wife* and *A Miss in Her Teens*, either of which would be a perfect vehicle to launch our first season."

Flushed, she placed the playscripts on the tea table, shoving the delicate china to one side to make room. The ensuing clatter brought a worried maid into the parlor, and Liz clucked her tongue reprovingly. "Careful, Rumor, you will break the family china." She shook her head, but said affectionately, "You are such a child, despite your new dignity as Lady Spenser."

Seeming not to hear in her excitement, Rumor babbled on. "Help me decide, please. There is much to do, the theater to refurbish, actors to interview, tickets to sell, and of course we must advertise—"

"Whoa, whoa, my spirited little filly," Liz expostulated, rising up and taking Rumor by the shoulders. "It is absolutely out of the question for you to engage in theatricals in your present situation."

"But you said in the autumn that as a married woman I would be accepted as an actress. You promised that I would be in charge."

"It will be at least a year until you can be seen at any social occasion."

Picking up the playscripts, Rumor drew back her arm as if to hurl them in the fire. Just in time, Liz grabbed her arm. The papers scattered on the flowered rug. Patiently, the maid who had remained, stooped to gather them up.

"Leave them, please," Liz instructed the girl. "I wish to be alone with her ladyship."

She turned to Rumor, "Darling child, you are distraught. Please, come, sit down again with me, and we will talk."

Rumor allowed herself to be drawn into the woman's arms. Huddling beside the perfumed mistress of

General Howe, who had become the mother she had lost, she moaned, "But I shall die of boredom."

"Why not travel to England," Liz murmured. "I will have Sir William find you a strong, safe ship. Take the waters at Sadlers Wells. It will certainly do Olympia a world of good. No one will comment on a young widow accompaning her relative on such a jaunt.

A mumble from Rumor was her only response. Mrs. Loring persisted brightly. "Why not visit Jamaica? The southern waters are not frozen over as in the north. It must be lovely down there this time of year."

"No!" The word shot from Rumor like a bullet. Her head came up defiantly. "I cannot leave America."

"But why not, for pity's sake? You can return when this pesky war is over and won."

"There is something I must do, dear friend, something I cannot speak to you about just now."

The finality about the girl's voice silenced Liz for a moment, then, drawing back, she exclaimed, "You seem ill yourself. Are you—" She smiled, her pretty face beaming, as if inspired. "Of course! You must be with child. What else would account for your erratic behavior?"

Tearing away from Liz's warm grasp, Rumor bolted up again and darted to the window. The sun had gone behind the clouds, and a cold wind had replaced the earlier warmth. She threw back her head, running her hands through her loosened hair. She began to laugh, but without mirth.

"Am I with child, you ask? How delicious!" She whipped round, and the pain in her soft brown eyes brought a wince to Liz's pretty face. "Would you be very much surprised to learn that I am still a virgin,

130

Liz? My titled husband was too drunk on his wedding night to consummate our marriage."

Thrusting her head out the window, she threw both hands up into the air, as if imploring help from above. "All those people out there, all over this vast city, have someone to love. Men and women climb into bed at night and turn to another who is warm and giving."

Turning back into the room, she fell into Liz's arms once more, her tousled head resting on the warm, silk-clad shoulder. "Must I wait years and years to hold a man in my arms? Oh, how can I bear it? I am so filled with yearning, at night I toss and turn, thinking of forbidden things."

She lifted her tear-streaked face as a voice from the doorway broke in harshly. "Slut, the world will know you at last for what you are." Olympia stood tall and avenging, clutching her wrapper about her nearly gaunt body. Her narrow face was red with righteous rage.

White-faced, Rumor gasped. "How long have you been standing there?"

"Long enough to hear that you have no right to call yourself Lady Spenser. I suspected that my brother was not able to perform his conjugal duty on his wedding night. Now that I have it from your own lips, minx, an annulment will be speedily arranged."

Coming forward, the sick woman thrust her face between a stricken Rumor and Liz. The foul, fetid air of the sickroom came with her. "I'll hire the best legal mind in the Colonies. In a few weeks at most you will find yourself back in the street where you came from."

"Annulment," Liz scoffed. "Absurd. Woman, you are a fool if you think you can cheat Rumor out of

131

her inheritance."

"But she said—" Olympia protested. "We both heard what she said."

Liz Loring lifted an imperious chin, and flicked a vagrant blond curl back in place beneath her bonnet. "I heard nothing, madam. I very much fear that your illness has affected your brain, dear woman."

"Argh-gh-h—" With a strangled cry, Olympia slid to the floor in a heap. She had fainted. Between them, Rumor and Liz got her back up to bed, where after being revived with smelling salts, she fell promptly back to sleep.

Despite her fainting spell, Lady Olympia set about her scheme to annul her brother's marriage immediately. Faced with both Liz and Rumor's firm denials of the conversation that February day in the parlor, the spinster's threat to expose her widowed sister-in-law as a virgin met with ignominious defeat. The best legal mind in loyalist New York City, a certain Judge Rivington, conducted a very short hearing in the Spenser gaming room. The laundress, a large, placid, well-spoken woman named Harriet, was summoned for questioning.

The judge, the witness, Rumor, and Liz sat around the whist table. Olympia stood at the window, aloof but alert. Her arms were crossed on her skinny chest and her patrician face was grim. The questioning lasted exactly five minutes by the eight-day clock in the foyer.

The judge began questioning the laundress. "On the morning of December 25 last, did you launder the sheets that had been taken from Lord and Lady Spenser's bridal bed?"

Harriet, sitting erect, answered in a strong, sure voice, "I did, Your Honor."

The judge continued, "What was their condition?"

"They was rumpled, and, pardon the expression, sir, full of stink and dried blood," Harriet answered.

"Blood, you say?"

She nodded. "A big round spot."

Judge Rivington leaned forward intently. "Tell me now, Harriet, was the smell one you are familiar with?"

The woman nodded, her plump face turning a rosy red. "Yes, Your Honor, it is the odor of a man when he has—"

She paused, staring down at her folded hands on the whist cloth, and the judge put in quickly, "No need to go on, Harriet. We take your meaning."

Olympia lunged forward, hovering over the table like an avenging angel. "She's a liar and a slut herself. The woman's obviously been bribed to tell this outrageous story."

The servant drew up indignantly, spitting words into Olympia's face. "I am an honest woman, madam. I do not lie. Until March last, I had a husband and three children of my own, but God saw fit to send the choking sickness and took them all." Harriet turned back to the judge. "I know well the smell of a man in the marriage bed."

Later, as she dressed for dinner in her bedroom, Rumor confided to Liz, "I feel like a fraud. I really am still a virgin." She puckered her brow. "Do you think I could be tried for perjury?"

"Harriet swore by the Bible, you did not. And furthermore, sweet, from what you've told me of the wedding night, you deserve all the good things you're getting."

Judge Rivington stayed for dinner in the grand dining room. Her natural vivacity restored, Rumor regaled both him and Liz with stories of growing up in the theater.

133

"I miss it so," she lamented. "I long for the day when I can once again trod the boards."

"Why wait," the judge asked. "Society is most anxious that you soon restore the dramas prohibited by the puritanical Yankees."

"But—would it not cause a scandal?"

"Poppycock. These are unusual times. The city has hundreds of widows and orphans who will benefit from the money raised by your productions." He lifted his wineglass, as if toasting her. "You will be much admired, my good woman, for conquering your own very great grief for such a worthy cause."

The very next morning, at sunup, Rumor found herself at the only theater in the city that had survived the great fire. An unsightly red-brick building, it was situated sixty feet back from John Street, a covered larchway of rough wood leading to it.

Inside was more cheerful, though, with a large auditorium consisting of a pit, two rows of boxes, and a gallery. The place was already filled with workmen, the sound of hammers and saws filled the morning air. They'd been there since midnight, they told her, on express orders from Judge Rivington.

Within a week, the widowed Lady Spenser had interviewed a hundred prospective thespians, had designed six playbills, had sent out advertisements all over the city. Rehearsals began. The first offering would be *The Jealous Wife*, with the noted Jamaican actress, Lady Rumor Spenser, nee Seton, taking the role of Lady Freelove.

She had never been happier. She fell asleep at the touch of the pillow on her head.

Happily, Olympia resumed her former role as mistress of Spenser House.

The formerly frustrated young widow had no time or energy for agonizing erotic yearnings. Rumor thrust all thought of hunting the Red Turtle from her mind. Vengeance was sweet, but it could wait.

It was April in Virginia, and the countryside was blooming. The morning sun was warm and bright on the Potomac as Aaron reined in at Mount Vernon. A smiling black slave came out to greet him and take the exhausted mare to the stables for much needed rest and fodder.

Inside the gracious white mansion, Aaron took the hands of Martha Washington in his own. He bowed deeply, then grinning, kissed her on both cheeks.

"The general, your husband, bade me greet you fondly as he longs to do," he said, his blue eyes twinkling.

The two were old friends, Aaron having been a frequent visitor at Mount Vernon in the days before the war. Placing a plump, motherly arm about his waist, the comely matron led him into the dining room for refreshment.

After a hearty country feast of baked Virginia ham, fresh garden vegetables, crusty bread, and wine from the well-stocked cellar, Aaron followed his hostess through a covered outdoor passage into an adjoining building used as an office.

"My husband assures me that you will be more successful than I in collecting these delinquent accounts." She pointed to a sheaf of papers and account books littering a wooden shelf against the wall. She sighed expansively her bosom rising and falling dramatically. "I am such a dunce at this sort of thing. How fervently I wish the war would end so that my dear husband can return to his family."

"Soon, madam, soon," Aaron muttered, pulling

up a high stool and bending over the papers.

His commander had been explicit. "The rascals who rent farmland from me have refused to pay my wife. Your job is to run them to earth and wring it out of them." He'd flashed a rare smile. "Use any means at your disposal—threats, intimidation, your trusty rifle if it comes to that. "Even get yourself up like a Mohawk Indian," he had added. "Scare the hell out of the rascals."

For more than a month, Aaron rode about the countryside and into the mountains to the west collecting the delinquent rents owed to General Washington. "You're the only person I can trust," his adopted father had said.

Aaron chafed to return to battle. The British were hammering at Philadelphia; the city could fall at any time, to join New York among enemy-occupied cities. But he relished the days and nights in the forest, the candlelit dinners and long conversations with Martha Washington and her large household.

At last he handed her eight hundred dollars in cash, a princely sum. He had not resorted to his Son of Liberty Indian garb, though he was sorely tempted many times. He had succeeded far beyond his expectations. His commander would be pleased.

As he stood in the pretty circular driveway, mounted and ready to travel north again, he said casually to Mrs. Washington, "Have you knowledge of a certain man who claims to be Beaumont Carter? His family once owned a plantation on the Pamunkey River to the south."

"Know him? Who has not heard of the scoundrel?" Martha Washington scowled. "His family and mine were neighbors. "We all thought him dead, but he showed up, like the bad penny that he is, last autumn."

"Where can he be found?"

"In jail, I hear, for carousing and running up debts at local taverns. Same kind of behavior that got him banished from his home twenty years ago." A pair of keen eyes looked up at Aaron. "What business could a gentleman and soldier possibly have with such a worthless person?"

"None of my own, but I know of someone who is anxious to find the man."

Aaron found Beau Carter at the boat-landing of Albemarle Plantation. Tall and strikingly handsome, there was no mistaking the strong family resemblance. The man, scroundrel and ne'er do well even at forty, was Rumor's father.

Beau and his companion, a man named Philip Stokes, were lounging on the dock, drinking cider from a jug. At his approach, Carter swung a welcoming arm. "Come drink with us, friend." He peered drunkenly at Aaron, who accepting the proffered jug, drank thirstily. "You look familiar, are you from around these parts?"

Dismounting, Aaron leaned on the splintered wooden dock post. The wooden column gave way, nearly tossing him into the river. Carter laughed. "The whole damn place is falling apart, fit for nothing but firewood."

"Why don't you fix it up?" Turning, Aaron gazed up at the once-splendid house atop a pretty hill overgrown with brambles. Chickens strutted on the wide front veranda and one side of the house was blackened, as if from a fire.

"I've got tenants in it now," Carter went on. "But I got plans." Pointing a long finger at his companion, he chuckled. "This here is Philip Stokes, and he owns the neighboring plantation, which, I might add, is in lots better shape. Soon's as I marry my

137

daughter to Mr. Stokes, we're going to combine the acreage and tear down Albemarle."

"How'd you do." Philip Stokes stuck out a hand to grasp Aaron's. A man in his thirties, Stokes was small and wiry, with a sly face like a fox. He was nearly as drunk as Carter.

The two men got even friendlier when Aaron told the men that he was born five miles from this very spot on the Pamunkey River, and that he had deserted from the Continental Army.

"The revolution can't last much longer, months at best," he informed the men, with an air of assurance.

Stokes jumped up, nearly falling into the water. "Blast, I told you, Beau, we'd best hurry on up North. First thing you know, that cousin in England will hie on across the waters and snatch Albemarle right out from under your big nose."

At Aaron's astonished look, a drunken Carter told the story. His grandfather had died last summer, leaving all he had, including Albemarle, to Carter's daughter Rumor. According to the will, if she did not claim her inheritance within a year, the property would go to an English cousin.

Beaumont Carter, wastrel, had been cut off without a penny. However, if neither the English cousin nor Rumor Carter showed up to claim Albermarle, Carter had been assured by legal minds that he could sue, and probably win.

"But all I have to do is find my long-lost daughter and marry her off to my good friend, Stokes," Rumor's father grinned. He lifted his head proudly, shaking the honey-brown thatch of graying hair that caught at Aaron's heart. It was the exact color of Rumor's.

"When you find her, what if this daughter is not

138

inclined to marry Mr. Stokes?" Aaron asked quietly. "What if she will not bend to your will?"

Carter's handsome face darkened, and a hard light came into his brown eyes. "My sweet lost baby will do what her daddy tells her. She's a mere eighteen, under age by Virginia law. If she doesn't, well, it will go hard with her." Ripping a piece of wood from the decrepit dock, he broke it in half over his knee. "Women in these parts have no more rights than slaves."

"If this won't bring her to heel," he added slyly, slapping the wood against his hand, "a bit of laudanum in her tea, or an accidental fall down a staircase—"

Puckering his deeply indented lips, Carter whistled. "Well, you're a man of the world, you catch my meaning."

The girl was in New York, acting on the stage, Carter then went on to say. That was the last he had heard of her before he was jailed in September of last year for nearly killing a man in a tavern brawl.

As Aaron looked at the face, so much like his beloved Rumor's, yet hard and set in cruel lines, his heart sank. The man was capable of killing anyone who stood in his way. He had killed once, long ago. He could kill again.

A toot from the river announced a tobacco boat rounding the bend, and as it neared the landing, Carter and Stokes waved it to the landing. "Come with us, friend," Carter urged. "It should be safe enough in New York for a Rebel deserter.

Shaking his head, Aaron remounted and turned his horse toward the road. The tobacco packet would sail into Chesapeake Bay before entering the Atlantic, and then northward along the coast to New York. They were going by water instead of stage or horse, the men had told him, because sheriffs were looking for Carter in every other town in Virginia and Maryland.

The cargo vessel would make several stops along the way, Aaron reasoned. He should be in New York days before Rumor's father.

Five horses and six days later, Aaron Fleming was in New York City, dressed in the nines as Sir Oliver Mowbray and standing outside the John St. Theater, studying the playbill. Rudely elbowing him aside, a British soldier read aloud. " 'The Royal Theater Company in performance tonight of Wm. Shakespeare's comedy, *As You Like it.* Doors open at six. Comedy and wild animal show follow the drama. Rowdies will be speedily evicted.' "

A list of players followed. Lady Rumor Spenser would take the role of Rosalind. Aaron was quite familiar with the play, and knew Rosalind would be attired as a boy during most of it.

The Redcoat whistled. "Blimey! The old bard right here in the Colonies? I 'ear as this Lady Spenser be a clever actress, Ever seen 'er up on the stage, gov'nor?"

"Aye, 'tis rumored she is magnificent," murmured Aaron, liking his own pun.

It was raining hard, one of those cold, determined April downpours that afflict Manhattan Island in the spring, and Aaron huddled into his wool cape, drawing the hood well over his head. He had no wish to be recognized as Sir Oliver, nor was he in a mood for idle conversation or questioning on where he had gone for four months.

He also had a additional problem. He had not reported to General Washington following his mission to Mount Vernon, and he did not intend to. He was now a deserter. The knowledge of his outlaw status did not trouble him, however. He would face his commander in chief when the time came. Now there was one vital, overriding passion in his life, a passion far outweighing duty to his country.

Rumor had to be spirited from New York tonight. Beau Carter might show up at any time, ready to take his daughter in hand and work his evil schemes on her.

With his sweetheart safe, Aaron might well return and resume his masquerade as Lord Mowbray, dandy. That should clear up any problems with his commander in chief about Aaron Fleming's apparent desertion. The Continental Army was still direly in need of inside information on British movements. What better place to obtain it than in New York society?

He looked around the crowded narrow street that swarmed with people, most of them clamoring to enter the theater. As usual, ticket scalpers milled about, asking outrageous prices. Without a thought, Aaron paid a man three pounds for a box.

Still desiring anonymity, he did not take the box once inside the theater, but melted into the crowd standing in the auditorium. With a fanfare of trumpets and a roll of drums, the play began.

The rude stage was done up prettily, if fussily, as the Forest of Arden where Rosalind, the heroine, takes refuge from her scheming uncle, Duke Frederick. Thunderous applause, foot stamping, and whistling greeted the entrance of Lady Spenser, disguised as a shepherd lad. The scene was of Rosalind, in disguise, hiding from an uncle who had torn her from her true love.

"Have I not cause to weep?" Her rich words resounded, and the crowd fell silent. The magic was still there, mused Aaron, the magic he had buried in the turmoil of war. In the bright light of the sconces, her lovely face glowed with inner fire beneath the peaked green medieval cap. The dark green doublet and close-fitting hose did little to hide the slim, seductive form. In truth, she seemed all the more desirable in the masculine attire.

As her beauty once more assaulted his senses, the love he had suppressed so long surged once more into Aaron's heart and soul and body, enveloping him in remembered heat. He felt exactly as he had those agonizing nights back in September, when a sweet Juliet had enslaved him.

Exactly? No, not exactly. His love was stronger than he had ever imagined it could be.

When the play was ended, the players took their bows, and the stage and pit as well were cleared for the circus to follow. Ropes would be strung around the theater to keep the audience from interfering with the horses.

During the performance, Aaron had devised a plan. He would go backstage, accost Rumor in her dressing room, inform her that her father awaited her in a nearby hostel.

He thought of what he would say. He would tell her that her father was anxious to see her and embrace her, that he begged her to forgive him for deserting her mother so long ago. Aaround would say that her father was changed man, had found religion, and that Aaron had met him quite by accident, and he had begged Aaron to intervene, fearing that Rumor would decline to meet him.

As he mused over his speech he realized it all sounded foolish, that she might not believe any of it. But, he reasoned, simple curiosity might induce her to accompany him. He would have a carriage waiting. He would insist she come alone. Despite his previous attempts to sell her into prostitution, she would trust him. She had to.

But as he elbowed through the crush, a high, female voice hailed him. "Why, Sir Oliver, how very odd to see you here! We all thought you dead, or come to some dire circumstance."

It was Lady Olympia Spenser, splendidly attired in mulberry wool, trimmed in black velvet. A thick velvet pelisse was slung over one shoulder, caught with a diamond brooch. Imperiously grabbing his arm, she halted his progress.

Aaron stifled a cry of annoyance. A pox on the woman. She had ruined everything. Forcing a smile, he bent to kiss her extended hand. "I am far from dead, your ladyship, as can be plainly seen. As to the reasons for my abrupt departure and long absence from society, I will regale you with that story at a later time—" He rolled his eyes expressively round the theater"—and in more private surroundings."

"But of course, Sir Oliver. I look forward to your tale. You were always an amusing reconteur." A look of utter joy suffused her plain features as she continued brightly, "But we are astonishingly well met this night."

Turning to two men who had been standing quietly to one side during the dialogue, she exclaimed, "You will be most delighted, as I most assuredly am also, to greet Mr. Beaumont Carter."

A sly look came into her brown eyes. "Does the name ring a bell with you, my friend? Surely you recall a conversation between us on my brother's wedding night. I showed you a handbill—"

"But, *certainement!*"

143

With iron control, Aaron suppressed the cry of anguish welling up within him. The tobacco boat had made spectacular time in reaching New York.

He took Carter's hand warmly, then that of Philip Stokes, thanking the gods above that he had taken care to powder his face well and paste on a couple of beauty spots. Neither man showed any sign of recognizing him as Aaron Fleming.

"But how marvelous," Aaron exclaimed. "Rumor will be transported with joy. She has spoken often of you, but thinks you long dead."

"Like yourself, your lordship," Carter laughed. "I am very much alive."

The cunning look in her eyes extended over Olympia's face. "But come, we waste precious time. Will you join us in Rumor's dressing room, Sir Oliver? I would not deny you the joy of witnessing her amazement."

He grinned from ear to ear, drooping one eye in a sly wink. "We are of one mind, madam. Once reunited with her true parent, I am certain Lady Spenser will want to visit her family home in Virginia."

Carter spoke up at last, in pious, unctuous tones. "I sincerely hope, God willing, that my precious child will comfort me at Albemarle for the rest of our lives together."

"She might even marry again—a local man of property," put in Stokes.

Thinking furiously, Aaron put a staying hand on Lady Olympia's arm. "Let me go before you, to pave the way. The shock of seeing one supposedly dead might bring on an apoplexy to our dear, sweet Rumor."

At her doubtful look, he added smoothly, "I've known it to happen, especially with volatile or artistic personalities. Further, she has just finished a most strenuous performance."

"Good idea," Carter commented. "I confess that I myself have some fears in that regard."

They would repair to a nearby tavern for refreshment, awaiting word from Sir Oliver. Warning that it might take some time to break the news to her, he entered Rumor's dressing room.

After her initial shock at seeing him after so long a time, Rumor listened attentively to the story he had devised earlier. He could not tell her the truth. What daughter would believe that her father awaited a few hundred yards away, and intended to kill her — if neccesary — to get Albemarle.

As he had hoped, she trusted him implicitly. Flinging a heavy brocaded cloak over her masculine costume, she walked with him into the dark alley behind the theater.

She looked around. "But where is your carriage, Sir Oliver?" she inquired.

"There is none. Come with me."

Without a word, he pulled the boy's peaked cap from her head, then drew the hood of her cloak up to cover her hair and most of her face. "Don't say a word," he hissed, as he heard a stifled cry of alarm. "Just listen, for God's sake."

Speaking low and urgently, he told her that her father was nearby with her sister-in-law, waiting to see her. "They both plan evil things for you," he said. "I have come to save you."

Locking his arm into hers, Aaron started propelling them both forcefully down the street. "There's a stable a block away, we'll hire a carriage there."

She screamed and pulled away violently, nearly toppling into the gutter in her haste. "I will go nowhere with you, Lord Mowbray," she spat at him.

Striking herself on the brow with the back of her

145

hand, she turned back toward the theater. "How could I be such an idiot? Will I never learn? This is obviously still another of your rascally schemes."

The hood fell away from her face, which he saw was flaming with fury and scorn. "Just who, what general—or perhaps it's an admiral this time—do you intend to sell me to?" She could not muffle the sob of rage that choked her. "Oh-h-h—dear God in heaven, is there no one—and to think I had begun to trust you—"

"You can, oh, my sweet little fool, you can! I swear on my mother's grave that your father intends to do you harm. You have fallen heir to Albermarle and he is capable of killing you for it." He groaned. "It's exactly as I feared. You refuse to believe the truth."

Leaning toward her, he attempted to take her arms again, but she drew back, shocked. "You don't even know my father, how can you say such—" She stopped, abruptly, as if struck by a sudden thought. Then, after a moment, she mumured wonderingly, "You called me 'sweet.' So what I suspect is true. You are not really what you pretend."

" 'Tis but an expression," he said coldly, retreating from her once more. "I think of you as a child, a very difficult child."

Desperately, he lunged toward her, but suddenly a tall figure loomed from the shadows. Olympia strode forward, accosting them. "So here you are, Sir Oliver, and Rumor, too. Splendid. You have been at your task overlong. Mr. Carter is most anxious, he cannot wait a moment longer to hold his child in his arms."

Rumor went white. "So it's true! My father is actually here in New York."

Flashing a look of contrition at Sir Oliver, she

146

implored, "Lead me to my father, Olympia. I have need of comfort—" Swaying, she fell against Olympia's velvet shoulder. "Sir Oliver has been telling me the most outrageous things—"

Rumor seemed near to fainting, but Olympia was oblivious to anything but her own elation. "Sir Oliver speaks true, your legal parent has come to fetch you home, where you belong. He will succeed where I have failed. Your fraudulent marriage to my brother will be annulled. You married without your father's permission."

The woman erupted into a mirthless laugh. "You will not be Lady Spenser, my girl, free to divert yourself as you wish, but the property of Beaumont Carter."

But Rumor heard nothing. Her senseless form slid to the cobbles, crumpling into a heap, looking like the child Sir Oliver had said she was.

"You idiot woman," Aaron snarled at Olympia as he stooped to lift Rumor into his strong arms. "You've frightened her near to death." Running with her back into the theater, he called back, "Wait here for me, I will see her tended to."

Once revived with smelling salts, Rumor looked up abjectly into the smokey blue eyes of Aaron Fleming. Her own were troubled. Smudges of fatigue and anxiety clouded her face. Rising up from her cot, she threw her arms about his neck. "Sir Oliver, I beg forgiveness for doubting you. Please take me back to Jamaica, as you often said you would."

"Of course," he said tersely, grasping the wooden legs of the cot to keep from drawing her fiercely to himself and kissing away the pain in her face. "But we must make haste."

"Yes," she replied softly, slowly removing her arms

from his neck. She was silent for a long moment, her face set in thought. Then, "But first, sir, I must—"

Mutely, she pointed to a corner of the tiny room where a curtain partially hid a wooden commode and a line of costumes on hooks.

With an understanding smile, he rose up. "Don't be long about it, I'll go back into the alley and stall Olympia and Carter. We can't have them bursting in here now."

When he returned, moments later, the dressing room was empty. Rumor had fled.

Chapter Seven

No one took special notice of the short man in the voluminous green cloth topcoat and a wide-brimmed grosgrain hat pulled low over his face. He seemed just another eager spectator pushing through the auditorium of the John St. Theater. All eyes were glued to the performing ring, where the famed Madame Roseanne was riding bareback, standing up on a splendid white horse. Madame Roseanne was also bare, or so it seemed. Her skintight spangled costume, the most daring ever seen in New York, did little to hide her supple body.

Grateful for Roseanne's magnetic appeal, Rumor kept her head well down until she was a block away from the theater. Then she began to run straight for the docks. She would board a Jamaican packet this very night, but alone. She needed no Sir Oliver Mowbray to act as her keeper. She was no sheltered Spanish senorita requiring a duenna. Rumor had cut the apron strings for good that tied her to Sir Oliver.

For a moment, there in the dressing room, she had been fooled by the warm, protecting look in the cool blue eyes. But only for a moment. She shuddered inwardly at her narrow escape. The man had more than his rightful share of devilish charm. And when the blue eyes took on that smoky look, it was all a silly girl like herself could do to keep from swooning.

The harbor swarmed with vessels of all description, both military and commercial. British sailors, soldiers, and the usual complement of prostitutes crowded the narrow streets around the wharf. Rumor asked a brief question in an affected masculine voice that brought a ready answer.

Chuckling at her easy success, she entered a tavern, and swiftly made arrangements with the captain of the *Mermaid* who was having a last drink ashore before sailing with the tide at midnight. The transaction was brief, eased considerably by the sack of coins Rumor drew from the pocket of her cloak.

The captain asked no questions. This war had made him rich. A multitude of folks were anxious to flee the Colonies—deserters from both sides, women fleeing their husbands, indentured servants, even a black slave or two. The captain was happy to oblige. His cargo of logs and beeswax was actually incidental to his main commerce—human flesh.

They were almost out of the harbor and Rumor was settling into the tiny space behind the wheelhouse where she would spend the next ten days, when a knock sounded on her door.

"It's the cabin boy, sir, with your chamber pot."

Opening quickly, Rumor came face to face with Sir Oliver Mowbray. Beside him stood the captain, shaking his head. "This gentleman swears you are his runaway indentured servant. I must ask you to leave my ship. I want no trouble with the authorities."

"But it's a rotten lie," she shrieked, forgetting to use her masculine voice, "I've never seen this man in my life."

150

But the captain was gone, already halfway down the deck. Without a word, Sir Oliver's fist came up, and she felt herself being enveloped in swimming darkness. When she opened her eyes, they were back on the docks. She was sitting on a horse, behind Sir Oliver, on a cushiony pillion.

It was raining, the green cloth man's coat she wore was sopping wet. The grosgrain hat was not on her head. Two lengths of sturdy hempen rope encircled their two bodies, joining them together at the waist.

Rumor groaned in despair. She had lost her wild bid for freedom. This detestable dandy would sell her into prostitution. She would spend the rest of her miserable life on her back, whilst lecherous, slavering men bent over her, using her body to slake their voracious appetites. Anything Beaumont Carter intended to do to her would be heaven, by comparison. Even death.

"Take me to my father," she muttered against Sir Oliver's wool-covered back. "Before he sets the law after you."

"The law!" he scoffed. "You're damn lucky I showed up and persuaded that money-hungry captain to let me have you. For twice the gold you gave him, the scoundrel. Once he discovered that you're a female, he would have sold you to the highest bidder at the very next port."

"You're talking nonsense. I don't believe you." Her voice rose to a shriek, causing a group of men at a corner to gaze up in alarm.

"Be still, you fool, or I'll be forced to knock you out again."

He spurred the horse to a gallop, and Rumor subsided. Her jaw still hurt from his first blow, and she had no wish to become senseless again. Odd, she thought, her mind wandering, the last time she had

151

been punched in the jaw, a blue-eyed Indian had administered the blow. Like that last time, during the fire, she had felt curiously safe as she did now.

The rhythmic movement of the horse was wondrously soothing, the hard feel of Sir Oliver's back was comforting. Her eyes refused to stay open. She was utterly weary. The past few hours had drained her of both energy and will. She felt eaten up—first two hours cavorting madly on the stage as a shepherd lad, then that dreadful, unbelievable business with Olympia about her father wanting to take her back to Virginia. And now the ever surprising Sir Oliver seemed determined to take charge of her life.

Too weary to lift her head or utter another word, Rumor settled her head between his broad shoulder blades. Eventually, by a clever ruse, she would manage to escape the blackguard. There was sure to be an unguarded moment, but she was too tired to think about it now.

Some time later, in that delicious twilight state between sleep and waking, Rumor felt herself being lowered onto a soft, cushiony bed. A blanket was being thrown over her. It was warm and fuzzy and, childlike, she curled her body into a ball, pulling the blanket over her head. If this is a dream, she mused, let it never end.

Aaron awoke with the buoyant feeling of a child on Christmas morning. His body felt as if every nerve had been touched with an elixir of life. Caught in the pleasant shadowland between dream and reality, his mind spun, seeking the hidden cause for his joy. He stretched, staring straight up into the interlacing branches of the cottonwood. His old friend the jay, perched on a leafy branch, stared back with beady eye.

Aaron shivered. The spring morning was chilly. Odd that he had gone to sleep without his saddle blanket.

The silly bird hopped excitedly from branch to branch, flapping its blue wings in pride. Aaron bolted to his feet, instantly alert, reaching for his knife. The bird was his scout, his pure animal instinct sensing danger long before the man. A soft noise at his feet caused Aaron to swivel, knife poised downward.

Wrapped cocoonlike in his missing blanket, Rumor had turned restlessly in her sleep. He chuckled silently, remembering. That bubbly feeling in his gut came from the knowledge that today was the day for which he had yearned, without knowing it, all his twenty-eight years. Today, Aaron Fleming would truly become a man; today he would possess the woman he loved.

A warm sun was already pearling the treetops but did not penetrate the bower where they had slept. She had not awakened last night when he lowered her limp form on the bed of leaves. How he had longed to take her then, at least to hold her in his arms. But it was too soon.

The eternal forest twilight reigned in Aaron's hiding place, this secret bower where for the last time he would discard the persona of Sir Oliver Mowbray.

A soft iridescent light fell on the sleeping girl. Her lovely face was tucked cunningly into her elbow, so that only one arching brow and one closed eyelid were visible. He stood a moment, struck by the simple beauty of the fringed brown lashes shadowing the curving cheek, imprinting it in his heart for all time. A tiny muscle moved in the smooth white brow above her eye, and Aaron clenched his hand to keep from dropping to his knees and kissing the spot with his lips.

Whatever came, however all this hellish business of war and flight from a scheming Beaumont Carter turned out, they would have this day — one perfect day in all their lives, to outshine all others.

So overwhelming was the young man's passion that he never entertained for a single fraction of a moment that the object of his intense desire would not love him back with a power to match his own.

Unconsciously, he flexed his powerful muscles. Fare-thee-well, Sir Oliver Mowbray, welcome Aaron Fleming, he thought to himself.

Lost in fantasy, Aaron imagined Rumor's supple flesh writhing under his as she strove in the sweet agonies of female passion. Her flesh would be soft yet firm, resilient yet tough, her mounded breast would spring beneath his touch.

The squawking jay started greeting the morning in shrill, scolding tones, interrupting his reverie. Reaching out, Aaron angrily shook the limb, sending the bird away. Miraculously, the racket had not awakened her. The ride from New York had been grueling. She was not only exhausted but certainly sore from riding astride, instead of sidesaddle as is customary for females. Aaron smiled, thinking of how the exercise he planned for her would banish the soreness from her sweet round buttocks.

Fearful lest she wake before he had changed, he loped, Indian fashion, down the reedy embankment to the stream. Doffing his soiled garments, he leapt eagerly into the cold water, chasing two fat beavers into their mud-daubed lodge on the other side.

On the bank again, he danced and leapt about like a deer in rutting season, drying himself in the crisp air, slapping his chest. Casting a blue-eyed gaze upon himself, he nodded with approval. His biceps and thighs were like tempered steel, his narrow hips cradling the ready manhood in its nest of dark hair. He felt like Adam on the day of creation.

The brown hair on his broad, rippling chest which he'd shaven off for playing Mohawk with the Sons of Liberty was as thick as before. He peered worriedly at the red turtle. She would have to part the hair to see it, and why on earth would she want to do that? There were so many other more erotic places on his manly body where she could kiss or stroke. He would simply have to be on guard that she did not glimpse the telltale totem.

Not today. Nor tomorrow. One day, when she was as enslaved by love as he was at this moment, when nothing on earth, certainly no silly vow of vengeance made in the heat of pain could separate them, they would laugh about it.

"To think, my love, that I once vowed to kill you," she would say in her throaty actress voice. "Imagine!"

He should have the telltale tattoo removed, he mused, but he had a superstitious fear that erasing the memory of his Indian years might bring bad luck.

Removing the skin-wrapped bundle from the willow, he shrugged into his buckskin. The shirt and long trousers reeked of mold and old sweat. Quite a change for her from Sir Oliver's raspberry cologne, he thought with glee. Now Miss Rumor Seton could fill her dainty nostrils with the animal aroma of a real man.

Quickly now, anxious, Aaron wrapped the dandelion-yellow satin breeches and quilted green coat in the bearskin and thrust it well back into the willow. He might need them again one day. Once his love was safely tucked away where Beaumont Carter could not harm her, he would report back to General Washington.

The old man would understand why his top spy had taken his leave. Hadn't the two of them talked many nights over the fire about what love can do to a man?

A silvery trout flashed in the sunlit water, and, lightning swift, Aaron bent his lanky form to scoop up the fish with his two hands. They would need breakfast before making love. All of their breakfasts, and suppers, too, must come from the land from this day forward. Even if he dared to venture into a town, he could buy nothing. That damn captain had taken all his coins.

As he quickly gutted the fish and started back toward the cottonwood, his mind dwelt eagerly on the coming intimacy. He hoped she wouldn't act coy, forcing him to play a courtly game of seduction. It was something he had never done.

The Indian maids he'd taken during his two years with the Shawnee had been more than willing. There was a simple, primitive pattern—the short chase through the trees, the capture, the coupling. Short, sweet, satisfying. No talk. No holding back. Just the natural joining of two young bodies in heat. The Indian girls had a way of wrapping a man between their legs which even now, in memory, set his loins afire. He often wondered if there were any little Indian babies with his blood in their veins.

There'd been no opportunity to play the courting game with highborn women. A man with no fortune is not welcome in respectable houses. As for prostitutes, the general had warned him against indulgence of that kind. "Most are diseased," he'd said. "Find yourself a clean girl, and marry her if you must."

156

Reaching the bower Aaron saw that Rumor still slept like a child who's played too hard and long. The blanketed bundle moved gently, rhythmically, up and down. Aaron hummed softly under his breath. It was a glorious morning for making love. He was happy that she was no virgin who expected him to arouse her to passion, to guide her gently, expertly, through her first sexual encounter.

Holy saints, but he was lucky. A woman of Rumor's obvious experience with men would have a lot to teach him. He frowned. He would make it absolutely clear that after him there would be no others.

He gathered twigs and stones for a fire. This part of Manhattan was no longer a combat area, both forces now being encamped in eastern Pennsylvania. There were few British patrols. As for Beaumont Carter, that scoundrel was halfway to Jamaica by now, following the false trail he had laid last night with the captain of the *Mermaid*.

His back to Rumor, he was turning the fish with a sharpened twig when he heard her voice behind him. "Where did you get those backwoodsman clothes, Sir Oliver?"

It was a sleepy voice, showing no fear. Without turning around, he stated simply, in his slow, Virginia drawl, "I am not Sir Oliver Mowbray. I am Aaron Fleming, of Virginia, a Rebel spy."

Pausing to let her absorb that much, he continued casually. "As for the clothes, I got them from a hole in that willow tree yonder by the beaver dam."

Deliberately keeping his back toward her, he waited. The fish had begun to take on a tantalizing aroma. Silence. Then he heard a sharp hissing sound, an indrawn breath, followed by a pleased, "I think I always knew you were no dandy."

"Did you now?" Half turning his face, he grinned

157

widely. "If so, you were the only one who suspected."

There was a shaky little half-giggle, half-laugh, as if she were struggling for control. "It's really a great relief to know you're not really a vain, conceited macaroni, but — Then she added, "Very clever disguise. My compliments, Mr. Fleming. You could go on the stage."

"Umm," he chuckled, and, rising, picked up a thick piece of sapling to boost the fire. "Americans disapprove of theatricals, remember?"

"Oh, yes, I know that only too well."

She had pulled herself to a sitting position, pulling the blanket tight around her. "But I — don't know if I can trust you anymore," she ventured. "Though I must confess I am grateful that you took me from that ship. It was a mad, impulsive — "

"Idiotic thing to do," he finished for her.

Pulling her hand from the blanket, she rubbed her chin. "It doesn't hurt much. I guess you had to do it."

"Certainement," he quipped, in Sir Oliver's high nasal whine. "But there is no bruise. Your chin looks lovely."

She obliged him with a laugh, then sheepishly threw him an owlish look. "Who knows what you may turn into by tomorrow?"

Taking a few steps from the fire, he loomed above her. She hunched over, hugging her knees with her arms, her piquant face upturned. Lifting a trembling hand, she brushed a lock of hair from her eye. The long ride had left her glorious mane all tangled and knotted.

"Not trust me?" Aaron's sandy brow went up to his reddish hair, and almost angrily, he returned to the fire, where the fat trout was crackling and turn-

158

ing brown and crispy. "I saved you from your father, didn't I, confound it anyway. And from the *Mermaid* captain. At considerable risk to myself, I might add."

"Why?" she asked simply.

The word echoed in the forest, and Aaron was struck dumb. How could he find words to explain his love? He shrugged, incapable of answering just then. She would find out soon enough. Irritation surged within him.

While he was grateful that she had not gone into hysterics at his sudden metamorphosis into a frontiersman, he was more than a little piqued that she had taken it so calmly. But then, she might be in genuine turmoil inside. After all, she was an actress, accustomed to feigning any emotion upon demand.

She had risen, and was standing by him now, clutching the blanket tightly around herself. The long hair tumbled untidily past her hips, or where he thought her hips would be if he could see them.

"We should cut your hair," he said sternly, "and find a cap to hide it. You must continue to travel as a boy, until such time as we are well out of Beaumont Carter's reach."

He rolled his eyes, and made a slicing motion with his finger across his throat. "Even under my protection, a beauteous female like yourself will not be safe."

At her continuing, staring silence, he finished lamely. "Well, we'll talk about it after breakfast."

Their eyes met and locked, as if joined by an invisible string. She didn't move. Two tiny, vertical lines appeared between the soft brown eyes which continued to stare at him like a puzzled young owl. With an effort, Aaron suppressed the hot yearning within him. Botheration, why should a female who

159

looks like she's been dragged through a knothole make him so randy?

Finally she spoke, shyly, hesitantly. "Are you—" Her mud-streaked cheeks turned the color of ripe strawberries. "I mean, Sir Oliver was not interested in women . . ."

She lowered her eyes, and the slender hands clutching the blanket at her neck tensed until the knuckles whitened. She looked so terrified, he wanted to reach out and enfold her trembling body in his strong, warm arms. But strangely, he could not move a muscle toward her. A wall of diffidence had arisen between them, even though they had been friends in a way no one else would understand. For nine months they had seen each other daily. My God, they had even ridden six hours astride the same horse, her body fitting into his from behind.

Now they could have been travelers, meeting by chance in the forest. Thinking about it that way added a spicy fillip to the coming adventure for Aaron.

"We'll also talk about my manhood—or lack of it—later," he snapped. "Now scoot down to the stream and wash up so we can eat."

As she darted fawnlike through the trees, he yelled after her in a loud voice, "Take off your clothes and bathe properly. Your virtue is safe with me, Miss Seton."

As she splashed energetically around in the beaver dam, Rumor's thoughts tumbled over one another, like a child's marbles rolling down a long, spiraling staircase. Ironically, she felt a keen sense of loss over the now defunct Sir Oliver. Despite his many cruelties and his freely expressed contempt for all females—especially pretty ones like herself—Rumor had seen through the facade. She had sensed that under the snobbish exterior lay an intensely complicated person.

True, he had sold her to General Howe, but she had been rescued mysteriously. Although Liz had taken credit, she was now convinced that the fake dandy was responsible.

For months she had thought that Sir Oliver was not—could not be—what he seemed. As an actress herself, a person who had assumed many roles, she had sensed that the man was playing a part. Expertly. To turn into a macaroni was a stroke of genius. She smiled. How she had agonized over her growing attraction for a man who was not a man!

That he was a Rebel spy had never crossed her mind, not once. She had thought the sparks of her desire for him to be aberrations of a girl unused to the ways of love.

Narcissus of legend had gazed into a stream at his own image until he turned into a flower. Sir Oliver Mowbray had, by a simple change of clothes, turned into a virile man with a brown, hawklike face, wiry hair, and muscles which bulged through the heavy buckskin. His hands at the fire were strong, calloused. His fingers were hard knuckled, with blunt ends and strong nails. A man's hands—hands that could clutch a woman by the shoulders, hurl her to the forest floor and ravish her within an inch of her life.

Fear—stark, primitive, and delicious—raced through Rumor's body as she paddled feverishly around in the icy water. She was alone in the wilderness with a man she did not know. A man she had thought to be somebody else.

She could escape while he was out of sight beneath the cottonwood. She gazed around her. Beyond the fringes of the stream, the forest seemed impenetrable.

Her choice was simple. Submit to his will, or perish because of wild beasts in the forest.

He had insisted that she bathe, and he would most certainly cut her hair because she was his prisoner. His captive.

Captive. The word made Rumor shiver with delight.

Her supple body glided through the clear water like a rare white flower, taking life from its invigorating coldness. As she swam, her churning thoughts seemed to straighten out, and one soared clear and strong above the rest. It was this: she wanted Aaron Fleming as a man, today, in this green world where no prying eyes would see their love. Why would she flee? Love awaited her.

Rumor continued to swim, feeding her desire, luxuriating in her growing passion, as the clear water lapped against her thighs and sucked into the tiny dark place between her breasts. As her wanting grew and swelled, her body began to go limp. She felt she no longer could control it. She cast her eyes down to her firm white breasts on which the rosy rigid nipples waited for a man's caress. She was tense with readiness.

There would be no need to "talk about it," as he had said. To think she had questioned his manhood! A throaty laugh escaped her, her breath caught in her throat. Aaron Fleming exuded virility—the way he squatted by the fire, sinewy thighs spread apart in easy strength, the implicit and thrilling, masterful way the broad shoulders spread outward from his neck.

Rumor was reminded of a panther she had seen

once from a moving carriage. It had crouched on a hillock, preparing to spring upon its mate, who squatted opposite, snarling, resisting. As the carriage had moved on, the high-pitched scream of the female was heard as the male mounted and entered her.

Rumor thought about his body. He seemed perfect. It was in the eyes, she decided, finally, that she had seen the brief flare of wanting, when he had been Sir Oliver. It had always been quickly suppressed. His eyes were still the eyes of the fop, but they were not hard and glittering as before. Through the curling wisp of smoke from the campfire, they had been soft, yet luminous, kind of smoky . . .

Smoky! The word raced through her brain like a flame. Rumor was seized with a revelation so powerful yet so true that she stopped breathing for a second. Diving beneath the water, she touched the slippery rocks in the stream bed, clutching them as if to assure herself that she was not mad.

That fiery and tragic September night when her life had changed forever, she had gazed into those very eyes. They had smoldered down at her from a painted Indian face. She had felt then, as she felt now, the fire of passion in her blood, the same fire she had felt upon occasion at Sir Oliver's touch.

Surfacing again, she treaded water. *Amazing, how it all fell into place!* Aaron Fleming was the Mohawk who had saved her from the fire, who had watched David die. Aaron Fleming, whom she loved to desperation at this moment, was the man she had vowed to kill.

As she climbed back into the green hose and doublet of Shakespeare's Rosalind, Rumor felt as though a heavy stone lay upon her heart. Her course was clear. She could not possibly lie in his arms.

How could she love the man she had sworn before God to kill?

First, she must make certain. She must get this tall Virginian to take off his buckskin shirt. Vengeance filled her heart, which moments before had been consumed by love. Her eyes aglitter, Rumor started up the embankment toward the fire.

"Sit down, eat," he said gruffly, through a mouthful of food. His long arm swept across the smoldering embers of the fire. Meekly, hoping he wouldn't hear the pounding of her heart, Rumor sat and ate from the piece of whitish bark that served as a plate.

He seemed nervous, and when he had consumed his trout, he got up jerkily, dropping his fish bones and bark into the ashes. "I'll be at the stream—ah-h, washing up." His eyes were downcast, as if he feared to meet her gaze.

Looking up calmly, she said, chewing as she talked, "I don't think I want my hair cut. It's a woman's crowning glory, you know."

He stared. His blue eyes flared in the sudden burst of flame from the burning bark. Then without a word, he turned and sprinted toward the water. Rumor gulped down her fish, hardly tasting it. Her desire to see the red turtle possessed her, and there was one sure way of doing it. She would seduce him.

Hurling her own bark into the fire, she raced to the stream. He squatted on the bank, his hands in the water. Softly, she crept up behind him and thrust her hands around and beneath the heavy butternut shirt. His flesh was hard and warm to her cold fingers.

Lightning swift, he reached behind him, and before she knew what was happening, Rumor found herself being tumbled head over heels into the water. As she surfaced, spluttered, she saw his angry face

164

glowering down at her, the glint of his hunting knife in his upraised hand.

"Goddamn it, woman, don't ever sneak up on a man like that." He lowered the knife, laid it on the bank, and reached out to grab her hand to pull her back up beside him.

She sat there, wanting to weep, wringing the water from her hair. "I—I just wanted to touch you," she sobbed.

"What for?" His hands were on her shoulders, the smoky eyes filled with the feverish glitter of lust.

"To—to—" She stared into his face, a sudden thrill of dismay coursing through her. Her hand went to her mouth, Perhaps he really was a man who felt no desire for women!

"I thought you wanted me as I—"

Her confidence crumbled, and blushing furiously, she bent her head in shame. As a seductress, she had failed miserably. Desperately, she racked her brain for lines from roles she had played—any words at all which could convey to him that she wanted him to love her. She had to expose that manly chest. She had to see the red turtle.

Finally, she burst out, "I want so desperately to feel your flesh on mine."

"Oh-h?" His sunburnt face looked astonished, then wary, then glad. "Oh, my God, Rumor, my sweet, my own—"

His arms were on her back, and she was being lowered to the marshy bank. He was on his knees above her, and his hands moved to cup her buttocks. With a loud groan, he brought her lower body up to his. His hips began to swivel and she felt the hardness of his manhood grind against her feminine softness beneath the tight-fitting green hose.

Frightened now, Rumor tried to scramble from

165

beneath his heavy body, but he held her fast. His eyes were closed, and he was panting into her ear, "Love me, please love me. Show me what you want me to do."

His lips came down on hers in a bruising kiss. Forcing her lips open with his tongue, he explored her mouth. She bit down. Drat the man, she was the seducer here, and whatever happened, she would not be raped by a clumsy oaf of a randy American patriot.

With a cry of rage, he was on his feet. Blood seeped from his mouth, running down his chin.

Springing up, she snapped, "You fool. I am not an animal to be mounted and pierced at your will." Getting to her feet, she ran to the hollow willow, hiding her burning face in its mottled bark, her arms outflung.

After a moment to collect herself, she turned around. "Your undue haste flatters me, Mr. Fleming," she said softly, "but please allow me to remove my clothes before you ravish me."

There was no reply. He had returned to the water, and lifting off his shirt, plunged in. With two quick movements, his breeches were also off, and he squatted in the water, naked, waiting.

Her heart began to thud as she stared at the dark place between his thighs. Then, forcing her eyes upward, she fixed on his chest at the spot where the red turtle should be. His sandy hair was thick and golden in a thin ray of sun which pierced the interlacing trees. Mindlessly, Rumor slipped out of the medieval costume. She was burning up, as if from a fever. Her entire body ached to be held. The tumult between her thighs would drive her insane, she thought, if she could not appease it.

Taking a steadying breath, she waded in. He came

166

to meet her, and clasping both her hands in his, drew her to himself. They knelt together on the rocks, the shallow water barely clearing her waist. Bending his head, he placed his lips on one taut nipple, holding it gently, firmly, within his mouth.

For long, exquisite moments, the two remained still as he plundered her breasts. Rumor closed her eyes, abandoning herself to pure sensation.

Releasing his hands, he began to make little stroking motions on her thighs, circling, circling, moving inexorably inward, until his hard, calloused fingertips reached the hair sheltering her womanhood. Then, very gently, his fingers parted the downy softness to discover the opening in her body, separating the warm, moist flesh like the petals of a flower.

Tiny spears of pleasure rippled through Rumor's hips and abdomen. The shock of these new feelings was so great, she could only fling back her head and stare up at the arching trees. Her mouth fell open, and her breath came and went in short, hot gasps. Instinctively, she moved against him, desperately needing to feel his hard manhood against her.

With a deep cry he stopped caressing her and drew her tight against his hard, thick shaft.

"No, no, not that — please." She wanted the stroking to go on. "I'm not ready for —"

His head was down as he concentrated on entering her. Pulling his head up, she forced his eyes to hers. "I am a virgin, Aaron, I — I am afraid —"

The blue eyes grew wide. "Nonsense. You're an actress, many men must have had you."

She shook her head vigorously from side to side. "No, never. I was always protected. Please, go more slowly." She paused, reddened. "I want you to kiss me, all over, to stroke me, to be gentle — when — it happens."

167

Rumor was intoxicated with desire. Despite the icy water, her body was tingling madly. She wanted this man to love her, to possess her, to ravish her. The red turtle be damned! She would forget about her vow. Sweet, nonviolent David would not want her to kill for his sake. She was no longer David's child, but a woman in need of a man.

The surprise on his face had softened somewhat, as with infinite care he drew her to him once again. Her eyes bored into his, and finally he exclaimed, "As a gentleman, I am compelled to believe you, but for a virgin, you show a remarkable amount of passion, my little vixen." He nibbled on her earlobe, and ran his big hands up and down her back, delving into the warm place between her buttocks, holding her fast. "But the proof of any pudding lies in the tasting."

The torment of her desire was so overpowering, Rumor's senses were whirling. Blindly, she reached behind and grabbing his hand, guided his fingers once again to her throbbing femininity. Brazenly, shamelessly, she thrust her nipple into his mouth.

Arching backward, she let her passion rise unchecked as a searing heat enveloped her. There was an unbearable sweetness in her blood, a clamor to be satisfied. When his finger found a sensitive place, she cried out with spasms of ecstasy, writhing against him like a woman possessed. Her legs left the bottom of the stream, and curling up and around his hard hips, she cried, "Oh, Aaron, love me, love me, I need you so. I swear I will go mad—"

"No." The word came out bulletlike from his mouth, as he abruptly released her. "Not this way. Let's go back on shore."

Shocked out of her semiconscious state, Rumor gaped. Her desire receded. She felt ill. Flushed, she lowered her gaze to his chest, and with a quick movement separated the curly hairs on his left nipple with her fingers. The tiny red turtle gleamed darkly against the glistening flesh. The tattooed shape moved in and out with his breath. It seemed alive. She felt all desire and love drain from her body. It was replaced by a cold fury—not at the man who had deceived her all these months, but at herself for being such a fool. She had let a crude bodily lust captivate her brain, making her forget her vow of vengeance.

Biting her lip to keep from crying out, she splashed to the bank, and picking up his discarded hunting knife, pointed it at him, holding it with two trembling hands. "You are the scum who saw my sweet David tortured and murdered," she gritted, "and I intend to kill you. Now."

Reaching her in two strides, he caught her by the wrist and twisted it until her hand opened up, dropping the knife. He was laughing, the smoky eyes filled with merriment. "I honestly regret your stepfather's death, Rumor, but I saved your life—not once, but twice."

Cocking a sandy brow, he loped up the embankment, not even bothering to grab his clothes. "I think that evens the score."

Bewildered by conflicting emotions, Rumor, unmindful of their nakedness, followed him to the cottonwood. His long rifle leaned against the tree, and, lifting it, he thrust it at her, almost knocking her to the ground.

"Here," he murmured, with a twinkle in his eye, "use this. You'll have to prime it, load it, and catch me when my back is turned, but it will do a more respectable job of killing Aaron Fleming than a skinny old hunting knife."

169

The weapon was so heavy, she could hardly hold it. Stupidly, she stared at the gleaming metal barrel, the shining wooden handle. He was rummaging in his saddlebag, throwing powder horn and a bunch of cleaning tow onto the ground. Just returning from her night in the forest, the sorrel mare gazed benignly at the two naked people who were making so much noise.

As he emptied the saddlebag, Aaron talked rapidly, though calmly. "Here's the bullet mold, you might prefer to make your own. Most marksmen do. I must warn you that my rifle has a nasty way of kicking back." He glanced up. "They're like horses, or women, they get used to one master. You may want to go off somewhere and take a few practice shots—"

He stopped as he heard a tiny whimper escape her. Flinging down the cumbersome gun, she ran off, weeping, back to the water. I'm a complete fool, she thought with agony. He would never love her now as a woman. He would take her, use her, tire of her, discard her. Or maybe even sell her to somebody else, as he had sold her to General Howe.

Following her, he caught her by the arms, and together they fell back into the water, clinging to each other like two drowning people. Turning her so that her head and shoulders rested on the bank, Aaron forgot about his lack of experience, and with unerring instinct, did to her what he sensed she wanted him to do. He plundered her nipples, her neck, her mouth, with lips and tongue and fingers. Her gasps of delight goaded him on to more and more daring explorations.

Every place he touched, it seemed, sent her into transports of delight. Her legs curled round him, tight, better than any Indian maid. Her slender arms

170

flung up and out and around, as she writhed like a snake with tremors of ecstasy. Once again, saving it till last, he touched the place which had thrilled her so before. Slowly, tenderly, he touched it with his lips.

"Caress me, I beg you," she implored.

His strong fingers persisted in the rhythmic stroking, until suddenly, she arched her body, her head on the marshy ground, while the ecstasy of fulfillment took its long, delicious, satisfying course.

Aaron had never seen a woman undergo such a powerfully wrenching climax. The young Indian maids had remained silent throughout the copulation, with maybe a grunt or two at the end.

Forgetting her plea to be gentle, he knelt above her on the bank, and plunged his aching manhood into her with all his strength. Inside she was warm and strong. The resilience of her seemingly frail body drove him to a frenzy. He hardly felt the tiny moment of resistance as the tissue of her maidenhead was torn. Nor did he heed the tiny cry as she felt his demanding flesh pierce her pliant womanly body.

Her fingers clutched his thatch of hair, and she moved against him, circling her hips to gain the greatest contact with his thrusting manhood. Again and again he thrust, ever deeper into her body.

Fixing her eyes on his, she moved with him as one body, riding the waves of passion, as his rhythmic plunging brought him to his own explosive fulfillment. Flinging back his head, he shut his eyes and opened his mouth in a hoarse cry of male triumph that echoed in the forest.

Rumor remembered the screaming of the panther as he had leapt upon his mate. When she saw the spasms rippling through the hard flesh around his

171

manhood, spiraling up into the taut muscles of his abdomen, her own fading desire resurged, and, kneading his ironlike buttocks with her hands, she whispered, "Aaron, please love me again."

"Soon, but first let a man catch his breath."

Chuckling, struggling for breath, he fell against her. Softly, her arms reached around to cradle him. Never in her life had she thought such rapture to be possible.

Tears of happiness coursed down her cheeks. Inwardly, she said farewell to the vengeful, foolish girl who had thought to kill the man she loved more than life itself.

Chapter Eight

The new lovers spent their first day in the forest of Manhattan Island making love. They were like two people who had been found starving on a desert island, who must now feed their ravenous appetites. The food they ate was not only that of love, however. At midday, they devoured a second fat trout. For their evening meal Aaron caught a possum with a snare.

"Let us never leave this paradise," Rumor whispered, replete with love and food, turning in Aaron's arms. "To think I once thought that dining on Sèvres china and sleeping on a feather tick was all a woman could wish for."

He laughed deep in his throat, covering her face with kisses. He, too, much preferred his dinner on a piece of bark and taking pleasure with his love on a fragrant bed of cattails and willow leaves.

But sobering, he said, "Sadly, this paradise, like the first, has a serpent lurking in it, my sweet. Two of them, in fact—your father and your sister-in-law. They will be searching for us with dogs and men with guns and swords, I'm sure."

He did not mention that General Washington might also be tracking down a certain major who had apparently deserted. Time enough for all that later. He would point his horse toward eastern Pennsylvania, where the Continental Army was now entrenched.

Once safely in that region, he would hide Rumor in a safe place, one where her enemies would not think of looking for her. Then he would take his chances with the general. Desertion from the ranks had become so severe that flogging, imprisonment, and even hanging were being meted out to stem the tide.

His longtime friend and foster father was a stern disciplinarian; he had to be strict, to keep his ragtag army from dissolving completely. Aaron could expect no special mercies.

The western sun had just left the horizon when he announced that they must resume their journey. After a futile try at stuffing her long hair into one of Aaron's beaver caps taken from the willow hiding place, Rumor submitted to a haircut.

As the shining locks fell victim to Aaron's sharp hunting knife, falling in a heap on the forest floor, Rumor found that she experienced a wondrous sense of freedom. Her head felt light, her arms and shoulders felt light. She felt light all over, as if she had been drinking wine.

"I could walk on air," she exclaimed, running about their bower like a child. A vagrant evening breeze blew on her neck and ears, a sensation completely new and wonderful to her.

"Women are such fools to tolerate that heavy burden all their lives," she cried.

Running to the stream, she threw off the doublet, and naked to the waist, splashed water on her breasts and shoulders, cleansing them of stray hairs.

Seeing her like that, her rosy flesh wet and glisten-

174

ing, the shoulder-length brown hair curling round her beautiful face, Aaron caught her to himself. Bending his head, he kissed the dewy drops from her rounded breast.

"Oh, Aaron, how is it possible to want you yet again?" she groaned, pressing hard against him. "Will I never be satisfied?"

"I hope not," he muttered. "But we have a lifetime to find out."

Anxiously glancing up at the flaring sunset, he pushed her from him regretfully. "Get dressed, we've got to be heading west."

Traveling by night to escape detection, and sleeping, eating, and loving by day in the forest, the fleeing lovers managed to get halfway through New Jersey before they saw another living soul.

It was an Indian, very tall and naked but for a very dirty breechclout. He was a deep, rich brown all over, a copper band encircled his wrist, there were long eagle feathers in his hair. A great knife hung down on a thong slung across his massive chest.

Stern and unmoving, he gazed with hooded eyes down on the sleeping man and woman entwined beneath a tree. Opening her eyes, as if she had felt the intent gaze in her sleep, Rumor thought groggily, "My, what a magnificent fellow. Why do they call them redskins, when they are such a handsome brown?"

A split second later she uttered a whooping, strangled cry of pure terror. Bolting up beside her, Aaron reached for his rifle, but immediately dropped it back onto the ground. Rising quickly, he faced the savage, speaking to him in the Indian tongue.

Rumor had fled into the forest, waiting. Aaron was defenseless, she thought. His knife and rifle were yards away from where he stood. If this savage killed him, she would be at his mercy.

Instinctively, she put both hands on her head, as if to protect it from being scalped. Aside from the fake Mohawks who had attacked the theater, she had never been so close to a native before.

Finally, after what seemed an eternity, Aaron turned, smiled, and gestured for her to come forward. When she hesitated, he bounded to her side and dragged her by the arm. When they drew close to the Indian, he pointed with his hand to the man's chest.

Rumor gasped, nearly fainting with relief. Over the man's left nipple, cunningly drawn in red, was the tiny image of a turtle.

"We are brothers in the Shawnee tribe," he said. "They adopted me when I was a boy." Shoving her roughly back toward the tree, he said loudly, "Now, go sit down behind the tree like a good girl and don't make a sound. Nymwha and I are going to make big medicine."

He winked without changing his stern expression and Rumor understood that where Indians were concerned, a woman was best not seen, nor heard, nor even thought about when serious talk was taking place.

Leaning against the rough bark of the sycamore, Rumor pulled the green coat she had taken from the theater over herself. The May day was warm, but the deep forest held a chill. She could hear their voices, low and earnest, interrupted at intervals by long silences.

From time to time she turned her head to see them. They were taking turns smoking from the pipe that Aaron drew from his saddlebag. Clouds of tobacco smoke rose into the air, weaving eerily in and out of the overhanging tree branches.

Finally, she fell asleep again, stretching her slender form out on the bed of leaves. When she woke, it was totally dark, and Aaron was shaking her. "We've got to get out of here."

The Indian was gone, and silently they remounted and resumed their journey westward. Aaron's face was grim, and he told her nothing that had transpired between him and Nymwha until dawn streaked the sky and they released their weary steed once more to graze and slumber in the forest.

He did not take her into his arms and ravish her with love, as usual. It was raining, and after hastily constructing a shelter of interlacing cattails and willow saplings, he held her tight and told her that Beaumont Carter was following them, closely.

"Nymwha says that a large bounty is being offered for your capture. General Howe has sent dispatches to all his troops, ordering them to pick up for questioning anyone even remotely resembling a tall man dressed in dandy's clothes, traveling with a beautiful brown-haired girl."

Grimacing, he continued. "The girl was reported to be wearing bottle-green tights and doublet and riding a sorrel mare."

Obviously they had been seen riding out of New York that fatal night. Rumor recalled with a twinge the men on the street corner, who had glanced up as they had passed.

"But why would General Howe become involved?" she asked, bewildered. "Surely Liz would persuade him that my father means to do me harm."

He shook his head. "Despite his former lust for you, the British commander is more interested in me, my darling. If he hasn't already discovered it, he surely must have strong suspicions that the man whom everyone called Sir Oliver Mowbray has been

177

spying on him all these years."

Pressing her painfully against his long body, he mumbled, with a little, hollow laugh, "He also surely knows damn well that Sir Oliver is more of a man than anyone thought."

It was imperative that she acquire new garments. But how, and where? To enter a town or hamlet was dangerous. "When I think of all those wonderful costumes hanging in the John St. dressing room," she mourned.

Aaron, doffing his buckskin, easily passed for an Indian. Wood ashes mixed with purple berries turned his short-cropped reddish hair a musty black. Once again, as in his Son of Liberty days, he shaved his chest with his hunting knife until not a hair remained. His beard, which had reached a goatee length, came off also.

He slung his rifle across his back, as Indians did, with a thong crossing his chest. It was a splendid firearm, he informed her proudly. Smooth-bored, double-barreled, and fashioned of the finest Spanish steel. He'd found it in the forest after a fierce battle during the Indian wars in the sixties.

Even with the shortened hair, it was insanity to continue passing Rumor off as a boy. "They'll expect that," Aaron said. "We'd best disguise you as a woman."

"Old and feeble and decrepit," Rumor suggested, humping her back and hobbling around the little clearing. She began to mutter in a shrill, cracked voice which astonished Aaron.

"If I didn't know better," he grinned, "I'd swear you were ninety if a day."

She would turn into an old squaw, they decided, but a skirt was needed, and a bodice or shirt to hide her firm breasts. As they neared the Pennsylvania

178

border, they spied a farmhouse where a woman was hanging garments on a line. She seemed to be alone, and when she walked into a nearby field where vegetables were growing, Aaron quickly darted to the house and removed a billowing skirt and bodice.

The skirt was thick gray homespun, the bodice a calico with a faded pattern of red-and-blue butterflies. After smearing both with forest loam to make them look worn, Rumor put them on and draped the saddle blanket over her shoulders, pulling it tight around herself.

With his knife, Aaron sliced off a strip from the overlong hem, and helped Rumor wind it round her hair. But not before she had given her shiny brown locks the ash and berry treatment also.

Rumor enjoyed the make-believe, relishing the ease with which they fooled people on the road. For now they could travel in the open once again. They had sold the horse at a roadside tavern and were traveling afoot, Rumor walking a good ten yards behind Aaron, head bowed, arms beneath the blanket in the manner of all Indian squaws.

For the hundredth time at least, she uttered a silent prayer of thanks for the sturdy men's riding boots she'd had the good sense to slip on when she had run off from the theater.

On the whole, Aaron declined to consider their masquerade a game. He had had a bellyful of pretending to be something he was most definitely not, he said with truculence. But as they boarded a ferry to cross the Delaware into Pennsylvania, he seemed to brighten.

Once on land again, he told her, finally, of his plans for her. "There's a house in Chadds Ford," he said, as they bathed and rested beside a pretty stream, "where I was once befriended. The husband

179

was killed early in the war, but his widow and numerous little ones maintain a good-sized farm."

He told her there were at least ten children, some full grown, with grandchildren running about, and visitors galore. She could simply blend in as a maid or visiting relative. At any sign of danger, he remembered a cellar, where she could run to.

"No one will think of looking for you in such a place," he said confidently. "Don't go into the village, or mingle in society."

She would have to work, of course, to pay her way, he warned, glancing down at her delicate hands.

"Thanks to Olympia," she replied, "I can sew and darn a silk stocking."

That fetched a grunt. "More likely they'll put you to spinning or wiping babies' bottoms."

She was fearful. "How long must I hide?"

"Until we are certain that Beau Carter has given up and gone back to Virginia."

Being among people once again, especially kindly folk such as he described, appealed to Rumor. But, still timorous, she asked wistfully, "When will you return for me?"

The thought of living without the man she had learned to love beyond all belief filled her with terror. The days on the farm would be filled with work, but how could she bear the long summer nights?

"Return for you?" he echoed. "When this fool war is over, one way or the other," he gritted. "Much as I enjoy our dalliance, my lovely, I cannot go on living as a deserter, whilst my countrymen are laying down their lives for liberty."

Arriving at his old friends' farmhouse, they stood behind the trees on the opposite side of the dirt road before approaching the house. A wise precaution, for they found it swarming with Redcoats. The sturdy three-story structure fairly bulged with men. Horses were tethered to every tree in the spacious yard, men in crimson-and-white uniforms, some with gold epaulets and tall, plumed hats, moved in and out of the house.

Rumor stifled a gasp of dismay. Aaron groaned aloud. They had seen a number of soldiers and provision wagons on the roads, but not until now did he realize that the countryside around Philadelphia had fallen so fast into British hands.

"They've taken over the house," he said. "God only knows what has happened to the Wagners."

Spying the two Indians standing on the far side of the rutted country road, an officer waved a hand and shouted, "Come here, savage."

A group of men seated at a plank table set up under an arching elm, started waving their arms about wildly, beckoning for Aaron to cross over.

Fearfully, Rumor crept up behind Aaron, close enough to hear him mutter, "Now we'll see if these damn disguises are any good."

"Get back," he grated to her, then loped across, as if eager. It would be unwise to let the Redcoats think he had anything to be afraid of. Rumor trailed behind, shuffling like an old woman, keeping her head well down.

While Aaron approached the soldiers, tall and erect, his rifle slung across his back, she stopped at a well at the edge of the yard, leaning against the raised stones as if weary.

She drew the filthy blanket tight around her, her heart beating fiercely. What if they saw through their ruse and took them prisoner? Aaron would fight, but what was one man against so many?

The soldiers were all drinking from pewter mugs,

probably rum, she figured. Drunken men were unpredictable, even well-disciplined soldiers.

An officer in gleaming epaulets swaggered up to Aaron, rudely grabbing his brown arm. "Turn around, redskin, let's see that rifle."

Obediently, Aaron turned. The officer examined the piece, running his hand reverently along the polished wood, the smooth, shining barrels. "Damn, if that's not the sweetest piece I've ever set eyes on. Real Spanish steel."

"Double-barreled, too," said another. "And smooth-bored, no doubt. Like all the damn Rebel rifles that are cutting our lines to ribbons."

Facing Aaron again, the officer said, "Where the hell did a savage like you get such a magnificent firearm?"

Aaron stared, as if uncomprehending.

"Stole it, Perkins, what else? They're all thieves and scoundrels," cried one of his companions in a voice slurred with drink. "Offer to buy it, I'll wager you can get it for a shilling."

"Or a string of beads," chortled another, slapping his thigh at his own wit.

Men were pouring out of the house, and in seconds the yard was full of soldiers, all anxious to see the fun. All Britishers feared Indians as savages, but this one was alone, not counting the old squaw, who seemed to be half dead over there by the well.

"Heap big money," Perkins said. Extending a hand with a small silver coin between two fingers, he shouted as if he thought Aaron deaf, "Heap big silver, big wampum."

Drawing back, Aaron shook his head, scowling fiercely. Suddenly, another soldier grabbed the rifle on his back and pulled. Aaron's head jerked back, but the leather thong did not snap, as the soldier

182

had expected. He had tied the rifle to the leather strap with a strong, Indian knot.

Silently, his face like stone, Aaron lifted up a fist and struck the thieving soldier on the head. The man fell immediately to the ground.

Perkins went white, dropped the coin, and gritted. "So you want to play rough, redskin?"

Turning to the crowd, he barked, "Pick up this soldier. If he's dead, bury him." He cast an angry look at Aaron. "As for you, you ignorant heathen savage, you'll find that striking one of His Majesty's troops will cost you not only your rifle but your head."

Perkins drew out his sword.

At the well, Rumor froze with fear, clutching the rough stones of the rim to keep from crying out. How much would Aaron stand for before he revealed himself as a white man?

Suddenly, like a clap of thunder, a voice rang out, "What the blazes is going on here? Why aren't you men at your posts?"

All the blood seemed to drain from Rumor's body. She went limp. They were surely lost now. The voice belonged to General Sir William Howe, who had emerged from behind the house with a beautiful, blond-haired woman at his side. The crowd of soldiers parted respectfully as they passed.

Sizing up the situation at a glance, Howe remarked, "Haven't I enough headaches playing tag with that damn Virginian up and down the Delaware, without my own men tormenting a savage?"

The general scowled at Perkins. "Put up your sword, you damn fool, you're not fighting a duel."

Facing the men, he spoke with the steel edge of authority. "The Indians are the king's loyal friends and subjects. You have been ordered to leave them

183

alone. That includes their rifles. He shot a glance at the huddled figure at the well. "Their women as well."

Chuckling mirthlessly, he added, "If any of you have ever seen a man who's just lost his scalp, or heard the screams of a man who's being slowly roasted on a spit—"

Turning abruptly, he faced Aaron, whose hawklike face could have been carved of stone. Smiling, Howe took his hand, shook it with vigor. "Go in peace, brother."

Then, almost as an afterthought, "Damn, I've never seen a blue-eyed Indian before." He smirked. "Probably some Viking took a fancy to an Indian maid long ago."

Bowing deeply, Aaron walked slowly to the well, imperiously swinging a long arm for Rumor to follow him.

Unexpectedly, Liz Loring called out, "Give the savage a drink of rum, at least, for all his trouble."

Running to the table under the elm, she picked up a stone jug, hurrying to where Rumor stood with Aaron. Frantically, Rumor pulled the blanket up to hide her face. She had smeared it well with loam that morning, but could she possibly fool her old friend?

Thanking her with a grunt, Aaron tilted the jug and drank deeply. But instead of handing the rum to Rumor, he pointed with his hand to the well.

"Water," he said gruffly. "Squaw want water."

Liz laughed. "Obviously he doesn't want to get his squaw drunk."

Although several men ran up to assist her, Liz took hold of the wooden bucket sitting on the stone rim and dropped it into the well. After a soldier hauled it back up by the rope, Liz offered a wooden

184

cup brimming with icy cold water to Rumor.

Rumor scuttled back, but Liz followed her. There was no escape. Forced to drop the blanket from her face. Rumor took the cup between her hands. Ivory white and firm, Rumor's long tapered fingers were not those of an old squaw. She realized with dismay that she had neglected to color them with berries for days.

Moving numbly, Liz planted her plump frame in its billowing silk summer dress in front of Rumor, hiding her from view. Blue eyes met brown over the rim of the cup, and Rumor's heart sank.

Her friend's clear eyes could not lie. Slowly, one blue-shadowed eyelid dropped in the merest suggestion of a wink. A rush of joy and tenderness suffused Rumor's being. Liz knew, but she would not betray her.

"That was a Christian thing to do," she heard Sir William say to Liz as the tall Indian and his wizened old squaw moved into the road.

"The old hag is obviously his mother," Liz remarked. "That Indian is also a Christian, I think, for I understand it is the Indians' custom to callously leave their old to die alone when they become too feeble to be of any use."

Shaken to the bone by their narrow escape from being found out and captured—he to hang and she to the clutches of her villain of a father—Aaron declared that they must find shelter.

Empty houses abounded in the region around Philadelphia, but most of them were occupied by troops, both Rebel and British.

All who could, had fled. Those who stayed lived in fear of being shelled or shot at by mistake. The long summer days were filled with noise of war—the crack of rifle and musket, the roar of cannons. The roads were jammed with marching men and wagons.

"We're in the midst of battle," Aaron said grimly. "But we're probably as safe from being found as if we were beyond the Ohio in the wilderness."

At dawn the day after Rumor had looked into Liz's knowing eyes, they stumbled upon an abandoned cabin in a river town called Barren Hill. Deep in the woods some distance from the road, it was almost smothered by vines and overhanging trees.

But it was snug and warm inside, with a large chimney corner. A great iron pot hung over the empty firepit and crude wooden mugs and trenchers sat on the plank table built into the wall. A low bed of rushes filled one corner, a quilted coverlet, thick with dust, on top.

Rumor was delighted. "It's as if we were expected," she said, sitting down on a length of sawed-off log beside the old fire. Her face clouded as she picked up a bit of knitting from the floor, from which two bone needles protruded. "War is so terrible . . ."

He was gazing out the oiled skin window into the forest. "This cabin has been empty for a long time. Probably an Indian massacre during the troubles in the sixties."

Her delight turning quickly to horror, Rumor dropped the wool, as if it had suddenly burst into flame. Running to Aaron, she buried her face in his chest. "Do you think the owners of this cabin were murdered?"

"Don't think," he said tersely.

Banishing dismal thoughts, Rumor set about making a home for herself and her lover. Although the former occupants had left some clothing in a chest—frocks, aprons, and stockings—they thought it best to continue their Indian disguise.

Aaron patched up the holes between the logs with wet clay, against the winter. "But I doubt we'll have to stay here more than a few months," he said.

Voices could be heard from the road, and occasionally a traveler stopped to beg for a drink of water from the clear spring behind the cabin. No one thought it strange that an Indian and his mother were living there. Whole villages and tribes were moving west before the encroaching white men. Many Indians were left behind, or did not care to leave.

Rumor was content. She put aside her fears of being found by her father. If he came, Aaron would protect her. She could face anything with Aaron at her side.

They did not lack for food. Aaron supplied game from the forest and corn flour from town for the johnnycakes she learned to cook over the fire. Fish of all varieties abounded in the spring-fed little stream that ran behind the house. Her once delicate hands grew rough from the unaccustomed labor.

But at night, when the dark forest closed in on them, they flung themselves on the rush bed and gave themselves up to love. When Aaron's strong arms drew her to him, when he stretched his taut body against hers so that every part of him touched every part of her, Rumor felt a kind of mindless bliss that banished every fear. She didn't care if they stayed until winter, or beyond. Rumor wanted to stay here forever.

When he thrust his hard manhood into her, she shouted with rapture as wave after wave of ecstasy shook all exhaustion from her body. After a night of love she went about her household tasks singing and

187

cavorting like a young deer.

The summer flew by on wings, it seemed. By August few rifle shots were heard. The war had moved elsewhere, apparently, north and east. Restless, and fearing no longer for her safety from Howe and Carter, Aaron began leaving the cabin for longer and longer periods, returning with news of the war. Howe had missed his chance at taking Philadelphia, but Congress had fled from the city.

Aaron's blue eyes were often troubled. He became grumpy, picking at his food, wandering about the place aimlessly. He spent hours standing in the little hard-packed dirt before the cabin door, staring at the trees that led to the road.

Guilt tugged at Rumor's heart as she held internal debates. Aaron wanted to be with his beloved General Washington, fighting to save his fledgling America from tyranny, and she was stopping him. She was a millstone around his neck. If he hadn't saved her from her father's murderous schemes, he would be shooting his rifle at the Redcoats right now instead of squirrels and possums.

One day, it all came to a head. Hearing a noise in the forest as she dipped water from the spring at dawn, Rumor ran to fetch Aaron. When they returned, a man was sprawled, face down in the water, as if trying to drink.

He wore a butternut-colored shirt and breeches, both of which were spotted with blackened, dried blood. He had no boots, but a scarlet feather was stuck into the tricornered hat that lay on the ground beside him.

"My God, he's an American soldier!" Aaron exclaimed, picking the man up and taking him into the cabin.

After several cups of Rumor's strong tea, the

188

stranger revived, and told a harrowing tale of defeat at a place called Brandywine. "Washington's army is done for," he said. "The men are deserting in droves. There's no food, no bullets or powder, no money to pay the troops."

He was trying to get home to Maryland before the winter. His wife and five children were without food themselves. In a few days, the man was fit to travel and went on his way.

Aaron's discontent worsened. Finally, bringing it out into the open, Rumor said, "I've been thinking, Aaron, that it's best that I return to New York and face my father. Albemarle is mine by law. I am a grown woman, able to fight my own battles. I've got the Spenser money—"

"Rot!" he exploded. "You're talking like a foolish woman, damn it. The man will tear you to ribbons, legally and otherwise. They'll be fishing your body out of the Pamunkey River." He snorted. "They'll call it suicide."

He looked at Rumor kneeling on the banks of the stream, dipping their one homespun bedsheet into the water and beating it with a stick on the rocks. He turned away and stood at the edge of the forest, listening.

"And you're talking like an arrogant man," she responded heatedly. "How can you be sure—"

He interrupted her, as if he hadn't heard. "The birds are noisy. That buck deer is back again. Think I'll go after it today. If I bag it, we'll have meat for the winter."

Shouldering his rifle, Aaron went into the forest. He would be gone for hours, perhaps all day. Spreading the sheet on the rocks to dry in the sun, Rumor ran back through the trees to the house.

The time for arguing was past.

Minutes later, she was dressed in a red-and-blue faded calico gown she'd taken from the chest. Stuffing her short ash-blackened hair into a poke bonnet, she took the few coins she had left from beneath a loose hearthstone, dropping them, along with a chunk of cold johnnycake and three windfall apples into a drawstring bag.

Next, she wrote with a blackened coal on the pale underside of a wooden plate.

"I am gone. Do not try to find me. Now you can fight for your America."

The road from Philadelphia was jammed with refugees. A massive British fleet was battering the city from the sea. Anyone who could do so had fled. There was also disease in the city—smallpox and dysentery.

A woman driving a wagon piled high with furniture, and three small children, huddled under a blanket, stopped where Rumor stood. "Get in," she ordered Rumor. "We're going to my sister's farm up North, and you're welcome to come along. God knows I could use the help with the kids."

The woman obviously assumed that the slender girl in the faded calico with a bag slung over her shoulder was also a refugee. Why not, thought Rumor, swiftly climbing into the wagon. Up North was toward New York.

There was no time for chatter, the woman shouted over her shoulder, expertly guiding her horse through the maze of vehicles clogging the road. Her name was Abby, she said, and her husband was fighting with General Washington. She hadn't heard from him for months. He could be dead. The whole damn Continental Army could be dead for all she knew.

"After I leave the kids with my sister," Abby said, "I'm going to join my husband, wherever he is. Maybe even do some fighting. I'm a mean hand with a rifle."

The children were quiet, obviously scared half to death at the noise and confusion. Soon they stopped at a river, swollen by recent rains, and waited in a long line of wagons to cross a narrow bridge. Suddenly, a scream was heard. The bridge had collapsed, tossing a wagon into the raging flood.

Standing in the wagon, Rumor saw heads bobbing in the debris-strewn river. People in waiting wagons or afoot stood about, gaping. No one was doing anything to help.

"They'll drown," she shouted at Abby.

"So will anyone who tries to save them," the woman yelled back. She yanked on the reins. "We've got to turn around. There's another bridge farther upstream."

Without another word, Rumor leaped from the wagon and ran to the edge of the stream. She was a strong swimmer, having spent her childhood splashing around in Jamaica Bay. Plunging into the swirling waters, she swam with powerful strokes toward a child who clung to its mother, who in turn clung to the overturned wagon.

They all floated downstream for a terrifying few minutes before being stopped by a fallen tree that had fallen from the bank and blocked their progress. Several men had also plunged into the river by now, and soon Rumor found herself back on shore with the mother and child.

She had lost her bag of johnnycake in the river, but aside from that was unharmed. A worried man came running up, dripping wet, to gather his wife and child into his arms. He thanked Rumor profusely. Dazed, she nodded, refusing his offer of money for helping to save his family.

They left, and Rumor found herself alone. All of the wagons were gone from the road. Sitting on a rock in the sun, she gazed upriver. It was the same river that flowed by the cabin where she and Aaron had been so happy, and where at this very moment Aaron might be reading her note.

She began to weep. How could she have been so blind? Abby said she would fight at her husband's side if she had to. Many women did. Many traveled with the troops, offering the kind of help and comfort only a woman could.

Picking herself up, Rumor ran back to the road. Luckily, she got another ride on a wagon, but it was dark before she reached the cabin. No light shone through the oiled window. No smoke spiraled from the stone chimney.

Tears of frustration and remorse spilled from her eyes and ran down her cheeks. She was too late. Aaron had already gone. Standing there in the mud before the little cabin, Rumor felt that her life had come to an end.

Wearily, she entered the darkened cabin. A faint streak of moonlight shone through the open door. A man was sitting at the table, his head down, as if sleeping. Overjoyed, she ran to him and threw her arms about his neck.

"Oh, darling, darling, forgive me," she sobbed aloud, "I'm such an utter fool. Let's leave this place, I'll go with you, wherever you go. I can't live a single moment without you."

The head that came up to bump against her chin did not smell of ash and woodsmoke, but of a sweetish hair oil. He also reeked of whiskey. To her horror, Rumor found herself embracing a stranger. As he stood up and faced her, she saw he was a British soldier, an officer. Gold epaulets adorned his shoulders, and there was gold lace on the gorget at his neck.

Hurtingly, he grasped her wrists, drawing her close. "That kind of love talk makes a man rise up good and proper," he hissed against her lips.

As if to emphasize his words, he pushed himself against her. Releasing her hands, he cupped her buttocks, pushing harder and grinding obscenely in little circles. His mouth came down on hers in a biting, bruising kiss.

When he drew back at last, he grinned. "How's that for an opening scene, Lady Spenser?" Drawing a flask from his pocket, he drew a long swallow and tossed the bottle into a corner.

Stunned, she stared into his face. "Who-ho-o are you?" she stuttered. "How do you know me?"

"For an actress, your memory is short, madam," he chuckled huskily. "Perhaps you were too wrapped up in your role as Indian squaw to take notice when we met."

That voice, she thought. Where had she heard it?

"There was a nasty business of a certain rifle—"

Her eyes widened in horror as she remembered. "That day at the farmhouse—"

She darted away, but with a strangled whoop he was upon her once again, pinning her against the wall. "Captain Perkins at your service, whore."

Taking her hands in his, he gently bit down on each finger, one by one. "It was your white hands that gave you away, and what I could see of your face as you drank the water. They looked mighty odd against that dirty blanket."

"Aaron will be home at any moment," she said,

"he's been out hunting deer—"

"Aaron, is it? No more Indian chief? Or perhaps your Rebel lover has gone back to being Sir Oliver Mowbray," he snorted. "Whoever he is, General Howe will be happy as blazes to receive him. The general's been bloody upset at being hoodwinked all those years by a simpering dandy."

As he talked, the officer lifted a pistol from a belt around his waist and hips. It was black with an ivory handle. Touching the black barrel to her head, he chortled, "It'll be more sport to put a bullet in his head, however. Squarely between the eyes."

After a long frozen moment, he laid the firearm on the table. "Much as I admire your charms, Lady Spenser, I wouldn't think twice about doing the same to you."

His eyes narrowed to slits, and his voice grew husky. "Now if you're as sensible as I think you are, you'll not give me any trouble."

Taking hold of her calico dress, Perkins ripped it from her shoulders, then with startling ease he yanked it down around her ankles. "Like 'em naked, stark naked," he mumbled, tugging at her chemise.

Transfixed, Rumor stared at the pistol. Even if she could reach it, she could not fire it. She couldn't even fire Aaron's big rifle, though he had tried long and patiently to teach her. She was terrified of firearms.

Whimpering with fright and repulsion, Rumor twisted from his grasp, and stepping out of her dress, ran across the cabin toward the door. Like greased lightning, he reached it a second before she did. Grabbing her by the hair, he spun her round and threw her to the floor.

"Don't try that again," he grated as he fell upon her. Grabbing her two hands in an ironlike grip, he held them high above her head. Then, pulling the bonnet off her head, he bound her hands together with the cotton ties.

Maddened at the sight of her thrusting breasts, Perkins started chewing on her nipples. He had pulled down his breeches and she felt him thrusting between her legs. Cruelly, parting the tender folds of her flesh, he quickly tried to push inside.

Shrieking, Rumor twisted and turned, almost toppling him over.

"Lie still, you bitch," he growled, reaching up to the low table for the pistol. He cocked it, held it once more to her head. "This sweet little thing can kill a man as surely as any rifle five times its size."

She could not possibly escape, Rumor thought, despairing. The man would rape her, again and again until Aaron returned. He was drunk, he might even kill her with the pistol. When Aaron came back, expecting no danger, Perkins would either shoot him dead, or capture him by surprise and deliver him up to the British to be shot as a spy.

Groaning, Rumor imagined her lover's bullet-ridden body being thrown to the dogs. That's what the British did to dead spies.

As she lay helpless, pinned beneath the Redcoat, she spied her note still on the table by the pistol. It was in exactly the same position as she had left it. Beside it lay Aaron's bullet mold and a bag of long bullets he had fashioned from powder. He would hardly leave without them. Her heart leapt. He was still in the forest. She must stay alive to warn him before he entered the cabin.

Laying the pistol once more on the table, Perkins resumed his vigorous assault on her nipples. Marshaling every ounce of inner strength, Rumor purred into his ear, "Please, sir, do not chew me to pieces

195

before we have our pleasure." She forced her voice to be low and sultry. "If you unbind my hands, I can show you how a real woman can love a man. I know tricks you've never heard of in England."

Colonel Perkins lifted his head in pleased surprise. "Aha, so it is true what they say. The famous Lady Spenser spreads her legs willingly." He laughed aloud gleefully, but in the next instant he seemed to hesitate. "How can I trust you?"

"Surely a British officer can overcome a mere woman," she purred. "I adore masterful men."

Easing back on his haunches, he stared down at her, openmouthed. She hoped fervently that his drink-befuddled brain was not too clear. The harvest moon shone brightly through the open door on his narrow face.

Recalling her wedding night, and Lord Spenser's appetites, she pulled herself up from the floor, leaning her head on his thigh, near his thrust-out manhood.

She inched closer, her lips nearly touching him. Then, shivering with disgust, she drew back, waiting.

"Oh, so that's what you like to do?"

"I know all the tricks, as I said. I can drive you wild."

Perkins arched backward, invitingly. "Show me. Touch me there."

"Release me," she taunted. "My hands can do wonders."

Frantic with lust, Perkins started tugging at the bonnet strings around her wrists. Her hands free, Rumor stretched out beside him, praying fervently that her agony would not go on all night. When Aaron was stalking a deer, he sometimes did not return for days.

How much could she bear to save her lover? She had never been intimate with any man but Aaron. The thought of touching this man's flesh turned her stomach.

"Come, sweet bitch—"

The Redcoat's words were cut off as a long shadow darkened the moonlit cabin. Aaron stood in the doorway, the carcass of a deer slung across his back.

Chapter Nine

It was like a scene from one of those naughty drawing room comedies theater audiences are so fond of, Rumor thought wildly. The absent husband surprising his wife and her lover in a more than compromising position. What was that Latin phrase the lawyers always used? Oh yes, *Flagrante delicto*. Red-handed, Rumor mused.

She was naked, lying free of her bonds, the Redcoat lounging at her side. Both seemed perfectly at ease. She was obviously not being raped. There was no screaming, no apparent struggle.

Nobody moved for a long, charged moment. Her eyes met Aaron's. His were unreadable slits in the moonlight.

At first Perkins froze, then as he realized that Rumor's absent lover had come home, he rose up. Sliding the pistol from the table with a swift movement, he pointed it at Aaron.

"I want no trouble, Fleming," he said easily. "I can take you to Howe dead or alive."

"No," Rumor screamed, throwing her body between the officer and Aaron. "You'll have to kill me first." If Aaron was to die, so would she.

With a pantherlike movement, Aaron knocked

Rumor to one side with a powerful hand, and dipping his head and shoulders low, hurled the heavy deer carcass on top of the Redcoat.

"Run," he shouted to Rumor, "outside!"

The officer's pistol hit the window, and went sailing through the oiled pane.

Darting past the two entangled bodies already rolling round and round on the dirt floor, Rumor scurried to the wooden stoop. She had seen men fighting before, but never like this. They were like animals. The two men seemed to be all over the little cabin. When they neared the door, she saw that the Britisher's breeches were off.

"Watch out," Aaron yelled. "I'm throwing out the deer."

She darted to one side a split second before the carcass came sailing through the cabin door. It landed face up, the four legs stiffly extended, the wide-open eyes staring glassily at her. The deer was a buck, the largest she had ever seen. Gingerly stepping round it, Rumor resumed her place at the doorway.

For some minutes there was no sound but the crack of fist on flesh and the slam of heavy bodies against the walls.

But then, words emerged, mostly from Aaron's mouth. Words she had never heard him use—man talk, profane words, mostly uncomplimentary words about the bloody damn Redcoats, about General Howe and his womanizing. Even the English king came in for his share of invective.

Despite the carnage inside, and her fear that somehow Perkins might get the better of her man, Rumor smiled. Aaron was using the battle to let off steam, built up over months of forced inactivity and absence from war.

Gradually, Rumor lost her fear. Extending her arms to either side, she clutched the doorjambs, craning her neck inside to watch. Actually, she told herself, there was never any doubt as to the outcome of the battle. Aaron topped Perkins by a head, as well as about thirty pounds of taut, sinewy muscles.

Rumor's would-be rapist was a typical British officer, well trained, well armed, with plenty of arrogance. But he was no match for an American woodsman, who'd learned to fight like a wild beast of the forest. His early years with the Shawnee had taught Aaron how to body wrestle to the death, if necessary.

Gradually it grew quiet inside the cabin. No more grunts and groans. Suddenly, Aaron stood before her, his body naked but for a breechclout, glistening with sweat. He filled the doorway.

The body of Captain Perkins was slung across his shoulders, just as the deer had been earlier. The Redcoat was totally naked, having lost all his garments during the fight.

Roughly, Aaron pushed Rumor ahead of him into the hard-packed mud in front of the house.

"Let's bury him," he said tersely. "Fetch the axe and spade."

As she darted back into the cabin, he grated, "And get some clothes on, hussy."

"Hussy?" she echoed, baffled. Her blood chilled. Horrors! Did he think that she and Perkins . . . No, he couldn't think that. He was teasing her. Often, in their loveplay, he called her names like that.

"Don't dawdle, whore" came a roar from outside. "His cronies will be looking for him."

This time his voice did not sound as if he were

teasing.

Hastily throwing on the calico over her nakedness, Rumor followed Aaron into the forest. He walked so fast she could not keep up, and from time to time he turned his head to yell at her—profanely—to hurry. The long-handled iron axe dug into her shoulder, the spade in her hand kept catching on outflung limbs of trees.

Finally they reached a place at the foot of a bluff that was bare of vegetation. There were no trees. It seemed to be all rock.

Halting abruptly, he lowered the body. "Give me the axe, strumpet."

"But there's no dirt," she said meekly, handing him the tool and stifling the words of explanation that danced upon her tongue. Wisely, she knew that his blood, inflamed by the fight—not to mention the heart-shattering sight of her with Perkins—had to be given time to cool down. When they returned to the cabin, she would take him into her arms and all would be well again.

He would apologize profusely, beg her forgiveness for assuming the worst. They would make sweet, tender, passionate love.

Calmer now, Rumor watched as he made a place in the plateau with the axe, prying up large rocks, slicing at the smaller ones, to make a hole big enough to hold the officer's body. Taking up the spade, he jumped into the hole and dug at a furious pace until, satisfied that it was deep enough, he climbed out and laid the dead Perkins into the hole.

When the dirt and rocks had been put back in place, Aaron rounded it off into a hump, as one does with any grave. Then, sitting on his haunches, he stared at her for a long time, apparently calmer.

After a while, Rumor ventured, "Aaron, I can't think that *you* could think—that you could possibly even imagine—that I was willingly making love with Perkins."

"Weren't you?" His voice was soft, deceptively so, she thought. Terror lanced into her heart.

"No," she said urgently. "I was merely pretending because he threatened to kill me. And you, too."

"Pretending!"

Rearing up to tower over her where she sat resting on a rock, he said, mockingly, "You're good at pretending, aren't you, you Jamaican strumpet. Quite the little actress. You should go on tour with your randy Redcoat. You make a handsome couple."

Chuckling, he added, bending over to glare at her, "And so loving, oh how loving!"

He made an ugly sound in his throat that was supposed to be a laugh. "I had always heard, but never believed it until now that you are good at spreading your legs apart and inviting any man you fancy to enter in and make himself at home."

As he spoke the long sentence, his face grew rigid with fury and his words dropped like nails onto her heart.

Choking with horror, she threw herself at his feet. He did not—could not—believe her story. Grasping his legs with both hands, she moaned, "Oh, Aaron, how can you—"

"Goddamn you, Rumor, you've killed the first decent feeling I've ever had for a woman."

Cruelly kicking her aside, he gazed down on her sprawling body. The calico dress had lifted up to her waist, and as she lay there, helpless, exposed, he drew in a long breath, almost like a whistle. His hand went to the breechclout, whipping it off, tossing it aside.

Then, falling heavily on top of her, he mounted her, lifting her up from the rock by her buttocks. Swiftly, he thrust his swollen manhood into her, thrusting deeply, cruelly, searing her with his masculine heat until she cried out with pain.

"Hurts, does it, my little Redcoat doxy? Well, here's some more."

Dawn was streaking the sky, setting the birds to chattering in the trees before he let her go. Through the night he used her, again and again, filling her so completely she felt as though they had truly become one body, and would remain so forever.

Each time he spent his seed into her womb, a sweet, agonizing sensation swept through her. Whatever his reasons for taking her, she welcomed the pain. She had hurt him unwillingly far more deeply.

Despite his animallike thrusts, the bruising, biting kisses, the feverish kneading of her breasts and soft thighs in the times when he strove to arouse himself once again, her own desire seemed only to intensify.

Arching to meet his searching lips, she offered her nipples to his pleasure. His tongue explored her mouth, then her face and neck. Where he touched, ecstasy followed.

When she saw him erect again, and ready, Rumor arched toward him once again, and drew pleasure from the sight of his beloved body moving on hers.

Is this what a woman really wants, she thought wildly, a man who loses himself in her?

For the man who battered her so mercilessly through the night in the midst of the forest was not Aaron Fleming, she told herself. Neither was it Sir Oliver Mowbray.

This man who loved her so desperately and wantonly was somebody else. A man whose pain was so great he must ravage his sweetheart to assuage the raw and bleeding wound.

Rumor gave herself to her love with wild, sweet abandon, knowing that in the dawn he would once again kiss her with tenderness. Though no preacher had said words over their union, she had vowed to love him forever, for better or for worse.

Shaken, but fulfilled as she had never been, she lay spent. Her back and shoulders were sore from the hard rock she lay on. No matter, she would have Aaron smear ointment over her entire body.

He rose, walked slowly to the place where his breechclout lay. He put it on, smoothing it into place over his now limp organ. His movements were those of a man who has just come back from a long, exhausting journey.

She sat up. "Aaron—"

The face he turned toward her was as cruel and indifferent as before. Her heart stopped for a moment, then began to pulse, rapidly, beating against her rib cage as if it wanted to fly out to him.

"Let's go home," he said quietly.

With feet of lead she followed him, a respectful distance behind, like a proper Indian squaw. Is this how it would be from now on, she wondered dully.

Inside the cabin, he began to straighten up, righting the upturned table, picking up Perkins's uniform, the plumed hat, his boots. He threw them into the smoldering fire, jabbing at the garments viciously with the iron poker until they caught fire.

In a far corner, wedged against the bed, Rumor spied the piece of bark on which she had written her farewell note. Picking it up, she tossed it into the fire.

Snatching it from the flames, he barked, "That's a good piece for writing on."

"I already have," she said quickly. "I wrote words that would free you to fight for your country."

He read the words, then tossed the paper into the fire and watched it burn. His face was grim, two deep lines were etched between his eyes.

"So you said. But first you thought to bribe a bastard of a Redcoat to take you with him. That way you wouldn't have to fret about food and drink and even fine dresses to cover your whoring back."

Rage surged within her. "That's enough," she gritted through her teeth. Her two fists came up to beat against his chest. "Now you listen to reason, for a change. I was not playing the strumpet with that revolting Perkins. I loathe the man. I was merely playing for time so that I could warn you when you returned. He meant to capture you, even kill you."

"For a captive, you didn't look too sad," he grated, thrusting her from him. "Your head was on his thigh, you wanton. Have you any notion what happens to a man at the sight of his woman so cozy with another?"

Drawing close again, she hissed into his face. "What if I told you that I refused him, he would have shot me? Would you prefer me dead?"

Turning away from him toward the gray dawn streaming through the open door, she uttered a strangled cry. "Merciful God, I actually think you would."

She began to sob. He made no move to comfort her. But when he faced her, she gazed with brimming eyes at him. He seemed to crumple for a moment, as conflicting emotions passed over his face. For the briefest fraction of a second, the blue eyes melted.

But instantly the hardness returned.

"Lies, all lies."

Whipping round, he started gathering up his bullets, his mold, some cold johnnycake and dried squirrel meat—stuffing them into a deerskin bag. She chased after him as he moved around the cabin, like a little dog whose master is leaving him behind.

"I'm no strumpet, you idiot. I was a virgin when you took me at the beaver dam."

"There was no blood."

"We were half in the water, you numbskull. Any blood would have washed away instantly."

"Bull. You weren't even sore, kept coming back for more."

To stung to reply to that, she listened as he ranted on. "You drove me clean out of my mind with your winning tricks. But I remember well enough that I had no trouble breaching your so-called maidenhead. Slick as a whistle, as I recall."

Bag in hand, he was out the door, then in again, with a rusty-looking musket. He threw it on the table. "I found this in the forest, beside a dead bugger of a Rebel soldier, probably trying to get back home when he was cut down."

"It's a flintlock," she yelped.

"Yep." He grinned maliciously. "Old, but trusty when used correctly. There's some powder and flint on the shelf. If you can't manage to load it properly, just point it at anyone or anything that tries to break in."

He laughed aloud, at his own wit. "Then again, if it's a man, you'll have no worry. Just get down on the dirt—" With that lewd advice, he was gone again, heading toward the forest. She ran after him. "Where are you going? What'll I do with that damn deer?"

His sharp, scornful laugh filled the morning air. A cold rain had started up, and when he turned around, his face was shining with wet.

"I'm going to hell, goddamn it. As for the deer, skin it, cut it up, and salt it down. It should last you all winter." Then came that awful laugh again. "But you should have no trouble getting another British bastard to help you out. For favors granted, naturally."

Incredibly, he was gone, his naked back swallowed by the thickening trees. The rain was harder now, and icy cold. She could not hope to follow him, she would only manage to get lost and get herself eaten up by a wild bear or a pack of wolves. Or captured by the British, she thought, running back home in panic. Perkins had found her. He may have told his fellow officers where he was going. The wisest and most sensible course was to leave this place, to seek shelter with friends. But who? And where? Her only friend, Liz Loring, was with General Howe, who was seeking to capture her.

The rain, mixed with her tears, was pelting down now, blinding her. Stumbling, she fell, hitting her head on something sharp. It was the Redcoat's pistol that Aaron had pitched out the window. Picking it up with horror, she ran to the spring and hurled the hated weapon into the stream.

Back in the cabin, Rumor closed the door. No wisdom in getting soaked, catching her death, and dying of pneumonia, she reflected wryly. Despite all that had happened, Rumor Spenser did not want to die. No man was worth that, she thought furiously, wiping the tears from her face.

Wearily, she tossed a log into the fire and flung

herself on the bed. She had to think. This was not the first crisis in her eighteen years on earth. She would make a plan. Aaron would come to his senses, he had simply been unhinged by what he thought was her brazen wantonness.

She managed a smile. His nasty words about her whoredom and all that nonsense had sounded exactly like Sir Oliver Mowbray in the days when he would rave and rant at her. There was more of the supercilious dandy in Aaron Fleming than he ever realized, she reflected.

Although he was a Virginian, her angry lover shared some of the puritanism of the New England Yankees. He hadn't even been willing to listen to her, but simply took appearances for reality.

Yawning, she flung back the quilted coverlet. There was no sheet. She'd left it on the rocks to dry this morning. Stretching out on the muslin-covered rusks, Rumor closed her eyes.

Her mind was calm. The minute her darling realized what an utter fool he'd made of himself, he would come running back through the forest, into her loving arms.

One week passed, then another. It was November, and the cold rains turned to sleet, then snow. The drifts piled up high around the little cabin, there were chunks of ice in the river. No one came near the place. The noise from the road seemed to lessen, few travelers willing to brave the wintry blasts.

Not a rifle shot was heard, nor boom of distant cannon, nor tramp of soldiers' feet on the road beyond the cover of trees. Perhaps the war had ended, she thought.

Although she could not bring herself to cut up the deer, leaving it for the wolves and vultures, Rumor had no lack of food. A crock of lard and two sacks of corn flour would last her for months. The girl who enjoyed delicacies of all kinds, who had dined on Sèvres china, learned to devour with keenest pleasure the hard corn cakes that were the staple of the frontier.

Windfall apples strewed the ground beneath the trees in the abandoned orchard by the spring. For meat she had salted bacon and several chunks of dried venison from a deer Aaron had shot the month before.

But it was not food that Rumor yearned for. As the wintry days grew shorter, and the nights grew long, she became desperately lonely. Missing Aaron's arms in the rusk bed, she writhed in the torment of physical longing.

As if fearing to view her own body that had brought such disaster into her life, Rumor never removed the calico dress. What bathing she did was sketchy at best. The stream behind the cabin had frozen over, and melted snow became her source of water.

Worst of all, she began to doubt Aaron's integrity. Had he lied to her? Was her father truly as evil as he had vowed? Forgetting that Olympia had also told her that Beaumont Carter would take her back to Virginia and make her do his will, Rumor convinced herself that there had been no need to kidnap her from New York.

Lust. Passion. Uncontrollable desire. That's why Aaron Fleming had carried her off into the wilderness. Any other reason he had given was pure flummery.

209

Men were all scoundrels. Amoral blackguards. Just as Mama always said.

One morning, Rumor woke from a fitful slumber to the sound of rolling drums. There were voices coming from the road above the cabin—a great many of them. Consumed with curiosity and loneliness, she decided to venture out. Anyone who was looking for the missing Perkins would surely have come by now, she reasoned. As for Aaron, she thought furiously, he could damn well go to hell, as he said he would.

Throwing on the old squaw blanket over the grimy calico, she darted out of the cabin. The blanket was filthy and reeked of smoke and earth, but it was the only covering she had against the weather.

The road was filled with British soldiers, all with rifles upraised, bayonets attached. They were running in and out of the houses on either side, shouting to each other. People stood about in little clumps, looking scared. Carts and wagons choked the narrow, rutted road.

An old woman leaning on a pushcart filled with walnuts and apples called to her. "Best git out'n the way, darlin', the soljers be all in a mean temper."

Sidling over to the cart, Rumor huddled against the old woman. "What be they lookin' fer?" she asked, instinctively imitating the woman's dialect.

"They be huntin' an off'cer what vanished. Mysterious like," the hag cackled. "Dead or alive. His pistol be found in yon river, stuck against a rock. They figger he musta bin took inside one o' the houses here."

"Do-do they figger he be hereabouts?" Rumor drew back, clutching at her blanket, fearing lest the woman hear the pounding of her heart.

"Yep." Another high-pitched crackle. "They niver find 'im, though. Redcoats what wander 'bout alone all'ays turns up dead."

Suddenly, a scarlet-clad soldier was poking Rumor in the belly with the tip of his bayonet. "And who are you, my pretty? You weren't here with the old woman last time I looked."

Rumor's face went white, her eyes widening in fright. She pointed a dirty finger to a fieldstone house directly across, at the side of which a mill wheel churned feebly in the nearly frozen water.

"Please, sir, I be a slavey in yonder mill."

Glowering fiercely at her, he jabbed the bayonet into the blanket. Winching more in fear than pain, for the blade had not pierced the flesh, she bit her lip and screwed up her face as if she were going to cry.

"I just came from there. The miller said naught about a servant." The soldier studied Rumor, pursing his lips, wrinkling his freckled brow.

"Orders are to look out for a young girl pretending to be an Indian squaw. Could be you. Why do you have that smelly blanket on?"

Ignoring the icy fingers of terror running up and down her spine, Rumor simpered, "This be me only cloak, sir."

The old hag spoke up. "She be jes comin' back from a night in town," she whinnied. "A bit o' more money, if'n ye git me meanin', sir."

A pair of gray eyes narrowed as the soldier regarded Rumor. He wrinkled his long hose. "Stinks as though she knelt down and let a few stallions have a go at her."

Bowing her head, Rumor remained silent, profoundly grateful for the reeking blanket.

Withdrawing his bayonet, but still entertaining doubt, the solder called to another. "Hudson, come over here." The second soldier came close to Rumor and the apple woman, grimacing and holding his nose.

Pointing to Rumor, the first one remarked, "You were there that day at the farmhouse when Perkins had that tussle with the big Indian over the rifle. He had a squaw with him, who we think was actually that Lady Spenser the general's after."

Putting his hand on Rumor's cheek, he turned it round. "Is this the one, d'you think? Pretty, brown eyes, fine features—"

Hudson peered into Rumor's face, frowning in concentration. He shook his head. "Absolutely not. I got a good look at that squaw. Let her go."

Both moved off. "Can't imagine Perkins cozying up to the likes of that," Hudson laughed. "The captain was always bloody fussy about his women."

After he'd gone, Rumor mumbled a hasty thanks to the apple woman, and silently blessed the departing Hudson's bad memory. She started across the road to the mill.

The soldier who had questioned her, obviously still not satisfied, was watching from a group of his fellows. She had to bluff it out. A tall gray-haired fat woman stood on the stoop, arms folded on her ample chest.

Praying that the woman had an understanding and merciful soul, and that she hated Redcoats as well, Rumor approached the house.

"So there you are, strumpet. I've been waiting for you." The fat woman's shriek could be heard by everyone in the road.

Tearing a branch from a thorny bush at the stoop,

the woman grabbed Rumor by the shoulders and knocked her to her knees. To the great amusement of the troops and people in the road, she cast off the blanket and lifted up the hem of the calico, exposing Rumor's bottom, covered by the white homespun shift.

Slowly, methodically, the miller's wife applied the twig to Rumor's buttocks, her strong, plump arm rising and falling rhythmically. She seemed to be enjoying her task, going about it with gusto.

Dutifully, playing along with the ruse, Rumor began to scream, then as the pain increased, the scalding tears came readily, pouring down her face into her mouth.

"I be sorry, ma'am, I be a black, black sinner," she wailed.

Finally tiring, the woman kicked Rumor for good measure, yelling, "Now fetch your bloody ass inside."

Crawling through the open door like a worm, Rumor thought, *I'm bruised and bleeding, but I'm safe.* The Redcoats would not question her again. Her bottom was afire, but what was a pair of fiery buttocks compared to being captured and hanged as a murderess?

Following her into a large hearth room, the miller's wife started giving orders to a passel of servants and half-grown children. Hot water, lots of it, was to be fetched from the kettle on the fire. Also a wooden tub, along with soap and linens. The young lady she had just beaten to the fare-thee-well with a twig must be bathed, anointed with salve, fed and put to bed. In that order.

While all these comforting activities were taking place, the miller's wife, whose name was Clara, talked to her unexpected guest. To her amazement, Rumor discovered that she and Aaron had been topics of speculation and gossip among the local citizenry ever since they had come to Barren Hill in the spring.

"We guessed you had run off from a husband, and that the tall handsome man playing Indian was your lover. We also guessed that he was running off from the war."

Gaping in amazement, Rumor exclaimed, "But it isn't like that at all. My husband died, and Aaron is a brave man. He's not afraid of anything, he even killed a bear one time—"

"He also killed Captain Perkins, that officer a whole blasted royal regiment's been looking for."

A merry girl named Janny, who was one of Clara's numerous daughters, had just stripped Rumor of the calico and shift and was lowering her into a wooden washtub. The tub was small, and Rumor's legs were up against her chin. For a moment, as she sank into the hot water, she felt a sense of great release. Then fear crept in.

"How do you know Aaron killed Perkins?" she said warily, as the girl began to scrub her back and neck with a cloth rubbed with lye soap. "You have no proof. Just because we were hiding—"

Clara laughed. She had sunk her solid body into a rocking chair and seemed to be enjoying herself immensely at Rumor's obvious astonishment.

Rocking furiously, Clara said casually, "We all saw the Redcoat go down the trail to your cabin and nobody saw him come back up."

There was a silence as a pail of warm water was poured on Rumor's head. Janny began to vigorously scrub the tangled brown hair with ten strong fingers.

When she emerged at last from the near-drowning, Rumor gazed without fear at Clara through her dripping hair.

"Aaron killed that British officer in a fair fight. The man was—"

She reddened, painfully, all over her naked body. Mercifully, at that moment, the daughter was dropping a nightshift over her head, made of that wonderful thick stuff the Americans called linsey-woolsey. Janny helped her out of the tub and sat her upon a three-legged stool by the fire.

"Don't want you to catch your death," the girl smiled sweetly.

Filled with warmth and love for these wonderful people, Rumor smiled back, accepting a pewter mug of warm cider from another girl. Cradling the mug in her hands, she sipped the tangy brew, looking around the large room. It was spotlessly clean—the plank floor and homemade furniture of pine was almost white from scrubbing. The rough stone walls were whitewashed with powdered lime and snowy curtains hung at the windows.

About ten girls and women sat about, sewing, knitting, spinning, mending. Rumor was reminded of the common room at Spenser House where she had been so unhappy. But this room emanated friendship. All wore colorful homespun frocks, with spanking white aprons tied around their waists. Several children played quietly in a corner. A babe slept peacefully in a cradle on the hearth.

They had been chattering like jaybirds when she entered, but as Clara began to question her, there was a sudden quiet. Ears became alert, heads inclined forward, eyes glistened. Now they would know the truth at last about the mysterious young couple in the old, abandoned cabin.

"No need to tell us what that British varmint did to you," said Clara gently. "There's one less Redcoat on this earth, for that we all thank the good Lord in heaven."

"Thank the young man, too," put in Janny pertly, with a quick glance at her mother. "Aaron. What a good name, biblical and all."

"Yes," Rumor responded.

Clara said nothing, Janny said no more. The babe on the hearth whimpered in its sleep. Rumor knew that all were waiting for her to tell her name, where she came from, where Aaron had got to. They were all almost slavering to hear the entire juicy story, down to every detail.

How much should she reveal? Could she be completely honest and truthful with these good people? They meant no harm to her. Like all women—and men too—they loved gossip—a good story.

Thrusting all fears aside, Rumor's dam of loneliness broke. The words spilled out. If revealing her identity brought Beaumont Carter sniffing round, she had no doubt that the formidable Clara would save her, even from a domineering father.

"My name is Rumor Seton," she began, staring at her mug, "and I was born in Jamaica. I don't sew or cook very well, but I can act. I used to be an actress on the stage."

She looked up, breathless, just as a muscular young man with a merry face like Janny's and arms like Clara's entered from the back of the house.

"Seton, you say? Tarnation, I saw you playing Juliet at a sugar house in New York." He crossed the room, limping badly. Rumor saw that one leg was considerably shorter than the other.

216

"This is my son Walter," Clara said.

Rumor met his gaze. "Were you in the audience the night the Sons of Liberty burned us out?"

His face lit up. "I sure was, Miss Seton." But his smile soon vanished. "I trust you were not injured by the flames."

"No. I was saved by a very brave man." She held his gaze. "Were you one of the scoundrels who attacked us so viciously?" she asked calmly.

"No, miss," he said vehemently. "Ma here would've tanned my hide if I had joined in such wickedness. She had no truck with shenanigans like that."

"Good." She paused. "They murdered my stepfather, David Seton. They poured hot boiling tar on him, then a lot of feathers, then put him on a rail . . ." She dropped her head. "Then he died."

A collective gasp rippled through the room. "How awful," Janny said, falling to her knees at Rumor's side.

Lifting her face again, Rumor swept her eyes around the room. She waited for the familiar vengeful feeling to fill her heart. But it did not come. No longer did she harbor the rage to kill the men who had danced about the fire that night while David suffered.

Rumor felt as if a great stone had been lifted from her chest. "I don't think they meant to kill him, they were just having fun, and we *had* been breaking the law . . ."

She trailed off, and Clara interrupted. "War itself is a terrible thing. It makes no distinctions. I've seen little children slaughtered who got in the way of the fighting."

"Amen," someone intoned piously.

217

Unable to speak any more, Rumor drained her mug. She felt as if she were under water, struggling for breath. She was feeling drowsy, for she had slept little last night. Through the drumming in her ears, she heard Walter's voice again.

"Say, pardon my asking, but didn't you marry Lord Lionel Spenser?"

Clara stopped rocking.

"Yes," said Rumor quickly, "I was Lady Spenser but only for a day. My husband was killed in battle immediately after the wedding."

Clara stood up. "What d'you mean, you *were* Lady Spenser. Ain't you still Lady Spenser?"

The woman wore a shocked expression, and Rumor's heart went to her bare toes. Now that they knew her for a tilted Englishwoman, they would throw her out. All American Rebels detested anyone who was called Lord or Lady.

She nodded. "I'm afraid so."

"What are your politics, madam?" Clara's voice was tight.

"I have no politics," Rumor replied without hesitation. "I believe in everyone doing what's right." Her words were clear, with the ring of truth in them.

After a long moment, Clara said, "Well spoken, Rumor." She spat into the fire. "We have no lords and ladies in America, we bow the knee to nobody but God above. Everyone's equal. If you remember that, Mistress Rumor Spenser, we'll all get along just fine." Taking a few steps across the hearth, Clara loomed over her. "Like any of us, you've got to prove your worth, young woman."

Tears filled Rumor's brown eyes. She was welcome. Fiercely, she said, "I want to help win your— our—freedom from the English king in any way I

218

can. Please tell me how."

Clara flushed, as if embarrassed at her patriotic outburst. "That can wait until tomorrow, Miss Rumor. Right now I want you up in bed. You got to be workin' hard tomorrow when those soldiers return to search again, as they're bound to."

There was no question of her returning to the cabin she had shared with Aaron. Not ever. It was too dangerous. The Redcoats would come again and again and torment her until she confessed.

As Janny showed her to a large bed in a roomful of beds upstairs in a kind of loft, she said, "I'll bring you some hot corn gruel and a chunk of bread."

No one had asked her what had happened to Aaron. When they did, she would say proudly that he was fighting in General Washington's army.

Rumor drew the rough sheet over herself, thinking, with wonder. *Now I am truly an American. Aaron would be proud.*

She looked forward to telling him. One day.

Chapter Ten

After the awful day when she'd nearly been captured by the British soldiers, life in the little river town of Barren Hill settled down to a routine. With everyone who lived at Clara's mill, Rumor ate, bathed, slept, and did her assigned chores.

Life was far from dull, though. People moved in and out of the tall stone building, in what seemed a constant stream, throughout the snowy days and often far into the frosty nights. Women came to sew and spin and boil the apples that abounded in the Schuylkill River valley into applesauce. Apple pie and tarts formed the dessert at every evening meal.

There were few men, even the old and very young having gone to war. Clara's husband had not been home for over a year. When the wheat and corn were ready to be ground into flour in the autumn, she had to run the mill.

At night as Rumor lay in bed, she heard the whinny of horses, and Walter's low commands to the beasts. Soon the rattle of wagon wheels on the frozen road told her that he and another young man named Ben had departed once again for Valley Forge.

That was the name of the tiny hamlet thirty miles

from Philadelphia, bordering the Schuylkill, where the exhausted Rebel Army had encamped for the winter. General Howe had removed his army and himself to captured Philadelphia, where he enjoyed the gaiety of high society—theater, balls, and more eager young women than he could possibly "taste" in two lifetimes. From what Rumor could gather from the free-flowing conversation around her, Sir William was playing a waiting game, confident that a long, hard winter would finish off what was left of the defeated Americans.

The wagons that left the mill were loaded with food for the starving American troops. Fish, game, vegetables, flour, lard, whatever could be spared. And a great deal that could not.

"Of all their miseries, hunger is the worst," said Clara. "We do what we can. That fool of a Congress thinks an army can live on air."

It was but a half day's journey to Valley Forge, but the wagon road passed through enemy territory, and there was always a chance that the two young men would not return. They were often stopped, and searched as spies.

Many times, the food they carried was commandeered by the British.

Each time they left, Clara kissed her son goodbye, bidding him godspeed. Ben was kissed by Janny, for he was her beau. He had been wounded in the lungs at the battle of Trenton and could not fight.

Watching from the house as the sweethearts embraced, Rumor felt little knives of envy twisting in her heart. Her longing for Aaron was so intense she could hardly bear it. Tormented questions skidded round and round in her brain.

Where was he, why did he not return or send a

message? How could he be so callous? Surely, he had recovered his sanity by now and realized that she was no whore. Was he at Valley Forge, starving, cold, and miserable? Was he dead, shot by a Continental firing squad? Perhaps his General Washington had turned a cold ear to his explanation that he had deserted his assignment for love of a woman.

Each time she passed a window, she stared out at the road until her eyes began to ache, as if her longing could somehow materialize his tall, sweet shape walking toward her.

One day she spoke to Walter. "Please, can you inquire at Valley Forge for a man named Aaron Fleming?"

He promised to do what he could. But upon his return, he said sadly, "Your Aaron is still listed among the deserters."

The boy—he was not yet twenty—gazed at her long and hard with his blue-gray eyes. "He left you alone and defenseless from what I hear. How can you still love the cur?"

Shrugging, she replied, "Love is blind, I guess."

Now that she had seen the devotion of these people to their new republic, Rumor longed to call America her own country. She yearned to perform brave deeds to prove her loyalty, to fight alongside her man. Like that Molly Hays, who had followed her man to war and carried water in a stone pitcher to the battlefield. When her husband fell, wounded, she loaded and fired a big cannon by herself.

Molly had been commended by General Washington himself, right there in the battle. Now everyone called the woman Molly Pitcher and her fame spread abroad.

Despite her dreams, however, Rumor's contribution to the cause was limited to caring for the numerous children in the mill. It was a task at which she excelled, all said. The youngsters were of various ages, both boys and girls, and Rumor wracked her brain for new and different games each day to keep them from pestering their mothers who were engaged in sewing quilts from scraps for Valley Forge.

One and all, the children loved to act out stories, she discovered. So did she. It worked out very well in the end. Each evening before bed, she and her passel of "younguns" wrote, rehearsed, and performed, to the delight of the adults.

As Clara had predicted, the Redcoats returned, ransacking every house as before. Hastening to the cellar, Rumor donned the filthy calico again, drew her hair across her face in an untidy tangle, and bent over a washtub filled with dirty garments.

The officer who had questioned her in the street grinned widely when he saw her. "Next time you come to the town, my girl, look me up. I don't mind a tumble now and then." He leered. "Now that you're cleaned up."

Grinning back, Rumor quipped, "It'll cost ye a shilling or two, sir, to buy me some ointment." Lewdly, she rubbed her behind with a sudsy hand.

When he'd gone, she chuckled. It had gone well. The role of slave was hardly Juliet, but she was enjoying it. As she dried her hands and walked upstairs to rejoin the children, she thought that her whole life had been like a melodrama, in which she was only playing a part, first one role, then another.

Which part—Juliet, Cleopatra, slave—was the real Rumor Seton? Last summer, when she and Aaron had been lovers in their little cabin, was that, too, a role? Had they been merely playing a game? No, she thought rebelliously, lifting the wailing infant from its cradle on the hearth to soothe it against her bosom. Loving Aaron was the truest and best thing she had ever done. As real as this babe on her breast.

One clear, starry night a week before Christmas, Rumor fell into her attic bed early after a hectic day. She awoke from a brief sleep to voices below and running feet upon the stairs.

Janny burst in. "Rumor get up, Ma wants you."

Hastily throwing on a quilted sacque and running quick fingers through her tangled brown hair, Rumor followed the girl down two flights of stairs to the cellar. The windowless space was dark and dank. Clara awaited them at the bottom step. Her broad face was anxious and she held a single candle in a saucer.

"What is it, Clara?" Rumor whispered. "Is one of the children ill?"

The woman shook her head. "No, thank God. It's some poor woman. She's over by the woodpile."

Baffled, Rumor walked across the hard-packed earthen floor after the miller's wife, trying not to think of the bugs and occasional rats that inhabited the dark, dank place. In her haste she had forgotten to slip on her woolly slippers.

There was a rusk-filled mattress in the corner by the woodpile, once used by the miller and his helper to catch sleep now and then. Clara had never used it, though, preferring her rocking chair in the hearth room for the rare minutes of daytime rest she dared to take.

Reaching the cot, Clara held the candle over it, and Rumor saw to her great surprise that a tall, black woman lay upon it. A motley-colored patchwork quilt covered all but the woman's face, which was so gaunt the bones stuck out.

"Is she dead?" Rumor asked, bending close. There

ZEBRA HOME SUBSCRIPTION SERVICES, INC.

P.O. BOX 5214

120 BRIGHTON ROAD

CLIFTON, NEW JERSEY 07015-5214

Affix
stamp
here

——— FREE ———

BOOK CERTIFICATE

ZEBRA HOME SUBSCRIPTION SERVICE, INC.

YES! Please start my subscription to Zebra Historical Romances and send me my free Zebra Novel along with my first month's Romances. I understand that I may preview these four new Zebra Historical Romances Free for 10 days. If I'm not satisfied with them I may return the four books within 10 days and owe nothing. Otherwise I will pay just $3.50 each; a total of **$14.00** (a **$15.80** value—I save **$1.80**). Then each month I will receive the 4 newest titles as soon as they come off the press for the same 10 day Free preview and low price. I may return any shipment and I may cancel this arrangement at any time. There is no minimum number of books to buy and there are no shipping, handling or postage charges. Regardless of what I do, the **FREE** book is mine to keep.

Name _____
                              (Please Print)

Address _____ Apt. # _____

City _____ State _____ Zip _____

Telephone ( ) _____

Signature _____
            (if under 18, parent or guardian must sign)

Terms and offer subject to change without notice.   11-88

ACCEPT YOUR FREE GIFT
AND EXPERIENCE MORE OF
THE PASSION AND ADVENTURE
YOU LIKE IN A
HISTORICAL ROMANCE

Zebra Romances are the finest novels of their kind and are written with the adult woman in mind. All of our books are written by authors who really know how to weave tales of romantic adventure in the historical settings you love.

Because our readers tell us these books sell out very fast in the stores, Zebra has made arrangements for you to receive at home the four newest titles published each month. You'll never miss a title and home delivery is so convenient. With your first shipment we'll even send you a FREE Zebra Historical Romance as our gift just for trying our home subscription service. No obligation.

BIG SAVINGS
AND FREE HOME DELIVERY

Each month, the Zebra Home Subscription Service will send you the four newest titles as soon as they are published. (We ship these books to our subscribers even before we send them to the stores.) You may preview them Free for 10 days. If you like them as much as we think you will, you'll pay just $3.50 each and save $1.80 each month off the cover price. AND you also get FREE HOME DELIVERY. There is never a charge for shipping, handling or postage and there is no minimum you must buy. If you decide not to keep any shipment, simply return it within 10 days, no questions asked, and owe nothing.

was something hauntingly familiar about the face, the way the dark brows came together over the nose, the sharp indentation of the upper lip.

"No, but she is very sick, and in a delirium," said a rich, low voice in a cultivated accent. The speaker sounded like a trained actor. Startled, Rumor lifted her head to stare into a shining face, as black as the one on the mattress, but not as gaunt. In fact, the man who was smiling broadly at her from the other side of the sick woman's body looked as sleek and healthy as a well-cared-for horse.

It was a face she knew and loved. A face she had not seen since that terrible night when a band of rowdy Rebels had set fire to the sugar house. A face she had not thought to see again in this world.

"Caesar!"

"Rumor!"

Man and girl spoke at once, and instantly were enfolded in each other's arms at the foot of the cot.

"I thought you dead! Where have you been, and why didn't you try to find me?"

Feverishly, she pressed his thick, warm body to herself, running her hands on the bearlike shoulders, the tough, sinewy neck. Caesar had always been her protector, her guardian angel. Caesar had been the big brother she had never had, as Calpurnia had been in many ways her sister.

He laughed, that deep rich sound she had missed more than anything she could remember of that wonderful, carefree life she had once known as a child growing up in Jamaica.

"Later, Rumor, later. All will be told and you will be amazed." Gently, he removed her arms from his neck. "First we must make Calpurnia well."

Tears rolled down the big man's cheeks as he perched on the edge of the mattress and stroked the brow of his beloved wife.

Numbed with shock, but near hysteria with joy at finding these two old servants—who were more like friends—alive, Rumor bent eagerly to the cot. She put her hands to her mouth, stifling a scream. Incredibly, this grisly skeleton was her beloved nurse and girlhood companion, Calpurnia.

"What happened to her?" She touched the lips that had kissed away her childhood hurts. "Her skin is like paper."

"I don't know. Nobody knows. I found her at a slave auction in Virginia. I had to buy her to get her back."

"But she's no slave, you're both free as air."

Rumor's voice had risen to a shriek of horror, and suddenly, awakening, Calpurnia sat up, jabbering in a shrill voice in a strange tongue.

Swiftly, Caesar placed his arms around Calpurnia's shoulders, holding her close against him. "She's talking in her mother's language, the one they spoke in Africa, before the slavers brought them to Jamaica."

His ebony eyes pleaded with Rumor. "When you were a child, and my wife a bit older, you and she used to talk in that dialect when you wanted to keep secrets from me." He grinned. "I never did catch on to the lingo."

Nodding, Rumor lifted a silencing hand. "It's really a patois, half-English, half-African. Not really a proper language at all."

For a few minutes, the sick woman and the girl spoke rapidly together, Rumor questioning, Calpurnia answering. The woman's eyes began to glitter feverishly, and she tried to rise, impatiently flinging off the heavy quilt.

Instantly, Clara was there, gently pushing Rumor

aside, and lowering the sick woman back onto the bed. "Talk is not what your friend needs right now. We must see that she does not die."

With Calpurnia once more lying quietly, and apparently asleep, the miller's wife turned to Rumor. "I sent for you because you had lived in Jamaica, and the husband here"—she smiled at Caesar—"said they were natives of that island. We both hoped you could understand her."

Clara headed for the stairs. "I'll fetch some victuals—some hot broth, bacon, bread and cheese. Since you two are such old friends, maybe she'll take some nourishment from you, my dear." The good woman shook her head, obviously awed at the miraculous reunion she had just witnessed. "The good Lord above sure works in mysterious ways, don't he?"

In the hours before day broke on the river, Rumor managed to get Calpurnia to take some broth. Calpurnia chattered some more, mostly about some men who had bound her and taken her south, Rumor informed Caesar.

"Maybe she will never be right in her head again," Caesar said, troubled.

"She will," Rumor vowed confidently, laying a comforting hand on his arm, "with good food and all our love and care. The wild talking eases her mind, and helps to relieve her of the bad memories."

Seated side by side on a bench, they ate and watched Calpurnia. Caesar told his story. After the sugar house fire, he had been shown a charred form which they told him was Calpurnia. Grief-stricken, he had tried to find Rumor.

"You were seen being carried off by a wild Indian," he said. "Were you—?" His eyes fell. "I mean, did he—"

227

Giggling at his obvious discomfort, Rumor supplied, "No, Caesar, I was not ravished by the savage, though I was held captive for a time." She could not suppress her giggles at the look of relief on his face. "Being captured was only the beginning, my friend. There is much, much more to tell."

But first she insisted on hearing of Caesar's wanderings, and how he and Calpurnia had so miraculously stumbled into Barren Hill.

He told it quickly, the words salted with humor. Fearing to be taken by avaricious men who made a living by picking up free Negroes in the North and transporting them to the south to slave markets, he had boarded a ship for England, working his passage as a seaman. Leaving the ship at Liverpool, Caesar had worked on the waterfront for nearly a year, loading cargo.

Grimacing, he muttered, "But I didn't like the English way." Standing up, he started to bow and scrape, as if on stage, murmuring in a silky voice, "Yes your lordship, no your ladyship, of course, your majesty, go to hell, your eminence."

Doubling up with merriment at his own antics, Caesar collapsed back onto the bench. "I decided that America was where I wanted to be."

"If we win this war," Rumor murmured.

"We will," he replied firmly. He took her hand in his. "So you, too, have become a Rebel," he grinned. "What would your mama think?"

Rumor's eyes clouded. "She always wanted me to remain in America and return to Albemarle."

Once back across the Atlantic, Caesar had decided to go west, away from men and laws and wars. But midway through Pennsylvania, he had met by chance the actor who had played Romeo that fateful night to Rumor's Juliet.

"Percy?"

He grinned. "The same. He's done well in America. He married the innkeeper's daughter."

From Percy Caesar had learned of Calpurnia's capture by slavers, and after months of searching through the southern states, Caesar found her. Starving, beaten, abused, but alive. Percy had promised help and shelter, but Calpurnia's grave condition forced them to stop at Barren Hill, a hundred miles from Percy's inn. Clara's mill was pointed out to them as a place where a stranger in need was always welcome.

"Amen," Rumor said fervently. "I can attest to that."

Smoothly, as if she were spinning a tale for the children, Rumor related what had happened to her since the fire and David's death. She skipped the part about the night of love with Aaron on the rocks, and his leaving her in a towering rage.

When she had finished, he said gravely, "This Aaron, whom you love and who killed a Redcoat for you—"

"Not for me," she bristled, "but for himself and his America."

"Of course." The deep laugh rang out. "Is he at Valley Forge with his friend the general?"

She hesitated, too mortified and embarrassed to tell this old friend the awful truth, but at that moment a great commotion arose upstairs and she was saved for now.

Janny came dashing down into the cellar to report that Walter and Ben had returned from Valley Forge with a Frenchman they'd found wandering around in the woods. Rumor and Caesar hurriedly followed her to the common room. The tall, aristocratic young man informed the astonished family in a

229

charming accent that his name was Charles de Borre. In truth, Monseuir de Borre fairly exuded charm notwithstanding the grimy, wrinkled uniform and lack of boots. His tight white breeches and lace-trimmed jacket were torn in a number of revealing places, a sorry-looking gold plume drooped from his hat, and his bare feet and toes were dirt-encrusted.

He stood in the midst of the hearth room crowd, while women and children gaped. All had heard of the "Frenchies," — or "frog-eaters," as the colonists called them. How wonderful to actually meet one of those wildly impulsive, romantic heroes who had left his own land and crossed the vast ocean to fight for America's freedom. It was enough to stir any patriot's blood.

Monsieur de Borre started to tell his tale of woe in a comic mix of rapid fire French and English until, despairing, Clara shooed everyone back to work like a mother hen.

"Later, later, later, we will hear all. The man is half starved, and needs a bath." She cast a sly glance at the Frenchie's manly thighs exposed in several places.

"Walter, fetch him a pair of your homespun breeches, and a shirt, too, if you can spare it."

"Later" turned out to be long after supper, when, after putting the little ones to bed, Rumor sat around the trestle table with Caesar and the family in the firelit kitchen. Rumor, who was fluent in French, acted as interpreter when needed.

Like Caesar's adventures, de Borre's story was long and complicated, taking many unexpected turns. He had fought with Washington on Christmas Day at Trenton, but then, hearing from his family in France that his father had died and left him heir to a large estate, he decided to return to his native land.

"But alas, my friends, my ship was attacked by the British, and I barely escaped with my life. I was taken prisoner, but managed, with some others, to escape. New York teemed with British soldiers, so I repaired to Philadelphia where my countryman the Marquis de Lafayette has established a residence."

Embarking for France in March, his ship was once again commandeered by a British warship, and once more he was under British control.

The Frenchman puffed out his cheeks, rolling a pair of very clear blue eyes to the ceiling. He shrugged his shoulders beneath Walter's butternut-colored woolen shirt.

"But I weary you, my kind, American friends."

"No, please, we are most curious," Rumor said, completely enchanted by the man.

He favored her with a dazzling smile. "Very well, I continue," he said. "The British took my, boots which were fashioned of the finest Moroccan leather, and turned me loose in the wilds of North Carolina. After many misadventures, I decided to return to the Continental Army at Valley Forge and resume the fight for freedom."

"And did you?" Caesar asked.

Monsieur de Borre turned a clouded gaze on the big black man. "Fortune was not with me, sad to say. As I neared my destination, I was set upon by robbers and lost all my money, and—"

Once again the pale-blue eyes turned upward, and the Frenchman's hands flew out in an expressive birdlike gesture. "If your young men had not found me in the forest, I surely would have perished."

"A remarkable tale," Caesar commented rather tersely. He rose from the bench. "I bid you all good night. I must see to my poor wife."

Caesar's black face was impassive, and Rumor,

who could always sense his moods, had the sudden thought that her old friend did not quite believe the Frenchman's story.

Janny and her sisters served hot mulled cider to the company, and the talk turned to the troubles at Valley Forge. Walter and Ben reported that conditions were worsening as the winter deepened.

"There is practically no food, and little firewood. Our daily deliveries are but a drop in the bucket. Our commander in chief is being pressed by Congress to sue for peace."

Walter stared at de Borre. "If only your countrymen would send the aid they have been promising for months. It would make all the difference. With France on our side—"

Monsieur de Borre sat up and blinked his eyes. "But how can that be? Our King Louis has finally made up his royal mind to send ships, arms, food, supplies—anything your depleted army requires."

There was a shocked silence. Then Walter said quietly, "Then why in the name of all that's holy doesn't he send word to our Congress? I myself heard General Washington say just yesterday that if he didn't hear from France in a month, he would sue for peace with the British."

The lad's voice broke at the end of his speech. He was openly weeping.

De Borre had risen and was pacing like a caged panther up and down the hearth room, his hands twisted nervously behind his back. "But this is monstrous, how can such a tragedy be possible?

"There is a treaty," insisted de Borre. "I heard the news from one of my countrymen who was bearing the official letter to your Congress. He traveled with me from North Carolina where his ship had docked."

"It could be a dirty spy trick," Walter said, doubtfully.

"Mais non," the Frenchman said indignantly, "the representative who carried the letter is an old friend of my family, he is very highly placed in the government."

There was a long silence, while all pondered this new development. Then, pounding her empty cider mug on the table, Clara said, "It's that fool Congress. There are many there who want to settle with the English. They are delaying telling the general, hoping that things will get so bad, he'll—"

"That must not happen!"

All eyes turned to Rumor in astonishment as she rose up and shouted out the words. "General Washington must learn of this."

Running to de Borre, who was staring glumly into the fire, she put her hands on both his shoulders. "You yourself will tell him, *mon ami,* tomorrow you will go with Walter and Ben to Valley Forge."

The man turned white as a ghost. Drawing back, he looked deep into her eyes. There was so much suffering and pain in the pale eyes that Rumor uttered a gasp of dismay.

"Much as I yearn to deliver the good news myself, I cannot show my person at Valley Forge," whispered the Frenchman.

"Why not?" came a chorus of voices.

"Sure, why not, you were on your way there, anyway," Walter stated. "Are the British looking for you?"

"No, it's General Washington I fear." Miserably, the Frenchman faced the family. "I am a deserter," he went on in a rush. "I ran like a beaten dog from battle last January." He paused. "I have been running ever since."

So Caesar had been right, Rumor thought. The Frenchman's tale of woe was all a pack of lies. She gazed at the man with compassion. Her own Aaron was a deserter. Deserters were flogged, or humiliated in some other way, Aaron had told her. Sometimes they were even hanged, or shot, if the offense were severe enough.

There was a pensive silence until the practical Clara announced, "Let's all sleep on it,"

As they all headed for their beds, Rumor touched Walter's arm. "Is there any word —" She reddened. It was a question she asked without fail every time he returned from Valley Forge.

The boy shook his head. "As far as anyone knows, Major Aaron Fleming has dropped right off the edge of the earth."

Suddenly, de Borre spoke up from the stairs into the cellar where he would sleep with the other two refugees. "Aaron Fleming? Tall, red hair, a painted turtle on his chest?"

Rumor gaped. "Do you know him?"

"We fought together at Trenton. A brave man, this Aaron Fleming." He hesitated before going on. "Is he your lover, my dear young lady?"

His long face took on a mournful aspect. "And to think I had begun to dream —"

"You can go on dreaming what you will, Monsieur de Borre," Rumor interrupted crisply from across the room. Tilting her chin into the air, she spoke through stiff lips, "Aaron Fleming is nothing to me. He lived among us for a time, and we are all concerned about his welfare."

That much was very true, she thought, disliking her evasion.

Heaving a great sigh of exaggerated relief, de Borre announced, "Then you will be happy to hear that he is in the best of health. I saw him barely a month ago. He was traveling with a band of young Indian braves and their squaws, and they were all heading west. Away from the white man's war. To a place called Ohio, they said."

War raged in Rumor's heart as she lay, tense and wakeful, at Janny's side in the big bed upstairs. Her body, beneath the scratchy homespun shift, was doubled up into a tight little ball of nerves.

Clara and the others had tried to be kind. "But how wonderful to know that at least Aaron is well," Janny said.

"They say that once a boy lives with the Indians, it's in his blood forever. He's spoiled for civilization." Sighing, Clara had laid a comforting hand on Rumor's cheek.

But the older woman, knowing that at a time like this mere words were little help, could not look into the girl's eyes.

Rumor fumed inside. Heading west, was he? To the Ohio? He had spoken of it many times, when they were curled up together after love on the rusk mattress. "It's a beautiful river, the great O-hi-o," he used to say, rolling the Indian word around on his tongue, as if it were a talisman.

"It waters a wilderness more bountiful than anyone has ever even imagined. Beyond the Pennsylvania border, there are majestic mountains, fertile valleys, and vast plains where a man can plant grain and corn and raise a dozen children."

One day they would go there, the two of them, together as pioneers, he had promised. After they sold his Virginia plantation and hers. They would free the slaves they owned, taking any who wished to come along to the Ohio country.

But at other times, he wove word pictures for her of life as a lady of quality in his mother's stately house on the Potomac. From time to time they would visit with General and Martha Washington who lived at beautiful Mount Vernon, just down the road.

"You won't be Lady Spenser anymore," he used to chuckle, "but you'll be a first-class citizen in the new America."

So he had finally gone west, she thought. Not with her, as he had promised, but with an Indian girl. That cunning little painted turtle on his chest had worked a kind of black magic on him. Despite his vaunted patriotism, he was going west with the Shawnee. Away from the revolution and all its problems. All the Indian tribes were leaving Pennsylvania for new hunting grounds.

Rumor pounded her fist into the pillow, then turning, buried her face in the feathery mass, fighting the ready tears. She would not cry, damnit—not for him, not for any man.

Charles de Borre was very interested in her. His roving eyes had told her so. She recognized the signs. She began to fantasize. Life in France would be lovely. Mama's family still lived there, in a villa on the Seine. Back in Jamaica Mama used to look at her little daughter and mourn, "If only we could return to my family! My little girl would be a countess."

Tomorrow morning, first thing, she would ask Monsieur de Borre if he had ever heard of a family called d'Estivet who had a villa in the province of Champagne.

As she let her thoughts wander into such delightful realms, Rumor's old cockiness returned. She was still attractive and vivacious. Not yet twenty, her body was lithe and supple. Good breasts, sweet curving thighs, with not an ounce of ugly fat. She had learned to make a man happy in bed.

So Aaron Fleming had rejected her. No matter. She would have the Frenchman on his knees proposing to her within the week.

A vision of herself in a magnificent silken peau de soie gown, her brown hair artfully tumbling about her shoulders, floated in her mind. She would sit for her portrait with a passel of beautiful blue-eyed children at her feet. There was a painting, just like that, hanging in the grand salon at Spenser House.

Afire with renewed vitality, Rumor slipped out of bed and fell on her knees by the window. It was frosted over, but warming a spot with her breath, she made a hole to see through.

She gasped with pleasure. A week-long snow had covered the Schuylkill river valley with a sparkling blanket of white. The sky was velvety black, and stars shone like diamonds down on the little Pennsylvania town.

Finding the North Star, she turned her gaze to the west. Across the frozen river the forest was a dark shadow on the horizon. Aaron had walked into that shadowy dark, turning his back on her forever.

Now she was in a shadowland of a different kind, she reflected wryly. The man to whom she'd given her whole heart and soul had abandoned her. She could love again, perhaps, one day, but not in that all-consuming way. Never in her life, if she lived to be a hundred, would she love a man with that devouring, bittersweet kind of passion that makes two people truly into one.

Rumor laid her head on the windowsill, praying for a light to guide her through the darkness of her soul. Aaron had found his way out of the forest with the Shawnee. Oh, dear God, she prayed, help me find a way.

When she woke to Janny's poke in her ribs, Rumor rubbed his eyes and stretched, lifting a smiling face to the girl. She gazed out at the snow. "Lord, did you ever see such a morning?"

"Mercy, you must have had pleasant dreams," exclaimed Janny with a hug. "I'm so happy you're not grieving overmuch about Aaron—"

"Not another word about that man," Rumor grinned, placing a silencing finger on Janny's lips. "From this day forward, I am free."

At breakfast in the cozy hearth room, Rumor announced to all that she would be leaving that very day for Valley Forge. The answer to her prayer for guidance had come to her as she had slept a few hours on the hard wooden sill.

Her brown eyes held a kind of feverish glitter as she said, "I want to work for my new country, I long to help General Washington in his time of trial in any way I can."

"Doing what?" Walter exclaimed. "You're not thinking of becoming—" He reddened.

"Walter, that's insulting!" Clara scolded her son.

Laughing, Rumor shook her head. His glib assumption that she would be a prostitute reminded her of her years on the stage, when everyone naturally took for granted that her talents lay in only one direction.

"No, Walter," she replied, "I will not become a camp follower, one of those women who give lonely soldiers pleasure in bed. You and Ben have told us that many wives and sweethearts live right there in the camp, nursing the sick and wounded, and lifting the spirits of the men in ways that only a woman

238

can."

Charles de Borre rose up, and coming round the table to where she sat, drew her gently to her feet. Kissing her soundly on both cheeks, he murmured huskily, "Please, deliver this French greeting to the general for me. Work your sweet womanly charm on this good man, and tell him that a repentant coward wishes fervently to return to the battle."

"I will also tell him that help is coming from your countrymen," she whispered.

"Pray that he believes my story."

"He will."

Drawing him close and boldly kissing him on the lips, she added, "I am still a fine actress, I can be very convincing when I put my mind to it. Never fear, Monsieur de Boree, we will be together at Valley Forge. Soon."

His mouth was warm and loving, and ignoring the amused stares of the family, they clung together like a pair of sweethearts. Though lacking the rocklike strength of Aaron's body, the Frenchman's back and shoulders were strong and manly. She waited for the familiar stirring in her loins.

Nothing. Well, it would come, she mused, as she reluctantly pulled away. Her memories of Aaron were too fresh.

There was still danger of the British picking Rumor up and handing her over to General Howe, who in turn would hand her over to Beaumont Carter. Walter had seen a sketch of her likeness on a bit of paper that had been sent to the various barracks in the region.

She would have to go in disguise. But as what? Her roles as Indian squaw and promiscuous slave had outlived their usefulness. As she stood pondering the matter with Janny and Clara in the yard, where the children had built a snow-block fort and were waging a snowball battle, a Quaker woman rode up on the back of an ox. She sat atop a bale of grain to be ground to flour between the great stones in Clara's cellar.

The kindly woman was more than willing to supply Rumor with one of her Quaker bonnets, a simple black frock and apron, and one of the broad white collars that women in her society wore. She would also sell the ox, she said, amazed, when Caesar—who had arrived at the mill with a bagful of coins—offered her a generous amount for the beast.

Within the hour, Rumor was attired in prim Quaker costume, her brown hair dusted with ash to make it gray. The problem of her clear complexion was solved by the ever-helpful Clara, who rubbed a foul-smelling ointment on Rumor's sweet face.

"You'll be not more than a mile on your journey before your face will be festering, as with the pox," the older woman stated. "It will be a foolhardy Redcoat who dares approach you then."

The disfigurement would disappear in a few days, Clara promised.

The winter sun was climbing to the treetops when Rumor finally settled herself on the beast's broad back. Behind her, Caesar firmly strapped a grain sack filled with Clara's dried medicinal herbs, windfall apples, and chestnuts from the trees behind the mill.

She had already bid a sad farewell to Janny and the family, as well as to Calpurnia, who still had not regained her memory. At the last, she leaned down to plant a second farewell kiss on the Frenchman's uplifted face.

Holding the memory of his warm and loving touch fast within her, Rumor headed north to Valley Forge.

Chapter Eleven

"Black Hawk, come, eat. The trout is ready."

The plaintive voice of the woman broke into his thoughts, but the tall bronzed man hunkering on the marshy riverbank of the southern river did not answer. Curling his toes into the loamy soil, he continued his brooding contemplation of the broad dawn-touched stream.

He let her wait. Aaron Fleming had been an Indian long enough to know that a man who treats a woman with too much deference was despised in turn by his fellow braves.

Naked but for a narrow bit of mooseskin stretched taut between corded thighs over his manhood, Aaron sought to be alone for yet a little longer. He had spent a long and tiring night copulating with the maid. Though she was far from that, he thought wryly. Her womb had been wide as a barn door when they'd first come together.

Her name was Dawnstar and she was one of a straggling bond of Algonquin who had attached themselves to the westward-bound Shawnees. They had been starving near to death, and were scrounging for bits of last year's grain in a snow-covered corn field.

The squaw had flung herself at Aaron's feet, closing her eyes and spreading her legs in whimpering invitation. She was willing to trade love for food right there in the middle of the dried-up corn stalks.

He'd been happy to oblige. Not there in the snow, but later, in a warm forest cave. After a bellyful of fresh beaver meat and some rum they'd stolen from a trader outpost, Dawnstar proved to be not only ready, but lusty as a mare in heat. At any hour, day or night, rain or shine, even on a blanket in the snow, her glistening copper body gave Aaron Fleming a vigorous and satisfying coupling.

Then, why in hell don't I feel good, he grumbled to a winter duck swimming around in a nearby clump of reeds.

The duck remained silent, but Aaron needed no reply. Hell's fire, he knew all too well. Relieving his agony in Dawnstar's arms was not enough. Each time he rose from pounding her willing body, he felt worse than before.

He could mount a thousand women, each more seductive and skillful than the last, and his heart and body would be with another.

But that one's a whore, he told himself. He had caught her with another man, her mouth and breasts and thighs open to his caresses. She had looked eager, almost slavering to get on with it.

Each time Aaron relived the hated image, a voice deep inside called out, *But you're wrong. She was only trying to save your life.*

Something very male and very stubborn in Aaron kept him from believing what he knew instinctively was the truth. The image of Rumor's body, which he had thought to be his alone, forever, stretched out so close and intimately near the Redcoat, seemed burned forever in his brain.

The dreadful scene in the cabin would haunt him to his death. Even beyond, he thought, miserably.

Now, as Dawnstar's nagging voice sounded once again, Aaron quickly invoked the old pain. The Shawnee believed that rubbing salt into a wound would make it heal faster. Sadistically, Aaron summoned Rumor's lovely face, and the soft brown eyes with the sweet, trusting love locked in their depths.

Strangely, he saw her at these times, not as they had writhed in passion on their bed of rusks in the cabin, but as he had seen her first and immediately fallen madly in love with her.

The slim, gauze-covered figure of Juliet danced before his pain-filled vision — a pure, white-hot vision of immortal, undying, unchangeable love.

"Ho, the dreamer!"

A loud masculine shout splintered Aaron's mood. Eagerly, he turned, and, bracing, caught the stocky brown body that hurled toward him. With an easy twist of his own well-honed torso, he tossed his old friend Nymwha over his head into the river.

The two men grappled playfully in the shallow water by the banks. Grunting, biting, digging into vulnerable places with knee and foot, they stirred up the mud like two young beavers at play. Toads and frogs and nesting ducks scurried in fright as the brawny young human giants splashed about. It was a daily game, entered into with much glee. As he wrestled, Aaron's moody tension seemed to vanish, and the tantalizing aroma of Dawneater's roasting made his stomach rumble. He was ravenous.

Catching Nymwha unawares, he dunked the shaven head of his opponent under the murky water, one hand on the black scalplock. Planting both feet on the Indian's torso, he pinned him to the river bottom.

Aaron held fast for a time, smiling wickedly, until the frothing air bubbles almost stopped and the flailing arms and legs grew still. Then, relaxing his hold, he helped the defeated brave to his feet.

As the two men climbed together up a little hill toward the thick grove of aspens where the women waited with food, Aaron felt as light and free as air. He felt cleansed. The bittersweet vision of Rumor Seton filled his brain no more. Wrestling, he decided, was a damn better way to pass the time than brooding about females.

They remained at the aspen grove for a week, hunting small game and filling their bellies with fish. The land watered by the southern reaches of the Ohio was bountiful. One of the women gave birth to a son, and Dawneater cast a sly glance at Aaron.

But that night, when the campfires burned low and the men lay with their women, Black Hawk found no desire in his loins. The night was warm, and as he lay atop Dawneater's now-plump body, the rancid smell of bear grease which she smeared on herself to ward off insects set his stomach to churning.

Sliding off to her side, he turned his face away from her. The eastern sky glimmered with stars, as if beckoning him. Toward dawn he slept, but a feverish dream of Rumor tormented him. In the dream she called his name—"Aaron, Aaron"—in a plaintive voice, as if she were ill. Snow lay all about, and he heard a voice saying, "Do you think she'll die?"

In the morning, as Dawnstar was at the river fetching water to mix her corncakes, Aaron rose, and throwing the blanket on which they'd slept around his shoulders, he slung his rifle on his back. Quietly, without a word, he slipped out of the aspen grove and headed north and east toward Pennsylvania.

He would return to his own people, to his commander at Valley Forge, and to Rumor. He prayed that both would forgive him.

Ten days later, traveling practically without sleep, Aaron reached the Continental encampment, and stood on a snowy peak called Mount Misery, surveying the scene below. The day was clear and cold, with a pale sun bravely shining down, but the smoke of myriad campfires cast a haze on the ragged mess of huts and tents.

No longer naked, he was clothed in leather breeches, homespun shirt, and a ragged cloak of sheepswool, having exchanged three fat beavers for the clothes with a local farmer's wife. She had almost kissed him for joy.

"My little ones have had no meat for weeks," she had told him. Her husband had been shot by Redcoats, when he refused them food. All of her neighbors had also been looted, and the once plentiful game in local woodlands had been slaughtered. Not even a skinny squirrel could be seen, and dogs and cats had all mysteriously disappeared.

"They took everything we had—stored grain, our two cows, all the hams and bacon in the smokehouse."

The entire countryside was impoverished, Aaron soon discovered. Washington's army was desperately hungry. Anyone who provided food for Washington's soldiers would be looked upon with favor by the general.

As he'd neared Valley Forge, his confidence in forgiveness had begun began to waver. Perhaps there was a way to get round his adopted father's stern nature. Even a deserter might be welcomed back with open arms, if he arrived dragging a slain deer or bear behind him.

The first sentry he encountered was standing in a half-barrel fastened high up in an oak tree, one of hundreds that bordered the camp. It was snowing so hard and furiously that the man could hardly see the hand in front of him, much less anyone approaching the camp.

Chuckling at his luck, Aaron crouched right under the tree, behind the man. He was talking in a loud voice with the man across the way in another tree.

"Hear there's naught but salted herring at the mess today. Prob'ly have it for Christmas dinner."

The other made an obscene noise indicating disgust.

The men parried back and forth, mostly dreamy talk about roast goose, plum puddings, crusty bread hot from the oven slathered with butter. If a band of Redcoats marched up right now and offered them a roast beef and pudding dinner, with all the rum they could drink, they would probably surrender, thought Aaron wryly.

Aaron headed north and west, to old Shawnee hunting grounds where he and Nymwha had roamed as boys. There was a place in a hidden gorge where the elk and deer were thick as flies. He stopped only long enough to fashion a pair of snowshoes from a sapling.

It took two days to stalk the bull he fancied. He was a mean old bastard, and would most likely be tough as hell to eat, but what a damn fine Christmas present he would make for General Washington and his staff. The beast was a thousand pounds at least, with great clumps of winter fat on his haunches.

Luckily, it was snowing when he returned to Valley Forge at midnight two days later. Strong winds and a blinding blizzard whipped the snow into drifts against the two-story stone house that Washington had made his headquarters. The roads were impassable, in any case, so the chances of enemy attack were down to absolute zero.

Boldly pounding on the front door with his gunstock, Aaron dug his sticks into the ground, pushing his snowshoes into a high drift behind a wide-girthed chestnut.

He heard a call—"Halt, who goes there?"—followed by a shaft of light from inside a log lean-to at the side of the house.

Nothing could be seen but shrouded figures, but he lingered long enough to hear the amazed shouts of two half-dozen sentries and a black servant as they dragged the carcass inside. The laughter he'd been holding in exploded as he made his way back up north.

The shouts awakened Rumor, who lay abed in an upstairs bedroom, swathed in a cocoon of Martha Washington's quilts. She had lain there, barely moving, for three days, while the fever and delirium brought on by Clara's disfiguring ointment abated.

Now, as she awoke, her mind was clear for the first time since the moment she had been stopped at the outskirts of the camp. It wasn't the Redcoats who had nearly killed her, but the Rebels whom she was coming to help.

Not a soul had stopped her or even come close, until she crossed a plank bridge spanning a small creek. For over an hour the pustules on her face had been itching fiercely, but she had kept her hands firmly on the hempen reins. "You'll scar if you scratch," Clara had warned.

She remembered having felt a little dizzy, but thought it was because she had not eaten since she'd left the mill. Amazingly, though it had been bitter cold and snowing, she had been very warm under the Quaker cloak. Almost feverish, she thought.

A soldier in a Continental uniform had emerged from a tent at the other side of the bridge and had pointed his rifle at her.

"All entering the camp must be examined," he had called out sharply. "Kindly step down, mistress."

A second soldier had emerged, and yelled, "Holy Mother, she's got the pox."

Rumor had opened her mouth to say, "Oh, no, I haven't," but no words had come out. She had been unable to make a sound. She had felt as if a wad of cotton had been stuffed down her throat.

The soldiers had backed away. A sentry from across the road had left his treetop platform to run toward her. "I've had the pox, I'll examine her."

Poking her with his musket, the man had ordered her off the ox. Suddenly, Rumor had been ringed by Rebel soldiers, all talking at once, from a distance, of course.

"It's a trick—"

"Those sores don't look like pox—"

"Most likely a spy got up like a female—"

"Let's find out. Strip her—I mean, him."

As the others watched from a safe distance, the sentry who'd had the pox had yanked the cloak off her shoulders. Then, as he lifted the bonnet with the tip of his musket, she had heard the sound of a horse approaching and a soft but very commanding voice.

248

"Well now, have we snared us a Quaker spy?" he had chuckled. "And a pretty one, to boot."

Glancing up, Rumor had seen a tall, incredibly handsome man atop a white horse. The tip of his long pointed nose had been red from the cold, and his high-boned face pitted from the ravages of pox. He had worn a sweeping dark-blue cloak and a tricornered hat with a cockade of red-white-and-blue ribbon stuck rakishly on the brim.

Pulling his prancing mount close to her and the sentry, the big man had leaned down. "What is your name, daughter, and why do you and your beast visit us?"

Rumor had known that the legendary commander in chief himself was addressing her, but her throat and mouth had become so swollen she could not speak. The world of snow and barren trees and leering soldiers had begun to spin—round and round, faster and faster, as if they were all on a gigantic carousel.

The red-white-and-blue ribbon in General Washington's hat was the last thing she had seen before the ground rose up to meet her.

Rumor knew vaguely from the start that she was in the commander's house, and that a sweet-faced woman had come from time to time to bathe her face with cool water. Words of thanks had tumbled about like waterdrops in her brain, but she could not be certain that she had uttered any of them. Someone had removed her Quaker clothes and slipped a warm nightshirt over her head. She had a memory of strong black hands upon her fever-scorched body.

Now, after the shouts, voices murmured from below. Steps sounded on the stairs. Something had happened to cause such a commotion, she mused drowsily, staring at the window. It was frosted over, except for a tiny place in the lower corner where a rush light candle in a saucer on the sill cast a glow.

Perhaps the shouts meant that war was over. Perhaps the heroic but beleagured General Washington had hoisted the white flag.

When Rumor woke again, the snow had stopped and the low winter sun was struggling to shine through the window. A fire crackled in the little grate.

The door opened to admit a short, dumpy woman in a ruffled cap. A starched linen apron was tied around her matronly waist over her gaily patterned morning frock.

"My word, I am happy to see you so alert," she cried in a cheery voice, turning back into the corridor to call out, "Sam, bring up a bowl of that good broth, I think we can persuade our guest to swallow a spoonful or two."

Despite her bulk, the general's wife tripped lightly as a sparrow to the bed, and laid a warm hand on Rumor's brow.

"Cool as a babe's," she exclaimed with obvious delight. "Though I must admit," she added with a tiny grimace, "not quite as smooth."

Rumor tried to raise her head, but the room began to spin. Sinking back, she raised a languid hand to one cheek, then the other, stroking fearfully. A few bumps met her touch.

"The pustules are gone, just a little roughness remains," Martha Washington smiled. "I fear you applied the disfiguring ointment with a too generous hand."

"Thank you for your devoted care," Rumor croaked, from a throat still raw and sore.

"Shush now, girl, don't try to talk."

A huge black servant entered with a steaming

bowl of broth on a tray. Handing it to her mistress, she said, "I strained it through a cloth, Lady Washington, jes' like you said."

"Fine, Betty, it's nice and clear."

Lady Washington was what all called the gracious wife of the commander, Rumor knew. She was in truth a lady, in the truest sense, Rumor mused.

"I feel that I am taking much needed food from the fighting men," Rumor murmured guiltily, as Betty's big, capable hands cradled the back of her head, tilting it so that she could take a sip of broth.

"Oh, miss, they's a whole kettleful of this lovely soup, with chunks of meat in it." The servant beamed, "Some bless'd angel from heaven has fetched us an elk, big as the side of a house, I swear."

Her mistress laughed, "Hardly an angel! Blessed, yes, and certainly mysterious. All we know of him is what a distant sentry reported when he spied him on snowshoes, dragging the beast behind him on a kind of sledge. He is tall, a young giant, and wears a mangy sheepskin cloak. He dropped the elk at our door last night and we cut off a hearty chunk for soup before giving it to the cooks to butcher."

"But how curious," Rumor murmured, too busy swallowing broth to say more. The gamey flavor of the meat had been enhanced by a judicious use of herbs and spices.

"The man was probably an Indian of the Shawnee tribe," Lady Washington commented. "The outline of a turtle was burned into the elk's hide, like a sign."

"A turtle?" A startled croak came from Rumor.

"It be one o' them Shawnee signs," Betty said, "what they paints on their skin."

Her throat hurt like the very dickens with each

word, but Rumor finally managed, "Was it red?"

Lady Washington cocked her head. "Why yes, it was, as if the man had rubbed a dye of some kind into the burned flesh."

After a time, when she'd drained the bowl, Rumor's inflamed throat felt better. Lady Washington left, and Rumor glanced up at Betty, who had just returned with fresh water in the washbasin, and linens over her arm. "This Robin Hood—elk hunter—could have been shot," she said hoarsely, brokenly. Her heart was pounding fiercely beneath the quilt, and she hoped her mix of joy and terror wasn't showing in her eyes.

She hadn't the slightest doubt that Aaron was the anonymous angel. He'd come back from the West. But why? For her—or for his beloved General Washington?

It was obvious that his elk was a propitiary gift, preparatory to begging forgiveness for deserting. But he had told her all deserters were shot or hanged, without fail.

"Yes'm," Betty replied, shaking her dark head. "He took an awful chance." She dipped a cloth into the basin and wrung it out before applying it to Rumor's face. "But you know somethin,' darlin', the general took a funny turn when he seen that red turtle on that stiff hide. He got all red and smiled with all his teeth."

Rumor held her breath. "What did he say?"

"Nothin' much," Betty said, with a shrug.

The maid was silent for a minute as she sponged Rumor's face and neck, then dried them gently with a piece of old soft linen.

"Well—" Rumor prodded.

"He say somethin' biblical, like he often does," Betty muttered. "He say—*the prodigal returns.*"

Rumor's brown eyes became so lively that a worried Betty fetched back her mistress to lay a hand on the girl's still bumpy brow to make sure the fever hadn't returned.

The entire household, if not the whole camp, knew all about the girl who had shown up at Valley Forge with an ox and a case of false pox, Rumor discovered to her dismay when she finally got out of bed. Walter and Ben had delivered several wagonfuls of grain and bread since her arrival, and had extolled her virtues to any who would listen.

Martha Washington smiled. "But we were aware of your identity from the start. You were quite vocal in your delirium. Despite our attempts to quiet you with potions, you raved and ranted and talked a blue streak."

"That's why you be so hoarse after," Betty commented.

Rumor paled, then turned a fiery red. "Wh-what did I say?" she gasped, dreading the reply.

They were sitting by the fire in the sitting room toasting bread baked in Clara's oven on long forks in the fire for their tea.

"You kept repeating, "My name is Rumor Seton, and I am a patriot, come to help." The general's wife's eyes twinkled. "As though you had memorized it, like a child in school."

"I had, but never got to say my piece," Rumor mourned.

"You also spouted a number of lines from Shakespeare's plays, especially from *Romeo and Juliet*."

The cultured male voice of the commander was followed by his immediate entrance into the room. It wasn't often that he honored them at tea, and Betty and her young helper scurried to pour him a cupful and toast him a crust.

253

The big man quaffed the brew with relish, smacking his lips and closing his eyes, as if the reddish stuff were not really dried sweet myrtle leaves pounded in a bowl with maple twigs. No patriot drank English tea, even when it was available.

Too tongue-tied to speak before this sainted man whom Aaron worshipped almost as a god, Rumor fell silent. She clutched her blue-and-white china cup with stiff, nervous fingers. This great, often austere man surely must have heard her delirious ravings.

Sensing her discomfort, General Washington began to chat in an amiable fashion about the theater, putting her at her ease.

"I saw your lovely, talented mother on the stage at Williamsburg many times before these troubles," he grinned. "And you, too, young lady. As a child, of course."

Blushing with pleasure, Rumor exclaimed, "Oh, that I could only bring back those wondrous times." Tears sprang to her eyes. "Alas, I fear my acting days are past."

The thin brows flew upward, and the general shook his head in vigorous denial of her statement. "Ah, but no, my dear young woman, far from it. The troops in charge of lifting the men's spirits hope to present some theatricals soon," he said with vehemence. "Skits, scenes from plays, some music perhaps—"

Grimacing, he added, "When our fever of hut building is over, of course, and we are all under roof."

He rose to go, but stopping at her chair, grasped both her hands, cup and all, between his own. "I look forward to seeing you perform."

There was a twinkle in his eyes that Rumor wondered at, and when he was safely gone, she turned to his wife. "In my fever, did I mention any name other than my own?"

Her hostess pursed her lips, pulling in a musing way at her tiny ear beneath the drawn-back graying hair. "Why, no—"

But to the chagrin of her mistress, the ever-helpful Betty, busy with the tea things, did not catch the signal. "Why yes, miss, you kep' jabberin' 'bout a man named Aaron. We all figger he's your beau."

"Oh-h-h."

Closing her eyes, Rumor emitted a long, drawn out sigh that was more of a groan.

A minor household emergency summoned Lady Washington to the kitchen, and Rumor was spared the embarrassment of explaining Aaron to her at that moment.

A never-ending stream of important official visitors poured in and out of the headquarters house. Rumor's bedroom was sorely needed, and she would have to move to another dwelling, Lady Washington informed her.

"When you are well, of course," her hostess murmured, "the end of the week, perhaps."

Ten woman, wives and sweethearts of the soldiers, occupied a sturdy stone farmhouse that had belonged to loyalists who'd fled to British New York before the Rebels. It would be crowded, she was told, she would have to share a bed with another.

"It's the best we can do," the general's wife said. "But you will be able to walk to the camp for the sewing."

"Sewing?" Rumor echoed, dismayed. "But I am all thumbs with needle and thread. Is there nothing else?"

There was the hospital work, but unmarried young ladies, especially those so gently reared as

Rumor, did not nurse the sick and wounded. Aside from the fear of contagion from the dreadful diseases suffered by the soldiers, there was another problem.

"Modesty," Betty snapped. "A sweet thing like yourself, miss, jes' don't belong in a place like that."

The camp was in a dither over a hundred bolts of fine woolen cloth taken from the cargo of a British ship captured in Delaware Bay. It would be fashioned into badly needed uniforms, and the farmhouse parlor that Rumor walked into on a snowy morning was packed tight as a herring barrel with sewing women.

A log blazed in the hearth, and the room was stifling. All were chattering merrily. Rumor's mind flew back to the common room at Spenser House, the hearth room at Clara's mill. Disheartened, she took her place on a long bench against the wall and picked up the breeches she was given to stitch.

Sewing with a gaggle of chattering women was not what she'd had in mind when she had come to Valley Forge. Her lips set in a determined line, and she began to push the needle in and out of the heavy stuff with a show of great industry.

Her stitching was so bad that Martha Washington threw her apron over her merry face in a fit of laughter, declaring that she had never seen the like.

"The poor man who dons these breeches at dawn will be naked at dusk," she giggled.

The Jamaican actress would be very useful in a month or two when the theater was scheduled to begin, the general opined, when asked for his advice. But for now, why not have her help with the children of the married troops?

Though she bowed meekly to authority, Rumor's heart was still set on the hospital work. But that

256

evening, as she entered the farmhouse where she was to live, a kindly fate intervened.

"You've a visitor in the parlor," said a broad-chested woman with a sweet but careworn face. She smiled. "A man." Her name was Stella, she added brightly, leading Rumor to a heavily curtained doorway.

Rumor's heart skipped a beat. It had to be Aaron. The gifts of game from the anonymous Red Turtle—as the general called him—had continued almost nightly since that first elk. Now Aaron had finally decided to show his face, beg forgiveness, and take his punishment for desertion.

But—oh, what joy—he would also beg to reconcile with the lover he left so cruelly months ago.

Forgiveness? How gladly she would give it. And more. Her love still burned with the same fierceness in her heart.

The parlor was also dark in the early winter dusk, and Rumor floated on air, it seemed, to the tall figure in the white homespun shirt, who stood gazing into a cold fire, both hands on the mantel.

Encircling him with her arms, she clasped her hands together at his waist in front. Leaning her head against his broad back, she murmured, "Oh, my love, my love, my love—"

"Ma chérie," he exclaimed, and taking her hands in his, whipped round. Before she could utter a sound, Charles de Borre took her uplifted face between his hands and kissed her long and passionately on the mouth.

Too startled to resist, Rumor returned his kiss, parting her lips and allowing his tongue to explore her mouth at will. It was the kind of kiss that was an invitation to further intimacies.

"Ah, *mon Dieu,* what a greeting. I had not dared

to hope that you cared so much," Charles muttered huskily, as he lifted his mouth from hers.

Dazed, Rumor broke from his embrace, sank into a chair. "I thought . . . I thought—"

But she could not go on. How could she tell this fine man that she had expected another? Charles's thin Gallic face was aglow with rapture as he drew her up again into his arms. Helpless, Rumor stood as if mesmerized, permitting the Frenchman to cover her face and neck with ardent kisses.

"But you are a deserter," she said at last, drawing them both onto a settee. "Have you seen the general?"

He nodded miserably. *"Naturellment.* I am to report tonight at midnight for a hearing. There will be punishment, but I hope for leniency."

He gazed solemnly into her eyes. "After your oh so courageous departure for Valley Forge, I could not prolong my cowardly absence. Especially when my countrymen will be sailing at any moment to aid—"

Rumor's hand flew to her mouth as she uttered a tiny shriek of chagrin. "Dear God, I never delivered your message. My illness drove it clean out of my head. Oh, Charles, can you ever forgive me?"

To her amazement, he whooped with delight. "Your forgetfulness has worked in my favor, *chérie.* I had the great pleasure of breaking the good news of the French alliance to his excellency the general myself. He was so overcome with joy that I am certain he will beg the court-martial officers for leniency on my behalf."

After a discreet knock, Stella entered, bearing a lighted candle in a bowl. Placing it on a little table, she cautioned Rumor that dinner would be served momentarily.

258

Stella cast a wary look at Charles. "Your gentleman is most welcome, of course, to our poor table. Will you dine with us, sir?"

There was no answer. Charles had slid quietly off the settee and lay in a senseless heap on the worn carpet.

"That's a nasty, festering wound in his shoulder," Stella commented, as she and Rumor, and several others, gazed down at a pale Charles stretched out on a bed.

"He said nothing about it," Rumor wailed.

When he had recovered his senses, the Frenchman explained that he had been hit by enemy rifle fire on the road to the camp. Being anxious to reach his destination without further incident, he had extracted the musket ball with his knife and staunched the flow of blood with his handkerchief.

The wound was black around the edges and thick with yellow pus. It would have to be lanced and thoroughly drained, Stella said grimly.

Rumor insisted on caring for Charles herself, cutting and gouging the opening in the flesh under Stella's skilled guidance. When she'd finished, both women gazed admiringly at the neatly bandaged shoulder. Stella was extravagant with her praise. "That's a fine job, Rumor. I can scarcely believe you've not done this many times before."

Charles's wound proved to be Rumor's blessing, for the admiring Stella—who worked in the hospital herself—persuaded the general to allow Rumor to become a nurse. At dawn next day, Rumor happily walked with Stella to the hospital, a long hut at a place called Yellow Creek. If only Calpurnia were here, she thought. The black woman was a wonder with the sick, using a combination of magic and native herbs to work her miracles.

Calpurnia could not be at Valley Forge, but Janny arrived to help. Clara's daughter waited at the farm-house when Rumor returned at dusk from her second exhausting day at the hospital. "Ben and I have come to help with the nursing," she said, with a sparkle in her eye.

The sparkle, Rumor shortly learned, did not stem entirely from the prospect of helping her fledging America gain its freedom.

"Ben and I are to be married," she announced, "within the month."

Until the nuptials, Janny would sleep with Rumor in a big bed under the eaves of the farmhouse. Rumor was overjoyed. "It's just like old times," she giggled, snuggling against the girl's warm body beneath the quilt as a near-gale shook the timbers of the old house.

"What about you and your frog-eater?" Janny inquired, archly. "It's all over camp that you and he are sweethearts."

"A gross exaggeration," Rumor grunted, groaning inwardly. "Charles is counting his chickens too soon, I fear," she grumbled.

To her dismay, Rumor discovered that the news of an impending betrothal between herself and the Frenchie major was indeed all over camp. In two days at the hospital having his wound cared for, the exuberant Monsieur de Borre had talked almost without ceasing to anyone, who was not too sick to comprehend about his lovely fiancée.

His wound also proved a blessing to Charles, for the doctors pronounced him too weak to run the gauntlet between two rows of men armed with clubs and sticks. That was the usual punishment for cowardly behavior in battle.

"I am to ride backward on a horse," he informed

Rumor, almost with glee. Then he added, chuckling, "Stark naked."

In addition, he would have to serve latrine duty for a month, digging trenches, cleaning out old latrines of filth and offal. It would be, Rumor realized, without being told, a grueling, humiliating ordeal for the sensitive, aristocratic officer.

They were seated on the settee in the candlelit parlor the night before his punishment was to begin. They'd partaken of a light supper of flour cakes and hot water laced with a dollop of cider. Such was the soldiers' fare in these days of depleted rations, stated Charles, and he must eat humble pie, quite literally, for a time.

Janny entered from the dining room with two pewter mugs of her mother's dark, sweet elderberry wine. "But you must drink," she protested, when Charles murmured a mournful refusal. "We and the others are toasting my wedding at next week's ball."

The ball would also celebrate the new French alliance, and promised to be the most festive event of the hard winter at Valley Forge. It would be held at a local tavern, and there would be music, dancing, and much merriment.

When Janny left, discreetly pulling the doorway curtains together tightly, Charles drank his wine in one gulp. He seemed nervous. Putting down his tumbler, he drew Rumor into his arms, kissed her fervently and long, and held her so close she could hardly breathe.

"Oh, my darling," he panted into her ear, "how long must I wait to taste your sweetness?" He groaned, as if in mortal pain. "Sometimes I cannot bear the waiting."

Grasping her buttocks with one hand, he lifted her from the hard cushion so that his great erection

261

thrust between her thighs. Capturing her lips again, he parted her lips and spoke hotly against them.

"You have stolen my heart," you darling witch, please say you'll be mine. Tonight. I know a place—"

His hips were swiveling obscenely against hers, and he was pushing her slowly but steadily down upon the settee. His body soon covered hers completely.

"Charles, please, the women!"

"They will not enter, they know we are lovers."

With all her strength, Rumor slid from beneath his squirming body, landing on the floor. Picking herself up, she confronted him as he sat up, dazed and flushed with passion.

"But this is madness, I cannot—"

Rising nimbly, he drew her to him once again. "You will tell me that your year of mourning is not yet over, that you cannot marry so soon." He stopped, and the look in his gray eyes was agonizing. "Is there another? I was given to think that you loved me. When I arrived—"

He hesitated. "Is it Aaron Fleming perhaps? I recall your asking Walter for news of him."

Not trusting herself to speak, Rumor shook her head emphatically.

"Who, then? Tell me, and relieve me of my agony."

Charles waited, his face a mask of pain.

Her head a jumble, Rumor sank into a rocking chair. Filled with remorse at allowing Charles to think she loved him, she rocked gently to calm her nerves, appraising the tall, slender man before her. He was attired in full French uniform again—a smart, close-fitting blue jacket with rose-and-silver lace on collar and sleeves. White and rosy plumes lifted from his grenadier's cap lying on the table.

He was a fine figure of a man, she thought. Calpurnia would approve. Mama, too. Fine old titled family, old money. Best of all, he adored her. When Charles looked at her, Rumor felt like a goddess.

There was absolutely no doubt that Charles was a man in every sense. He had returned to take his punishment, had been willing to accept even death if so ordered by his commander.

Unlike another, who continued to hide, and whose intrusive image she now pushed ruthlessly from her mind. Aaron Fleming made a poor showing against Charles de Borre. Aaron had sworn to protect her from her father and Olympia Spenser. Aaron Fleming had sworn to love and cherish her forever.

Instead, he had fled his duty to her and to his country. Afraid to face the music, he threw pitiful offerings of turkeys, geese, possum, squirrel, and the like at his commander's door.

Like a naughty child, she thought furiously, who'd been caught with his hand in the cookie jar.

On the other hand, a stalwart, loyal, faithful man like Charles would shield her from her father, from Olympia, from General Howe. From Aaron, too, if and when he decided to return and plague her once more with his lust.

Charles did not arouse in her the mindless passion that Aaron did. Merely thinking of Aaron set her blood to simmering. But enough of that. It takes more than simmering blood to build a life upon.

During her silence, Charles sank back down on the settee, and gazed across the room at her. After a minute, he began to talk, hesitantly at first, but then all in a rush, as if the words had been bottled up inside him.

"There is something I must tell you, Rumor, before you agree to become my wife. It is not true that I am the heir to a landed estate in the Loire valley. I am merely a fourth son, and will inherit nothing. Aside from wanting to fight for America, I came to your country to make my fortune." Spreading his expressive hands outward toward her as if beseeching her, he finished. "I am penniless, my darling."

Long before he had finished his confession of duplicity, Rumor was on the carpet by the settee, hugging his knees.

She lifted a radiant face to his. "Dear, dear Charles, I love you all the more for your honesty. I am still Lionel Spenser's widow, and will share my fortune with you."

Tugging at his rose-colored lace, she pulled him down until his lips met hers. Kissing him passionately, she exclaimed in a loud voice, hoping that everyone in the dining room would hear.

"I will be honored to be your wife," Monsieur de Borre.

Chapter Twelve

"You're a truly perfect couple," Martha Washington proclaimed in her bright, cheery voice, kissing Rumor on both cheeks and clasping the girl to her full bosom. She smiled. "So handsome, both of you. What lovely children you and Charles will produce."

Curiously, however, her husband the general, was not so enthusiastic about the engagement. His high-boned face was thoughtful, even a little grim, as he grasped Rumor by the shoulders. "Charles de Borre is a fine man, and will make a superb husband, I am certain. But—"

His blue eyes narrowed piercingly, and Rumor felt that the man was looking into her soul. "I strongly advise that you wait the full year of your mourning before standing up before the preacher," he continued.

Somewhat unsettled by the wise man's ill-disguised disapproval of her engagement, Rumor dressed for the ball to be held that night in the Spread Eagle Tavern. The hostelry was a full mile from the camp, but was the only domicile with a room large enough for dancing.

Washington and his adopted son were so close. Had Aaron confided in the general about their love affair, Rumor wondered as she slipped a length of white gauze over the mint-green gown the camp seamstresses had made for her to wear tonight. She was to play Juliet, and a marvelously authentic costume had been whipped up in a day.

It was no longer a secret that the mysterious huntsman who deposited game at the general's back door was the truant Major Aaron Fleming. The mark of the red turtle appeared without fail on every carcass. The game arrived daily. Clearly, Aaron was in camp, or nearby and the general was in touch with him, and for reasons of his own did not choose to tell her.

The two men — George Washington and his former head spy — were playing some kind of devilish game. Was she to be the pawn? Why else would the commander beg her to perform the dagger scene from *Romeo and Juliet* tonight, as part of the entertainment following Ben and Janny's wedding?

Did he hope to lure the Red Turtle from his hiding place? Why not some other scene, from another, more cheerful play? The bard had also written many comedies.

The dagger scene was his favorite, the general said.

Had Aaron told the man who was a father to him that this scene where Juliet kills herself for love of Romeo was his favorite, too? And that it was not with Rumor Seton as herself, but Rumor Seton as Juliet, that he had fallen madly in love that terrible night in the sugar house?

Fitting the pearl-encrusted Juliet cap on her springy, shoulder-length curls, Rumor stood in front of the window of her bedroom at the farmhouse. A January rainstorm had drawn a veil across the hori-

266

zon, and the smoke from the soldiers' campfires added to the haze.

The whole world beyond the window seemed an impenetrable cloud of mystery. Like my future, like my whole life, mused Rumor pensively.

Shaking her head to clear it of such gloomy thoughts, she joined the other women of the house in the wagon that would take them to the ball. Orders had been issued to everyone — troops, officers, wives, sweethearts — to be merry.

Rumor laughed aloud, as if practicing. She would have to get through this difficult night alone, Charles being forbidden to see her — or anyone — socially, until his latrine-cleaning punishment was over.

But as the wagon bearing her and others to the Spread Eagle bumped along the rutted roads of Valley Forge, her spirits lifted. Cider from a cellar hoard captured by the forage detail had been distributed to every tent and hut. Sounds of singing and crude musical instruments rang out into the rain.

Forgotten for a few brief, blessed hours was the fact that bellies were never full, that feet were often bare, and that loved ones were far away.

Every window of the Spread Eagle blazed with light. Inside, Rumor found a gay crowd. The brilliantly colored uniforms of the French officer volunteers moved in and out of the more subdued American uniforms like flowers blowing in a field of grain.

Many, both officers and their ladies, wore masks, as was the fashion. Unconsciously, Rumor's brown eyes flitted about the room. The capricious Red Turtle was audacious enough to appear right here in public, in mask and costume. Perhaps as Sir Oliver

267

Mowbray?

You ninny, she told herself, that would be too obvious for the biggest trickster of them all. Aaron would be more subtle.

Gritting her teeth, Rumor stood against a wall, watching the brief ceremony as Janny married her Ben.

"Do you vow to love and cherish—"

"I do—"

"I do—"

Swallowing a lump the size of a lemon in her throat, Rumor hugged the bride. "Love him, with all your heart, darling, and trust him, no matter what."

The toasts rang out, endlessly it seemed, as French and Americans linked arms in friendship. Rumor forgot her own miseries and cheered along with the rest.

"Vive le France!"

"Huzza, huzza for America!"

"Yankee Doodle went to town—"

Everyone was getting very drunk. Even the austere face of the American commander was strawberry colored, and he was heard to burst out in frequent laughter.

In her graceful Juliet costume, Rumor danced, with this one and that, first a jig, then a minuet with the dazzling Marquis de Lafayette himself as her partner.

The musicians struck up a lively country reel, and Rumor danced about the room, tripping from one man to the other, as though her feet had wings. Her blood grew hot, and beads of sweat formed on her brow and lips, pouring down in a shiny trickle between her unbound breasts.

Every nerve and fiber in her body tingled. She felt

more vibrant and alive than she had for many months. Many admiring glances came her way. Many a soft invitation to dalliance—mostly in French—was whispered into her shell-like ear.

Smiling radiantly, she refused one and all, confident in her beauty and sexuality. She was Rumor Seton of Jamaica, actress extraordinaire. She was her own woman at last. No man would ever enslave her again.

Aaron Fleming be damned, wherever he was.

"Where is my lord, where is my Romeo?"

An ethereal Juliet wafted onto the makeshift stage from behind a hastily constructed stage.

As the plaintive, sultry voice of Shakespeare's tragic young heroine lifted into the smoky rafters of the Spread Eagle, the audience leaned forward as one. A collective sigh went up, moving through the packed tavern like water over stones.

"She's incandescent," breathed a captain in the blue and gold of the Virginia militia.

"Mais oui," mumbled the bewigged and beruffled French officer who lounged alongside in a narrow doorway at the side of the huge firepit.

"Bien sur," *"mais oui,"* *"très charmante,"* and other simple French phrases had been the extent of Aaron Fleming's mumbled conversation all night. From the start, he had put on quite a show of being too intoxicated to partake of intelligent talk.

When he'd decided to attend the ball as a Frenchman, he knew that the less he spoke the better. His schoolboy French would come immediately under suspicion.

Discreetly, he pulled at his black satin mask with a

white-gloved hand, making sure it covered his long nose completely.

"Just this once," the general had sighed, when he'd yielded, wearily, to Aaron's plea to have a rendezvous with Rumor. "The risk of your being discovered by others is very great."

It was vital that everyone at Valley Forge remain under the impression that the Red Turtle and the general were still playing the game of hide-and-seek. Actually, after the first week of throwing animals at the headquarter's back door, the mysterious Robin Hood had resumed his spying duties. A backwoodsman from Tennessee had been given the task of catching and depositing the animal carcasses at headquarters door.

"All will think that Aaron Fleming, alias the Red Turtle, is too cowardly to show his face," the general said. "That will be your punishment."

Aaron had groaned. "I would prefer to run the gauntlet, even to clean out latrines, like poor de Borre."

A gasp from the Virginia captain was followed by a poke in Aaron's ribs. "Pay attention, she's lifting the dagger."

By God, she hasn't lost her touch, Aaron mused as he watched Rumor stab herself and fall dead upon Romeo's still form. He longed to shout proudly, "She's mine, this beauty belongs to me. To me, Aaron Fleming, she has yielded her charms— and to no other."

In the rush of memory, his scalp began to itch, as it had that night at the sugar house. He slid a finger under his wig, scratching vigorously to keep his mind from his growing erection.

Damn it, but it was still the same. Even far away,

up there on the stage, so far away he couldn't even see her face clearly, the woman still had the power to stir him as no other.

After a moment two watchmen made their entrance on the stage, and one proclaimed in a loud voice, "Alas, here is Juliet, bleeding, warm, and newly dead."

"Dead, dead, dead," echoed the other.

The Virginia captain was weeping into his hanky, but the masked French officer beside him sidled out into the rainy night. The word "dead" had reminded him painfully of the real reason he was here tonight.

Merely wanting to hold his sweetheart in his arms was not sufficient reason to grant permission for a meeting, the general had said.

Beaumont Carter had finally arrived in Pennsylvania in search of his daughter. At this moment, Rumor's father was residing at the Crooked Hill Tavern, a few short miles from Valley Forge. According to Aaron's informants, the blackguard, together with his henchman, Philip Stokes, was getting rich from the American and British soldiers in the region by drawing them into gaming, cockfights, and other forms of diversion.

Carter's sly face had haunted Aaron since the day he had seen him on the rotten dock at Albemarle, the man's rundown plantation on the Pamunkey River.

"My sweet baby will do what her daddy tells her," Carter had vowed. "Women in these parts have no more rights than slaves."

Aaron was as certain now as he had been then, gazing at the man's evil face, that the father Rumor had never seen would murder his own daughter if necessary to obtain Albermarle for himself.

Rumor must leave Valley Forge. Nothing else would save her from Beau Carter's schemes.

In a pantry room behind the tavern kitchen, Rumor sat on a wooden bench, eyes closed, trying to think of nothing. She was emotionally and physically drained. The other actors had rejoined the dancers, but she had begged a few moment's rest.

Janny and Ben had already left to spend their bridal night in a farmhouse where they had been given a tiny room. The wagon for Rumor's farmhouse would not come for her and the other women for two more hours.

Bunches of drying herbs hung from the rafters, imparting a woodsy fragrance to the little room. There was no fire, and feeling chilly, she hugged herself, lifting up her legs to stretch out on the hard bench.

The sharp voices of the cook and her helpers came through the wall as they busied themselves with the supper for the officers and their ladies. Music and shrieks of laughter could be heard above the general roar emanating from the hearth room.

Rumor had spent a grueling day at the camp hospital, and she found her mind dwelling somberly on Mack, the young soldier who was dying slowly and painfully from his wounds.

"Don't leave me, miss," he kept begging, as Rumor sat by his cot and held his hand. She reminded him of his sister in far off South Carolina, he said. Her work with the sick consisted mostly of giving comfort—holding hands, writing letters, talking of this and that. Mack never tired of listening to her stories of Jamaica.

On occasion she performed scenes from plays she had acted in, standing in the rude hut between the rows of beds and declaiming dramatically as if she were in the grandest of theaters.

The end was near for Mack, she should be with him now. Nobody should die alone.

Drowsily, she thought of fetching her cloak from the hook to cover herself. The herby smell in the room reminded her of the forest of Harlem Heights where she and Aaron had first made love. Now it all seemed like a dream. She imagined Aaron's arms around her, his smoky eyes gazing at her with adoring love.

Ruthlessly, she shut the image from her mind. Like all dreams, it was over, never to come again.

She must have dozed, for when the young scullery maid touched her shoulder, Rumor bolted up, frightened, rubbing the sleep from her eyes.

"Yer wanted at the hospital, miss."

"Mack?"

"I dunno, some soldier's dyin' and is callin' for ye."

Her cloak was fetched, and pulling it tightly round her shoulders, Rumor ran out to the waiting horseman. The short nap had refreshed her, and she held on fiercely with both arms to the soldier whose mount and saddle she was sharing.

"Please hurry," she urged. "I want to get there before Mack dies."

He spurred his horse, and they proceeded at a gallop down the muddy road. Occasionally they were forced to slow down as small bands of celebrating soldiers blocked their way.

But at last the hospital hut came into sight, and Rumor removed her arms from the soldier's back, preparing to dismount. But the soldier did not slow down, continuing his rapid pace.

"They moved Mack to a tent at the edge of camp," he explained. "They needed his cot for someone else."

At length they arrived, and, sliding off the horse, Rumor fearfully pushed open the flap of the animal-hide tent. A small fire crackling in a pit, of stones emitted both warmth and the only light. A long shape lay under a blanket on one of two cots. The second cot was empty.

Mack was lying on his side, and falling to her knees, Rumor gently cupped his chin, turning his face to hers. Leaning close, she brushed his brow with her hand.

"I won't leave you, Mack, I promise—"

Rumor heard a kind of yelp as the blanket was pushed away. Two strong hands pulled her down by the shoulders, and she found herself being kissed passionately on the mouth by a masked stranger. There was no mistaking that intimate touch, the bold thrust of the arrogant tongue into her mouth.

Though her brain yelled "Pull away," Rumor clung to the man whom she knew full well was Aaron. Hot waves of emotion swept through her love-hungry body, and the lovely, familiar, sorely missed warmth crept rapidly into her hips and thighs.

Marshaling every ounce of strength in her tired body, she did pull away finally, straightening up and running toward the flap. A strong arm yanked her back before she reached it, and she found herself pressed against Aaron's manly chest, her face uplifted to his.

"Your escort has his orders," he grinned down at her wickedly. "He'll stand guard lest we be disturbed,

274

and will take you back to the tavern in an hour. In time to catch the wagon for your farmhouse."

"You wretch," she choked, nearly blind with rage. "This is the dirtiest trick I have ever—"

Her angry outburst was cut short as his head came down and he captured her lips again. Her struggles for release only served to increase the iron-like pressure of his arms about her.

"Give up," he mumbled against her lips. "Save your strength for the sweeter battle to come."

"Is rape your weapon again?" she stormed when his lips lifted at last.

"Rape?" He cocked a skeptical brow. "If you refer to that night on the rocks after I killed the Redcoat, I don't think you were entirely unwilling."

Flicking off the Juliet cap with a long finger, Aaron curled his fist into her hair, pulling her head back. He laid a trail of tiny kisses up and down her arching neck, paying special attention to the tiny pulse that fluttered like a little bird right in the center.

"Stop that," she moaned. "You know what that does to me."

"Uh huh," he chuckled, cupping her buttocks with his other hand and drawing her close to his lower body. His manhood was full and ready for love. Her feminine parts were moist and warm. As he was well aware.

His arms no longer held her in a vise. She could easily break away and run outside. The area was jammed with tents. She could hear voices, singing, laughing. But she was powerless to move.

A delicious languor possessed her. She had not known such a wonderfully exciting feeling since the last time she and Aaron had made love together. Her knees turned to water, her arms went limp, and her head was spinning in mindless circles.

Rumor began to feel light as air, intoxicated, as if she had taken a sleeping potion.

"That's more like it," he said, forcing her eyes to look directly into his. "Be honest. Was it rape then?"

"No-o-o," she groaned.

"Is it rape now?"

"No, you bastard. You know I want you every bit as much as you want me."

She managed to pull away. "But we must talk," she said shakily. "You owe me an explanation."

"Later."

Drawing her by both hands to the cot, he sat down, and removing his mask, untied the strings of her cloak. She shrugged it off and quickly, urged on by mounting passion, they undressed. Rumor slipped off the loose gown and gauzy sacque with ease. With trembling fingers, she helped Aaron unbutton his blue officer's coat and breeches.

Naked, they sank back together on the narrow cot, she on top of him. His hard-muscled, sinewy flesh against hers was warm and vital, and she moaned in unrestrained pleasure as her hands roamed freely, stroking, grasping, clutching, kneading.

Nearly sick with passion, she kissed the tiny red turtle on his breast, as he kissed her breasts and nipples.

With the slow, deliberate moves of memory, they played on each other's bodies like musicians tuning up for a concert. Wantonly, she fondled his masculine hardness as it thrust against the soft flesh of her inner thighs.

Dimly, through the roaring in her brain, Rumor

caught a fleeting thought, "I am promised to another. This brief hour is all I will ever have of my true love."

But then all thought was gone as he skillfully fondled the throbbing flesh of her innermost femininity, driving her to the brink of ecstasy, only to teasingly withdraw his caressing hand.

"Beg me," he crooned into her ear. "Ask me for release."

"Oh, damn you, damn you," she gasped. "Take me, take me, take me—"

With a pantherlike movement, he drew her from atop his body to lie beneath him. Parting her thighs and lifting her legs to encircle his buttocks, he took her then, this man to whom she was a slave of love. He entered her with the deep, powerful thrusts that filled her fitful nightly dreams. With each rhythmic movement, Rumor felt as if her insides were turning inside out to receive him, to capture him forever.

When he exploded within her, spilling his seed into her churning womb, Rumor's body convulsed in a passion so intense she muttered, "Oh, I could gladly die right now."

He chuckled hoarsely, gasping for breath. "No, not that, my love. You must live for me, and for the child I have surely given you tonight."

"Child?" she murmured. "But we cannot marry."

"Why not, my sweet?"

Rolling off her warm body onto the dirt floor of the tent, Aaron squatted for a moment, staring at her as she struggled up to a sitting position.

"Is it because you are the rich and titled Lady Spenser and I am nobody?" he inquired in a sarcastic tone.

"Of course not," she replied, angrily reaching for

277

her clothes and starting to put them on. "I have promised to marry Charles de Borre."

Combing her short hair with her fingers, she continued, with some asperity. "Loyalty may be something you know little about, Major Fleming, but—"

A voice came suddenly from outside. "Almost time, sir."

"Yes, Sergeant," Aaron shot back.

Already in his breeches, he shrugged into his blue military jacket. Gold lace edged the high collar and sleeve ends, and, absently, Rumor reached out to straighten out the wrinkles.

Grasping her by the wrist, Aaron said flatly, "Charles is a charmer. I'm fond of him myself. I trust you are aware that he is counting on Lady Spenser's wealth to keep him in the high-flown manner he cannot afford as a penniless fourth son."

"I know all that. Charles has been straightforward with me."

"Good."

Slipping on his mask, he tied it securely from behind his wig. He couldn't afford to be recognized as he rode back through the camp.

"All the same, you will never marry that Frenchie."

"Whoa, Aaron Fleming of Virginia," she stormed. "You are not my king, nor even my keeper. You have no power to say yea or nay to anything I do with my life."

He touched her nose with his, rubbing playfully, but there was no lightness in his reply. "Any woman who denies the power of love such as we have just experienced is a bigger fool than most of her ilk."

Releasing her, Aaron waited for her to finish dressing. At a loss to think of a scathing rebuttal to what was obviously true, Rumor fastened her cloak, setting the Juliet cap back on her head and tying it under her chin against the wind.

He was right as rain. She *did* love him, madly. When she was in his arms, she was helpless as a babe.

"Now listen, listen hard," he said, pulling her down on the cot beside him and taking her hands in his. "General Washington is much concerned about the rash of gambling and dicing that the troops are engaging in. For many reasons, such activities are detrimental—"

"Oh, hell," he exploded, as the soldier called again from outside the tent.

He continued, talking rapidly and low. "Various gambling dens have been raided by our military police this past month, and from their reports it is almost certain that your father, Beaumont Carter, is the ringleader in this nasty business."

Paling visibly, she stood up, stunned. "My father is here, near Valley Forge?"

"A man answering his description has been seen."

"Then why has he not tried to murder me, as you claimed he intends? It would be a simple matter. Any soldier can tell him where I live."

Grim-faced, he rose up and took her by the shoulders, regarding her with slitted gaze. "It's not his way to be so direct. Believe me, I know the man. I've talked to him. When the time is ripe, he'll strike."

"No, no!" She spat the words into his face. "I don't believe you. I don't believe you have ever seen my father. It's all a lie. Our whole relationship has been a tissue of lies."

"Rumor, please, stop and think—"

"No!"

279

The word was a shriek, she was near hysteria. Despite her angry words, Rumor flung herself at Aaron, burying her face in his chest.

"I want to see my father," she moaned. "If it's money he wants, he can share the Spenser wealth. I'll set up a house anywhere he wants, and we'll live together, as nature intends."

Aaron groaned aloud as he pressed her to him, encircling her protectively with his arms. "You sweet little ninny. Has your lawyer not told you that to claim the Spenser heritage, you must live in England on the ancestral estates? Lionel was in the Colonies only because he was serving in the Royal Army."

He hesitated, as if his next words were hard to say. "Your father committed a crime against the Crown. In his youth, he killed a man. He fled Virginia, thus escaping punishment at the time. But English law has a long memory, and if he sets foot in England, he will surely be brought to trial."

Drawing back, he lifted her tearful face to his. "He might be hanged, or sent to prison. Do you want to take that chance?"

"I don't care what you say. I want to see the father I've never known. When we come together face to face, all will be well. We will embrace. I feel it in my bones. You can't deny nature."

"You blind, silly woman," he exploded, thrusting her from him in disgust.

With his hand on the tent flap, he continued urgently. "Stop dreaming about what cannot be, Rumor. Your dreams of setting up a house with your father are but childish fantasies. You will end up destroying yourself."

"Loving you will destroy me," she countered. "I cannot believe a word you say."

As if he hadn't heard, Aaron went on implacably. "Return immediately to Barren Hill. Clara and Caesar will protect you from Carter until such time as I am free to do so."

Livid, Rumor hastily wiped her wet face with the edge of her cloak. "I need no one to protect me from my own father. It's all a bare-faced, outrageous lie, and when I find him—which I will if I have to search every square inch around Valley Forge, I'll prove it."

"The general will order you back to the mill," he said flatly. "You'll have no choice."

As they went out into the night, she could not resist a parting barb. "Courage to face a difficult situation is also something a coward knows nothing about. You may despise Charles as a fortune hunter but he came back to face his commander and take his punishment like a man. He doesn't throw dead animals at his commander's feet and hope for mercy."

"Go back to Barren Hill," Aaron yelled, leaping onto his mount, which the soldier had been guarding.

"I can't," she called back as she put her foot in the stirrup of her own horse. "They cut up my ox and made it into stew," she added irrationally.

A laugh erupted from Aaron's chest, but his heart was heavy as he watched her riding away behind the soldier. Oh, God, how he longed to tell her that he was no coward, that he was risking his life for his country every day in a variety of disguises.

But her very life might depend on her not knowing. If she were ever captured by the British—as she was likely to, if she searched for Carter—they could easily torture any information about Aaron Fleming

281

out of her.

The general had said that being thought a cowardly deserter in the eyes of the camp was cruel but sufficient punishment.

The general was dead wrong. To have the one you love despise you is hell on earth.

The stars shone down like diamonds on Valley Forge, and the celebration was still in full tilt in the huts. But Major Fleming was oblivious to everything but his own resolve to save this willful, childlike woman he loved so desperately from her scheming father.

If Mohammed won't go to the mountain, he mused wryly, the mountain will have to come to Mohammed.

Big black Caesar was the nearest thing to a mountain Aaron could think of. Flicking his reins, he turned his mount toward Barren Hill and Clara's mill, where Caesar and Calpurnia still resided.

Chapter Thirteen

A month passed. A freezing, snow-filled January slid into a slightly warmer but muddy February. Cold rains fell almost every day, with now and then a thaw.

The makeshift roads of the Valley Forge encampment often were more like rivers. Rumor's daily half-hour wagon journey home from the camp hospital was sometimes an ordeal of an hour or more.

Mud-spattered and almost giddy with exhaustion, she sat at the farmhouse kitchen table at midnight of a day that had begun for her at dawn. Her eyes were closed, and her still hooded head leaned back against the wooden back of a chair.

"Rumor, how long have you been sitting there like that with your cloak and hood on?"

Calpurnia's clear, softly Jamaican-accented voice preceded her as she walked across the dark, low-ceilinged room, shielding a candle with her hand. Her handsome black face was concerned, as she set the candle on the table and moved to stand behind Rumor. Gently removing the damp woolen hood, she placed two strong, skilled hands on Rumor's neck, and began to knead in rhythmic circles.

Choking back the tears, Rumor thought of the

many times the capable, warm-hearted black woman had worked this soothing comfort to both her and her dear dead mother.

"Do you think we will ever see our dear island again, Calpurnia," she asked wistfully.

"Yes, I do," said the other firmly. "Soon's your man comes back from the war."

With characteristic stubbornness, Rumor's former nurse persisted in referring to Aaron as Rumor's "man."

"Your muscles are like rope," Calpurnia muttered. "Too much tension. You've got to stop these eighteen-hour days at the hospital."

Rumor's hand came up to grasp her old friend's wrist. "Mack died tonight," she said dully.

"Bless the Lord, he's better off in heaven," Calpurnia intoned piously.

Gradually, the warmth engendered by the nurse's massage spread to the tense muscles of Rumor's entire body, and she began to breathe more easily.

"What would I ever do without you, dear Calpurnia," she exclaimed with a little laugh. "These three weeks since you and Caesar came to live here with me have made me feel like a carefree child again."

"That man of yours gave us orders to watch over you, every minute. Though I don't know how I can do that when you stay at the hospital so long each day. Anything could happen to you—your wicked father could do you harm."

"Nonsense," Rumor responded sharply. "And may I remind you for the thousandth time that Aaron Fleming is not my man. He's not my anything. I am going to marry Charles."

Calpurnia's pert reply was muffled by her vigorous poking of the coals in the hearth. Rumor caught the last words, "not much of a man, he's never here."

284

"Charles has gone to the shore to prepare for the imminent landing of the French fleet," Rumor said wearily. "Much needs to be done, in an official way."

"Uh huh," Calpurnia mumbled, returning with a steaming cup of herbal tea. "Now drink this and no more talk."

Obediently, Rumor drank while Calpurnia squatted, pulling off Rumor's mud-encrusted boots. Then, rising, she pulled the girl to her feet, undressing her—first the wet cloak and then the linsey-woolsey frock, turning her round and round like a sleepy child.

Caesar's wife had fully recovered from her nightmarish experiences between the night of the sugar house fire and when she was found at a slave auction, alive and starving. Thanks to Clara's care and hearty cooking, the skeleton that Rumor saw months before in the cellar of the mill had filled out into the substantial womanly figure now moving with authority about the kitchen.

Though she no longer raved in delirium, Calpurnia's illness had served to blot out the terrible things that had happened to her.

While Rumor sipped a second mug of the delicious, strengthening tea, her childhood nurse vigorously brushed and sponged her garments, hanging them on chairs by the hearth to dry.

The marvelous heat of the tea coursing through her veins, the comforting sounds of Calpurnia fussing about the kitchen, the familiar, mother-daughter kind of nagging repartee between them—all combined to infuse a sense of well-being Rumor remembered fondly from her childhood in Jamaica. The loving care her former servants lavished on her filled the void created by Aaron's abandonment—almost.

She grudgingly admitted, though not aloud, that Aaron's fetching her old friends to Valley Forge made up in part for all the terrible lies he'd told her. One day, soon, she'd begin to look for her father. Several soldiers had reported seeing a man named Beaumont Carter at a certain tavern where gambling was rife.

At least that much of Aaron's wild stories was true.

Now that Mack was dead, and she was not bound to camp by any special dying soldier at the hospital, she was free to scour the countryside. Rumor dared not admit, even to herself, that part of the reason she had delayed looking for Beaumont Carter was the fear that perhaps Aaron's story of her father's evil intent held a grain of truth.

Caesar had promised to help her. In truth, the big black man forbade her to go anywhere without him, lest Beaumont Carter or his henchman take a pot shot at her from behind a tree. He accompanied her everywhere, except to bed, when Calpurnia took over the watchdogging task. Today, however, he had asked a soldier friend to take her back and forth to the hospital.

"I have an errand to run," he had grinned, adding with a twinkle, "a secret rendezvous."

The constant watchfulness, though oft annoying, was more often comforting. The couple's overweening devotion was balm to a heart sorely bruised by Aaron Fleming.

Later, as the two women lay abed in the loft room, back to front like spoons in a drawer, Rumor mumbled into Calpurnia's plump shoulder. "You'll love Charles, once you get to know him."

"Hope so. Though why you want to marry a Frenchman when a perfectly good American like Aaron Fleming is around mystifies me."

"Aaron's *not* around. God only knows where he is."

Irritated, Rumor turned her back to the older woman. Angrily, she punched her pillow until she

286

made a hole in which to bury her face. That sneaky Virginian had worked his devilish charm on Calpurnia and Caesar, too. Neither of them would hear anything said against him.

"You've only seen him once," Rumor protested.

"That's all it takes," Calpurnia replied blandly, "Manhood shines out of that one like he invented it."

Long after her bedmate was snoring peacefully, Rumor lay awake. There'd been no word from Aaron since that night in the tent. He was spying, he'd said. But as far as anybody could tell, he was still playing games as the Red Turtle. Dead animals still appeared at the Washingtons' back door. "Oh, botheration," she moaned to herself, "if I only knew what to believe!"

She must have slept, because toward dawn she was awakened by the sound of wagon wheels behind the house. Slipping out of bed, she crept to the window and peered out.

A wagon was just pulling away from the tiny sleeping tent that Caesar had constructed under a large chestnut bordering the brook behind the house. Through the heavy mist she saw Caesar's black hand above his bulky shape, waving to the departing driver. Then, quickly, he slipped inside.

Returning to the bed, Rumor mumbled teasingly to Calpurnia, just waking up, "I wonder what your husband has been up to. He's been out all night."

"He likes a good card game now and then," replied the other equably.

Both women found out what Caesar had been "up to" soon enough. They had just settled themselves in the crowded hospital wagon when Caesar emerged from his tent, pulling a woolly cap over his tight black curls. The cap was one that Calpurnia had knitted for him, and had a jaunty red ball at the top. "So's I can spot him in a crowd," his wife had joked.

"No nursing today, ladies. You're both coming with me," the big man called out.

"Oh?" asked Rumor, her brown eyes puzzled. Climbing back down from the wagon, she asked pertly, "And might I ask where we are going, and what is more important than the nursing?"

Caesar's ebony eyes fairly danced with excitement. "I'm taking you to your father," he said. "He is extremely anxious to see you again after all these years."

"The man's never seen me. I was born after he abandoned my mother."

Now that the longed-for time had come, Rumor found herself holding back. Calpurnia had climbed into the cart that Caesar had ready for them, but she held back, standing by the chestnut, her gloved hand on the trunk.

"Are—are you certain he is—"

"It's him all right. He is your father, Rumor Seton. The resemblance is amazing. You and he are stamped from the same cloth."

Caesar nodded so energetically that the red woolly ball bounced up and down in the chilly air. The weather had suddenly turned cold again overnight and frost covered the ground.

"The likeness is in looks only, you can be certain," snapped Calpurnia. "Now get in, child. You've got to face it, whatever that rascally man has in mind."

Face it. The words rattled around in Rumor's brain as they bounced along in the rickety old farmcart out of the camp and onto the Schuylkill River road, past the place by the bridge where she had been stopped by the Rebels and had fainted at George Washington's feet.

Snow was falling softly, whirling out of a gray sky in big white flakes, when Caesar slowed down and turned the horse into a lane bordered by giant oaks. They were about ten miles from camp, far past any American sentries.

A flock of chattering black snowbirds flew up into an overhanging tree, causing a drift of snow from a bare branch to plummet down on Rumor's head and shoulders, nearly choking her. Brushing off the heavy stuff, she felt a sudden, unreasoning fear of entering the tavern.

Leaning forward, she called out, "Caesar, let's go back. This region is too close to British territory." Her eyes darted around the snowy hills that bordered the road, half expecting a troop of Redcoats to storm them with bayonets flashing. But Calpurnia's ironlike arm was around her shoulders, pushing her inexorably out of the cart.

The Crooked Hill tavern was three stories high, and sat imposingly behind a spacious cobbled yard with a dozen hitching posts. Walls of thick gray fieldstone gave it a fortresslike appearance. A wide stone porch ran the full length of the building.

Her eyes glued to Caesar's broad back, and holding tightly to Calpurnia's hand, Rumor entered the tavern. She gasped audibly, slapping her gloved hand to her mouth to stifle a scream. Her worst fears had been realized. The taproom fairly swarmed with British soldiers.

Three men seated at the long, polished bar turned round to stare. The low chatter at the many small tables abruptly ceased as the newcomers received full attention.

The narrow room was ablaze with light. Candles burned on every table as well as on the walls. The smoke from a tremendous log crackling in the firepit added to the drift from cigars and pipes and curled round the already blackened rafters.

"Come, child, don't dawdle. They won't shoot us.

We're not Rebel soldiers, but peaceable citizens," hissed Calpurnia, tugging at Rumor's arm.

"Confound it, if we haven't got a rustic beauty come to pay us a visit!" A scarlet-covered arm belonging to an officer with epaulets darted from a table as Rumor passed, halting her progress. A hand closed on Rumor's wrist. "What d'y think, O'Brien?" the officer inquired of his companion, with whom he was playing cards.

A slow grin curved O'Brien's mouth as he puckered his lips and emitted a shrill, appreciative whistle. Then, leaning back, he swept Rumor up and down with a pair of narrowed green eyes. "Confound it, Higgins, if she ain't a beauty!"

Snickers ran through the taproom. The visitors promised to be great sport. Fresh, young, American ladies were a rarity at the Crooked Hill. You could hardly count the ones who came at night to trade a bed tumble for a shilling.

"Sir, you mistake us," proclaimed Calpurnia wrathfully, attempting to move forward.

Throwing his hand of cards on the table, the officer rose, grasping Rumor's other wrist. "Out of my way, Negress," he snarled, kicking her shin with his boot, "I want to view the merchandise."

Caesar was on the hearth talking in low tones with the aproned innkeeper, but as the laughter swelled, he whipped round and charged across the floor like an enraged gorilla.

The innkeeper rang a large bell. Instantly, the commotion ceased. "Unhand him, blackamoor," the man yelled at Caesar, who had Officer Higgins by the collar and was growling doglike into a very frightened face.

"I'll have no brawls in my tavern," the innkeeper said to Caesar, "unless you'd like to get handed over to the Rebels who'll likely sell you as a slave."

Then, angrily, "Higgins, you damn fool, the girl is Beaumont Carter's daughter. Any tomfoolery with her will fetch you pistols at dawn with a man who's never lost one."

"Never was word more truly spoken, innkeeper," said a modulated voice in the slurring, fluid accents of the South. The voice belonged to a man standing on the open wooden stairs at the far end of the room.

Rumor, who was shakily holding on to Caesar's arm, glanced up. A tall, slender, extremely handsome man no more than fifty, walked with easy grace down the remaining steps. Reaching the bottom, he paused dramatically, his pale hand on the newel post, as if waiting for applause.

Entranced, Rumor gaped. Her father—there was no doubt as to his identity—bore the graceful, confident mien of an actor on first entering a scene.

There was absolutely no doubt that Beaumont Carter stood before her. Caesar had been right on the mark. The creator had used the same cloth, same pattern, for both of them. His brown hair curled in soft waves to his shoulders, just as hers did. Brown eyes gazed imperiously from above the thin, aristocratic nose, a mite longer than her own.

It was the set of the head, as he cocked it slightly to one side, and the childlike gaze of the wide-spaced eyes, that—catching at her heart—convinced her.

Her mother's voice echoed from the past. "You hold your head just like your father," she used to say. "And you both have that bewitchingly innocent look in your eyes—"

Though far from splendid—he was no macaroni—his attire was fashionable and scrupulously clean. Brass buttons adorned the superbly tailored velvet cloak in cinnamon brown. Knee breeches of the same hue sported silver buckles. Gaiter boots of soft leather gleamed with polish.

"He's a gentleman, every inch," Rumor breathed proudly.

She did not hear Calpurnia's snappish response, for she found herself moving as if on invisible strings toward the man who glided gracefully across the taproom to her.

"Have I caught thee at last, my child? He that parts us again will bring a brand from heaven down upon him."

Through the pounding in her ears, Rumor recognized the poetic words of Shakespeare's King Lear. So he was an actor, too, or a very learned man! Her heart swelled until she feared it would burst her rib cage.

With a choking, "Father, Father," she hurled herself against him, weeping against the narrow brown velvet chest.

Cupping her chin with cool tapered fingers, he kissed her on the brow and cheeks, his tears mingling with hers.

"Come, Daughter," he said finally, glancing haughtily at the boldly staring soldiers, "let us repair to my quarters, where we will talk our hearts out."

Despite Caesar's vigorous protests, Rumor walked up the stairs alone to the tiny cubicle of a room.

"We'll not move from the taproom, child," shouted Calpurnia, from the foot of the stairs. "If you feel you're in danger, just scream, and we'll come running."

"Danger?" murmured the wonderful man with his arm tightly about his daughter. "The woman must be mad."

Giggling, Rumor laid her head on his velvet sleeve. "She thinks every man who looks at me intends to ravish me. Even my own father, I suppose."

Though he'd been near Valley Forge for weeks, Beau had not sought his daughter out, he explained, because he was not ready.

"I arrived in Pennsylvania without a sou, as they say in France," he said ruefully. "My clothes were in tatters, I was a wretch. I could not have my only child see me thus."

Fortunately, he'd had a lucky streak at the Crooked Hill, and by the time Caesar discovered him, he could present himself like a gentleman again.

Her father lived in a world of fantasy, like an actor constantly on stage, Rumor learned as the day wore on. All her attempts to find out about his life in the past twenty years since he had left her mama were futile.

Beau Carter spoke little and never to the point. He answered none of her probing questions. Instead, he spouted verse, fending her off. He had a quote for every occasion, it seemed.

Supper was brought—roast fowl and cakes with a good, hearty claret. A fire was lit in the tiny grate. Though barely wide enough for two people to move around in, the room was tastefully furnished, with a narrow bed and chest of drawers in Queen Anne style. There was but one chair, so father and daughter sat on the bed, close together.

Far from being discouraged at her father's evasions, Rumor was ecstatically happy. Just being with the father she had so often dreamed about was heaven enough for now. Later, when they were more comfortable with each other, she would find out why he had left her mother alone, penniless and pregnant so long ago and why he had never sought her out all these years.

When she pressed him about it, he had gazed into the fire before replying in his wonderful, dulcet voice, "A cruel, inscrutable fate is the master of us all."

She avoided mentioning his ancestral home, Albemarle, or why it was rumored that he was ready to kill her to get the plantation for himself. She could not bear to even suggest such a terrible thing. How that kind, sensitive face would blanch! Even a hint of such vicious gossip would banish the love from his expressive brown eyes.

Once said, she could never retract the awful suspicion. They could never be close again. He might even run away, disappearing from her life forever.

The storm had worsened, and there was no question of their returning home that night.

"You may have my bed," Carter insisted. "There is nothing else but the common sleeping room for the women, and" — he shuddered — "you'll arise with vermin, and some obscure but dreadful disease that you'll pass on to your aging father."

Screwing up his face so that Rumor laughed aloud, Beau Carter danced about the narrow room, scratching himself like a prancing monkey.

How utterly charming he is, mused Rumor, as she kissed her father good night. To think that he was capable of murdering his own flesh and blood was ludicrous. Aaron was out of his mind for even imagining such a terrible thing, and wicked for telling her of his evil thoughts.

Her father told her that he supported himself by gambling. To Rumor, there was nothing innately sinful about card games and such. Every man she knew liked to gamble, even otherwise upright Caesar. Aaron, too. As for the drunkenness that Aaron had mentioned, she would curb that excess once they were living together.

There was no lock on her bedroom door, so Caesar insisted on stretching his giant body across the doorsill as she slept, like a big black watchdog. Disdaining the straw-strewn female dormitory, Calpurnia wrapped herself in a blanket downstairs on the kitchen floor.

Four glasses of the heady wine had made Rumor tipsy, and gratefully she sank back on the comfortable bed, falling asleep instantly.

She woke to mountains of snow outside her window. As far as the eye could see the world wore a dazzling cloak of white. Great drifts piled up against the stone walls of the Crooked Hill and obliterated the road.

"We're snowbound," the innkeeper announced, a jolly Pennsylvania Dutchman named Joe.

Rumor and her father could not spend their second day quite as intimately as the first. "I have agreed to pay my chit for room and food by keeping the men occupied with games of cards and billiards and the like," he said.

Giving her a good-morning kiss and hug, he added, "I will pay for you, too, my dear. From this day forward, we are a family."

Rumor spent most of the day with Calpurnia on a bench by the big fire in the taproom. Purchasing a few skeins from the innkeeper's wife, the nurse busied herself with knitting stockings for the soldiers.

Fortunately, Rumor had in her possession three playscripts that she had intended to read from at the hospital yesterday. As she began to recite the lines in her resonant voice, some of the tavern guests made a circle around her, listening avidly.

Unfortunately, her first selection was a somewhat rowdy comedy, entitled *The Kept Mistress*. There was much ribald laughter at certain suggestive lines, and when Rumor read "Give me a kiss, sir, before I go out," Colonel Higgins leaped forward to boldly plant his lips on Rumor's.

Once again, Joe the innkeep was forced to ring his bell as Caesar sprang like a lion at the Redcoat.

Calpurnia demanded that the reading stop, but,

yielding to Joe's pleadings that it provided superb diversion, Rumor continued. But with a different, more sedate offering.

Thinking to make the drama more lifelike, Rumor innocently asked for a volunteer to read with her, taking parts. Higgins eagerly stepped forward, but was discouraged by a fiery look from Caesar who stood nearby, arms folded, standing guard, like a Roman sentry.

"May I suggest my good friend, Philip Stokes?" Beau Carter smiled down at his daughter, his hand on the shoulder of a short, wiry man with a shock of sandy hair and a thin, pointed foxlike face.

"He's partaken of amateur theatricals in Virginia," Beau continued. "His plantation borders ours, my dear, and we have been traveling together for some time. Since we are neighbors, it behooves you, my dear, to cultivate his friendship."

Suppressing a tremor of panic, Rumor studied the man before speaking. Philip Stokes was the man her father would force her to marry so that their plantations could be joined. So Aaron maintained. But she had stopped believing in any part of Aaron's fanciful tales about her father.

Smiling graciously, she extended a hand to Stokes. "What are you doing so far from your home, sir?" she inquired.

A look of infinite sadness came into the man's gray eyes. " 'Tis a long story, madam, and one that would cast a pall on the good spirits of all present, were I to tell it to this jolly company," he murmured.

His words had the ring of truth, and ashamed of herself for convicting the man without a proper hearing, Rumor patted the space beside her on the bench.

"Pray, join me, sir. We must read from the same page, I fear."

His thin face turning bright red, Stokes took his place. "I am most honored, madam."

Calpurnia pursed her lips, and Caesar glowered. Surely they cannot think that such a distinctly unattractive person will endanger my virtue, reflected Rumor, smiling sweetly at both of them.

Despite his apparent lack of charm, Stokes proved to be a talented actor, rendering the lines with spirit and conviction. Rumor warmed to the little man, and when supper was brought, courtesy of the innkeeper, she sat with him and her father at a table next to the big hearth.

Over wine and country cheese and apple pie, Stokes told his story reluctantly at Rumor's prodding.

With eyes downcast, he began, speaking slowly, hesitantly, in his low, cultured voice. "My family has been on the Pamunkey since 1750, long before the Indian wars. The land was deeded to my great-grandfather by George the Second, grandfather to our present monarch, for glorious services rendered in India."

Looking up at Rumor, he said quickly, "I am under the assumption that you are not in sympathy with the rabble that has rebelled against our beloved King George?"

"I have no politics, sir," Rumor lied smoothly. She had no wish to start an argument with this obviously unhappy man.

"I married young, at eighteen," he went on, "but lost the wife of my heart in childbirth. A pestilence snatched my parents from my side, as well as my only brother."

Tears crept from his eyes. He wiped them with the back of his hand. "I am left alone, with a house so big I rattle around in it like a lost soul. My slaves are out of hand, they rob me blind, the fine furniture and china and silver that was my mother's pride and joy are in such a state—"

Overcome with emotion, Philip Stokes dropped his head on the table and wept like a child, his hands splayed out helplessly.

"Your poor, poor man."

They were alone, Carter having left them to fetch more wine, and impulsively, her own eyes brimming, Rumor placed a sympathetic hand on his.

There was a loud cough from Calpurnia, who sat on a stool nearby. As Rumor glanced her way, the older woman shook her black head vigorously, mouthing, "Poppycock."

Caesar came forward with a large red cloth. He pushed it at Stokes. "You sure can spin a tale to make the stones weep, Mr. Stokes. You could make a fortune on the stage."

"Caesar, how very rude!"

Rumor's sharp words were lost on Calpurnia's husband, however. Chuckling, he walked quickly to the bar to refill his tankard with Joe's rich, dark ale.

Rumor cast a withering look at Calpurnia. Her two watchdogs were so wary of everyone, she thought angrily, that they would suspect the most innocent child of perfidy.

"Well, I believe him," she mouthed back at the scowling Calpurnia.

Stokes's hand was clasping hers tightly now, and suddenly becoming aware of the curious glances of the other guests, Rumor gently extracted her hand from his.

Lifting his wet face, and wiping it vigorously with Caesar's handkerchief, Stokes sniffled, "I sincerely beg your pardon, ma'am, I am making a fool of myself."

Leaning forward, she peered into his eyes. They were

298

wide, innocent of guile. "My father and I will return to our beloved Albemarle when the weather clears and the roads are passable," she said warmly. "We will help you get on your feet again."

The eyes that met hers glistened with gratitude. "Oh, if only such a wonderful thing could happen—"

"It can, sir. You have my word on it as a gentleman." Rejoining them at that moment, Beau Carter refilled their wine tumblers. "I am certain that my daughter's generous nature will extend to helping you regain custody of your son—"

"Son? You have a son?" Rumor's rich voice resounded like a bugle in the crowded taproom. All heads turned her way.

"Please, Daughter, you are shaming the man."

Carter put a reproving hand on Rumor's arm. "The subject is a painful one, so I will speak for my friend."

In low accents, her father spun a sorry tale of a child born to the now dead wife, of the mother's relatives snatching the boy from the grief-stricken father.

"The lad is three," Carter finished. "A handsome child, despite his handicap. But, sadly, without a profitable plantation, and a new mother for the child, my dear friend cannot sue for custody in the courts."

"Handicap?" Rumor asked.

"A slight deformity in one leg," Carter said.

Regaining his composure, Stokes stated flatly, "No woman in the world would take on another man's child. Especially one who has a gimpy leg." He stared fixedly at Rumor. "Would you, madam? Would you devote your fresh young beauty to such a task?" He spread his hands out beseechingly.

Her heart full, Rumor exclaimed, "Any loving woman would. I would—"

At that moment Joe rang his bell again, announcing that it was high time all were abed. The taproom was closing for the night.

Calpurnia was livid.

"You're a bigger ninny than I thought," she grated. "You're being hoodwinked. That Stokes is in collusion with your father. The two of them will trap you into marrying that sniveling weasel."

"Fiddlesticks," Rumor spat back, thoroughly out of patience with the woman. "His story rings true, nobody is *that* good an actor."

The two women had been arguing heatedly for some minutes while Rumor undressed for bed in the cold bedroom. Caesar had mysteriously vanished and his wife would take his place outside Rumor's door that night.

"But where could he possibly go in this snow?" queried Rumor, with a glance at the mountainous drifts still piled up outside the window.

The nurse shrugged her plump shoulders. "I don't know. All that carrying on you did tonight with that lying Philip Stokes got him so riled up, he probably went off somewhere to cool off."

Yawning widely, Rumor climbed into bed, pulling the heavy quilt up to her chin. "How odd. He swore he wouldn't let me out of his sight." She slid down into the bed, mumbling, "I pray he doesn't get lost out there and freeze to death."

"Or get shot at by a stray lobsterback," mumbled Calpurnia, gazing worriedly out the window.

As she was leaving for the corridor, Calpurnia couldn't resist a parting word. "Now tomorrow I want you to stay away from that man. Don't let him tell you any more fabricated tales of woe."

Grunting in annoyance, Rumor pulled the coverlet over her head, shutting out the scolding voice.

The third day of their unexpected stay at the Crooked Hill passed quietly. She could hardly avoid Philip—they were on first-name basis now—because they were implored by the innkeeper to resume their play reading.

That night at late supper before the fire, Philip Stokes spoke no more of his troubled life. Instead, he and Carter talked with animation about plans for refurbishing their neighboring plantation.

"You'll have free hand in choosing new furniture, or refinishing the old," her father told Rumor. "As for the garden, that will be yours, too. I trust you have a green thumb."

"I never had a garden," Rumor mourned. "Mama and I were never in one place long enough." Her eyes sparkled. "But I look forward to the challenge."

At bedtime, Caesar still had not returned, and a very worried Calpurnia prepared to spend a second night playing watchdog at the door. The weather had relented, and a warm breeze began to blow from the south. The drifts were still high, but as Rumor climbed into bed, she could hear the steady drip, drip of melting snow from the roof.

Despite the excitement of making plans for Albemarle, Rumor found herself very drowsy. "I don't know why I'm so sleepy," she yawned to Calpurnia. "Must be the lack of my usual activity at the hospital."

"You drank far too much wine tonight," the other snapped. "Now go to sleep, I feel powerfully sleepy myself."

Seconds later, Rumor heard several bumping noises as Calpurnia slid her heavy body into place in front of the door. Despite her snappishness, Rumor was grateful for the nurse's careful attention.

In Caesar's absence, that pesky Colonel Higgins had flirted outrageously with her all day. A bold one

like that one might even try to enter her bedroom He
had gotten very drunk.

Lulled by the wine, the dripping roof, and the
comfort of Calpurnia a few steps away, Rumor drifted
into a dreamless sleep.

The wind had arisen, and at first she thought the
rattling of the window had awakened her. But gradually, as her senses cleared, Rumor became aware of a
hand on her bosom. Her eyes flew open. A naked man
stood at her bedside.

"Higgins?" It was barely a squeak.

The man laughed, and bent low. It was not the brash
Redcoat but Philip Stokes whose hand began to wander over her breast, reaching under his nightshift to
cup it lewdly.

She bolted up. "Get out of here, you're drunk."

Where was Calpurnia? She attempted to slide out of
bed on the other side, but swiftly he fell on the bed,
pinning her down.

"Calpurnia," she screamed.

"The Negress is in the kitchen, my sweet — dead
drunk. She won't hear you."

Revulsion mixed with terror put enormous strength
into Rumor's arms, as with a mighty push, she thrust
the man away and scrambled out of bed.

"You bitch, first you lead me on a merry dance, and
now you won't pay the piper."

Before she could reach the door, he was at her again,
hurling her to the floor and landing on top of her
again. Cruelly, he spread her legs apart, attempting to
push between her thighs.

"Calpurnia, help —"

A bruising hand came down on her mouth, stifling
her. The other spread out beside her head, as he
balanced himself.

"Now be nice, Miss Rumor, this is what your daddy

wants for both of us. We will marry, never fear, but I just want a little taste beforehand."

He was moving vigorously, and despite her vigorous squirmings, he was perilously close to entering her.

"I won't scream," she managed to mumble into his palm. "You just surprised me. Go ahead, I want it, too."

"You lovely, lovely little bitch," he murmured, removing his hand from her mouth.

Slowly, so as not to arouse suspicion, Rumor turned her head, and, bracing herself, rose up to bite down hard on the flesh of his upper arm.

Bellowing in pain, Stokes reared back. Blood began to seep from the wound, trickling down into the crook of his elbow. He stared at it, as though mesmerized.

He really is very drunk, thought Rumor, he'll hate himself in the morning for this.

Knocking his skinny body against the bed, Rumor ran to the door, glad for once that it could not be locked.

There was no sign of Calpurnia, drunk or sober. Not knowing whether to laugh or weep, Rumor ran downstairs in her nightshift.

Chapter Fourteen

Calpurnia lay on the cold stones of the tavern kitchen, arms flung out, staring through slitted eyes at the smoke-black rafters. Her half-closed eyes stared vacantly at the bunches of dried herbs hanging from the rafters.

Orange embers glowed in the cavernous firepit, but there was no one in the place when Rumor entered. The cooks had been in bed for hours.

She's dead, thought Rumor, as she fell to her knees and frantically shook the limp shoulder. "Calpurnia, wake up," she yelled into her face.

"Slap her, that'll bring her round."

Joe, the innkeeper, came toward them from the doorway. "I heard somebody creeping down the steps a while ago. Your maid probably wanted a nightcap—"

"No, no," Rumor wailed. "She's not that kind. She had a cup or two of wine with her supper, but she was perfectly sober when we went to bed."

Recalling her hospital work, she lifted Calpurnia's wrist and held it to her ear at the pulse point. A faint but regular beat reassured her. Putting a fingertip to one eyelid, she lifted it, peering intently at the ebony-and-white eyeball. She wasn't sure what she was supposed to look for, but the doctors always did it.

Instinctively, Calpurnia winced, then blinked.

"Praise God," Rumor wept.

The innkeeper's wife had arrived in her nightshift and cap. Squatting on the other side of the prone woman, she put her nose into Calpurnia's face.

"She's been given a sleeping herb," she stated. "There's no mistaking that skunklike odor."

"Stand back," Joe said, taking a dipperful of water from the hearth bucket and pouring it in a stream on Calpurnia's face. The unconscious woman started mumbling, and encouraged by his first attempt, Joe repeated his watery treatment.

Coming round at last, Calpurnia sat up, staring stupidly at Rumor. "Are you trying to drown me, child?" she spluttered.

Laughing with relief, Rumor shook her head, clasping her old friend to her chest. "No. We thought you were dead."

Clamping the sides of her head with both hands, Calpurnia moaned, "I feel like a whirling stone at the end of a string."

The innkeeper's wife thrust a brittle sprig into Rumor's face. "Smell this. It's what was given to your maid. Someone's been at my herbs. There's a powdery bit on the floor under this bunch."

Suddenly, like a flash of light in a very dark tunnel, everything became crystal clear to Rumor. Stokes and her father had carefully set up the entire performance — the intimate talk between her and Stokes, the happy planning to refurbish the two plantations, the attempted rape.

It was laughably easy to get rid of her human watchdog. She remembered how gracious her father had been to her childhood nurse at supper, pouring her wine, asking if there was anything special she cared to eat.

The three-day snowstorm had made it so easy for the plotters, she thought wryly. All of them had been housebound, forcing them to become much more intimate more quickly than they might have been ordinarily.

So it was true! The black sheep was still black. Beau Carter was the same wickedly charming scoundrel Mama had described so bitterly.

Groaning, Rumor dropped her head into her hands while the innkeeper and his wife helped Calpurnia to a bench and stirred up the fire to make some tea.

By this time the commotion had aroused the entire inn, and the kitchen quickly filled up. Rushing forward, Beau Carter grasped Rumor by the wrists. His face was stark white and his thin nostrils were flaring with barely controlled rage.

Glancing coldly over his shoulder, Rumor snapped, "Where's your partner in crime, Father dear? Or has he perhaps found a more willing bedmate than I?"

"Be still, wench," Carter hissed. "Don't add lying to your sins. Poor Philip told me all about it — how you lured him with your eyes and suggestive talk throughout the play reading, and when he, filled with ardor and confident of a warm reception, came to collect on your promise—"

Wrenching from his grasp, Rumor stormed, "Stop the playacting, Father. It's time to draw the curtain. What a wonderful production you put on, though. My compliments to you. I've been a complete and utter fool, but now that my eyes are open at last, I'm leaving you forever."

Forcing back the tears that pressed behind her eyes, she ran to Calpurnia, who was drinking strong tea under the anxious eyes of the innkeeper's wife.

"Your slave will be fine, miss," the woman said. "But it was close." She shrugged. "Another five minutes—"

"Oh, darling Calpurnia, to think I almost lost you," Rumor wept, cradling the woolly black head against her bosom. The tears that she had held back for her father's wickedness now poured out for her childhood nurse.

Then, turning round to face the crowded kitchen, she announced, "I'll give a full pound sterling—not continental, mind you—to anyone who will take us back to Valley Forge as soon as day breaks."

She didn't have a full pound, but she would get it somehow. From Lady Washington, perhaps.

"Gad, I might just take you up on that, young lady," a mocking voice called out. "But I'll have to trade my crimson jacket for some Rebel rags."

Amid much laughter and some cheers, Colonel Higgins stepped close to Rumor and Calpurnia. "But no need to waste your money, ma'am. I'll take out my fee in trade."

Winking lewdly, he placed an arm about her waist. With a withering look, she stepped nimbly aside as more ribald laughter trickled among the men.

A stentorian voice rose over the din. "My daughter oversteps herself," Carter yelled, "she is going no-where—certainly not back to that Rebel rabble at Valley Forge."

Drawing himself up, he announced, "By nightfall, she will stand before a preacher and make an honest woman of herself."

"Wh-at?" Rumor shrieked in a voice to match her father's in power. "You are talking rot, Beaumont Carter. Nothing happened between me and Stokes."

Laughing shakily, she walked with a forced nonchalance to where her father stood tall and wrathful in the center of the room. He was playing the role of out-raged parent to the hilt, and doing a wonderful job at

307

it, too.

How magnificent he is, thought Rumor with grudging pride. Who would think he is a hound of Satan?

She swallowed a lump in her throat the size of a lemon. She would not weep for the man. "It seems to me," she said, standing a scarce few inches from his rigidly erect body, "that you have discovered your parental duty a bit late. Where have you been, Father, all this time when I needed you? Who do you think was shielding your little girl from disgrace for eighteen years?"

Her composure cracking, she continued brokenly, "What you did tonight is far worse than any dalliance you accuse me of. You could have killed poor Calpurnia with that drug you put into her wine."

"Nonsense, girl," he snorted, "the woman left her post to snitch a little brandy from the cooking stock. I heard her heavy steps on the stairs as I was tossing about on my pallet in the men's sleeping room."

A voice from the crowd was heard. "That's the truth. I saw the woman, myself, sliding past my door."

Directing a contemptuous glance at Calpurnia, Carter finished, "The darkie got so drunk she passed out in the kitchen."

Keenly aware of his audience, Beau Carter ran a graceful hand through his thick, gray-brown hair, and flashed a winning smile. "Would you take the word of a blackamoor slave over mine as a gentleman?"

Knowing smirks appeared on faces, several shook their heads, doubtfully. I'm losing ground, thought Rumor, panicking. In another moment, this supreme actor will have them eating out his hand.

"Fetch Stokes and let all see the wound I inflicted on him when he tried to force me," she said. "That should prove that I did not welcome him to my bed."

"A wound? How delightful!" Higgins doubled up

with merriment. "The plot thickens."

Leaping on a bench, the officer flung out his arms, addressing the room like a pitchman at a carnival.

"A wedding, a wedding, come one, come all, to the nuptials to be held on these premises ere night draws her velvet curtain once more. I promise you a lusty, unblushing bride, a wounded bridegroom—"

He paused, and turning to Carter, put hand to mouth in mock terror. "The wound, oh wrathful Father—I trust that it was not inflicted on a part of the groom's anatomy that might prevent him from pleasing his blushing bride in the bridal bed?"

As if on cue, Philip Stokes appeared. His foxlike face was pale, but he was smiling broadly. A filthy rag was wrapped around his upper arm. He strode to where Rumor stood facing her father.

"Your love bite is deeper than I thought at first, darling. You'd best find some clean lint and a soothing ointment, else it might fester."

"You swine," Rumor grated, "you tried to rape me."

Stepping out of the crowd, one of the tavern doxies spat at Rumor's feet. She turned to Stokes. "All 'er kind cry rape, pet, but oncet ye gits 'er fer yer legal wife, ye c'n whip 'er into shape."

Taking the wounded man by the hand, she cooed, "Come, I'll clean yer wound, dearie."

Suddenly, voices sounded from all over, hostile voices.

"You agreed to marry him—"

"You said 'I would,' plain as day—"

"You held his hand and gazed like a lovesick calf into his eyes at supper—"

Hands over ears to shut out the awful, incriminating words, Rumor fled across the room to Calpurnia.

The innkeeper was shouting from a tabletop for the crowd to get back to bed, that he had a wedding feast to prepare, that he needed his sleep. With the help of his wife, Rumor got Calpurnia upstairs and onto her bed.

"Maybe I was wrong about the herb," the innkeeper's wife mumbled, shuffling off.

Calpurnia slept peacefully till dawn, but Rumor cuddled against her big, warm body, weeping steadily, helplessly, as if her heart were breaking. In truth, she mused, when she finally began to think rationally again, a part of her had died tonight.

Through the years, despite her mother's persistent and scathing diatribes against her father, Rumor had harbored a nagging affection for the man who had conceived her. Childlike, she had stubbornly refused to admit that he was as black as painted.

The shocking disclosures of the past hours had shaken her faith in her own judgment. Her childlike faith in humanity had been shattered. Beaumont Carter's callous manipulation of her had made her grow up into a woman. Far more effectively than Aaron had, she reflected, that day in the forest when he had taken her virginity. The mere tearing of a bit of tissue does not make a woman of a girl.

Suffering does that. Suffering such as she had known this night. To discover a father, to love him blindly, to reach out to him. Then to have him betray her so foully.

She had condemned Aaron as a liar. Her heart shrank in self-recrimination. How could she doubt him, while loving him so much? She wanted to weep, but had no more tears to spill. Instead, she shook her bedmate by the shoulder impatiently.

"Calpurnia, I must find Aaron. I must ask him to forgive me. What if he dies in battle or is caught by the Redcoats and shot, and dies, thinking I don't trust him?"

A strangled sob escaped her. "Oh, I want to die!"

There was a grumble from the servant as she struggled up, stretching and rubbing her eyes. She cast a bleary eye on Rumor, staring at her almost vacantly. "Don't die. Aaron will forgive you, I promise, if you'll forgive him for doubting you about that Perkins."

"How do you know about that?"

"He told Caesar and me all about what happened in the cabin at Barren Hill. He said he acted like a damn fool when he saw you naked with that British officer."

Leaping out of bed, Rumor dashed to the window, pushed it open, and thrust out her head. "It's warm out there, a real thaw. The snow is almost gone. We can travel." She turned eagerly back into the room. "Are you well enough, dear? We must try to find Aaron."

Ever practical, Calpurnia was on her feet and pulling off her nightshift. "We wouldn't get off the front porch, you booby. Beau Carter will have soldiers posted everywhere. He intends to see you married to that viper Stokes, come hell or high water."

"If only Caesar were here—" Rumor's eyes dilated in sudden fear. "You don't think—oh, no, he couldn't have—oh, Calpurnia, that wonderful man of yours might be lying out there, dead, in the snow."

"Take more than a weasel like Beau Carter to kill off my Caesar."

"What are we going to do?" wailed Rumor.

"Wait for Caesar" was the calm reply, as Calpurnia secured the final button on her bombazine gown. "There now," she grinned, "I'm still a mite shaky from that herb, but I'm ready for anything the day will bring."

Walking to the window, the nurse thrust her head way out, staring into the woods behind the inn. Her plump, strong hands grasped the wooden sill. "My husband will return before this shotgun wedding,

311

child, I promise."

Despite the woman's confident words, Rumor noticed that the servant's knuckles were white and the sweet face was no longer smiling.

A knock on the door brought Rumor flying to throw it open, crying, "There's Caesar now."

But it was the innkeeper's wife, with a voluminous garment slung over her arm. "Since you came to visit your father with naught but a middlin' bag of things, I hoped you would honor me by wearing this."

Entering the room without being asked, she slid the gown onto the bed, spreading it out proudly. "It was my own wedding gown, twenty years ago, and cost a mighty sum for those days. A bit out of fashion, for a highborn lady such as yourself, but — "

"Thank you for your kindness, madam, but there will be no wedding," Rumor snapped.

As though Rumor had not spoken, the woman darted back into the corridor, returning with a gigantic pair of bone hoops. "Your blackamoor here can stitch these back in place."

Standing back from the bed with arms folded on her chest, she viewed the spread-out gown with pride. "You'll be a picture in it."

Rolling her eyes in exasperation, Rumor glanced at Calpurnia, who stood by the window, arms akimbo, her round face inscrutable.

"Play along," she mouthed silently.

"It's lovely, truly," Rumor said sweetly, suppressing a mad desire to laugh out loud. Her life had become a melodrama, she thought, event piling on event, each more grotesque than the last.

Truly, the gown was one of the ugliest she had ever seen, reminiscent of some of Olympia Spenser's horrendous and unstylish costumes. Too much lace, too many furbelows weighted down with mauve crepe

312

fabric. Worse, a distinct odor of stale sweat emanated from the fabric. Distinct yellow circles surrounded the armpits.

A quick burst of noise from downstairs brought the woman's head up. She darted to the door. "That will be the parson, I must hasten to greet him." She giggled. "I just love weddings, don't you?"

Her hand on the knob, she added, beaming, "Officer Higgins and the others are donning full dress uniforms. They've sent a lad to fetch them from the outpost. Swords and all."

She clapped her hands together. "Lord, who would have thought to see such a grand event in our backwoods inn."

When she'd left, Rumor tossed the smelly garment off the bed and flung herself down. Arms outstretched, she lay, corpselike, staring at the ceiling.

"I'll have to go along with this farcical melodrama, Calpurnia," she said tonelessly. "Else my father will murder us both."

The road along the Schuylkill lay under a foot of muddy water, and the two riders splashing their way west and north past Valley Forge bent their heads against the incessant rain.

Approaching a covered bridge where a stone sentry house guarded the arched entrance, Aaron turned to his companion. "Now watch your temper, Caesar, you almost got us caught the last time."

Caesar, huddled over his horse's neck, grunted in response. "The dirty lobsterback called me a gorilla." His tone was grumpy. They'd been riding three hours in the rain. One length of rope bound his wrists together, another encircled his thick neck. Both were knotted to a third length that was attached to Aaron's reins. It was damned uncomfortable.

Jerking the reins of the white stallion he had stolen from a Redcoat who had carelessly left the animal untended while he relieved himself in the woods, Aaron snapped, "They'll be calling you dead if you're not more careful. You're supposed to be a captured darkie Rebel, but when you open your mouth and those cultured Jamaican accents spill out, anyone gets suspicious."

A British soldier stood in the open door of the little house, his body sideways so that the shoulder bearing the rifle escaped the rain. Aaron could see a second, inside, by a little fire.

"Atlas," he said sharply.

"Solon," replied the sentry, saluting smartly.

It was the proper password, delivered by the officer with an air of such aplomb that the sentry put aside any fear that this bloke might be the Rebel spy they'd been warned about.

"Washington's top spy, Aaron Fleming, has been reported in the area," the official report had read. "He's a master of disguises, and may even appear in British uniform. He favors officer dress."

Well, this one was in a grand uniform, for certain, the grandest the sentry had ever seen. He wore it as if he'd been born in it. The flowing heavy fustian cloak was parted just enough to reveal gold buttons on waistcoat and jacket both. Lace edged the neck, silver buckles gleamed wetly on the high black boots.

Even mud-spattered as he was from head to toe, the man was every inch the military gentleman.

Noting the man's hesitation, Aaron spoke quickly, supplying the poor fellow with his name, rank, and business. Many of the Britons serving in the Royal American Army were raw recruits, all from the lower classes and surprisingly ignorant of protocol.

314

"I am Colonel James Armstrong, Sixtieth Regiment, Fourth Company," he said, lifting his head into the air, and speaking in the languid, affected accents of Sir Oliver Mowbray.

Cocking his head toward Caesar, who slumped dejectedly at his side, he added, "This is an American deserter I'm delivering to Colonel Higgins at the Crooked Hill tavern. We think the man's been working with Aaron Fleming, and Higgins is a master at extracting information from the most unwilling subjects."

The sentry stared at Caesar, who lifted his head, taking care to let his mouth hang open stupidly.

Drawing out a hanky from an inner pocket, Aaron flicked it in his best Sir Oliver style, and wiped his nose with an elaborate flourish. "The fellow actually says he wants to join His Majesty's forces. Imagine!"

He gave a mocking little laugh, and the sentry politely smirked in return. "We don't need his kind, sir. Looks like he's a runaway slave."

The sentry heaved a sigh of relief. No matter how clever this Fleming trickster was, he could never talk like this bloke. So refined, and haughty-like. A gentleman born and bred. And that hanky! These crude colonials didn't know what a hanky was. The barbarians just honked their noses with two fingers, right onto the ground.

Curious, the other sentry had come to the door. "How are conditions at Valley Forge, sir? As bad as they say?"

"Worse, soldier," Aaron intoned, returning the man's salute. "No food, no arms, no real discipline. The cocky Virginian can't hold out past June. General Howe is making plans to return to England."

Putting a hand inside his jacket, Aaron said casually, "Here are my orders." He glanced at the sky. "Try not to get the paper wet."

"That won't be necessary, Colonel Armstrong. You may proceed."

Craning their necks out the door, both sentries stared anxiously at the bridge. "That water is too high for comfort. Better hurry before it decides to sweep the bridge away."

Shaking his head morosely, Aaron flicked back a sodden plume from the brim of his tall hat with his gloved hand. "Have you ever seen a more godforsaken country? Pray God we'll all be back in merry old England come summer."

After a quick exchange of salutes, Aaron flicked his reins and moved slowly into the covered wooden bridge.

"Can I talk now?" Caesar asked.

"Yep."

"That was the damnest performance I ever saw in all my years in the theater. You missed your calling, Major Fleming."

"Much obleeged," Aaron returned in his finest Sir Oliver lingo, bowing his head in his friend's direction.

Soon, there was an end to talk as they left the river road to turn inland toward the hilly section surrounding the Crooked Hill Tavern. Aaron was still filled with amazement, and not a little awe, at his tremendous luck in running into the big black man at dawn.

He'd been in the forest north of Valley Forge, on the far side of Mount Misery, leading a small detail of soldiers on a foraging expedition. They had been on the road for two days, getting victuals for the camp.

Heartlessly turning a deaf ear to the most pitiful tales of hardship, they had searched and plundered every farmhouse and inn. Nobody escaped. The inhabitants of the region were by and large of Tory persuasion and had been niggardly in offering food to the starving Continentals.

The fact that the raiding party were all in British crimson and white almost ensured their success. Choosing from the stockpile of uniforms taken from prisoners of war at Valley Forge, Aaron happily became a dandified Colonel Armstrong.

By midnight of the second day, three wagons were already filled with a variety of farm produce—grain, corn, flour, apples, salted meat, lard. Two loudly complaining milk cows were tied behind. They were especially proud of two hogsheads of sugar and one of real Jamaican coffee taken from a profiteer farmer who had been saving them for even leaner times.

The soldiers headed back to camp, all in high spirits and looking forward to an extra ration of rum, when a buck deer was spotted in the woods bordering the road. Shouldering his long Pennsylvania rifle and ordering his men to go on back to camp without him, Aaron began to stalk the buck.

An hour later, in the murky rain, he saw his prey in a thicket of aspens. Taking careful aim, he fired. The shot rang out. Someone yelped, and there was a great thrashing in the aspens as a man ran toward the road.

"I surrender," Caesar yelled, when confronted by the British officer who had caught up with him quickly enough.

Then, with astonished recognition, Caesar exclaimed, "Godamighty, is it you, Aaron Fleming?"

"None other," the fake officer grinned, lowering his firearm. "And what might you be doing here, Caesar? I might have killed you." Frowning, Aaron added tersely, "I left you in charge of Rumor. Why are you so far from Valley Forge? Has something happened to her?"

Quickly laying Aaron's fears to rest, Caesar described the trouble with Beaumont Carter at The

Crooked Hill. Both thanked the deity for arranging the fortuitous meeting. Otherwise, Caesar might not have found him for another week.

Praying that his long-suffering commander in chief would forgive—again—his adopted son's taking French leave for Rumor's sake, Aaron headed immediately toward The Crooked Hill. Only he could save the naive Rumor from her father's nefarious schemes.

Blast the woman. Though he loved her to distraction, she was an idiot to believe anything a man like Beau Carter would tell her. Caesar had said the man was transparent, every word that came out of his lying mouth as worthless as the paper money issued by the Continental Congress.

The little fool, she was obviously so eager, so desperately hungry to have a father of her own at last she'd hid her brain under a bushel. He cursed himself for being unable to make her believe the truth about Beau Carter.

Apparently, though, it wasn't all Rumor's fault. To hear Caesar tell it, the man could charm a rattlesnake.

"Well, here we are," Aaron said grimly, as they turned into the lane for The Crooked Hill. "Better dig up some more of those prayers you said earlier."

The plan was simple enough, Caesar would hide in a cave behind the tavern where ice was stored in summers. Nobody went there this time of year. In his persona as Colonel Armstrong, Aaron would bluff his way into the place, announcing that he had been sent to fetch a certain Lady Spenser, nee Rumor Seton, who was wanted by General Howe for helping to kill a British officer named Perkins.

They would hand her over without question. He had completely fooled a vigilant sentry—two of them. Surely, he would have no trouble convincing a group of half-drunk soldiers.

After they delivered her to him, he would order her tied up with Caesar's ropes, mount her on Caesar's horse beside his own at the hitching post, and gallop away.

An hour later, Caesar was to appear inside the inn, begging Calpurnia to forgive him. He had carefully rehearsed his story during the hour-long ride in the rain. He would tell her that he had gone into the hills to the trees to relieve himself. She knew how he hated commodes, when he was caught unawares with his breeches down by a thieving bunch of rascally American deserters. They took what money he had in his pockets, then forced him to ride with them a long ways before leaving him in the road.

He would appear suitably bruised and battered, having taken a few punches in the face from a reluctant Aaron. Caesar was a superb actor, he could convince anyone that the moon was made of green cheese.

As Caesar scuttled to the ice cave, Aaron boldly walked across the stone porch of The Crooked Hill and pushed the door open with his silver-buckled boot.

Chapter Fifteen

Imperilously, glancing neither right nor left and dripping water all the way, the tall, powerfully built, mud-splattered British officer strode into the tap-room.

The innkeeper bent over the firepit, wielding a poker to the logs. Poking Joe's posterior with a long, gloved finger, Aaron said, in his best Sir Oliver voice, "Have I the honor of addressing the keeper of these premises?"

Straightening up, the innkeeper turned round and gaped as at an apparition. In that long, glistening black cloak the man loomed like a messenger from hell. His craggy face was stern and forbidding, the shoulder-length white wig curled in soggy tendrils around his neck.

"You — you have, sir," Joe stammered. "How can I be of help, sir?"

"I am Colonel James Armstrong, of His Majesty's Royal Americans, adjutant to General Sir William Howe, supreme commander in the rebellious colonies."

Giving time for that much to sink in, Aaron whipped out a gold snuff box, took a hearty pinch and applied it to his nostrils, whilst covertly surveying the room. Five officers, three of them half drunk, two blowsy women, a tall, elegant man in brown velvet, conferring in a corner with another man in black, very pale, who looked like a parson.

"You are reported to be harboring within these walls a woman who stands accused of a heinous crime against the Crown. Her name is Lady Spenser, nee Rumor Seton, of New York City—" he paused to sneeze into his white hanky—"though she may be known to you under an assumed name."

Pleased that all eyes were upon him, he continued crisply. "My orders are to fetch her posthaste to General Howe, presently quartered in Philadelphia."

The gentleman in brown velvet stepped forward. "I beg your pardon, Colonel Armstrong, but what may I inquire is the nature of the crime this woman is said to have committed?"

Looking down his long nose at Beaumont Carter, Aaron repressed with difficulty a desire to flatten the handsome face with his fist. "My good man," he said, cocking a brow, "do I assume that you have an interest in this notorious woman?" A faint smile crossed his features. "I have never seen her but she is reputed to be a great beauty."

Flushing with quick anger, Carter snapped. "The woman of whom you speak so contemptuously is my daughter and is the epitome of feminine virtue."

Placing both hands on his hips, Aaron fondled the hilt of the pistol strapped to his breeches. He had hidden his long rifle under the saddle blanket. He had thought it unwise to enter the hostelry looking as though he were ready for a fight.

Happily, he noted that none of the Redcoats was armed, except for dress swords. Several long British rifles stood in a corner. If a scuffle developed, it would take them a minute to fetch a firearm while he held them off with his pistol, which was capable of firing three shots without reloading.

After a long pause designed to discomfort Rumor's father, Aaron sneered. "My good man, this daughter, whom you claim to be so very virtuous, together with her paramour, killed an officer of the Royal Army in cold blood and buried his body in an unknown grave."

Simply looking at this poor excuse for a parent riled Aaron so that he was beginning to lose his cultured accent. Careful, Aaron, an inner voice warned. You're losing your aplomb. Just a few more minutes . . .

Pausing dramatically, Aaron swept the room with his eyes. "Colonel Perkins was my best friend, we were schoolmates at Eton." His voice broke a little at the end, suggesting grief.

The effort was lost on Carter. "Indeed!" Rumor's father haughtily replied. "My sympathies, sir. However, you are mistaken about my daughter. The idea that she could be capable of such dastardly deeds is ludicrous."

Sweeping the room with an amused glance, Carter chuckled. "Were it not that I am loath to trouble her with such vile gossip on her wedding day, I would fetch her to confound these absurd charges."

"You're just in time for the wedding, off'cer," cried one of the doxies from a nearby table.

Suddenly, a hearty voice called out, "Colonel Armstrong, what tremendous luck!"

Turning, Aaron saw a ruddy-faced British officer coming rapidly toward him from a door behind the bar.

"What the blazes are you doing here in this godforsaken backwater?" Colonel Higgins inquired taking a wide-legged stance in front of Aaron. In his hand he held a gold-encrusted cutlass.

Grinning widely, he waited, running a thumb up and down the cutlass blade. Turning his head slightly, he shouted gleefully to the others, "This tall gentleman and I are great good friends."

The good-looking British officer was dressed to the hilt for the wedding festivities. A long, powdered wig rippled handsomely beneath a plumed peaked hat, gold buttons gleamed from jacket and waistcoat. A black satin gorget was wound about his neck.

Warily ogling the cutlass, Aaron caught his breath, stalling for time. This man was a total stranger. Was it a trick? Or was it possible that a Colonel Armstrong actually existed among the British forces?

Without waiting for a response to his greeting, Higgins began to sweep the cutlass over his head in wide circles. "A beauty, is she not? Got it from a dead Mohammedan in India—"

Executing a kind of twirling dance, Higgins started to circle Aaron, dipping, swaying, the cutlass whistling over his head. Both Aaron and the innkeeper ducked to keep from having their heads sliced off.

"Splendid," Aaron exclaimed, with enthusiasm, scuttling with bent head toward the bar, trying to avoid the vicious blade. "Spanish steel, is it not?" Then casually he added, "But you mistake me for another, sir. We have never met."

"Oh, yes we have, Colonel Armstrong—sometimes known as Major Aaron Fleming, sometimes known as Sir Oliver Mowbray."

Moving with catlike swiftness, Higgins sliced the sodden plume neatly from Aaron's hat. It dropped to the floor, and kicking it aside with his foot, he poked the point of his cutlass up and under Aaron's wet wig.

The hairpiece lifted off, together with the hat. Laughing fiendishly, Higgins hurled them both over the bar.

"Aha," he chortled, "the notorious Rebel spy, unmasked at last. Short reddish hair, blue eyes, hawkish face. Could pass for an Indian. But I'd know you anywhere, Fleming, even in hell. It was the voice that gave you away. Your rendition of a London dandy has never been surpassed."

Playing for time, his eyes on the cutlass, Aaron quipped, "So I've been told. I am thinking of pursuing a theatrical career when this nasty war is over."

"It's all over for you now, Fleming. There'll be no theatrical career for you, unless it's in hell. As to how I know your rendition of Sir Oliver, I am pleased to tell you that Lionel Spenser and I were in the same regiment, and I attended many soirees at Spenser House."

The five officers in the taproom had all taken up their rifles, and were busy pushing musket balls into the long barrels. That Higgins was a genius with the cutlass. His head would be off before he could even get the pistol out of the holster.

Aaron thought fast. If he were killed, or even wounded, Rumor would be at their mercy and her father's. Either way, he would have failed in his mission.

Throwing out his hands palms up in a helpless gesture, he said mournfully, "The game is up. I lost. This should mean a commendation for you, Higgins."

"Take him, men." Flushed with victory, Higgins sheathed his blade at his belt, watching with narrowed eyes as Aaron was encircled by British officers.

"You've had your sport, Fleming," he said, "You had the beauteous and lusty Jamaican piece to yourself for months in a rustic love nest in Barren Hill."

The frightened innkeeper had returned to the fire, poking it vigorously with a great noise to calm his nerves.

"Fetch some rope from the stable, Joe," Higgins ordered.

Strolling behind the bar, the victorious Higgins

poured himself a tankard of ale from the hogshead, quaffed it hurriedly. Setting the tankard on the bar, he said musingly, "I attended Sir Lionel's wedding to Rumor Seton. I envied him his luck in finding such a wonder."

The officer shook his head. "But at this moment I'm happy he's dead, and cannot know that his sweet young bride has turned both harlot and killer."

Calmly accepting his defeat in the face of so much evidence—not to mention the British guns pointed at him—Aaron grinned. "Since you are undoubtedly aware of Lady Rumor Seton's presence at this inn, why have you delayed in delivering her to justice?"

Higgins chuckled and cocked his head toward the stairs. "Why hurry? I thought to have some sport with the delightful piece first. Why should Howe have it all?"

He glanced at a white-faced Carter, who was sitting at a table, drinking whiskey, visibly trembling. "I am forced to tell you, Carter, that I went along with this wedding nonsense because it promised to be great diversion. It's dull as Hades serving in these backwaters."

A shriek from the top of the stairs was followed by the appearance of the lady in question. Still in her muslin nightshift, her short hair uncombed and flying about her face, Rumor flew down the wooden steps.

"Aaron! Oh, my darling, darling, you've returned—"

Sobbing hysterically, Rumor thrust through the officers surrounding Aaron, hurling herself into his arms.

Oblivious to pointing rifles and knowing stares, Aaron bent his head. "My beautiful, beautiful love," he groaned into her hair, enclosing her shaking body in his arms.

325

Silently, the lovers kissed, and even the scoffing Higgins must have felt the blazing power of their love, for the smirk on his ruddy face was replaced by a bleakly envious expression.

The lovers kissed as if possessed, straining toward each other, striving with the meeting of their lips to erase the pain of past separation, as well as the sure knowledge of agony and death to come.

Aaron was certain to be hanged. As for Rumor, she would suffer a living death as the captive of the Royal Army. She had heard of captured American women being raped to death.

Drawing back, Rumor gazed into the smoky blue eyes that had burned into her soul, the night of the sugar house fire, captivating it forever. "Nothing will ever separate us again, my darling, nothing in the whole universe."

Proudly, head erect, Rumor walked like a queen to the bar, as if dressed in satin and jewels instead of a rumpled muslin nightshift.

"Colonel Higgins," she said to the man on the other side, spreading both her hands out on the polished wood, "take me, I surrender. Tie me up with my lover."

Capturing both her offered hands, the officer touched them to his lips. "Take you, madam?" A slow grin crossed his ruddy face and a glaze of lust came into his eyes. "With pleasure." Chuckling, he flicked his eyes to Aaron, encircled by Redcoats. "I might even tie you up, but most assuredly not with your lover."

Inhaling sharply, Rumor tried to withdraw her hands, but he held them fast. What a fool she'd been to think this one a man of honor.

Her father strode toward them angrily. "This farce has gone on long enough. Nobody is taking my daughter anywhere. Not as long as I have a breath in my body."

Like a wild man, Carter sprang behind the bar, and leaping at Higgins, put both his hands on the officer's throat. He began to throttle him, muttering incoherently.

Alarmed, Rumor ran around behind the bar to grab her father by the arm, tugging fiercely, desperately trying not pull him off. "Father, don't, don't, please, they'll kill you, too—"

The two men were on the floor by now, rolling round and round, snarling like two mad dogs. The men who were guarding Aaron came to help, and Aaron, seeing a chance at escape, yelled, "Rumor! Quick!"

Hearing his shout, Rumor's head came up. Aaron was at the door, signaling frantically. But she couldn't move. Her father was being held by two brawny soldiers and Higgins was on his feet, nursing his throat.

Aaron cried again, "For God's sake, Rumor!"

"Run the bastard through," grated an enraged Higgins. "Don't waste your powder. He almost finshed me. For an old man, he's got a powerful grip."

"No, no, don't kill my father!"

Rumor threw her body against her father's, shielding him from a sword a soldier had taken from his belt. She could hear her lover's agonizing call for her to escape with him. She knew that she could easily flee while Higgins was still helplessly clutching his bruised throat and the other officers were still flustered and off guard. But her legs seemed rooted to the floor, as a new and heart-shattering emotion swept through her. *She loved her father.* Amazingly. Wicked scoundrel that he was, she could not leave him to die without his daughter's love. Instinctively, she had placed her body between him and the men who would kill him risking her own.

Higgin's next words confirmed her fears. "Kill the slut of a daughter, too, if you have to."

327

Shaken, she cast imploring eyes on Aaron, who had walked slowly back to the bar. "I can't, Aaron," she wept, running her words together in a tearful jumble. "Dear God, run, darling, run. I'll be fine. They dare not kill me, I'm not a spy, and General Howe wants me alive."

His features seemed to turn to stone, the blue eyes that moments before had been filled with love and tenderness became like ice. "You fool, you've killed us both with your blind stupidity."

Recovering, Higgins grabbed Rumor roughly by the arms, and tore her away from Carter. "Kill the bastard and get that spy Fleming before we lose him altogether."

"Let her go, or I'll shoot you dead," Aaron gritted. pointing his pistol at the officer. "I'll come peaceably."

The two remaining Redcoats glanced uncertainly from their superior to Aaron. He would shoot them, too, if they rushed him. That firearm was a Spanish type that contained three shots. A number of high officers had them.

Suddenly there was the loud sound of feet on the stone porch, and the door burst open to admit a band of soldiers, water dripping from helmets and cloaks.

Their sodden uniforms were crimson and white.

"By Lucifer, you're just in time, fellows," grinned a relieved Higgins, rushing from behind the bar to meet the reinforcements. "We caught us a spy, but we need all the help we can get to keep him."

"Happy to oblige, Colonel," one said, who appeared to be the leader. "But our orders are to forage. We got to bring two wagonloads of food back to Barren Hill by nightfall, or it's our necks."

Aaron turned, gaped a moment, then whooped, "Jackson, Lang, it's me—"

His heart soared. It was the same foraging detail

328

from Valley Forge that he had left this morning before discovering Caesar.

"What the —?" Halting in his tracks, Higgins whipped out his cutlass, advancing toward the men. "Damned Rebels, had me fooled there for a minute."

All hell broke loose, as the Redcoats, the real ones and the fraudulent, launched into a brawl. A single rifle shot was heard, but landed in the wall. Sheathing his pistol, Aaron waded in with his knife and fists. A wild shot might hit Rumor or another innocent person.

It was knives, and swords and fists. It was an even match, Rumor noted hopefully, with equal numbers on both sides.

She really had no time to be frightened, though, for her father had knocked her to the floor, falling on top of her, to shield her. But immediately, he began to push them both toward the open door of the little storeroom behind the bar, through which Higgins had come earlier.

There was a small window in the place, and pushing Rumor toward it, he hissed, "You go first, then help me climb through."

Though her lover's life was in mortal danger, Rumor's only feeling at that moment was one of supreme happiness. Despite his nefarious schemes to marry her to that hated Stokes, her father truly loved her. He did not want to see her dead so that he could inherit Albemarle.

He had proved his love beyond measure, in the last minutes. First, he had tried to throttle Higgins. Then, instead of running off alone up the stairs or even through this window, he had delayed, helping her, and risking his own life again.

"But Aaron —"

"You cannot help him now, Daughter, he's a good

fighter and will win or lose as the fates decree."

Rumor had squeezed through the narrow window opening, and was squatting on the wet ground outside with hands extended to help her father up and out, when she felt strong hands on her hips.

"The jig's up, trollop."

A triumphant Higgins grinned down into her upturned face. Then, before she could cry out, he thrust a heavy cloak over her head and shoulders, at the same time scooping her up into his arms.

She was being carried away, to God knows what, but her immediate terror was of suffocating. As she felt the air leave her lungs, she began to kick and squirm and beat her captor with her fists. Just as her head was spinning dizzily, and she felt that each breath would be her last, Higgins threw her onto a pile of straw.

The straw was in the bed of a farm wagon that began to move immediately, out of the tavern lane and onto the road. It had stopped raining, and casting off the heavy cloak, Rumor gazed blankly up at a blue sky.

She was alive, captured but alive. With each breath she took of the fresh spring air, she was filled with the wonder of life. But Aaron and her father? What about them?

Two men sat behind the two horses, who were galloping so fast along the rutted road that Rumor was tossed back and forth on the dirty straw. One sat in the wagon, guarding her. Her heart plummeted. There had been six British against six Americans. If three Redcoats had managed to survive, that meant the Americans were surely all dead.

Rearing up, holding onto the slatted sides of the wagon with both hands, she groaned in a loud voice, "Aa-aa-ron —"

Turning round, Higgins yelled, "Your lover's dead, wench. You can call for him till doomsday."

Then, he addressed the soldier guarding her. "Get up here, Jones, I'll guard our prisoner."

The two officers switched positions, and Rumor found the detestable Higgins at her side. The sun was shining hotly now, and sweat was pouring down his ruddy face.

Pulling her from the side of the wagon, he shoved her down into the straw. Spreading her arms out on either side, he knelt above her, holding her fast by the wrists.

"We've a long journey to Philadelphia," he grunted, lowering himself to her, "plenty of time for me to sample what Howe and Fleming and who knows how many others are so mad about."

"You viper," she grated, gathering her spittle and blowing it into his leering face.

Backing up, he brushed the back of his hand against his wet face. He grinned widely, the insulting gesture seeming only to inflame his desire. "I like my women full of fire. Spit all you want, lovey."

His body fell upon hers, and releasing her hands, he put them on her buttocks, raising them to meet him. His head came down to her breasts, and pushing aside the flimsy muslin with his nose, he clamped his lips on her nipple. He sucked fiercely, bruisingly.

One of his companions called out from behind the horses, "General Howe might not look with favor on someone sampling his prize before he does, Higgins."

Lifting up his head for breath, the colonel yelled back, "You can take your turn, Jones."

"No thank you, sir. I got a nice little wife at home, and don't want to take a chance on catching a disease from this one. The Jamaican's free and easy with it, I hear."

They were traveling at breakneck speed through a dark wood, and had just passed a log farmhouse. As she gazed up at the overhanging trees, and saw the passing log house, Rumor was suddenly reminded of Colonel Perkins, who, like this one, had tried to rape her in the cabin at Barren Hill. But this time there was no Aaron to save her.

"You know," she said levelly, "history does have a way of repeating itself. Once before, just last summer, as I recall, another of your ilk—he was a colonel, too, I believe—tried to force himself upon me."

Higgins fixed her with an icy stare. "I know full well what happened in that rustic love nest. You lured poor Perkins inside with promises of sport, then your lover killed him. Perkins was my good friend."

"Your information is wrong. Aaron did not kill Perkins." She paused, then said coldly, "I did."

His eyes widened. "How?"

"That's for me to know and for you to find out," she murmured silkily, hooding her eyes. Although his hands hung loosely at his sides, she made no move to get away from him.

Clearly uncomfortable, he regarded her through slitted eyes, rubbing a place on his arm where he had apparently taken a knife wound in the tavern.

"You're lying."

"Try me."

"You have no weapons, and—" he swept his eyes to her waist—"can't weigh more than—"

"I don't rely on my muscles, sir."

"What then?"

"As I said," she smiled, "you'll find out when it happens to you. All I will tell you is that as a child in Jamaica I had a nurse well versed in native voodoo."

"Calpurnia?"

"Yes."

Fear had crept into his eyes, as he brought the huge black servant to mind. He slid off her body. "Think I'll

332

wait till we get to Philadelphia. Safer there. I'll have to put you in the prison for a time, until General Howe calls for you."

Turning on his side, he leaned on his arm, looking at her with a kind of respect. "The prison is a filthy place, and a few days in there might change your mind about me. I can make it easy for you — food, blankets, other niceties."

"My voodoo will work just as well in the prison as in this wagon," she said, turning on her side away from him. "In fact," she yawned, "even better. The more challenging the environment, the better the magic."

Higgins fell silent, brooding. That he had swallowed her cock and bull story amazed Rumor. Voodoo was rampant in Haiti, not Jamaica. He seemed so intelligent. But then, the fight might have exhausted him, muddling his brains. And Jones's caution about General Howe might be troubling him, also.

At any rate, blessedly he turned on his back and fell sound asleep. After a while, Rumor closed her eyes, covering herself with the cloak. She felt calmer than she had in days. Aaron was dead, but she felt nothing now. She would think about it later.

Rumor fell asleep, not waking up until Higgins jostled her to tell her that they had arrived in Philadelphia.

General Sir William Howe was not pleased, when the girl was brought to him at dinnertime. He looked up from his roast beef. "Well, who is it that can't wait till a man can finish his meal?"

"Miss Rumor Seton, sir. That is, Lady Spenser of New York, the infamous murderous of a royal officer. You sent for her."

Colonel Higgins blushed, stammered, as he felt the full weight of his superior's displeasure. It was not exactly the reception he had expected. Perhaps he should have cleaned up his prisoner, but he'd been in such haste to show off his prize.

"What?" The man peered at Rumor, standing arrow straight, before him. The muslin nightshift she'd worn on the journey from The Crooked Hill still hung on her slender figure. The upper part around the neckline was ripped almost to shreds, exposing her rounded breasts.

Her feet were bare. He had a sudden image of a play he had seen once involving Roman captives.

Six days and nights in the foul royal prison had done little for the gown's appearance. A rank prison odor of excrement and urine emanated from the mud and filth-encrusted garment.

Her brown hair was in tangles about her face. She'd not been given a comb or brush. Soap and water had also been denied her, and her beautiful face looked like an urchin's from the dregs of London.

Greedily, she eyed the crusty bit of meat on the silver fork in the general's hand. She'd had nothing but moldy crusts and brackish water since a disgusted Higgins had delivered her to her jailers.

"We meet again, General Howe," Rumor said, boldly taking a seat opposite him at the wooden table. "So kind of you to ask me to dine."

Attack was the best defense, Aaron used to say.

"What?" the man said again, stupidly. Then, recovering from his shock at seeing the woman he had once desired enough to pay good money for her, he handed her his fork.

"You look half starved," he said. "My God, where have you been?"

Rumor was too occupied with devouring the meaty morsel to reply, but Higgins, alarmed at the turn of events, spoke up. "She's been in the prison, sir, with the rest of the Rebel vermin."

334

Howe turned a contemptuous face to his subordinate. "You blasted idiot, she's not just anybody. She's the widow of a lord of the realm. If she had died in that rat-infested place, it would have meant your head." Cutting a second piece of meat, he handed it to Rumor, who smiled her thanks. "And mine, too, perhaps. One of the Spensers recently married one of the king's daughters."

Higgins backed away, his eye on the door. "How was I to know?" he bleated. "Our orders were to bring her in." He cleared his throat nervously. "I am happy to report that her paramour, the notorious spy Aaron Fleming, whom you knew as Lord Mowbray, was killed by my own hands."

"That so?" responded the general absently, his eyes on Rumor. He handed her a chunk of crusty bread. "My heartiest congratulations. Now get out of here, you nincompoop, before I have you put in chains for your idiotic bungling in handling Lady Spenser."

As Rumor continued to eat, quaffing large quantities of rich, dark ale from the general's silver tankard, two women entered from the door that Higgins had just scurried through like a scared rabbit.

"More pretties?" Howe inquired, rising from his chair to greet them. Both wore harem costumes, consisting of spangled, billowing pantaloons and turbans on their heads. Gold and silver bracelets jingled on their wrists.

"How do you like our costumes," they giggled in unison.

"Perfect," he exclaimed, gathering the two of them into his big arms. "Now leave me, you sweet little bonbons, I have some important business to take care of."

He cocked his head at Rumor, who continued to eat as if she were alone in the room.

The girls left, and Howe rejoined his odiferous dinner companion. He put two plump fingers to his nose. "Only the milk of human kindness keeps me from banishing you to the bath before you've had your fill, madam."

Rumor smiled up at him prettily. She would have to pay in bed for the feast, but Aaron was dead. Who else would care? She herself was beyond caring. She'd spent the last six days fending off her randy jailers, cleverly employing the voodoo story that had stymied Higgins.

The zest for life was strong within her, even if it meant giving herself to this mountain of blubber. Her ordeal, in any case, could not be for long. Howe was due to leave Philadelphia, in fact, the Colonies themselves, shortly.

"I've been called back to England," he said amiably, as if reading her thoughts. Lighting an ivory pipe handed him by an orderly who stood at attention a few feet from the table, he inhaled deeply. "I have no interest in you, my dear, other than seeing you delivered safely to my successor."

She nodded. "You do not care to spend a night with me then?" Her tone was casual, as if they were discussing the weather.

"Ah, sadly, no. Though once cleaned up and perfumed, you will no doubt tempt me. I admit to being quite annoyed when you were literally snatched from my bed on Staten Island. But times have changed."

"The talk in prison is that you are being replaced, sir."

He drew up huffily. "At my request, allow me to point out. When I agreed two years ago to the king's plea to command his forces in these blighted colonies, I thought it to be a matter of months. The trouble had all the earmarks of a simple, ill-advised uprising."

336

Sucking thoughtfully on his pipe, he added, musingly, "The king's advisers told him that it was simply a matter of shooting them down like mad dogs."

"But it hasn't quite turned out as you thought," put in Rumor slyly, "has it, General? The ragtag, yapping herd of mad dogs has become a raging lion."

A wide grin ceased his swarthy cheeks. "Zounds, you are a witty one, as well as the most striking beauty I've come across since my journeyman days in Jamaica. My successor Clinton is not a ladies' man, but he just might take to you."

Replete, Rumor sat back. She decided to ignore the threat of turning her over to General Clinton. "Who were those women? Theater people?"

"No. The men are giving me a grand send off. They are part of a fete to be held in a week or two." Leaning over the table, he waxed enthusiastic. "It'll be the biggest production these provinces have ever seen. They'll not soon forget William Howe."

There would be a medieval tournament, he told her, with jousting knights and fair ladies in distress, and a regatta on the river, featuring a parade of decorated barges. A poem was being composed in his honor. In Latin.

He pursed his fat lips. "I think I'll have you fitted for a costume. You deserve a bit of fun after what you've suffered in the prison."

"I—I don't think," she started, but the door opened at that moment to admit Mrs. Elizabeth Loring.

"Rumor?" she said, bending over the smelly figure in the brocade chair. "Rumor Spenser?" she gasped, grasping the thin shoulders. "Can it really be you? I heard that you were here, but could not credit such a story."

Lifting her head, she cast two angry blue eyes on Howe. "What in heaven's name have you done to the

337

poor girl? She looks half dead." She paused, then said in a low voice, "Have the men been at her?"

"No one has touched me, Liz," Rumor breathed against the perfumed hand on her shoulder, covering it with kisses. "But I would dearly love a bath."

As the women walked rapidly toward the door, Liz almost carrying the exhausted girl, the general called out, "Let's order a costume for her for the fete. You decide, darling."

"Go to hell, you booby, Rumor's not taking any part in your confounded celebration. I'm cleaning her up and taking her immediately to New York in my private chaise, with six horses for added speed."

Upstairs in her scented bedroom, the older woman paused long enough between staccato commands to the maids to inform Rumor that she was going back to royalist New York and Spenser House. The Rebels were advancing on Philadelphia faster than she liked for comfort, stated Liz grimly.

"Our mutual friend the general may be caught with his pants down, right in the middle of his damned medieval tournament," she added. "I have no intention of sticking around for the fun."

Several wide-open trunks were strewn about the room. The maids who were not scrubbing the dirt from Rumor's body in the wooden tub were busily packing Liz's extensive wardrobe.

"Are you really leaving Howe?" Rumor asked.

"Yes. For good this time. Now that the French are in it, the Americans are going to win this war, and I don't want to be caught on the wrong side."

She paused in her packing. "We'll both be safe from the New York Tories under the protection of the Spenser name. I trust I don't presume in expecting to be housed at Spenser House until I find a house of my own. They tell me that since the fire and occupation of the city by hordes of royal soldiers, that getting a room to sleep in is an exercise requiring weeks of effort and a great deal of money."

"Forget the effort and the money," murmured a deliriously happy Rumor from behind a tangle of soapy hair. "There will always be a place in my home for Liz Loring. . . . and in my heart as well," she added.

Chapter Sixteen

New York City
Summer, 1778

The Fly Market at Maiden Lane and Pearl swarmed with shoppers this muggy August morning, all seeking to have first pick of the farm-fresh vegetables and fruits brought in from the countryside. It was six clock: the sun was barely up. Rumor and her retinue had already filled five straw baskets with the choicest produce they could find in the covered wooden stalls and from sidewalk vendors.

One basket perched — mysteriously without support — on Calpurnia's cushioned head, while two more dangled from her sturdy black arms. The two Spenser House kitchen maids trotted behind, each with one full basket and one empty.

"There's still the fish to buy," muttered a harried Rumor. "Perhaps we should have stopped there first."

"No, ma'am," Calpurnia responded firmly. "There's always plenty of fish. You forget that this town is surrounded by water. The greengrocers will be sold out by eight o'clock."

British-occupied New York was having considerable trouble feeding the hordes of loyalists, refugees from battle zones, Rebel deserters, mercenaries of every description, and general hangers-on — all of whom had swelled the normal population to more than twice its size.

The weekly market boats from England fell victim, with maddening regularity, to American raiders. To aggravate the situation, Rebel armies stopped many of the victual wagons from New England and Pennsylvania.

Strict regulations had been imposed on hoarding. An extra basket of flour or sugar in the cellar meant a heavy fine, if not a day in jail. It was necessary to visit the market every day. Early, and with a pocketful of money.

The fish market was on Dock Street so Rumor walked the few short blocks, daintily lifting the skirt of her gaily flowered chintz well away from the filthy gutters. Heads turned to gape as she passed, broad smiles replaced early morning grouchiness.

Few highborn ladies were to be seen in this part of town, especially one so beautiful to behold as Lady Rumor Spenser. One white-gloved hand held her skirt up from the street, the other poised a bright red silk parasol over her head, shielding her alabaster complexion from the slightest ray of the morning sun. Huge red roses marched round the brim of her leghorn straw, and her narrow feet were shod in pure white kid.

"Our royalist ladies must do their part to banish the depressing effects of war's hardships," Governor Tryon had decreed. "They should dress always with thought in mind to gladdening the eye of the soldier who has been long in the field, facing death."

The wartime city found many ways of diverting itself. Theaters, taverns, racetracks, assemblies, balls — entertainments of every conceivable kind — made life bearable for the civilian and military popula-

341

tion.

Invitations to the musicales hosted every Tuesday night by Lady Rumor Spenser were avidly sought after, as were the amateur theatricals presented every Friday in the third-floor ballroom of Spenser House.

Today was Wednesday, though, and Lady Spenser would not be at home. A grand public concert was to be given at Trinity Church, the proceeds from which would go to loyalist families who had been forced to flee Philadelphia in June when the Continentals had marched in.

"Mary Smith is coming at nine to fit your gown for tonight," Calpurnia nagged her from behind, as the town hall clock struck the quarter hour. They had just left the fish market with two baskets full of lovely fat shad and flounder.

Rumor sighed. "There is still the apothecary. Olympia was very insistent that we not forget her headache powder. The chaise will meet us there at eight-thirty sharp."

Smiling at a green-jacketed dragoon who had just executed a sweeping bow in her direction, his plumed hat against his chest, Rumor gritted, "My sister-in-law awoke with another of her migraines. She had the entire household astir through the night with her loud outcries and demands. If we don't want our day as well to be ruined by her ill-spirits, we had better fetch home a goodly supply of the medicine."

"I could fix something herbal that would cost her nothing and be far more effective," grumbled the nurse, "but Lady Olympia will have no part of anything I concoct."

"She's afraid you'll poison her," Rumor giggled, sidestepping a wandering pig.

Despite the servant's warning to hurry home for her fitting, Rumor slowed her steps along the two blocks

342

to Hanover Square from Dock, then stopped altogether to watch a group of street acrobats who were undergoing astounding gyrations with each other and an African monkey. There was also a little dog who danced and actually sang, yowling in various tones to approximate a tune.

The little kitchen maids, neither of whom was more than fourteen, laughed and shouted their delight. Calpurnia roared also, holding her sides, her hearty belly laugh echoing up and down the street.

Seeing her old friend so happy and carefree brought a warmth to Rumor's heart. Caesar had brought his wife to New York exactly a week after Rumor had come from Philadelphia with Liz. But immediately he left to join the Continental army in the South.

Calpurnia missed her lifetime companion sorely, and fretted daily about his well-being. Word from the battlefront was hard to come by, especially in a British town.

As for Rumor, she had no such concerns. The man she had loved so terribly was dead. Before leaving The Crooked Hill after the skirmish with the Redcoats in February, both the Negroes had seen Aaron stretched out on the tavern floor, blood streaming from several wounds in his head.

"Are you sure he was dead, not merely wounded?" Rumor had pressed.

Both mournfully shook their heads. "God knows I wish I could say differently, Rumor," Caesar declared. "But there was no time to make absolutely sure. The British would have killed us, had we tarried. All of the American soldiers were slain, including Aaron."

Despite eyewitness evidence, Rumor continued to doubt. Colonel Higgins had told her Fleming was dead. Calpurnia assured Rumor that the blood was pouring from her lover's head with such ferocity that he could not have survived for more than a few minutes, at most.

The black woman was forced to remind her mistress of this cruel fact from time to time, for Rumor persisted in a desperate hope that somehow Aaron was still alive. It was a feeling in her heart that could not be denied.

Lady Spenser had a heartbreaking habit of peering into every crowd, of answering every knock on the door without waiting for the butler to do so, of examining every bit of post that came into the house, even letters that were not addressed to her.

The New York Gazette, a newspaper that delighted in printing the most trivial of American setbacks, had duly reported that "Aaron Fleming, the infamous Rebel spy, was killed by enemy action north of Valley Forge. Many will remember Fleming for his cunning masquerade as Sir Oliver Mowbray."

But the editors of the four-page loyalist newspaper were notorious for inventing stories to cheer their loyalist readers, Rumor had reminded Olympia when they argued about Aaron.

"Everybody with an ounce of sense knows that that loyalist rag prints more lies than truth," she had said defiantly.

"You're addlepated, girl," Olympia had snapped. "The man's dead as mutton. Your scandalous affair is over. You couldn't have married him, in any case, for as the wife of a traitor to the king, you would never have seen a penny of the Spenser money."

Olympia had not forgotten that she was one of many who had been completely hoodwinked by Sir Oliver Mowbray.

Relations between Rumor and her dead husband's sister were strained, though not as chaotically violent as they had been prior to Rumor's being carried off by

Aaron the year before. Olympia was a sensible woman. She accepted the inevitable. The annulment attempt having come to nothing, the Jamaican chit was her brother's rightful widow.

Furthermore, the girl was living comfortably in New York under the protection of no less a personage than King George III himself. This, despite the girl's having lived willingly with the Rebels at Valley Forge, and having conspired with her spy lover in the murder of a British officer.

Especially galling to Olympia was the fact that Rumor had managed to add the new British commander, that trifling fool, Sir Henry Clinton, to her list of admirers. The general who had succeeded the departed Howe appeared frequently, uninvited, at Spenser House, where he made no bones of his high regard for the wicked girl. All because the king's daughter had married a Spenser cousin. Lady Rumor Spenser could do no wrong. Even murder went unpunished.

To Olympia's utter consternation, the wicked actress who had snared her poor brother into marriage was regarded by all as the queen of New York society, a title that Olympia herself had once claimed as her own.

All this ill feeling on her sister-in-law's part was well known to Rumor. During her frequent headaches, the fortyish spinster relieved her physical agonies by tirades of verbal abuse directed mainly at the new and radiant Lady Spenser.

Rumor's almost daily expeditions into downtown New York served a dual purpose. It got her away from Olympia for a few hours, and her presence in the marketing retinue made Calpurnia feel less nervous about being picked up again by slavers. The nefarious trade in selling Negroes snatched right off the street and transporting them to the South, flourished in the crowded city.

But even without these pressing excuses, Rumor loved driving downtown in the chaise. The city teemed with life. She loved the bustle of activity, the assorted varieties of people who played, worked, argued politics, or simply sat on the old Dutch stoops, watching the passing parade of humanity.

The Spenser footman was helping Rumor into the green-and-gold family chaise when she heard a newsboy shout, "Bloody news, bloody news, where are the Continentals now?"

Ordering the footman to purchase a paper, Rumor settled back in the leather seat beside Calpurnia, the housemaids opposite. The paper printed half-truths more often than not, but it was Rumor's sole source of information about the war.

After scanning the brief article on the war in the South, and the usual blather about the French ships sunk by the British sailors, she flicked to the society pages. These, at least, could be taken with a degree of faith.

Lady Rumor Spenser is happily once again in residence at Spenser House after a harrowing period of captivity among the Rebels. She has graciously consented to take the lead in the royal theater production of Shakespeare's *Macbeth*, to be presented in late October. Rehearsals will be underway . . .

She read on. Her musicales were a continuing pleasure, the theatricals planned and staged under her direction were the finest in all the Colonies. Rumor Spenser was a star in the New York firmament, the editor prounounced.

"One would hardly guess that this lovely widow underwent such cruel travail at the hands of the Americans . . ."

General Howe, together with a gossipy Liz Loring, had spread it abroad that she if she had not been heroically rescued by a certain Colonel Higgins, Rumor would surely have perished in American hands.

The fanciful stories were designed to please the king, Liz assured her. If it were known that the exalted Lady Spenser harbored kind feelings for the rebellious Colonists, the Crown would be embarrassed, and her life in New York might become unbearable.

Quelling a surge of anger at the blatant lies, Rumor handed the paper to Calpurnia to peruse the columns for the tiniest reference to anything that might conceivably concern the regiment of her absent Caesar.

What did it matter anymore, Rumor thought dully, closing her eyes and resting her head back on the seat. Nothing mattered now. She had lost the only thing that made life worth living—a man who even in death possessed her whole being.

Until death claimed her, too, she would have to go through the actions of what others call living. She might well marry again, for she dearly wanted children and a family of her own. But as for the kind of passionate love she and Aaron had shared . . . "No," she said aloud, "no, no-o-o."

Her cry startled the housemaids, and quickly, Calpurnia covered her mistress's hand with hers. In the months since Aaron's death, Rumor often cried out at unguarded moments, as if in mortal agony.

As they reached home, Rumor's happy mood returned. Liz Loring stood waiting in the open front door as Rumor stepped out of the chaise at the entrance to the brick mansion overlooking the Hudson.

The fiftyish widow—her cuckolded husband had

347

died last year — looked half her age and fresh as a daisy in sprigged dimity, with tiers of chintzy flounces on the skirt.

The motherly ex-mistress of General Howe had proved to be a godsend in these difficult first months after Aaron's death. Her good spirits rarely flagged. Her wisdom and experience with people were invaluable to Rumor in her demanding role as official hostess of a titled house.

Though a sunny bedroom was set aside exclusively for her, the pretty blond woman was seldom there. She was much in demand for houseparties and social affairs throughout the city.

She drew Rumor inside quickly. "You have a letter."

Rumor's heart leaped. "From Aaron?"

Liz's blue eyes clouded, as she pecked the young woman on her smooth cheek and led the way into the music room and closed the door. The pleasant tiny room with the pianoforte where Lionel had proposed almost two years before was one of the few places in the big house where they could be reasonably free of Olympia's annoying eavesdropping.

The waxen seal holding the thick parchment together bore the Spenser crest. Though solicitors assured her that she was in line to inherit once she removed to the ancestral house across the Atlantic, Rumor was uncertain that she would be welcomed.

She imagined their aristocratic noses in the air. "My word! An actress? From Jamaica?"

While her companion listened raptly, beside her on the settee, Rumor read the letter written in an elegant hand in rich, black ink.

To the Lady Rumor Spenser, cousin.

Mere words cannot convey our feelings upon the joyful news that our beloved Lionel has left us a precious remembrance of his dear self. We had all but given up hope that our cousin would remarry after the sad death of his poor Mary.

Overcome with relief, Rumor turned a weeping face to Liz. "Oh, Liz, they want me."

"Naturally, you little ninny, who on god's green earth would not?"

Mrs. Loring finished reading the two-page letter aloud. Rumor was to come to Spenser Castle in Scotland the moment—the very moment, mind—that ocean travel was once again safe for civilians.

The letter was signed by Lionel's two female cousins. There was no mention of Olympia.

Liz's merry laugh rang out. "Something tells me that her nibs upstairs—" she pointed a finger at the ceiling—"is not exactly popular with her Spenser cousins."

Joining in the laughter, Rumor wiped her eyes. "She has been predicting a cool reception for me over there, if not downright hostility."

Hugging her friend fiercely, she exclaimed, "Oh, Liz, how marvelous to have a family once again. I can hardly wait until I sail. Bother this war."

The woman whom Rumor regarded as a second mother stroked the smooth young back. "What great sorrow to have found your natural father at last—only to lose him again."

Rumor fell silent, as her thoughts dwelt on Beaumont Carter. Like Aaron and the unfortunate innkeeper, he, too, had fallen to British swords at The Crooked Hill all because he tried to save her. Like Aaron, who had returned from sure escape through the door to plead with her to flee with him.

Sensing her inner agony over two deaths she blamed herself for, Liz murmured, "Life makes no sense,

349

sometimes, darling. Where the heart leads, a woman is forced to follow. Your father died knowing that you loved him."

"But Aaron did not," Rumor wailed, weeping afresh. "He died with the knowledge that I placed a scoundrelly Beau Carter over him."

"Sh-h-h, now, don't start all that—"

"The seamstress is here" came Calpurnia's stern voice from the other side of the door.

Drying her eyes, Rumor prepared to resume her life.

"After your fitting, let's tell Olympia the good news," Liz urged. "What an unholy commotion she will make! I can hardly wait to see the expression on her face."

"You spiteful wretch," Rumor joshed. "There's no time today, and besides, it's the kind of pleasure one like to put off—" she smiled wickedly—"like a spectacular dessert after a hearty dinner."

The remainder of the day was spent in the elaborate preparations of both ladies for the concert at Trinity Church, which promised to be the highpoint of August social life. Olympia would remain at home, nursing her migraine.

Since the war, wigs had declined in favor because of the scarcity of human hair, and disdaining to refurbish her old ones, Liz kept two hairdressers occupied on her own blond tresses.

Fashions in hair had soared to the absurd, and Liz appeared for the journey downtown in a truly fanciful creation. Fat sausage rolls on each side of her round face drew up to a cloudlike frizz on top, the whole crowned by a feathered hat.

"No one will notice, I hope," she grinned to Rumor, "that my turquoise lawn is two years old."

Rumor had never owned a wig. Her silky brown hair, which had grown past her shoulder blades since

Aaron's cutting in the forest a year ago, was simply but elegantly coiffed. Honey-colored ringlets danced around her cheeks and smooth brow, accenting her wide-spaced brown eyes. In back there was just enough hair to form a small chignon. Her hat was simple to match — white gauze and rich embroidered lace with tiny satin rosebuds interlaced.

In a dimity sky-blue quilted gown, and starched lawn cape, she was in Liz's words, "like a breath of fresh, mountain air in this muggy town."

Heads turned and chatter ceased as they took their seats in the front row before the wooden bandstand set in the chancel of burned-out Trinity Church. Like many other edifices, the historic structure was still in ruins from the fire started by the Sons of Liberty at the sugar house in 1776.

Smiling and bowing graciously to the many greetings, and in deference to the sultry August night, they snapped open their fans and settled back to enjoy the evening.

Midway in the concert, while sipping a cool lemonade, Rumor sat up, as if transfixed. She poked Liz in the ribs.

"The drummer," she hissed, "the one next to the flutist—"

"Yes?" Liz had been dozing. A Haydn symphony always had the disastrous effect of putting her to sleep.

"Don't you think he looks like Aaron?"

Dutifully, Liz sat up. Extracting a quizzing glass from her reticule, she fixed it on one eye. Squinting, she peered for some seconds at the very tall man in green satin who sat in his chair with his two hands folded, steeple fashion, on his knees.

"Looks like he's praying," Liz commented dryly.

Rumor sighed, exasperated. "The point is, he's not playing. I haven't seen him hit those drums once."

351

"Not too many drums in this kind of music," murmured Liz, putting her glass away.

"It would be just like Aaron to masquerade as a musician," Rumor whispered. "He doesn't know one note from another, cannot even carry a tune."

It was one of her recurrent fantasies that her lover was not dead, but must appear so for reasons of spying. He was an acknowledged master of disguises, and she dreamt that one day he would make himself known to her here in the city.

Frequently, as she went about her work, or in the midst of a soiree or musicale, she would stop and look about her at the guests. Maddeningly, there were so many bewigged gentlemen of fashion, so many with exactly that affected accent that Sir Oliver Mowbray had cultivated.

Perhaps he would pose as a workman. Every drayman, every horseman clopping along the street, every proprietor of every stall at the market got her brief attention.

After a thoughtful silence, Liz said, gently, "Granted, the drummer's face has got that Indian look — long nose, with a kind of eagle hook to it. But this one is too fleshy, just a mite. Aaron was like a whippet, lean and not an ounce of fat."

"He could have gained weight as part of his disguise," Rumor insisted.

"Please, dear, don't torture yourself with impossible imaginings."

The selection ended, and the audience rose for intermission. Rumor was bent on seeking out the drummer, but, almost forcibly, Liz restrained her.

"You'll make a laughingstock of yourself," she said sternly, "and make a shambles of your own masquerade as loyalist Lady Spenser, if you go up to a perfect stranger and ask him if he is Aaron Fleming, the famous American spy."

The drummer remained on Rumor's mind, however, until they arrived home and found the household in an uproar. A stranger had appeared at the door, begging refuge as a refugee from Rebel Philadelphia.

"Miss Olympia has him in the kitchen," stuttered the parlormaid.

Calpurnia entered, her ebony eyes like saucers. "It's God's own miracle, I swear. He's come back from the dead."

After a stunned moment, to make sure it wasn't a dream, Rumor breathed, "Aaron, oh-h-h, I knew he could not be truly dead."

Her heart stopped, then began to race, and every fiber of her being began to sing. Had any human being ever known such happiness?

Thrusting her reticule at the maid, Rumor tore off the lacy hat. She wanted Aaron to kiss her hair, as he always loved to do. Her lips grew soft, preparing themselves for the touch of his mouth on hers.

Breathless, she fled down the long corridor past the music room and back parlor, through a tiny pantry into the kitchen. Was ever a corridor so long?

Calpurnia was at her back, mumbling something she could not distinguish. Only when she pushed open the heavy door, did the woman's words become clear.

"Wait, wait. It's not Aaron, pet, it's your father."

Rumor stopped dead, just inside the door, her hand clutching the brass knob. A swordthrust of anguish sharper than she had ever known cut through her, tearing her insides to shreds, in a burst of brilliant agony. She stood, as if paralyzed, unable to move or speak.

Two cavernous brown eyes stared back at her from a skeletal face. His garments were in tatters, the once glossy velvet jacket was encrusted with filth and mud.

The hands that clutched the brandy glass were those of a wraith. Rumor had seen corpses that seemed more alive.

But it was Beaumont Carter in the flesh — or what was left of it. The man Calpurnia and Caesar had sworn to have been mortally wounded at The Crooked Hill was very much alive.

He sat in a chair at the long wooden table, a crystal glass of brandy in his long, bony hands. Behind him hovered Olympia Spenser, looking tall and mussed, but very much in charge.

A taffeta wrapper had been flung carelessly over the muslin nightshift, and tendrils of graying brown hair straggled from her lacy nightcap. This was a woman, Rumor thought, amazed, who never appeared without every hair in place. On those days when she lay abed, and must perforce be served by maids, she ordered her bedroom curtains drawn and no candles to be lit.

But as her sister-in-law met Rumor's quick, startled glance, Rumor caught her breath. The haughty, often bitter face was transformed. The harsh lines had softened, the hazel eyes shone with tenderness and concern and something else. With a shock, Rumor saw love in Olympia's hazel eyes.

"Well, Rumor," she said sweetly in her high soprano voice that usually sounded like a whine. "Don't stand there like a ninny. Come, greet your father. He has traveled a very long way to see you."

"Father," Rumor burst out at last, falling to her knees by his chair. Burying her face in his lap, she wept, uncontrollably, as if her heart would break. But deep within her, she was burdened with guilt. Her tears were not so much for the man who had come back from the dead, but for the one who had not.

Beau Carter had apparently drunk several glasses of brandy on an empty stomach, for when he spoke, his cultured voice was thick, the always precise theatrical accents slurred. "Don't press me now, Daughter, for an account of the horrors I have experienced since you were taken from me at the tavern. I thought many times that I must surely perish."

Olympia, respecting Rumor's time with her father, had been fussing with the cook at the fire. A kettle of soup was simmering, and as she brought a china bowl of steaming broth to the table, she said sharply, "Your father needs nourishment, girl, not talk."

"Yes." Rising to her feet, Rumor wiped her face and blew her nose in Calpurnia's large handkerchief. How desperately she wanted to ask him for any word of Aaron. If her father had survived the tavern battle, then it was possible that Aaron, too, had somehow escaped.

Wisely, though, she checked herself. The man was clearly at the end of his tether. "We can talk in the morning, Father dear," she said firmly. "Now that we are together again, there will be many, many lovely days to talk. All our lives."

Kissing Beau Carter on his gaunt cheek, she smiled. "You will always have a home with me, father. Never, never, until death, will we be parted."

His hands clasped hers, and he tried to speak. But instantly his hold loosened, and he fell back into the chair, drained. The aristocratic face was chalky.

Bending over the slumped figure, Olympia lifted a spoonful of broth, attempting to part his lips. "You must take some of this, Mr. Carter," she begged. "Else I fear you will not live through the night."

He sipped obediently, two swallows, then pushed the spoon aside. "There is something I must tell my daughter — "

Rumor had backed away to the other side of the table, but at his words, leaned forward, her hands on

355

the edge of the smooth, hard wood.

"Please, Father, no more tonight," she pleaded. "It can wait."

"No." He sat up straight, suddenly appearing to revive. "I was told that your fiance, de Borre, has been wounded, and begs to see you . . ."

The few words had drained him again, and a very cross Olympia beckoned the footman. "Let's get this poor man into bed." Together, she and the servant lifted Carter bodily out of the chair, and supporting him under the arms, half-carried him to the door.

"Charles?" Rumor asked quietly. "Where is he? I will go to him." There had been no word of Charles since he resumed his active service with the French contingent in late winter.

"I don't know."

Ignoring Olympia's black looks, Rumor persisted, trailing them to the doorway. "Who told you, Father? Perhaps I can—"

"That Fleming fellow, the spy who started the ruckus at the tavern—"

The doorway was too narrow for three people to push through at once, so the footman released his hold for a moment while Olympia helped Carter into the corridor.

"Aaron? Where did you see him?" Rumor's blood was hammering in her ears.

Her father's head was lolling about on his neck, and cupping his gaunt cheeks with her hands, Rumor forced his slitted eyes to hers.

"Are you mad?" Olympia tried to push her out of the way. "He's raving—"

Carter giggled, and started to hiccough.

"He's drunk," Rumor said tersely.

A second giggle from her father was followed by, "The man was in this green satin and was toting a set of drums . . ."

At that moment, the brandy took its toll, and Carter slumped, falling against Olympia. The footman and Olympia carried him upstairs, one at his head, the other at his feet.

He would be all right, Rumor thought. When the brandy wore off, she would question him further. She followed her father and the others up the stairs, thinking that this was the happiest day of her life.

Aaron was alive!

Chapter Seventeen

It was maddening.

No matter how desperately he tried to remember, Beau Carter could not recall the place where he had seen Aaron. Rumor's father reclined on a damask-covered Chippendale chaise, his magnificent brown eyes trained on the ceiling. A burgundy-colored silk dressing gown covered his thin frame, and he was sipping whiskey from a gold-rimmed tumbler.

"It was a public house in a smallish town some distance from New York," he said, pursing his deeply indented lips. "But as to its name—"

"Yes, Father, please try to remember," Rumor prodded gently. "The landlord might know where Aaron went."

Dear Lord, she thought, how many pubs in how many little town would she have to visit?

Even if her father remembered the name, and she found the place, Aaron probably would no longer be there. But there was always a hope that the innkeeper would know where he had gone.

Snapping his fingers as if suddenly inspired, Carter lowered his gaze from the ceiling to look cheerfully at Rumor, perched on the edge of the bed. "The wooden placard bearing the name of the hostelry had blown down in the wind," he announced excitedly. At her crestfallen face, he exclaimed, "That should be of some help, Daughter."

"Yes, Father, truly it is." Rumor bent to kiss him on the cheek, and left the room as Olympia entered, followed by a maid with still another tray of food and drink.

"My father drinks far too much alcohol," she frowned, glancing at the tall glass of whiskey and water beside the platter of meat and vegetables.

Her sister-in-law favored her with a complacent smile. "The man is thriving under my care, is he not? The Irish whiskey is better than any medicine."

Biting her lip to suppress her irritation, Rumor fled to the music room, where she sat down at the spinet and began to play, loudly, vigorously. Pounding on the pianoforte was her favorite way to vent the frustration she felt at her failure to extract information on Aaron from her father.

She was convinced that the constant alcoholic haze encouraged by Olympia was befuddling her father's brain more than it needed to be. He could not even recall what had happened to Philip Stokes, the man he had tried to force her to marry. His eyes grew puzzled when Stokes, who was his neighbor in Virginia, was even mentioned. Everything after the moment she was snatched from his arms by Higgins had apparently been blotted from his mind.

Perhaps because her father chose to remember only pleasant things, she mused, he had forgotten everything else. He was a man who dwelt in a world of his own making.

But to give the devil her due, Olympia Spenser had worked a miracle. In scarce three days from the night he had literally stumbled up the lane to Spenser House, Beau Carter had almost become his old self.

359

His face had filled out, the cavernous look was gone from the brown eyes, and there was little danger now that he would die from malnutrition.

The tattered velvet he had worn upon arrival had been burned, and Olympia ordered her brother Lionel's garments altered for her charge. Beau Carter appeared the picture of a gentleman of leisure as he reclined in the costly imported fabrics that the dead Lord Spenser had worn.

Turning away the physician Rumor had summoned, the spinster had taken complete charge of the man, canceling all her social obligations and letting it be known that she would not be at home for visitors until further notice.

Olympia did, however, send a notice to the editors of *The New York Gazette* to the effect that "Beaumont Carter, esquire, of Albermarle Plantation in Virginia is now residing at Spenser House. Mr. Carter is the father of Lady Rumor Spenser, widow of Lord Lionel, fallen in battle at Trenton."

Beaumont Carter had captivated the woman, who, as far as anyone knew, had never had a beau even in her youth. He in turn seemed devoted to his new friend and nurse. By the second day of his stay, they were calling each other "Olympia" and "Beau."

"It's a perfect match," Calpurnia had grinned. Then, she had said more soberly, "They deserve each other. One's a bigger scoundrel than the other."

Truthfully, Rumor was supremely grateful to her sister-in-law for restoring her father's health. Olympia had bloomed also. The habitual frown on the plain face had vanished, she went about the big house, smiling, humming under her breath. The dowdy garments she was accustomed to wearing had been replaced with softer, gayer gowns. Two seamstresses were working full time in the sewing room, fashioning the woman an entirely new wardrobe.

"This is the skinflint who complains continually about expenses," Rumor had commented to Liz. "Every time I return from market, she rushes into the kitchen to inspect my purchases, clucking her tongue in disapproval at my extravagance."

"Well, pet, you *are* living on borrowed funds," her friend had reminded her.

"I am fully aware of our straitened financial circumstances," Rumor had nodded glumly.

Lionel's will had provided both her and Olympia with a moderate allowance, until such time as Rumor could return to England to claim the full inheritance. Thereafter, Olympia's living allowance would derive from Rumor's largesse.

But money was the least of Rumor's concerns at the moment. Aaron's callous behavior troubled her. He was alive, and had not informed her of his whereabouts. She was certain that he had been in the city, at the concert, posing as a drummer, just days ago, not twenty feet from where she had sat with Liz.

Charles de Borre also preyed on her mind. Shamefully, she admitted to herself that she had all but forgotten the charming Frenchman whom she had promised to marry. He had left Valley Forge last winter to rejoin the French contingent under Lafayette, and no word had come to her since then. Aaron had returned from the West, soon after, driving all else from her mind.

Now, as her fingers ran up and down the keyboard, she tried to sort out her emotions. She still loved Aaron, and now that he was alive, she was driven to find him even if he apparently had no wish to seek her out.

Was he angry still at her refusal to escape with him at The Crooked Hill?

But there was poor Charles, wounded, perhaps dying . . .

A touch on her shoulder brought her fierce playing to an abrupt halt. Liz stood behind her.

"I knocked, several times," Liz apologized, embracing Rumor and drawing her to the settee. "Olympia begged me ask you to desist in your loud music. Seems her patient would like to take a nap."

"It helps me forget," Rumor replied, "for a few moments, at least."

"Soon, you will be too occupied for foolish brooding," Liz announced. "We leave immediately for Philadelphia."

"Oh-h, splendid! Then it is all arranged that you will accompany me?" Childlike, Rumor clapped her hands together for joy.

"*Certainement,* my dear," Liz laughed. "La, do you imagine I would allow you to travel alone? Besides, the Americans and French will still be celebrating the return of the Continental Congress to their capital and it promises to be a gay time."

Rumor's face fell. "I pray that Charles has not died from his wounds before I reach him."

She halted, brushing away a tear. Dear, sweet Charles. He truly loved her, not like that other arrogant one, who had never even asked her outright to marry him.

Cupping the girl's chin in her hands, Liz gently shook Rumor's face. "Now, stop this gloom, my girl. I simply will not allow you to go about a moment longer as if your life were over."

Assuming her best stern mother look, she added, "You've got to make an earnest effort to forget that man. He's not worth mooning over."

"I'm not mooning, I simply want to beg forgiveness for the way I acted at the tavern. If I had fled with him

362

when he called out to me, everything would have been different."

"You did what you had to at the moment. If he cannot understand that you were protecting your father from being run through by the British, he is not the man you claim."

Liz pressed her hand. "He was actually here, in the city, and never—"

"I know," Rumor said miserably.

Then, swallowing her tears, Rumor hugged her friend. She had asked the more experienced Liz to make discreet inquiries about the possibility of a loyalist lady visiting a wounded enemy officer in the city now occupied by Washington's forces. It was a delicate matter, but with her many high-placed connections, she was certain Liz could smooth the way for her to visit Charles.

In order that Rumor's loyalist image not be tarnished, Liz would spread it abroad in the city that Lady Spenser had embarked on an errand of mercy to the loyalist wounded in the American hospital in Philadelphia.

As the friends chatted, Olympia's voice sounded from the open door. "Your father has managed to recall more particulars about the public house where he saw your lover Fleming."

"Oh-h?" Rumor took a deep breath as Liz squeezed her hand, signaling that she must remain calm. "What did he say, Olympia?"

Obviously relishing the suspense she was creating, Olympia hedged. "Now let me try and recall his exact words."

Screwing up her face, Olympia began to fuss with her hair, tucking a few stray tendrils under her lacy cap. Not only had her wardrobe become more sprightly of late, but she had begun to frizz her hair with a curling iron in the latest fashion.

"Yes, dear Olympia?" Rumor's gorge was rising, and only Liz's restraining hand on hers kept her from leaping off the settee and throttling the woman.

Her hair tucked away to her satisfaction at last, Olympia beamed at Rumor, though there seemed to be more maliciousness than loving concern in her smile.

"The man with whom you carried on so flagrantly last year was playing cards at a little table by the fire," she said. "He was eating supper from a tray, and—" she stuck out a pink tongue to lick her lips—"oh, yes, he was traveling with a female companion. Your father vows that the two went up to bed together after supper."

Leveling a pair of guileless hazel eyes on Rumor, Olympia remarked, "The woman was definitely not a person of quality. Your father says she was a lady of the night, such as one always finds in taverns."

Pausing, she added softly, "I sincerely hope that this report will put an end to the bothersome questioning of your poor father about that confounded rascal of a spy."

"It will, dear sister," Rumor answered faintly.

In the silence that followed the closing of the door, Rumor held on to Liz's hand like a lifeline. Something was happening within her. The heart that moments before had still yearned for Aaron was turning numb. How could she have been such an utter fool!

A fury began to fill her heart and soul, making her blood run cold in her veins. She shivered. The numbness in her heart had turned to stone. She felt a heaviness in her chest, as if someone had punched her with a powerful fist.

Liz was right. No man was worth mooning over like a sick calf. Least of all a man who was so cruel that he would allow her to go on thinking he was dead when all the time he was very much alive and most assuredly not mooning over the woman with whom he had amused himself, off and on, since 1776.

How he and that "female" traveling companion must have laughed about her as they tossed about in bed upstairs in that nameless tavern. She conjured up an image of Aaron, naked, with that woman. She was sure to have large, full breasts, and wide-spreading hips, and when they came together, she would be on top, dangling her nipples in his face.

"Rumor, wake up, it's not the end of the world."

Liz's sharp words mercifully cut off her masochistic imaginings. She must not think of him again. Ever.

The eight-day clock in the foyer struck nine. Turning a composed face to her dear friend who sat anxiously at her side, Rumor said, "I'm fine. Let's start packing, Liz. I'll have the footman order a four-horse carriage to carry us to Philadelphia."

"Bonjour, Lady Spenser. Bonjour Madame Loring."

The smiling young officer, who opened the door of the Philadelphia house to which they had been directed, bowed deeply from the waist. "I am Lieutenant Laurens, and I bid you a very warm welcome to Philadelphia."

Batting her heavily painted blue eyes and simpering like a schoolgirl, Mrs. Loring extended a gloved hand, which the officer promptly lifted to his lips. Liz had drunk more wine than was prudent at the enormous dinner they had been served at the house of the French commandant.

The officer was a truly splendid sight, reflected Rumor, in his sky-blue jacket trimmed with yellow. A yellow plume on his black tricornered hat brushed her face as he straightened up from his bow.

Her spirits lifted. The day's long journey had exhausted her, but now, as they were ushered into a grand, candlelit foyer, and more smiling Frenchmen—each in colorful dress uniform—came to greet them effusively, the trials of the nightmarish journey vanished.

Though nearly midnight, the house streamed with light, and music sounded from a room off the foyer. Tucking her hand inside her cloak to avoid being kissed by a dozen or so gallant Frenchmen, she asked, "Please, show me to Major de Borre."

"Taking her by the elbow. Lieutenant Laurens smiled. "You will be pleased to hear that your fiancé is no longer a lowly major, but has risen to the rank of colonel, having shown great courage under fire."

Several other officers descended upon the enchanted Liz. "So you are the celebrated Mrs. Loring, who managed to keep the British Howe captivated for so many years!"

With a wave to Rumor, her friend allowed herself to be propelled into the parlor from which the sprightly music was emanating.

The house was enormous, and Rumor passed numerous closed doors behind which she heard trilling female laughter, and the kind of low, intimate chatter that two people make when engaged in dalliance.

The dashing French soldiers might have come in force to help the Americans win their freedom, she mused, but they did not come alone. Those whose wives and sweethearts had not accompanied them, Officer Laurens informed her, had little trouble finding eager American girls to keep them occupied when not in battle.

Rumor was led by Laurens up a flight of ornately carved stairs and down a long corridor to a room nestled in a kind of bay. The polished wooden door was wide open, and as she walked inside, she halted in surprise.

It did not look or smell like a sickroom. Lush oil paintings, opulent landscapes in gilded frames, adorned the gaily papered walls. Flowered chintz hung at the bank of wide-open windows through which Rumor could see the moonlight on the Delaware. Several bouquets of fresh-cut red roses stood about in tall vases, imparting a wondrous fragrance.

Charles himself lounged on a damask-covered chaise longue, chatting with a pretty yellow-haired girl of eighteen or so. As Rumor entered, they were laughing, but as Laurens came forward, the laughter died, and they turned, expectantly.

There was a short silence, as Rumor stared in astonishment. Charles seemed the picture of health. A broad smile creased his patrician face, and his eyes shone with pleasure.

"Chérie, chérie," he burst out at last, extending both hands in welcome.

Getting to her feet, his blond companion drew to one side. Her face was impassive, but the eyes that stared at Rumor were filled with curiosity.

As Rumor walked slowly across the thick carpet toward the chaise, placed in the curving space of the bay windows, the Frenchman's smile vanished, his thin face crumpled, and he burst into tears. Alarmed, Rumor quickened her pace, and reaching Charles, threw herself into his arms.

Neither spoke as Charles continued to weep, softly, his hot tears falling on Rumor's cool cheek. They kissed, not in passion, but as two old friends meeting after a long absence.

"Darling Rumor, I have dreamed of this moment so very long," he said at last. "General Washington promised to see that you could visit me here, but I had not dared to hope—"

The blond girl handed him a clean handkerchief. After blowing his nose loudly, he gave it back to her. "Yvonne, this is my darling Rumor. We were to be married, but—"

He shrugged in his inimitable Gallic way, and Rumor saw, for the first time, how very ill he was.

Yvonne stepped forward and put a hand on his brow. "Charles must not overtax himself," she said in a lilting French accent. "He is quite ill. During the day, he seems fine, but fever returns at night."

There was an edge of reproof in the girl's voice, and standing up, Rumor faced her. "Now that I am here, mam'selle, you can be assured that my fiancé will receive my full and constant attention. I have had much experience tending the Rebel wounded at Valley Forge."

"Indeed she has." Lieutenant Laurens spoke up. Taking Yvonne firmly by the hand, he drew her out of the room.

Exhausted by the excitement, Charles had fallen back on the chaise, eyes closed, his white hands dangling over the sides. Alarmed, Rumor prepared to get him into bed.

Laurens had returned, and together they removed the silken overwrap from the emaciated body and got the sick man into bed.

"Where is the wound?" Rumor asked as she tucked the chintz coverlet firmly into place beneath the mattress.

The officer shook his head. "There is none. It is a nasty, recurrent fever caught from the dreadful miasma that pervades this coastal area."

He pointed to a row of brown bottles on a little table. "Here is medicine to help him sleep. Sleep and rest is the only hope for his recovery."

Rumor frowned, glancing at the open door. "This place sounds like a public house. With so much revelry in the house, and young female visitors to excite him."

Laurens sighed. "Your fiancé is such a naughty boy. He has a mortal fear of being alone, demanding companionship, preferably female, every moment that he is awake. He also insists that his door remain open at all times so that he will feel part of the life in the house."

Smiling, he put both hands on her shoulders. "But now that his adorable Rumor has come at last, that nonsense can cease. You are the best medicine of all for our very dear friend."

She would sleep and dress across the corridor, Laurens told her, escorting her to a charming replica, even to the rose, of Charles's bedroom. After the officer left, she stood for a long time, gazing out the open windows at the river. The Delaware was broad at this point, and teemed with boats, many of which seemed to be alight. Distant sounds of music drifted over the waterfront.

Liz was right. Though in the midst of war, the American capital was certainly gay.

A cry from across the hall brought her flying back to Charles. Yvonne was there before her. Apparently she had remained close by.

"I brought you some refreshment," the girl smiled sweetly, placing a tray on a little table. "Some cakes and cheese and lemonade."

Charles was sitting up in bed, wild-eyed. "Are you really here, *chérie?* I thought perhaps I had dreamed it."

"It is no dream, dear one," Rumor cried, darting to the bed. Holding him close, she kissed him on both cheeks before lowering him gently back on the pillows.

Yvonne drew close, a brown bottle in her hand.

"Here is an effusion to bring the fever down." Her gray eyes were frightened. "But he refuses to take the bitter stuff."

"You are burning with fever, darling," Rumor scolded the man on the bed, her harsh tone cloaking her very real fears for his health.

Warming to the girl, and contrite for her earlier curt dismissal, Rumor took the bottle from her hands. "That nonsense is going to end. Perhaps with your help we can manage to get a few spoonfuls into this bad boy."

The two women worked through the night, for despite a few swallows of the medicine, the young man's fever raged. With the help of Laurens and a male servant, they wrapped the thin, burning body in linens wrung out in cold water.

Charles refused to let Rumor leave his side. She sat on the bed, through the long hours, holding tightly to his hand.

The house had grown quiet eventually, the partying officers and their guests having gone to bed about one o'clock. Dully, Rumor speculated as to whose bed Liz Loring had climbed into. The promiscuous woman rarely slept alone, and almost always with a full colonel or even a general.

"He's cooler now, thank God," Yvonne said, removing the last damp sheet from the emaciated body. She walked to the window, looking out. "The river is lovely at dawn," she said quietly. "War seems very far away at this quiet hour."

She turned, her slender arms holding the wrapped-up sheet against her chest. How very young and fragile she looks, thought Rumor, startled. A shaft of sun broke through the overcast, bathing the girl in an aureole of gold.

"You love him, too," she stated tonelessly.

"With all my heart," the girl exclaimed. "We have been betrothed since birth. Our two families have been friends and neighbors for hundreds of years in the Loire Valley."

Rumor's heart contracted with pity. The girl had obviously traveled across the ocean to comfort her fiancé, only to learn that he loved another. "I didn't know," she groaned, lifting compassionate brown eyes to the girl. "Charles never said a word about you."

Yvonne smiled faintly. "You dazzled him so that I am certain every sensible thought departed from his mind, Lady Spenser. Love comes, when least expected, and often with a certain happy violence. Like a summer storm after a long, sultry day."

Casting a fond glance at the sleeping man whose wan face was turned toward the windows, she added, "My only wish is that my sweet Charles get well and is happy."

"Mine, too," Rumor sighed lamely, wishing she could find words to comfort the spurned girl.

"He worships you as a goddess," Yvonne said, walking to the door. She managed a rueful grin. "He thinks of me as a loving sister."

Until that moment, Rumor had been unsure in her own mind about what she would tell Charles if he pressed her for marriage.

"The moment he is well enough," she told the girl, "Charles and I will be wed."

Hesitating at the door, the French girl said slowly, "If for any reason you should change your mind about that, please, I beg you, do not tell him until he has completely regained his health. The shock might well kill him."

The girl ran down the corridor, leaving a bemused Rumor behind, perched thoughtfully on the chaise, studying her folded hands. Despite her avowals of love, Yvonne had intuitively guessed that the beautiful Lady Spenser's heart lay elsewhere.

Blessedly, she was so engrossed in caring for Charles, forcing him to take his medicine and keeping him amused in his waking hours, that Rumor had no time to think of whether or not she truly loved the man. True, she did not feel the quickening of the blood or the tightening in the loins that Aaron Fleming's touch had caused.

But that turmoil of the body was not love. His callous desertion of her, not once, but twice, had proved that conclusively. True love survives all setbacks, even those that seemed, on the surface, to be betrayals.

Her mama's words came back to her, as they had not done for years. "Passion is a deceiver, look rather for tenderness and gentle feelings."

Only occasionally, as she stretched her weary body on the chaise for a few hours of much needed sleep, did she allow a tiny doubt to enter her mind. Her dreams were of Aaron as a Mohawk carrying her from the sugar house fire, as a superficial but caring Sir Oliver, as a buckskin Virginian in the forest, revealing his true identity and taking her maidenhead.

The idyllic months in the secluded cabin at Barren Hill came back most often to disturb her rest. No matter how fierce her defenses during the day, in her dream she surrendered again and again to the hard, muscled body of the man who had enslaved her forever.

Sometimes, in the hot Philadelphia nights, she would awake in torment, her nipples taut and seeking for a mouth that was not there. Her loins were often moist and aching, yearning for a body that would never possess them again.

She prayed that she did not cry out in her sleep, but

when she dared to sleep in her own bed across the way, Charles's tortured cry would send her back again to the chaise.

One morning, as she and Charles bent over the chessboard before the sunny windows, Lieutenant Laurens burst into the room.

"Mon Dieu! My prediction that our ailing colonel would recover rapidly after your arrival has come true with a vengeance, my dear Lady Spenser. You are not only beautiful and good, but an angel as well. You have worked a miracle."

Crossing the carpet in two long strides, he clapped his hands on Rumor's shoulders. "I declare you a saint, and will duly see that a church is named after you."

"A cathedral, perhaps," Charles added happily.

The jesting brought a belly laugh from Charles and a flushed smile from Rumor. Charles was indeed transformed from the man who had barely survived her first night in Philadelphia. The feverish pallor was all but gone, and the light-blue eyes fairly sparkled.

The impishly charming good looks that had first enchanted Rumor at Clara's mill house in Barren Hill were once more in evidence. His irresistible good humor and chivalrous manner had also returned. Blowing a kiss at Rumor opposite him on the chaise, he said, "I am fit as a fiddle, and ready to stand up before the priest tomorrow—"

"Not so fast, my eager swain," Rumor joshed, reaching out to tousle his light-brown hair. She herself felt a sense of happy well-being that had been absent from her life for a very long time. This would be her life, caring for a wonderful man who would never forsake her.

Standing between the two of them, his hand behind his back, Laurens cleared his throat. "It warms my heart to see you looking so well, Colonel de Borre," he said, "because I intend to ask a very great favor of you."

"Yes?" Two little lines creased the sick man's brow. "Anything that doesn't take my darling from my side."

"Well-l, there's the rub, my friend." He began to speak very fast, tumbling his words together lest Charles interrupt. "There is to be a grand celebration today in the town — a genuine fete — and I thought, perhaps, well, damnit, man, you've kept her prisoner long enough. I insist that you permit your devoted nurse to attend. All of the French and American dignitaries will be present, and music, sport, and dancing will mark the festivities."

Leaning over, he cupped Rumor's delicate chin. "Your fiancée will make a very pale and dispirited bride if she is not given some respite. You have kept her prisoner long enough."

Charles was, of course, soon persuaded. "Look beautiful for me, *chérie*. I want every man in Philadelphia to be positively green with envy."

Yvonne appeared, and was delighted to pass up the fete and keep the housebound Charles happy for the day. She immediately took Rumor's place behind the chessboard. As Rumor left, neither seemed to notice.

Making little effort to hide her excitement, Rumor went off eagerly across the corridor to her bedroom to dress for the fete. For six days she had seen no one but Charles and Yvonne and the maid who brought them food. Liz had seemingly vanished.

The unfortunate loyalist lady, wife to a wealthy shipbuilder, who had been the mistress of this house had made a hasty exit upon the arrival of the Americans to the city had left an entire wardrobe of gowns behind.

The young lieutenant would call for her in half an

hour, he said, "Although," he added, "sadly, duties call me elsewhere during the fete."

He would see that a dashing escort was provided for her, to amuse her during the festivities as well as protect her from the crushing mob that was already filling the streets.

Softly humming a jaunty Jamaican tune, Rumor ignored the gowns still neatly folded in her traveling trunk. Instead, she dashed into the small dressing room and flipped through two armoires hung with twenty or more silks, satins, voiles, dimities, and brocades, trying frantically to decide.

Discarding the more sophisticated, elaborate hooped and jewel-encrusted creations, she chose a heavenly voile in palest rosebud pink. Cascades of three-point creamy lace fell from the elbow-length sleeves, a demure handkerchief of the same lace covered the shoulders. It was fastened at the back with a huge satin ribbon.

"A second miracle of the day," she breathed into the mirror as she slipped it over her undershift, whirling round and round in her delight. The gown fit as if made especially to her order. Her full white breasts thrust vibrantly from the low-cut décolletage.

"Up, up, up," she murmured, recalling the words of the Irish maid at Holy Ground as she was being dressed to meet General Howe that first time. The rose areola around her nipples showed a tiny bit, and, modestly, she flicked the creamy lace to cover. The close-fitting bodice hugged her body like a doeskin glove, tapering to a tiny waist belted by a silver ribbon.

As she struggled with the back fastenings, Yvonne appeared at the door. "Allow me," she murmured, coming forward into the room.

When the last tiny bone button was secured, the girl stepped back. After a moment, she said, "I suggest that you do not show yourself to Charles before you leave, milady, or I fear he will become so excited he will suffer a relapse."

Her tone was light, but the pale eyes were somber.

Laughing somewhat self-consciously, Rumor vowed to slip past his door unnoticed.

On her head she wore a wide-brimmed straw hat, weighted down with blowing roses and several feathery plumes. There was no time to frizz her thick, honey-brown hair or arrange it in stylish curls. Dipping her comb into a water-filled porcelain basin, she ran it through her hair, causing the damp tresses to cascade over her neck and shoulders in soft, wide waves.

Even the usually nonchalant Lieutenant Laurens was almost speechless as he took her arm, escorting her out of the house. "I called you an angel, Lady Spenser, but, truly, I swear I have never seen such a vision."

Rolling her eyes flirtatiously, Rumor smiled, and followed him into the carriage waiting at the curb. "I am no angel, my gallant lieutenant," she replied, "but merely a mortal woman, looking forward to enjoying myself as only a young and healthy female can."

Chapter Eighteen

"Damn it, Wilson, whose harebrained idea was all this blasted foolishness?"

Answering his own question, the tall, good-looking American officer in the dress uniform of the First Virginia Regiment mumbled, "Some jackass of an adjutant with nothing better to do, I'll wager."

Major Aaron Fleming was hot, hotter than he had ever been in his thirty years, even as a boy in tidewater Virginia. This sprawling Philadelphia that the new republic had chosen for its capital was a bigger swamp than the Potomac basin.

Lifting his cocked hat for the fifth time in as many minutes, he ran his fingers through his reddish thatch. His scalp prickled from sweat, he was sweating all over his muscled body. It ran down his chest, settled in his navel. Warm rivulets of it slithered over his hard belly, then bathed his haunches under the linen breeches before settling into the white silk stockings tucked into his black, gold-buckled boots.

The borrowed blue and gold-lace trimmed outfit was too tight for his giant frame, especially at the crotch, where the linen was stretched taut from hip to hip. Pray God he didn't have an erection, or the ogling ladies would really have reason to feast their eyes.

There was little danger of *that,* he thought wryly. His normally quick-surging desires seemed to have grown dormant these past months. He might as well be a monk.

Rumor herself would have to come along before he might have cause to worry about an embarrassing bulge. "Not likely," he muttered, with a snort, half under his breath.

"Pardon?" Wilson murmured, who amazingly was not sweating at all, but stood tall and elegant, his white-gloved hand resting lightly on the hilt of his sword.

"I said, I do not like this costume party."

"Oh, yes. Well, it's the damn Frenchies, you know," Wilson replied mildly. "The Gallic temperament, I suppose." He turned his plumed head in a half circle, surveying the crowd of chattering ladies and officers already seated. In their colorful frocks and parasols, they seemed like an animated summer garden.

Rolling his eyes in apparent ecstasy, he added, "Ah, to be a flea among this beauteous crowd. What I wouldn't like to nibble at."

Then, he said in jocular vein, "Where is your patriotism, Major, not to mention your red-blooded American appreciation of feminine beauty?"

"I savor a pretty female as much as the next fellow," Aaron replied acidly, "but I prefer them in a wide bed, without all the fancy garments. All this falderol is setting my teeth on edge."

"If you'd eaten some of the hearty breakfast our hosts provided, you'd feel more amiable," Wilson replied. "Those three cups of strong black coffee laced with rum are simply encouraging your mighty sweat."

The two officers stood behind four cushioned wrought-iron chairs, guarding against their being taken by any of the vast throng that swarmed on the

378

green, looking for seats to watch the festivities.

Filling the square itself, upward of two thousand French soldiers were in formation. All wore spanking, dazzling white, and with their red, white, and blue cockaded hats were a stirring sight to behold.

"Stop frowning," Wilson scolded, "and cease your infernal fidgeting with that hanky. Our commander in chief is glaring daggers at you."

Instantly alert, Aaron glanced swiftly at the raised wooden platform where General George Washington sat with the Marquis de Lafayette. The noble face of his adoptive father was indeed turned in his direction, and a slight frown disturbed the smooth, high brow.

"Thanks for warning me. I promised the general to be on my good behavior today."

Captain Wilson was city born and bred of a socially prominent Boston family, and therefore vastly more experienced in matters of decorum than the Virginian Major Fleming. Without being asked, he had assumed the role of Aaron's mentor in proper social behavior.

"They look almost comical together, our two supreme leaders," Wilson remarked with a titter. "Rather mismatched, more like father and son. One tall and lean as a giraffe, the other short and squat as a toad."

"Together the toad and the giraffe are tearing the whiskers off the British lion," Aaron quipped, suddenly turning sober. "I wouldn't trade places with either of them." He paused, covertly wiping his face with his palm. "I envy them the two darkies behind, though, with the palm leaf fans."

"You are a hero, my boy," the general had told him last night when he'd summoned Aaron to his headquarters. "One of the first in our brief history. Act like one for a change. And look like one."

Reluctantly, Aaron had agreed to don full dress uniform and to show himself to the adoring populace.

But he drew the line on wearing a powdered wig.

"It's enough that I must dress up like a trained monkey on a leash," he had grumbled to his grinning commander. "If I have to clap on one of those hairy fleabags—"

His careworn face breaking up into a broad smile, Washington had raised a hand in surrender. "Sometimes Aaron, you don't act a day older than the callow youth I plucked from the Shawnee in '63."

Aaron drew his hanky from his sleeve, only to have Wilson grate through clenched teeth, "Put it back."

"My scar itches like the very devil."

Replacing the offending linen square, Aaron drew his finger to the jagged, pinkish scar that cut a path across his throat, swerving past his chin to his left ear. That Redcoat Higgins had used his cutlass with telling effect. It had been three days after the tavern skirmish before Aaron had managed to see a surgeon, only to have the man shake his head. "Too late to suture, Major. The flesh is already congealed."

"Barely touch it with your fingernail," advised Wilson, "lest you encourage infection." Then he added with compassion, "It will take a year before it stops itching. You're suffering now, my friend, but I assure you that a scar like yours, won in battle, works like a love potion on most females."

Cheers from the people hanging out the windows up and down the street signaled the arrival of a group of formally dressed men who now took seats on the platform behind the two commanders.

"There's our Congress," Captain Wilson said. "This affair is being staged mainly for the benefit of those old men. They've never quite believed that France would ally herself with us, but when they see real, flesh and blood French troops en masse, they might be persuaded to loosen their iron grip on the purse strings."

"Perhaps the general will stop staring at me now," Aaron said hopefully. "He's too busy shaking hands with all those solemn lawmakers."

"But there's the women, my friend."

Smirking, Wilson winked at a young French girl in blue who had just walked by, so close that she brushed against Aaron's breeches with a fluttery, *"Excusez-moi."*

Absently, without even looking at the girl, Aaron mumbled a reply.

"As I say," Wilson prattled on relentlessly, "the females can't get enough of ogling the notorious Aaron Fleming. Your story is oh so romantic! You have narrowly escaped death many times, your adventures are legend. You are like a son to our beloved general. There is even a ballad celebrating that famous tavern brawl where you barged in on the lobsterbacks bold as brass, in one of their own uniforms."

"Any more of this claptrap, and it's pistols at dawn," Aaron said, tightening his lips. A muscle twitched in his cheek, rippling the scar.

Not to be denied his sport, Wilson ranted on. "And what about your *affaire de coeur* with the beauty of the century, Lady Rumor Spenser?"

Aaron doubled up his fist, thrusting it into the officer's smirking face. "So help me, Wilson, if you don't keep your tongue in your head, I'll flatten you right in front of all the generals and admirals and any other damn fool who's watching."

"Sorry, old pal. No offense intended. I've never seen the lady in question. I joke about it only because I'm fairly green with jealousy."

"Here's Laurens now, with our ladies," Aaron said with relief. The officers without women of their own had been asked to act as escort for any unattached

381

females who were important enough to be seated on the green.

"They've probably a couple of old maids, from fine old Quaker families, going all the way back to William Penn," Wilson grumbled, as Lieutenant Laurens walked across the cobbled street toward the green, a woman on each arm.

Aaron craned his neck. "Hm, I don't think so. They don't walk like old ladies. In fact, the one in pink seems to be quite young, the way she walks ahead, as if she can't wait to join the party."

His heart contracted. Rumor walked like that, always a step or two ahead of him or anybody she was with. As if she couldn't wait for life to come to her, but insisted on reaching out, overtaking every new adventure.

Her lovely head was always in the air, the brown eyes sweeping about eagerly like the Juliet she played. Sometimes she would stumble, over a rock or bit of refuse.

Damn it, stop it, Fleming, he told himself. He had almost gotten his face slapped for staring at every tall, slim, brown-haired girl who crossed his path during the few days he'd been in the capital.

If only it were actually his own sweet Rumor, walking toward him so eagerly! But that was nonsense. Why would she be here in Philadelphia. Even if, by some miracle, she had received his message about de Borre from her father, the Frenchman was in a Maryland hospital, a hundred miles from here.

The girl on Laurens's other arm, who was wearing lavender, stopped to put up her parasol, an undertaking that seemed to take a long time. Something wrong with the mechanism, no doubt or perhaps the girl was nervous about meeting her unknown escort. Not like the other one, who appeared to be impatient, standing there so sweet and fresh looking, swiveling her head about with distinctly unmaidenly boldness.

As the trio halted midstreet, Aaron let his mind wander, ignoring his own command to banish Rumor from his thoughts.

Where was she now, at this very moment, two hours before noon on an August Friday? At the pianoforte in the little music room at Spenser House? More likely she was consulting with the cook on the menu for tonight's formal dinner where the British chief, General Henry Clinton, might well be a guest. Or she lay late abed after a night of love with a handsome bastard of a British officer. Despite a frantic effort to thrust it from him, the image burst forth in all its agony on his tormented brain. The two would be kissing good morning, her lips would be soft with sleep and remembered love. They would probably debate whether the captain or the colonel or the general perhaps had time for a last quick tussle in the rumpled bedsheets.

As a blind rage shook his gut, Aaron told himself that he had no right to even think about the lusty Lady Spenser. She thought him dead. A woman of her passionate nature could not be expected to live like a nun in his memory.

Perhaps Carter had reached New York, and reported him alive. But chances were slim that the man had even survived the fifty miles to New York from the tavern where they'd met. Beau Carter had been half dead from fever and a nasty knife wound. He'd been drinking heavily and had not a penny to his name. Aaron had given him supper but could do no more for Rumor's father. He had his own pressing business to pursue for the American forces.

Even if by some wild quirk of fate this vision in pink walking toward him under the enormous hat were Rumor, he was forbidden to tell her what was in his heart. He could not beg her forgiveness for the many months of silence. He could not tell her that he did not hate her for choosing her father over him at The Crooked Hill.

In New York at the Trinity concert, nursing those silly drums, he had longed to run to her, to fold her in his arms, to wipe away the pain of separation with his kisses.

"No dalliance this time, Aaron," the general had said sternly. "You are in New York to deliver congressional papers to one who will convey them farther to Philadelphia."

The papers, spirited away and hidden during the enemy occupation of the capital, had been in the drums. It was an almost foolproof disguise, even if he'd had to learn to pound the damn things enough to fool most people. Traveling with the woman had distinctly not been his idea, though. "Musicians always have a woman around," the general's advisers had insisted.

Luckily, the woman chosen for him had a loving husband in the army and expressed absolutely no interest in Aaron as anything but a companion.

There was to be no contact with Lady Rumor Spenser, Washington had warned. "Twice you've nearly lost your neck at a hanging party for that woman. If it happens again—" The general had left the sentence unfinished, but the set of his Roman senator face had been enough to frighten Aaron into strict obedience.

"You're no knight in shining armor," he'd added, with a smile to soften his harsh words. "You don't even own a white horse, let alone a suit of armor. So leave the fair damsel alone. Let her get out of her own scrapes."

Nudging Aaron with his elbow, Wilson exclaimed, "My word, what luck. They're both beauties, though I lay claim to the redhead in lavender. I like 'em plump, and the pinkie is a mite too skinny for my taste."

As they drew near, Aaron saw that the girl was slim almost to gauntness, but the breasts were full enough. Not that he had anything in mind but to pass the day as painlessly as possible and partake of supper later.

Laurens and the girls had stopped, two feet away, waiting for Laurens to make the introductions.

The proud head of the one in pink that had been sweeping about the crowd as they'd walked was now unaccountably lowered. Aaron could see nothing of her face for the enormous wide-brimmed hat that dipped low in front.

"May I present —"

Aaron paid no attention to the redhead's name. Without bothering to glance his way, she moved eagerly to Wilson, who took her hand in his. The two moved off, in deep conversation. The attraction was obviously mutual.

Lift up your head, damn it, girl. Aaron thought impatiently as he waited to be introduced.

Laurens was muttering something, but to his complete surprise, Aaron was so nervous he could not make out the man's words.

He caught the last of it, "Though of loyalist persuasion, she has left her crowded social calender in New York for an errand of mercy —"

Bowing from the waist, and clicking his heels in what he thought was a courtly gesture, Aaron quipped, "Beautiful ladies need not concern their pretty heads with politics."

"Oh, but I beg to differ, sir," she replied in a clear, resonant voice. Every word was distinct. "This is the eighteenth century, Major, and females are neither slaves nor children that they cannot choose sides in the wars that men make."

He had taken her extended hand, suddenly conscious of his rough fingers. His borrowed gloves had sprung several holes, and there had been no time to stitch them.

"Lady Spenser is of decided opinions, you'll discover," Laurens laughed. "As a Virginian, Fleming, you may find some of them not to your liking."

Her head came up at that, and he saw her face in full. The wide-spaced brown eyes were in shadow, but her face was so still, it could have been made of wax.

No one spoke for a long moment, and Laurens said, puzzled, "Have you two met, perchance?"

Somehow, from somewhere in his roiling brain, Aaron found words. They came out parrotlike, as if he had rehearsed them. "No, Lieutenant, the lady and I have never met. Once viewed, such beauty could not be erased from any man's memory."

"What a pretty speech," she murmured, but did not smile. She turned to Laurens. "You may leave us now for your other duties, Lieutenant, the major and I will get along famously."

When the officer was out of earshot, Rumor said, very softly, "So it is not a false report, after all. You are very much among the living."

He nodded, still holding her hand. She did not try to pull away. If only her face were not so pale and devoid of emotion! A bit of wind blew the brim of her hat away for a brief second, and the light-brown eyes stared back at him vacantly, as if he were a stranger.

Ever the superb actress, he mused.

In all his fantasies about how they would meet, and where, it had not been like this. In a milling crowd, with martial music blaring, all eyes upon them.

"Prithee, did the British cut out your tongue as well as disfigure your face?" she queried pertly.

For the briefest fraction of a second, the glassy eyes

386

softened, but then, quickly, they hardened once again. "Or has the proverbial cat got your usually wagging tongue," she added acidly.

Her mocking words came out in a rushing, breathless manner. The hand that now began to tug at his for release was trembling. The white bosom was moving in and out and the sweet little indentation in her throat that he always loved to kiss was palpitating like a little bird's that was fallen from the nest.

"Oh, my love, what cruel fate has parted us!" The anguished words were in his heart but what he heard himself saying was, "No, madam, my speech is very much intact."

"And the rest of you is healthy, I trust. Aside from the scar, of course."

"Courtesy of Colonel Higgins," he said sardonically.

Her eyes melted at that. "Calpurnia and Caesar swore you were dead."

"So it seemed. I was unconscious for a time, but when I awoke, I managed to struggle out of the place."

"I prayed—"

"Thank you."

Rumor's brown eyes were glowing now with a kind of luminous happiness mixed with pain. God, how was he going to get through the day without spilling out his guts to her? Had the general never been in love? What agony to withhold from the one you love the very thing that would ease her pain. If he could only shout, Darling, I love you, but cannot tell you how much. If he had any sense, he would beg to be relieved of this escort duty. Laurens could easily find another man.

A sudden blare of music from the platform precluding further speech, Aaron led her to the chairs. Laurens threw them a curious look, but mouthed silently, "Well done, friend."

387

A smiling mademoiselle, the one who had batted her dark eyes at Aaron earlier, pressed lemonade and cakes upon them. They sipped and nibbled, staring silently at the platform, where a man in black velvet was making a speech.

"He's the president of the Congress," Aaron offered helpfully.

She nodded distantly. Apparently she intended to make it difficult for him. Good. His chore as escort did not require him to be also entertaining.

During a lull in the festivities, she said coolly, "What brings you to Philadelphia?"

"My business is always secret," he replied. "You should know that better than anyone."

The soldiers on the green proceeded to execute a manual at arms, wielding their rifles and bayonets and swords with skill and ease. Curtly thinking she expected it, he explained the various maneuvers.

There followed a parade featuring cavalry on prancing horses, dignitaries in gilt carriages, and foot soldiers marching smartly in step to the music.

Her face remained impassive through it all, but when a group of captured British soldiers paraded by, she put her hand to her mouth in pity. "How sad, to be a captive."

His gorge rose. "It's them or us."

So it was true that she had become a turncoat, he reflected bitterly. Her vaunted Rebel sympathies had proved very fragile, like her love for him. If she were truly happy to see him alive and well, she could not possibly remain so composed.

After the formal program, the officers and their ladies walked to the river to observe the gaily decorated barges and warships. Because all were on military alert, boarding was not possible.

"I know little of ships and naval battle," he said

apologetically.

She smiled faintly at that. "As always you are too modest, Major Fleming."

A breeze cooling the river area, he suggested they promenade with the many others who were walking about, admiring each other's attire, as well as the fine old stately houses on the cobbled streets.

"Oh, what a beautiful house!" she exclaimed, pulling on his arm in front of a sprawling frame house with a sweeping veranda on front and sides. Roses tumbled down the terraces and trumpet vines shrouded the white-painted pillars.

"Reminds me of Golden Hill," he said, "and Albermarle."

She whipped round, eyes wide. "Do you know Albermarle?"

He hedged. "I've seen it. The Pamunkey River is not far from my own home on the Potomac."

Her face grew pink with excitement as she said softly, "One day, when this war is over at last, I intend to return to Albemarle with my dear father. My principal residence must be in England, of course."

So it's "dear father" now, he thought. That rascal Carter had ensnared her for certain.

"I hope your dear father is prepared to wield a hammer and saw and work from dawn to dusk," he said, casually rubbing at his scar. "There is little of Albemarle to come home to."

Her eyes grew wide. "I realize that it is in disrepair, but—"

"A British raiding party burned it to the ground, took what livestock there was, and set the slaves free. If it's any comfort to you, though, they gave the same treatment to Golden Hill."

Her carefully nurtured coolness vanished as the tears started from her eyes, coursing down her cheeks

389

unchecked. "Oh, Aaron, how terrible for you. You loved your home so much . . ."

She swayed toward him then, as if to fall, and with a groan, he caught her to him, holding her against his linen vest with both arms. Standing thus, she continued weeping, and to his consternation, Aaron found his own eyes watering. It was so like her to think of his tragedy, and not her own.

People were staring at them. A woman halted. "Is your wife ill, soldier?"

Shaking his head, he drew out his hanky, and thrust it into her face. Taking it, she withdrew to stand under an arching willow whose low-hanging branches half hid them from view.

"Forgive me for being such a fool. I don't understand myself. What with Charles so ill, and everything else."

Inhaling sharply, he waited for her to go on, to explain what "everything else" might mean. The general had demanded cruel silence from his subordinate officer. But not even George Washington himself could stop a woman from saying what was in her heart.

Dry at last, she turned a flushed face to him. "We had better return to the fete, Major Fleming," she said calmly.

"No—not yet."

She glanced up at him. "Was there something else you wished to say?"

"Only this," he half stammered, "you still have the land, it's a considerable frontage on the river. I offer my services and advice upon my own return to Golden Hill."

Favoring him with an icy stare, she stated, "Thank you, Major, but my husband Charles will take complete charge of any renovations that are needed."

Fortunately, they were not paired at dinner in the French pavilion. Aaron sat between two plump Philadelphia dowagers who regaled him with a point-for-point narrative of their respective family histories.

Away from his gloomy company, Rumor became her old charming self. From where he sat, Aaron had full view of her. She sat between a French admiral and an American cavalry officer, and smiled and flirted with her customary Jamaican aplomb. Both men looked completely captivated.

Dancing was announced on the several flagged terraces and in the grand ballroom. Dreading, but at the same tingling with the prospect of holding her in his arms, Aaron approached Rumor, who was chatting in rapid French with the admiral.

"I believe we are partners," he stated loudly, rudely interrupting the flow of French.

She looked surprised. The admiral scowled.

"Well, an escort is at least entitled to the first set —"

"I don't think I should partake of the dancing," she said, looking abjectly at her admiral. "My fiancé has been alone all day, and is looking forward to my tucking him into bed."

The admiral appeared devastated at the news but he took it gallantly. "Of course, Lady Spenser." He sighed. "Your Charles is a lucky man, to be the object of such devotion."

As they left the pavilion, she put a staying hand on Aaron's blue-coated arm. "Please, Major Fleming, I can walk home alone. I wouldn't dream of depriving you of the dancing."

"Nonsense," he snapped. "You know I detest dancing."

"Sir Oliver Mowbray turned a lively heel, as I recall," she replied impishly, squeezing his arm.

It was obvious that the lady had imbibed considerable wine at dinner. Her eyes sparkled, her cheeks were rosy, and the smile she gave him was soft and alluring.

Act quickly, Fleming, came a stern voice from within his heart. Or all is lost.

They were on the street now, and drawing her into a doorway, he took her by the shoulders. "Listen, Lady Rumor Spenser, soon to be Mrs. Charles de Borre. Sir Oliver Mowbray belongs to the past. So does Aaron Fleming as you knew him."

Taking a deep, hurting breath, he continued. "Damn it, woman, you and I and anything that passed between us is history. I will be grateful if you do not speak to me in intimate ways that might suggest to others that such is not the case."

With that, he all but pushed her into the street, and walked so rapidly that she was forced to run to keep up. She was quiet, like a child who's just been scolded severely. She clung to his arm, for that was the custom, and at this frantic pace, what else could she do?

"Here we are," he said with relief. The house was all alight, and rang with music and noise of revelry. "Please convey my warmest regards to Charles."

Without a word, she fled up the porch steps and into the house.

Just as she was closing the door, he shouted out, "I'll come to your wedding."

Then he turned, melting into the city.

"Rumor, come in here, girl."

Liz's merry voice rang out from the parlor where a party was in progress. Hesitating, Rumor prepared a little speech but as she moved into the crowded room, and saw the happy faces, all turned toward her expectantly, she thought "why not?" The night was young, and she was young. Life was not over just because a heartless man had said he no longer loved her.

The vivacious Mrs. Loring was surrounded by adoring swains. She introduced them to Rumor in turn, but the names flew past her, one merging into the other.

"Ah, so this is the angel of mercy whose name is on all tongues," commented a wickedly handsome naval officer.

"She's spoken for," Liz interjected. Taking the man's arm, she leaned against him in a distinctly proprietary manner. "And so are you, my pet."

The look that passed between the two told Rumor more than any words that Liz had found a man to share her bed. The officer was much younger than the matronly Mrs. Loring—not more than thirty. Shrugging, Rumor accepted a drink from another sailor, and launched into a polite patter about the heat, the parade, the simply marvelous French army.

But soon she found herself becoming restless, as she moved about the room. Seeing a pianoforte in a corner, she sat down and began to play.

Others drew round, and an hour passed before she was permitted to stop, begging fatigue. Liz had disappeared, along with her captain. Someone was kneading her shoulders suggestively from behind the piano bench.

Suddenly it all seemed sordid, all this pairing off for casual encounters. As if love were nothing more than a joining of flesh and a pleasure of a moment.

Blindly, fighting tears, she ran upstairs. Charles awaited her. Their love was pure and unsullied as yet by lust. She would spend the night on the chaise in his room. In the morning, she would urge that their marriage be celebrated within the week.

The second-floor corridor was quiet, only faint murmurs emanating from behind the closed doors. Surprisingly, the door to her fiancé's bedroom was also closed. It was always open, if only an inch or so, throughout the night. Was something wrong?

With thudding heart, she turned the knob, pushing gently so as not to waken him if he should be asleep. No candles were burning, but the moon was shining brightly through the open bay windows, lighting up his bed clearly.

Two heads lay on the pillows, or rather on *one* pillow, they were so close together. Yvonne sprawled face up on the coverlet, naked, her arm flung across Charles, who was also naked. His head was turned to one side, and his skinny legs were spread apart. Yvonne's one hand lay loosely atop his limp manhood in its nest of dark hair. Yvonne's light hair, unbound and gleaming goldlike in the moonlight, cascaded over her small, upthrust breasts. Through her slightly parted lips came the sound of her gentle, rhythmic breathing. On her face was the ineffably lovely look of a woman who has just been thoroughly and soundly loved.

As she gazed, transfixed, at the lovers, a line of poetry she'd once read crossed Rumor's mind. "Gather ye rosebuds while ye may, for old time is still a-flying."

Shrewdly, Yvonne had made the best of her day alone with Charles. Desperately in love, she had flaunted the rules. But all's fair in love and war, reflected Rumor. And rules were made to be broken.

The two looked so natural together. Rumor felt no rage or jealousy, or even very great surprise. Her only feeling was one of great relief. Another chapter in her life had closed.

Shutting the door without a sound, she stepped across the corridor to her own room. It had been closed up all day, and was stuffy. Moving to the bank of windows, she threw open the three panes, letting in the somewhat cooler night air.

Absently, she brushed aside some leaves from the sill. The housemaid had apparently closed the windows on the rampant vine that covered this side of the house. The vine was as old as the house, the maid had told her, and had a central trunk as thick as a young tree.

The city lay before her, vibrantly alive. Voices could be heard on the streets, couples passed to and for beneath the lanterns, stopping now and then to kiss.

A boat hooted from the river. Stars glittered in a summery sky. Life was going on its inexorable way without her. Aaron had abandoned her, Charles, whom she had cherished as a safe harbor, had been easily seduced by another.

Moaning in sudden fright, she shut the window against the pulsing city, then immediately opened it again. As Liz had said so often, her life was all before her. Carry on.

Slowly, moving as in a dream, she began to undress. The straw hat, the silk parasol, the satin shoes went first, thrown into the dressing room. Then, standing before the mirror, she unfastened the tiny buttons of her voile gown, whimsically counting them, one by one. There were thirty of them, down the back to the waist. She had to twist and writhe to get at the ones in the middle. It fell to the floor in a pink heap, followed quickly by three rustling taffeta petticoats.

Wriggling out of the loose muslin body shift, she stooped to pick up the lot, and stepping to the door of the dressing room, hurled them onto the pile of gowns already there, covering the floor. In her haste to dress this morning, she had slid the gowns from their hooks, examining them in turn, then let them fall to the carpet in an untidy pile. She would have the maid pick them up in the morning. Now she simply longed for bed and oblivion.

Standing a moment before the mirror in her white silk stockings banded by a pair of blue silk garters, Rumor appraised herself. So, two men did not want her. She would find another—that one, true, loving, caring man Mama had always talked about. Somewhere, sometime, he existed, and waited for her.

Cupping her white breasts with her hands, so that the long, firm nipples extended rosily, she slowly turned to one side, then the other. Too thin, she decided. The thighs needed more flesh. A man liked something to fill his arms. Calpurnia was always after her to eat more.

Yawning, she stretched so that her breasts uplifted. Shivering with delight in a sudden cool breeze from the windows, she watched as her nipples grew taut. A faint stirring of desire disturbed her loins. Shaking off the brief sensation, she bent swiftly and began to pull off her stockings.

"Allow me," a voice said softly, and to her amazement, the rangy figure of Aaron Fleming stepped out of the dressing room. Before she could straighten up, he put his hands on her hips and leaned down to kiss her buttocks, first left, then right.

"Swift attack is the best defense," he quipped.

Enraged, she whipped round and slapped him across the face, forgetting about the still tender scar. He winced with a quick pain, but instantly it was gone.

"How dare you. Oh, oh—this is the height of—" Taken by surprise, she could not find words to express her outrage. Her buttocks burned from his touch as if from a brand. Darting for the door, she put her hand on the knob. "I'll call the house steward—"

"The man is in bed with the housemaid. I doubt he'll be overjoyed at being disturbed to protect a lady's virtue."

Reaching her in a bound, he pulled her tight against

396

him, forcing her head back to meet his gaze. "Especially one whose virtue is a matter of history, having been taken long ago with much pleasure by a naked man in a stream in a certain forest in Manhattan."

"You're drunk," she muttered, but then his lips came down on hers, cutting off further speech.

It was the kind of kiss that shook her insides with a tiny earthquake. The kind that involved his tongue on hers, circling her mouth as if it were a cave he were exploring.

Desperately, she tried to break loose, but her struggles only served to intensify the pressure of his mouth on hers. She felt as if she were being consumed.

When it was over, he seemed shaken, too. Moving away, he mumbled, "Let's get into bed before I take you standing up with one stocking on and one stocking off."

"You're drunk," she said again, running to the dressing room to fetch a gown.

A maddening grin creased his hawkish features. His straight, even teeth showed dazzling white against against his deeply tanned skin. The jagged scar was pulsing vividly, as if it were alive.

Averting her eyes from the intensity of his smoky blue gaze, she stared at the hairy triangle between his white linen shirt, open at the neck. Her heart began to pound at the sight, and, fearfully, she slid down to gaze at the white breeches. That was no better. There was a prominent bulge in the stretched fabric between the sinewy thighs. Bits of leaves and twigs clung to the soiled white linen.

She gasped with sudden knowledge. "You climbed the vine, right into my room, like a—" Forgetting the robe, she ran to the window to peer out at the vine. "You could have fallen," she said, exasperated, "or someone could have seen you and summoned the police."

"I thought that you might be charmed if I played Romeo," he said gently. "So romantic, don't you think? I could have walked right in the front door and up the steps, but—"

Tilting back his head, he spread out his arms in a sweeping dramatic gesture, reciting in a loud voice, as if performing on a stage, "With love's light wings did I climb these walls, for stony walls cannot keep love out—"

It was the speech that Romeo made to Juliet after he had scaled the walls to her balcony by moonlight, and Rumor could not suppress a giggle.

"Shh," she cautioned. "Lower your voice, you'll wake up the house."

"Charles, perhaps?" He cocked a brow.

Her nostrils flared as she replied, "My fiancé is too weak to fight you, as you well know."

He pursed his deeply indented lips. "Well-l, perhaps Yvonne and he together might succeed in vanquishing me and throwing me back out the window."

Sighing with exaggerated resignation, he strode to the window, and placing his arms around her waist, drew her close. The blue eyes held a mocking glint. "Of course, they would have to take a few moments to don a garment, at least a robe or wrapper. Last I saw them, they were both mother naked."

"You wretch," she grated, trying without success to push him away. "You peered right into their window!"

"Yes." Brushing his lips on her cheek, he murmured, "You don't seem very heartbroken about being betrayed by your betrothed."

"They belong together," she admitted. "What Charles felt for me was infatuation."

His lips were at her ear, his tongue flicking along the tender lobe. All the blood in her body seemed to rush to the spot. She felt weak and helpless.

"And what did you feel for him, my love?"

Sudden anger cooled her rising blood, and pushing at his chest with two hands, she gritted, "What I felt for Charles is a kind of love beyond your understanding, Aaron Fleming."

A deep and throaty laugh rumbled in his chest, rising to his lips. "I suppose not. I know only what you feel for me."

"And that is?"

"Desire—mad, surging lust. It's in your eyes, Rumor, and the quickening of your breath. Your lovely face is flushed, and if I threw you on that bed right now, you would open up to me, like a flower to a marauding bee."

Blinded by fury, she yelled, unheeding of who might hear, "Then why in the name of all that's holy did you tell me in the street that all was over between us? That we were history?"

Their glances locked as a series of conflicting emotions passed over Aaron's bronzed face. She detected fear, agony, tenderness, wariness, pleading. The expression in the smoky blue eyes reminded her of the way Sir Oliver used to look at her when caught off guard.

Most of all, as she devoured the face of the man she would love forever, Rumor saw love. All the words in the world could never explain its power. She felt that she was swimming in a powerful stream, while irresistible currents swept her toward a destiny that would not be denied.

He did not reply to her question, offering no explanation for his callous words in the street. He wanted her, she wanted him. It was enough. This was no time to talk of the past, or the future.

The city throbbed behind them past the window.

Rumor's blood was pounding in her ears, demanding life.

"Let's stop talking," she muttered against his throat. "By this time, Romeo and Juliet would be in bed."

The first thing he did was take off her remaining stocking, sliding it down slowly, kissing each section of her leg as the smooth flesh was revealed.

"I hope you are in no hurry," he said, with a catch in his breath, "for I intend to love you within an inch of your life."

Next, he plundered her breasts as she lay outstretched, her head arched back. With each tug on her nipples, she groaned, feeling the response in her lower body. Her own breath was coming in fits and starts.

"Oh, please, Aaron, it's been so long, I cannot wait."

He took her then, savagely, poising his body over hers and quickly entering her. He filled her completely, resting a moment. Then with deep, powerful thrusts, he drew in and out before she spasmed and cried out. Her entire body seemed in torment, as her fingers dug into his buttocks, clutching the hard flesh as if in pain.

With a long, drawn-out sigh, he allowed himself to climax, his seed spilling into her for a very long time.

When it was over, he brought his face to hers. Both were moist with sweat. He spoke soberly. "When nature sends such ecstasy to a man and a woman, they are fools to prate about what is right and what is wrong."

They rested, then began the rituals, the sweet, tender, exciting play that they had practiced in their many times together in the past. His long fingers stroked every inch of her soft flesh, circling, circling, not only on her vulnerable breasts, but on the exquisitely tender flesh between her thighs. Teasing, he touched the sensitive place until she writhed and pleaded that he enter her again. But maddeningly, he desisted, playing coy. Again and again, he drew back until she was nearly mad with desire and forced his manhood between her thighs with her two hands.

She caressed him as he reclined, resting from his exertions, on the coverlet. For long periods, she would gaze at his powerful man's body, enraptured at the sight. This wonderful human being was hers, at least for tonight. Whatever happened in the future, if they never met again, if he took another to marry, he was hers for this night. All hers.

Kissing the tiny red turtle with her wide-open mouth was her special joy. She loved seeing his limp manhood become erect again as she caressed his sinewy flesh.

A warm, pearly dawn was silvering the windows when he awoke from a brief sleep and moved upon her once again.

"This has to last for a long time," he said, drawing her legs apart gently, raising her knees. Putting his strong hands on her buttocks, he lifted her to him so that their bodies touched.

Drowsily, she murmured, "I love you, Aaron. When you are gone, I am as if dead."

With exquisite slowness, he slid into her warm softness, then moved his hips in a circle, so that every part of her touched every part of him.

He did not thrust in and out with the harsh movements that would bring a swift fulfillment, but continued his circling, increasing in speed and intensity until they were both whirling their lower bodies in a kind of mad dance.

The tingling, sharpening sensations that accompanied each circling brought little cries of ecstasy to Rumor's lips. He did not touch her on any other part of her body. His hands were spread out on either side, as he loomed over her.

Throughout this last coupling, he gazed steadily at

her through hooded eyes, breathing heavily as he waited for her cries to reach the point of agony.

The sun was full up before her rapidly spiraling spasms brought a blinding, world-blotting fulfillment. Dimly, through the thundering clamor of her own body, she heard his shout of triumph and release as he stopped his circling to lie palpitating within her.

They lay together in the dawn, both drained and exhausted, as if they had been running for miles in a trackless forest.

Chapter Nineteen

Aaron stood at the window, arms extended to the wooden frames, gazing out at the waking city. In the street below a vendor called out, "Hot bread and sweet potatoes, tea, coffee—"

"I'm famished," Rumor said from the bed. "Call down to the vendor. Perhaps he has real tea."

She was still naked, lying in a dreamy mood beneath the coverlet, watching as Aaron had dressed.

"Sorry, real tea or not, our amorous interlude cannot extend to sharing breakfast," he replied absently. Turning round, he faced her across the room. He seemed distant, as if the intimacy of the past night had been a drama, staged for an unseen audience.

"You say that you are no loyalist, but remain faithful to the American cause," he stated. But it had the earmarks of a question.

"Yes," she said heatedly, sitting up. "Why is it so impossible to convince you? You forget that I was taken prisoner by the British and subsequently brought much against my will to occupied New York. It is difficult to change my residence. A lone woman cannot simply—"

Waving a silencing hand, he half turned to the

403

window, speaking stiffly, formally, his hawkish face in profile against the light.

"Prove your patriotism," he said curtly. "We need to know whether General Clinton intends to evacuate New York before winter and march with his regiments — now in the city — to the south."

"Don't you have many spies in New York who can easily find out," she asked, puzzled.

He laughed, dryly. "None that we can trust completely. Sadly, the Rebel army is ill-paid, if at all, and our men, many of whom unlike myself have families, are easily won over by British money. Reports have been conflicting, and General Washington fears that many are deliberately false."

"Well, General Clinton comes often to Spenser House, and talks freely."

"Listen hard to whatever he says. When you venture into the town, observe whether you think the number of soldier seems to be diminishing. If he moves, it will be in utter secrecy."

"I'll try—"

He whipped round, almost angrily. "To try is not good enough, Rumor. You must be absolutely certain."

At her frightened look, he added, "I will tell the general that you are to be trusted, as he trusts me." A wry grimace crossed his face. "I am certain he knows by now that I spent the night with you in dalliance against his express command. Your willingness to spy for us will go a long way toward his forgiveness." Coming to the bed, he took her by the shoulders, boring into her eyes. "Can I trust you, Rumor?"

Without hesitation, she replied, "Yes, my love. If it means my death, I will do this for you — I mean — for my country."

"Good. You are honest, whatever your other

404

faults." he said emphatically, brushing her cheek with his hand.

Quick anger surged at his condescending words, but repressing it, Rumor slithered back under the covers, remembering the night of love. Nothing else mattered.

She asked, "But how will I get the information to you? Will you come to New York to see me?"

A faint smile curled his lips as he replied, "I'll be there the night of October third. It is a Saturday. You will deliver your message during a drama you will be acting in."

"How clever," she breathed, "We are doing *Macbeth*. I am playing Lady Macbeth, of course."

"Of course." Planting a quick kiss on her brow, he jumped up again, and began to pace back and forth on the thick carpet. His big hands knotted together tensely behind his back, and two deep furrows of thought appeared between the smoky blue eyes.

"I know the play well," he said, "I saw it many times as a child with my mother in Williamsburg."

"I'd forgotten how much of a scholar you are on Shakespeare," she said admiringly.

"Don't speak, I'm thinking."

In the ensuing silence she could hear the sounds of the house waking up, the voice of the maid bringing morning tea to those who required it, the sound of footsteps on the stairs. What if the maid — or even Charles — should burst in upon them?

Facing her again, he said, "Is there a place in the play where the word 'north' or 'south' appears, spoken by Lady Macbeth?"

"Why yes, in the scene where she awakens at midnight and is walking though the dark, gloomy castle. The audiences love it, it's so dramatic."

Warming to her subject, Rumor chattered on. "The poor woman is wringing her hands in torment because

405

she has helped her husband murder his rival and—"

"Damn it woman, what does she say?"

Aaron's impatient shout was surely heard throughout the house and probably in the street as well.

Miffed, she replied, "She says—'There is a knocking at the south entry.' "

"Perfect."

Bending low to her again, he said, making each word distinct, "Now if Clinton is taking his troops from New York, say the line as written. If not, change the word to 'north.' Few will notice; those who do will think it a mere slip of the the tongue."

Kissing her briefly on the mouth, he strode to the door. "Farewell, darling, until October third."

"Wait!" Sitting up, she swung her legs over the side of the bed. "But what if something happens, what if I cannot say the line?" She took a deep breath. "What if the drama is postponed, or something happens that I cannot perform?"

For an instant, his face hardened, then a twinkle suddenly warmed his eyes. "See that all goes as planned, your ladyship. Are you not the queen of the New York theater? Can you not twist any man you meet around your dainty little finger?"

After he had gone, tramping boldly down the corridor, and pelting down the stairs as if he belonged here, Rumor sat a long time on the edge of the bed, thinking. The whole idea was absurd. It was another of his confounded games. He loved to tease her.

Surely the course of the war will not depend on whether I say "north" or "south" in a silly play, she mused.

Why could not the oh-so-clever Aaron Fleming infiltrate the New York social scene and find out himself? For a full year, he had done a masterful job as Sir Oliver Mowbray, fooling everybody, moving about the city with ease. If he had not decided to save her from her father's scheme, and been forced to uncover his disguise, he might still be there, wearing those outlandish clothes and talking in that ridiculous way.

Now that he was gone and she could straighten out her tumbling thoughts, she argued inwardly with herself. The man could not be serious about her becoming a Rebel spy. Her lover was testing her, to discover if her declarations of loyalty to America were genuine.

A sudden chilling thought came to her. Was it possible that he might decline to marry her if she should fail? Despite his great passion for her body, a rabid patriot like Aaron Fleming would be appalled at fathering children in a loyalist womb.

Her blood began to boil from her own imaginings. Did he take her for a fool? Men like Aaron always treated women as if they hadn't an ounce of brains. Why should she risk her neck just to prove a point?

Rising up, she dashed to the washstand. Pouring water from the ewer into the basin, she buried her burning face in it, till she cooled off. She was standing with the towel covering her face, when a sharp voice deep within her cried out, "Stop making mountains out of molehills, you idiot, the man has never even mentioned marriage — not once."

Casting the towel aside, she entered the dressing room, gazing helplessly at the pile of garments on the floor. Giggling at the thought of Aaron's huge body skulking beneath all those silky, scented gowns, she rummaged for a wrapper to cover herself.

She walked back into the bedroom shrugging into a pink silk peignoir. She would ring the maid for tea, then drop in on Charles, giving him time to dress and pretend innocence when she confronted him with what she had seen last night.

It promised to be great sport. Rumor imagined it in

407

her mind, thinking up choice words of accusation. "You and Yvonne are welcome to each other," she would say, wiping away a tear or two.

Her hand was on the embroidered bell pull when the door opened and Charles appeared, fully dressed. In fact, for the first time since his illness began, he was brilliantly attired in the powder-blue jacket and gold lace of his regiment. He looked the handsome soldier, though his Gallic face was still a little pale.

Walking toward him eagerly, she stretched out her hands in greeting. "I thought you still asleep."

"Let's not waste any time on evasions," he sneered, stepping nimbly out of her reach. "Yvonne and I both saw Aaron Fleming leaving your bedroom moments ago. It was apparent that he had spent the night with you. Do you dare deny it, Rumor? His light-gray eyes were hard. His entire body was rigid. He was the picture of outraged manhood.

The dramatic little scene that she had been rehearsing in her mind suddenly vanished. A huge sense of relief replaced it. You are honest, Aaron had said.

"I deny nothing, Charles dear. Aaron still lies within my heart, I fear. When I met him accidentally at the fete, I easily yielded to his blandishments."

Dropping her arms to her sides, she stood abjectly, her head slightly inclined, like a child being scolded. Then to enhance the image of contrition, she moved to the bed, pressing her cheek against the bedpost. Wrapping two hands around the polished wood, she inhaled, catching it at the end, as if suppressing a sob.

Seemingly unmoved by her display of emotion, he said, "In another time, I would challenge him to a duel, but we are patriots both, we fought together at Trenton."

His hand was on his sword, drawing it out a little from the scabbard. For a terrified moment she feared that, being unable to kill Aaron, he might run her through. No one would fault him. Unfaithful women were often slain by their cuckolded lovers, and society turned its head.

Speaking quickly, she wept, "Kill me, Charles, if you must. I am a harlot, victim of my own unruly passions. Lady Rumor Spenser is not worthy of a duel fought between two old friends."

His thin face showed his genuine surprise. He had obviously expected denial, defiance, evasions — anything but this abject confession. Sheathing his sword, he stepped to the bed and gently drew her hands from the post.

Holding them in his, he said gently, "I forgive you, Rumor, your passionate nature is one of the qualities that first attracted me to you." He sighed. "But as you freely admit, it is also a road to sin."

He kissed her lightly on the brow, as a priest might do to a penitent sinner. "Go in peace, my dear, and God bless you. Let us hope that some good man will marry you and save you from yourself."

Charles left then, hurriedly, seemingly anxious to be gone.

Rumor did not raise her head until she heard the door to his room opening and closing. She felt no anger toward the man, only pity. He's a fraud, she thought sadly. Weak, where Aaron was strong. Weak men cannot bear to be faced with the truth.

She felt ashamed of her earlier plans to make a scene about Yvonne. Aaron would be proud of her for sparing his old friend the humiliation of telling him that she knew about his own infidelity.

Her face wreathed in smiles, Rumor opened the door to the maid bearing a tray with a teapot and several cups. The girl looked around, surprised at finding her alone.

"I thought a gentleman had spent the night, milady. Will he be returning?"

Taking the tray and placing it on the bed, Rumor replied, sighing, "Eventually, my girl, eventually."

But as she drank the rich, dark, substitute brew of maple leaves and spices, and ate all four fat scones slathered with strawberry jam, Rumor did not feel as confident as her words implied.

In this world, nothing is certain, except that while one is living, life is good. With that consoling thought, she began to pack for the journey back to New York.

"What do you mean, I am no longer playing the role of Lady Macbeth?"

White with astonishment, Rumor faced her sister-in-law in her sunny bedroom. She had been home for scarce ten minutes, and was in the throes of unpacking with Calpurnia's help when Olympia had burst in, unannounced.

"My statement means exactly that," Olympia replied testily. "You can hardly expect to leave the city for three entire weeks and expect everything to be as you left it."

She drew herself erect. "You are not the important person you think, my girl. The officers in charge of the theater have appointed a new managing director."

"Who?" Rumor asked stiffly.

"None other than your own father" came a voice from the doorway. "Welcome home, my darling daughter."

Beaumont Carter rushed into the room enfolding Rumor in his arms, kissing her on both cheeks. Drawing back, he peered at her intently. "How pale you are, my dear. Frankly, I had expected a blushing bride. When will you and Charles marry?"

"Never," she replied crisply. "But more of that later. What is this I hear about your becoming theatrical director? You are hardly qualified."

Almost dizzy with shock and fatigue from the long journey, Rumor sat down on the bed, her hands knotted together tensely in her lap.

Stepping forward to take her father's hand, Olympia drew him to her side, her arm around his waist. "Isn't it the most stupendous news," the woman chortled. "The entire city is so pleased to have a genuine professional in charge at last."

"Professional?" Rumor raged, bolting from the bed. "What do you call my many years on the stage?"

Casting a withering look at her father, she spat, "Leave us, Olympia Spenser. I think my father and I have matters to discuss that do not concern you."

"Ah, but you are wrong, Rumor," her sister-in-law replied sweetly, with an adoring look at Beau Carter, who beamed in return. "Everything that concerns her husband concerns a wife."

"Wha-at?" Rumor's gasp brought Calpurnia from the armoire where she'd been arranging the wrinkled gowns. The nurse caught her mistress before she could slump to the floor in a faint, lowering her gently to the bed.

Rumor must have been unconscious for a few moments, because she awoke to the sharp tang of smelling salts in her nose and Calpurnia's worried countenance in her eyes.

"Father," Rumor said weakly.

"He's gone, and that fool woman with him," Calpurnia snorted. "I shooed them both out of here with orders not to come back for a week. The idea — springing all that bad news on you when you are barely home after a hard trip in the stage."

Meekly allowing Calpurnia to undress her and slip a

411

muslin shift over her head, Rumor murmured, "But a wedding is good news, my friend. They both look very happy."

"Humph. For my money they deserve each other."

The kitchen maid entered with a tray of tea and cakes. Dismissing the girl, Calpurnia took some dried leaves from a paper in her apron pocket, dropping them in an empty cup.

Pouring tea from the pot into the cup, she brought it to Rumor. "There's a sleeping herb in this," she said grimly. "I expected you would need it, what with all this excitement, so I had it ready."

As Rumor sipped the bitter brew, Calpurnia went about the sunny room, putting things in order, mumbling under her breath, "No more sense than a donkey, those two, acting like a couple of alley cats . . ."

Smiling, Rumor settled her head into the familiar pillows. She was home, Calpurnia was here, bustling about in her wonderfully capable way, and muttering threats against one and all who would dare bring unhappiness to her darling "child."

She should have a baby of her own to coddle, reflected Rumor drowsily. Or a dozen. She must inquire, first thing when she awoke and could speak rationally, if there had been any word from Caesar.

As for Olympia's nagging, she refused to worry about it. The triumphant bride and her handsome groom would be extremely busy cavorting about in the big bed down the hall. Newlyweds, especially ones well past their youth, as they two certainly were, couldn't get enough of each other.

As for losing her leading role in the play, and her father taking over her job as director, she would think about it later when she woke up.

* * *

It was three days before Calpurnia would permit Rumor to dress and resume normal life. Feeling refreshed, she sat down to a huge family breakfast with her father and her new stepmother. Briefly, without embellishment, she narrated all the events in Philadelphia, except for meeting Aaron and Charles's betrayal of her with another woman.

"Monsieur de Borre and I simply realized that what we feel for each other is not strong enough to base a marriage on," she stated.

From the look on Olympia's face it was obvious that she did not wholly believe her. "You poor dear," her stepmother exclaimed, placing a comforting hand on Rumor's as it lay on the snowy cloth. "Please feel that you can come to me at any time for—"

"Comfort?" Rumor interjected pertly.

"Of course, dear. What is a mother for?"

The woman's hazel eyes held not sympathy, but a glittering triumph at what she assumed to be her new daughter's humiliation at being spurned.

Tearing her eyes away, Rumor stared at the yellowing maples leading to the river. "Now that I am no longer in the play, I shall have to find other diversions to fill my empty hours. I cannot sew or knit for the soldiers, or even bake them cakes."

Her face alight, she stared at Olympia. "I have it. I love the outdoors. I shall take up gardening. Those maples are sadly in need of pruning."

Her plain face skeptical, Olympia withdrew her hand. "Our spacious park has in truth been neglected these war years. We had to let many of the outdoor staff go, for lack of ready cash. The able-bodied men have become soldiers. But perhaps you can hire a boy or two to help."

She turned to her husband. "What do you think, Beau? Shall our darling Rumor take up the hoe and

413

pruning shears?"

Carter put down his fork, and drained his coffee cup before replying. His voice was authoritative, as befits the master of the house. "Nonsense, dear wife. Simply because General Clinton's wife has been given the role of Lady Macbeth in our forthcoming production does not rule out the possibility of Rumor's appearing in a minor role."

"As a maid, or a stable boy?" Rumor snapped. There is no other feminine role of substance, save for the three witches."

"Ah, but I have a great surprise for you," exclaimed her father, leaning forward, his brown eyes glowing. "I have invented a role for you, my dear, that is guaranteed to bring down the house."

She would play the part of an angel, wafting down from heaven on a cloud, he explained, as both she and Olympia listened, astonished. He had been working with the carpenters for a week, devising a mechanism of ropes and pulleys that would bring her down from the rafters above the stage, and take her back again.

"I have seen it done in Charleston," he said, "and New Orleans as well. It never fails to rouse the audience to wild applause. You will be attired in gauzy white with a silver halo and glittering wings as wide as this." Standing up, her father spread his long arms wide to indicate the size of her projected wings.

His bride's rigid face made it clear that she did not entirely approve of all this glory for her stepdaughter. "It does sound rather tiring, and much too risky," she said tentatively. "What if the mechanism should not work. Rumor would crash to the stage and—" She put her face in her hands. "I forbid it, absolutely."

"Nonsense, dear wife," Beau Carter said again "Would I endanger my own sweet child's life?"

Rumor had other concerns. "Where does this won-

414

derful celestial being appear, Father. In what scene?"

Wringing his hands together dramatically, he began to pace back and forth on the dining-room carpet before the wide porch windows. "Lady Macbeth has awakened at midnight, and torments herself for the murder she has just committed. She thinks there is blood on her hands and she says, 'Out, out, damn spot—'"

"And then a knock sounds on the door, and she says, 'There is a knocking at the south entry,'" Rumor interjected.

"Yes, that's it."

"But, Father—an angel at that time? It is a dark, dismal scene."

"Precisely," he almost shrieked. "She has sinned, dreadfully, and thinks her soul is lost. She cannot pray. But a merciful God sends an angel down to earth to assure the woman that forgiveness will come."

Moving to her chair, her father turned her to one side, and grasped her by the knees. "It will bring down the house, my precious darling."

As she gazed into the luminous eyes so like her own, Rumor saw love and excitement in their brown depths. But she also saw a kind of wildness that struck terror in her heart. The man lived in a dream world. He always had, and probably always would. At this moment he seemed entirely divorced from reality. It would do little good to point out the absurdity of putting an angel in a scene meant to be dark and sinister.

"What does the angel say, Father?" she asked wearily, tenderly placing her hands on his.

Rising to his feet, he spread out his arms in winglike fashion once again, intoning softly in a comical falsetto—"'Your sins are forgiven, Lady Macbeth. This day thou shalt be with me in Paradise.'"

415

There was nothing she could say without hurting her father's feelings, if not offending him outright, so Rumor simply nodded. "Very good. As you say, the audience will adore it."

Rehearsals had been under way for a month, but the new manager required that all actors, no matter how small their roles, be present at all times. He was doing a magnificent job of directing, Rumor admitted grudgingly, commanding a respect, especially from the men, that she had never been given. He looked so handsome and debonair as he leapt about the stage, demonstrating the exact manner in which each scene was to played. Not only had her father invented an angel on a movable cloud, but had manipulated with breathtaking freedom many of the other scenes and lines. William Shakespeare is surely rolling in his grave, she mused.

As she lounged about the John St. theater waiting for her cue, Rumor kept her eyes and ears open as Aaron had advised. Not that her promise to spy meant anything now. She could not say the magic word "north" or "south" at the proper moment. If the whole scheme were no joke — if Aaron actually came to the theater on October third — it would be a waste of his time. He would assume that she had changed her mind, and she would never see him again. If she could only reach him to tell him the truth!

But how? He had said that New York teemed with Rebel spies. But who were they? How could she know them? Which of the many officers and merchants who were involved in the theater as actors or technicians was not a loyalist, as he claimed to be?

Tortured by uncertainties, Rumor went about her ordinary life in a trance. Calpurnia was worried.

"Are you pregnant by that Charles?" she asked in her customary blunt manner one morning as Rumor

416

woke with a blinding headache.

"No, you dirty-minded woman. The dashing Frenchman and I never got that close."

"Well—" Calpurnia's ebony eyes narrowed. "You didn't by any chance meet up 'accidentally' with Aaron in Philadelphia, did you?"

"I am not pregnant, by anybody," Rumor shouted, leaping out of bed and streaking, hand on mouth, to the washbasin, into which she retched for a long time.

Calpurnia's arms were about her. "Something's troubling you, child, you can tell your old nurse."

But she couldn't, Rumor thought miserably. A spy, even an unsuccessful one, is sworn to secrecy. Nobody must know.

Although her father had granted her leave from rehearsal for the regular Tuesday evening musicale slated for that evening it was called off.

"There were only ten here last week," she told a surprised Olympia. "Seems hardly worth the effort."

Disturbingly, more and more of Lady Spenser's invitations were returned with regrets. The one soiree she planned brought only five carriages to the broad driveway.

"Wherever you are, Aaron Fleming," Rumor had mumbled, as she'd climbed into bed that humiliating night, "you will be pleased to know that her ladyship Rumor Spenser is no longer the belle of New York."

She had not seen nor heard from General Clinton at all. Even if she could have said the magic word on October third in the play, she had not the slightest notion of the Royal Army commander's intentions to stay or go from the city.

"I think, Rumor, that you have cooked your goose as far as New York society is concerned," Olympia had remarked acidly one afternoon. "Running off like a camp follower to the American capital, brazenly chasing after a wounded French officer. No one can trust you now."

"I cannot help what people think," Rumor had replied evasively. "My politics have not changed."

Olympia had pursed her lips. "So you say. But there are those who take you for an American spy. Your claims of being held captive at Valley Forge are being seriously questioned by many in high places."

"Me a spy?" Rumor had laughed aloud. "How ridiculous!"

It was just as well the way things turned out, mused Rumor. She could not carry out her mission in any case. Aaron would despise her forever, but at least she would not arouse suspicion for changing a mere word.

Olympia Spenser and Beau Carter appeared to be supremely happy. Family breakfasts and long, cozy dinners in the spacious, portrait-hung dining room were not the tiresome affairs Rumor had anticipated.

The two were genuine lovebirds. The formerly haughty woman hung on her new husband's every word as if it were a pearl of wisdom. She, too, had been given a small part in the play, and made herself indispensable backstage helping with the many props.

Only one cloud darkened the general bliss. In a word—money. At least once at every meal, Olympia would gaze out the windows at the still unkempt garden.

"Ah, to think that this beautiful house will be lost to me. I've been so happy here."

The first time it happened, Rumor had asked, "Lost? What do you mean, Stepmother?"

Turning a look of pained surprise on Rumor, Olympia had almost moaned, "Why, darling, when you return to England to claim your part of the vast Spenser money, you will surely sell this place. You surely will not want to have it a millstone around your neck."

"Who said anything about returning to England?"

Beau had looked at them both over his wine. "What my bride is trying to say is this, Daughter. You have all the money, while we—my wife and I—are penniless."

"But you have an allowance," Rumor had gasped.

"A pittance," Olympia had spat out. She had burst into tears. "If only we could keep Spenser House."

Feeling somehow overwhelmed with guilt at being rich, while these two deserving people were poor, Rumor had leapt to her feet, and coming round the table, embraced her stepmother. "Everything I have is yours, Olympia. I thought you knew that."

Glancing with brimming eyes at her father, she had almost wept. "When the war is over, we are all sailing back to England on the first ship that crosses the Atlantic."

Olympia had sobbed out her gratitude. "Oh, what joy to see my childhood home again, even if it can never be mine so long as Rumor lives. It's such a beautiful castle, people come for miles to gaze at the Norman turrets and stained-glass windows."

But Carter's face had darkened. "You must see it alone, dear wife, for England is a country to which I can never go."

Olympia had gaped in genuine astonishment, but Rumor waited for the story, her face impassive.

In low, dramatic tones, he had related the story of the murder, which Aaron had hinted at to Rumor. "As a youth, I was wild, spent my days gaming, womanizing, riding fast horses through the Virginia countryside."

One day at dawn, he had lifted his rifle and shot a young neighbor, mistaking him for a deer. Her father's brown eyes had been wide and shining with torment, as he had moaned, "The boy I shot was Jack Tarleton, an only son." He had paused, swallowing his tears. "He was the last of his line."

The Tarletons were a vengeful lot, he had continued, not only banishing him from the commonwealth, but writing to their kin in England that if Beaumont Carter ever set foot on that island empire, he was to be summarily imprisoned and tried for murder.

Rumor had kept her eyes downcast, lest her father had seen the question in them. Aaron had said Beau Carter had killed a man in a duel fought over a woman. Whatever the real truth, it was obvious that her father was terrified of living in England.

"We will hire the finest lawyers," she had ventured.

He had shaken his head, running his long fingers through his graying brown hair. "My informants tell me that the English Tarletons are twice as powerful and wealthy as the Spensers."

"Oh, botheration," Rumor had yelled, slamming her fist on the table, "all this talk of money and where we are to live is giving me a headache. To hell with England and old castles in Scotland."

Olympia had looked shocked, and Beau simply had gaped.

Leaping from her chair, Rumor had faced them both with flaming face. "We still have Albermarle. The house has been burned out, they tell me, by the British. But we can rebuild. The land is there."

Magically, her father's thin face had been transformed. He flashed a beatific smile. "Oh, Daughter, that is my dream."

Childlike, he had clasped his hands together in the air. "Oh, to ride to the hounds again through the lovely woods, to glide in a birch canoe on the beautiful Pamunkey—"

"But I thought you were banished by the Tarletons," his wife had exclaimed. "How can you possibly live in

420

Virginia? The family will surely want to avenge the boy's death."

"Oh—that." He had gotten up and hugged her from behind her chair. "The Virginia Tarletons are all dead, have been for years."

From the evasive tone of his voice, Rumor had guessed that there had never been any Tarletons at all in that section of Virginia. The whole story had been a figment of her father's fertile imagination.

Stiffly, her stepmother had spoken to Rumor, her hand clutching her husband's. "You own Albemarle also, as you do the Spenser castle, Rumor. You will marry, and bear children. How can we be sure you will not turn us out?"

Thoroughly exasperated, Rumor had groaned, Nothing is absolutely sure in this life, Stepmother dear."

Carefully, Olympia had pried her hands loose from her husband's, and pushing back her chair, had walked out of the room, with measured step, as if she were a condemned prisoner going to her execution.

October third dawned brilliantly clear and warm, a lovely Indian summer day. Gazing out over the rooftops of New York from her window, Rumor said dully, We'll have an overflow crowd at the theater tonight, Calpurnia."

As she turned back into the bedroom, the other clucked her tongue, shaking her head in her ruffled white house bonnet. "Listen to me, child. Don't go on stage tonight. Have you taken a good look at yourself in the mirror?"

Lifting up her thin arms, Rumor drew off her nightshift, mumbling under her breath, "I'll be fine. Stop your fretting."

421

But deep within her she knew Calpurnia was right. She needed no mirror to tell her that she was rapidly becoming a shadow of her former blooming self. Deep shadows underscored her brown eyes, her once lustrous pale-ivory skin was pale and brittle to the touch.

If worry could kill a person, she mused, then she was not long for this world. What's more, her daily retchings into the washbasin confirmed her fears that she was carrying Aaron's child. Of course the nurse knew it also, but wisely did not question her about Aaron's whereabouts.

"You're likely to slide right off that wooden cloud tonight," she muttered, half angrily, as she went downstairs to fetch Rumor's morning tea. "And not only injure yourself but that poor, innocent babe as well."

As they breakfasted in the sunny bedroom together, Rumor tried to reassure the servant. "That cloud mechanism is perfectly safe, dear one. We've rehearsed the procedure fifty times at least."

"Don't know why you have to do it at all."

"The show must go on," Rumor quipped.

Though the curtain would not rise until eight o'clock, the theater was already filled by five. Those who were not privileged to purchase box and reserved seats, arrived hours early to get seats in the pit, bringing families and dinner in a basket.

Because tonight's performance was for charity, the usual rule forbidding babies and children had been suspended. As Rumor moved toward the stage through the theater, the place resembled a country fair. A carnival atmosphere prevailed.

Anxiously, she scanned the sea of heads, looking for anyone who might conceivably be Aaron in disguise. But there were so many tall men, so many with hawk-like faces. Even if she were able to say "north" or "south" as they had plotted in that Philadelphia bed, oom, he would not have been able to hear her in all his din.

Backstage, in a large common dressing room, Calpurnia helped her get into the intricate angel costume. A beaming Olympia ran about importantly, issuing orders to the volunteer technicians and carpenters.

"Just checking your cloud for one last time," she smiled at Rumor.

Looking strikingly handsome and professional in a superbly tailored black velvet suit, Beaumont Carter glided about, giving last minute directions, reassuring the nervous amateur performers.

When the second act curtain went up, he was at Rumor's side, helping her onto the wooden cloud. It was a piece of hard pine, carved out in the outline of a puffy cloud. The top had been roughened by a saw to ensure that Rumor would not slide on a slick surface. Underneath was an arrangement of humps and sharp places to further enhance the realism of a cloud.

Fearfully, Calpurnia had inspected the ropes and pulleys herself, running her strong brown hands up and down and around. "They all seem strong enough," she grumbled to Rumor. "The ropes are not made of hemp that might fray, but of a strong, resilient reed that has been highly waxed."

The wooden pulleys through which the reeds must pass were reinforced with leather. Sandbags provided the needed ballast.

"Though I hate to admit it," the nurse said grudgingly, "your father is a genius. The whole affair is very clever. You'll be fine. Just hold on tight."

As Rumor climbed onto the wooden cloud, her father arranged her body and hands in the exact positions they had rehearsed.

"Now don't hold on so tight, you'll look tense," he

cautioned. "And please, please, don't look so grim
Angels of mercy should come down from heaven
smiling and floating on air."

She was raised, with her cloud, to the rafters, await
ing the cue for her to descend and say her line.

Amazingly, when the curtain went up on the dark
castle scene, the crowd had settled down to a breath
less quiet. The wailing babies were apparently all
asleep. Maud Clinton made a somewhat fatter than
usual Lady Macbeth, but came onstage wringing her
plump hands in suitably tragic manner. She walked
stiffly to center stage.

"I hear a knock at the south entry," she cried in a
loud voice.

"Now," Beau Carter hissed.

As the wooden cloud began to lower toward the
stage, Rumor felt as though she were really coming
down from heaven. The part was a cameo, but she
would give it her best, as always. She forgot her
troubled stomach. If Aaron was out there, waiting for
an answer that could not come, she refused to think
about it another second.

The cloud stopped a few inches above Lady Mac
beth's head, and Rumor said her line in her resonant
stage voice. " 'Your sins are forgiven, Lady Macbeth
This day thou shalt be with me in paradise.' "

Not a sound came from the packed house, then a
uproar such as Rumor had never heard erupted from
every box and throughout the pit. Those who were no
standing stood up and stamped their feet.

Flushing beet-red under her stage makeup, Maud
Clinton took a deep bow. But it was the marvelously
beautiful angel that audience wanted.

Though waves and waves of applause resounded
mixed with bravos, Rumor did not move, remaining
statuelike, as befits a heavenly being. But within, she

exulted. Father had been so right. The un-Shakespearean angel was the triumph of the evening.

Slowly, the applause thinned out, and the cloud began to lift upward once again. As she neared the rafters, Rumor felt a tiny tremor, but passed it off as dizziness. Too much excitement, Calpurnia would say.

But in an instant, just as she cleared the framework at the top of the stage, she felt a second tremor, this one more decided. It was definitely not her stomach this time. At this point the curtain would close for a few seconds, allowing time for her cloud to be lowered again so that she could remove herself. She could hardly stay up there throughout the entire scene.

The stagehands were at the curtain ropes, ready to pull, when, unexpectedly, the cloud began to descend. The audience, thinking the angel was coming down for a bow, renewed its noise.

"Please, Father," Rumor groaned. "No more of this."

But — no — she was up again, and swaying from side to side. Suddenly, with a violent jerk, the cloud tilted sharply almost overturning. Despite her frantic clinging to the sides, Rumor slid off, plummeting to the hard boards below.

Falling on her back, her glittery wings outspread, she gazed helplessly at the jagged bottom of the cloud as it hurtled down toward her. Dimly, through her terror, she knew that she would die. Her last thought was of Aaron. "Oh, darling, forgive me, it's just as you said it would be. My father has managed to kill me after all."

She closed her eyes, murmuring, "Father I forgive you." Rumor Seton would not go into eternity with the sin of unforgiveness of her soul.

But instead of the sharply carved ridges and bumps of the cloud's underside, Rumor felt the bruising impact of a body on hers. There was a muffled groan, then nothing.

Her eyes flew open. At first all she could see was the top of a graying head just under her nose. A face had pressed so tight against her mouth she had to gasp for breath. As she did so, the head lolled to one side, and she glimpsed her father's still features.

The stage erupted, as shouts rang out.

"Don't move her—her backbone may be broken."

"Get this damn cloud off Carter."

"Careful, he's bleeding like a stuck pig."

Misery such as she had never known filled Rumor's heart as she realized what had happened. She had thought him a murderer, when her father had given his life to save hers.

She tried to raise her head as they lifted her father's limp form from hers. "Father, Father, forgive me," she moaned.

"Shh, darling, don't try to talk, or move a muscle."

"Aaron?" Ignoring his command, Rumor tried to rise, but was promptly pushed back down by her lover's strong hands. Then, his beloved face, the stage, the noise—all dissolved into a world of darkness.

When she regained her senses again, another face was bending over her. "I'm a surgeon," he said kindly. "Be still, Lady Spenser, whilst I examine you."

Quickly, gently, the man moved his fingers, probing at various places in her body, reaching under the billowing boned skirt and numerous petticoats. His hand on her neck, he lifted her slightly, feeling her backbone.

The wings were fastened to a thickly layered padded cloth between her shoulder blades. Impatiently, he nodded to Calpurnia. "Remove this thing, please."

Kneeling, the nurse unfastened the cumbersome wings.

426

"You may not be an angel from heaven, young woman," the doctor muttered after some minutes, "but you surely had one watching over you tonight. A fall such as you took could easily have broken your neck. As it is, you seem to have suffered only a few bruises from when your father's body hit you."

He nodded to Calpurnia. "You may remove the skirt now, but be gentle, so as not to jar her." To Rumor he said, smiling, "You may thank the thickness of your costume and the cushion that bound those wings to your back for saving your life."

"Aaron," Rumor whispered, clutching the doctor's arm, "is he really here, or did I only dream it?"

"I'm here, darling, I'm certainly no dream." Swiftly coming from backstage, he bent to kiss her on the brow, then softly on the lips.

The doctor smiled. "You may clasp her hands," he said to Aaron. "They suffered no injury."

"Father, is he—?" Stiffly, Rumor moved her lips to ask the painful question.

"He died almost instantly, darling, one of the jagged edges of the cloud went right through his heart."

"Damn dangerous thing," the doctor muttered, getting to his feet. He shook his head. "I always knew that theater people had little sense, but devising a fool contraption like that cloud is begging for an accident to happen."

With instructions to Aaron and Calpurnia regarding Rumor's care for the next few days, the doctor left. Calpurnia fetched a light cloak to cover her, and gently, as if she were a basket of eggs, Aaron lifted her up into his arms and carried her out through the stage door into the Spenser chaise.

"Where's Olympia?" Rumor asked, as the horses started toward Spenser House. "Is she with Father? How she must be suffering!"

"Last I saw her," Calpurnia commented cryptically, "she was wringing her hands just like that Lady Macbeth, and wailing that your father was a damn fool and that they could have had it all."

There was a stunned silence, then Aaron said quietly, "Rumor, this was no accident. While the surgeon was examining you, I inspected the mechanism."

Pausing, he held her tight against him as she sat on his lap. "One of the sandbags had been slit. As the sand slowly filtered out, the cloud began to tilt. The cut had to have been made while you were halfway up listening to the applause."

"It was no accident," Calpurnia broke in.

No one said a word to that, fearing to express the horrible thought that Beau Carter had tried to kill his own daughter, then, repenting at the last minute, gave his own life to save her.

Finally, as they drew into the curving driveway, Calpurnia muttered. "It was that she-devil, I know it. Your father didn't go near that cloud or the ropes or pulleys the whole time you were up above in the rafters."

Inhaling deeply, she pronounced, "Beaumont Carter was at my side, just beyond the curtain, beaming, whilst the audience was applauding. I've never seen a man prouder of his daughter than he was at that moment."

Aaron groaned, as he inched backward out of the chaise, holding tightly to Rumor. "That's what Olympia meant when she said that your father was a damn fool."

"Don't," Rumor begged. "Please don't talk about it now. Just take me up to bed and hold me tight all night."

While Calpurnia undressed the shaken Rumor, Aaron slipped out of the ribbed, cotton vendor's su

428

he'd been wearing. He had come to the John St. heater with a sack of candied apples on his back, a rumpled felt hat on his head.

"I looked through the crowd," Rumor groaned, "and missed you completely. I expected something much more fanciful from you—a clown or a grand-duke or something equally outrageous."

They talked no more, but lay naked, side by side, bodies touching, kissing now and then. It was enough for now. Aaron did not speak of the future. He would have to leave by morning.

They would be married, he promised, at the first opportunity. "If only I could take you with me," he muttered into her hair. "Some wives travel with their men, but I never know from day to day where I will be."

"Calpurnia will care for me, sweet," she responded. "You are with me always."

Covertly, she touched her stomach, praying that the fall or the impact of her father's body had not injured the child within her womb. He must not know about the child, not now. Her lover had a war to fight.

Seconds before they fell asleep, when the house was quiet and the moon shone brightly through the window, she murmured into his ear, "North, darling."

"What?"

"Your newest spy is giving you the information you asked for. I think General Clinton is keeping his army in the north."

"You silly goose, of course he is," Aaron chuckled, holding her so close she could hear his heart pounding in her ear.

The following Monday, an item appeared in *The New York Gazette* reporting a tragic accident at the

John St. theater, Saturday last.

"The life of the director, Beaumont Carter, was snuffed out, as he heroically saved that of his daughter, Lady Rumor Spenser."

The item was lengthy, extolling the achievements of the late Mr. Carter and his talented daughter. The mechanism that had failed was described in detail. The editors cautioned that no such risky stage arrangements should be attempted ever again.

"Perhaps it is a judgment," the writer pontificated. "Creating angels and wafting them up and down in the air is flying in the face of God. Man—or woman—was not meant to fly."

Burial would be private, in the family cemetery in Virginia, the item concluded. The widow, Olympia Carter, was prostrate with grief and was under a doctor's care.

Weeks later, one of the kitchen maids reported to Calpurnia that she had seen Mrs. Olympia Carter in the kitchen that fateful night, shortly before Lady Spenser had returned home with Mr. Fleming.

Calpurnia relayed the story to Rumor. "The woman was putting a knife back in a drawer."

Since the night her husband died, Rumor's step-mother had kept to her darkened bedroom. Her meals were brought to her, and according to the servants, she never moved from her bed.

"Leave her to heaven," Rumor sighed. "I'll not seek earthly justice for my father's death."

"She killed him," Calpurnia retorted, "and almost killed you, too. She should hang."

Rumor put a hand to her gently swelling belly. The babe was intact and growing. The hoops and bones in the skirt, added to the numerous petticoats, had saved it.

"What punishment," she murmured with brimming

eyes and aching throat, "what degree of suffering devised by man can be more excruciating than having to spend the rest of your life without the one you love?"

She did not have to add the obvious — that knowing you have killed your lover must be untold agony.

"If God is kind," she whispered, "he will afflict poor Olympia with madness."

Epilogue

Rain had fallen heavily throughout February, and the Pamunkey River had overreached its banks. Rumor stood on the Albemarle Wharf in the chilly dawn and gazed down into the swirling water. Kneeling down on the damp wood, she bent low, lowering the long measuring stick in her hand to hold it tightly against the piling.

The wharf and pilings were brand new, having been constructed last November by Caesar and a crew of volunteers from neighboring plantations. Fearfully, he drew it up, examining it in the pearly daylight. Her heart leaped for joy. The watermark was down at least a foot from yesterday. The Albemarle Wharf was safe. The pilings would not be swept away by the swift current.

Caesar had assured her that the cedar pilings were here for eternity and beyond, and would outlive anybody now residing on the Pamunkey. But stubbornly Rumor walked down each dawn to the river to gaze rapturously at the long, pitched-daubed wharf, reasuring herself that it was still there.

433

Dawn was her favorite time of day. The world seemed newer, the smell of the fresh-plowed earth more pungent. She loved to gaze about, alone, at the rolling countryside, the wide river, the branching trees along the banks.

It all seemed like a dream.

The first year that she and Calpurnia had lived at Albemarle, there had been no wharf. There had been little else of anything at all. Two rooms of the mansion were still under roof, the barn and tobacco curing shed were burned-out hulks. The chicken house was a pile of rubble.

That first hard winter they had lived on turnips, carrots, and potatoes dug out of the ground and two bags of flour the raiders had overlooked. The furniture gone, they had slept on the floor. Now and then a chicken wandered down the road and was roasted over the firepit in the kitchen.

In the spring, Martha Washington had sent some provisions by boat, along with some dinnerware and a few bolts of cloth from her store at Mount Vernon.

Rumor rarely thought of those hard times now. The spring of '79 had brought other blessings. Aaron and Caesar had arrived by horse in April, accompanied by a preacher from Alexandria. The preacher had lost a leg to a musket ball whilst ministering to a dying soldier, but a grinning Aaron had announced that "his marrying parts were still intact."

Rumor had been Mrs. Aaron Fleming two weeks when she gave birth to a son, whom the preacher (who had lingered for a long visit) christened George David, after Aaron's adopted father and Rumor's stepfather.

Having lost an arm in battle, Caesar remained at Albemarle as overseer. In May, one short week after his son was born, Aaron returned to the war. In the three years since, Rumor had not seen her husband. Exactly two letters had arrived, both less than a page in length.

"Not a cloud in the sky, the men think they can start plowing the wheat field." Calpurnia's musical voice preceded her down the path from the house.

Turning, Rumor smiled affectionately. Far advanced in pregnancy, the woman walked slowly these days, and had developed the habit of throwing her voice ahead of her. Rumor was still on her knees, her cotton skirt spread wide about her.

As the nurse finally stepped onto the wharf, she scolded, "You should not climb down that rocky path, darling. If you should fall—"

"Not going to fall," Calpurnia retorted tersely. She grabbed hold of a young cherry tree, one of an avenue planted two springs before. "It's best to stay on your feet till your time comes. Makes for an easier birth. In Jamaica the women have them in the cane fields, and get right back to work."

"Well, there are no cane fields here, and you're one Jamaican who's going to have her child in the proper way. In a bed, with a midwife and a doctor, if you need it." Calpurnia was well into her thirties and was having a difficult pregnancy.

Together the two women walked back to the house, the older leaning on the younger. Albemarle now had five rooms fit for habitation. Caesar had worked wonders with the charred bricks and timbers from their own woodlot. Many of the slaves who had been driven off by the British had returned, and were more than willing to work for a bed and what food they could be given. Rumor had freed them all, spending a bit of rare cash to have papers drawn up for each.

The father-to-be himself met them on the veranda. 'Got four hogsheads of cured tobacco for the boat tonight," he announced proudly.

"Wonderful," Rumor exclaimed, clapping her hands together. "Four? How much money does that mean?"

"No money," he replied, "but I'm getting a stud bull and plenty of seed for clover and hay from the folks at Elm Hill."

Rumor laughed, throwing up her hands. "Forgive a stupid woman, Caesar. I clean forgot that cash has become a forgotten commodity in these parts."

Everything was obtained by barter, as the families who had suffered the ravages of war struggled to rebuild, trading what they had for what they needed.

Casting a worried glance at his wife's distended belly, Caesar kissed her, hugging her fiercely with his one strong arm. "Send a boy the minute you feel a pain."

Grimacing, Calpurnia pushed him toward the veranda steps. "As if you'd be any help!"

Three-year-old George was in the kitchen, being fed breakfast by Sue, a dusky fourteen-year-old. He was excited as a caged monkey, jumping up and down in his little chair.

"When will the boat be here, Mama?" he asked as Rumor gave him a morning kiss.

Smilingly, she smoothed down his stubborn reddish cowlick. "By nightfall, we hope. It all depends on when it leaves the last plantation."

Child and maid left for the river, where they would probably spend the day, playing endless games of tag and hide-and-seek in the willows with the children of the Albemarle servants and the neighbors who had no wharf.

Rumor saw that the wharf and shoreline were already filling up with other watchers. A ship arrival meant a celebration, a holiday. Cargo from the North meant tea, coffee, cloth, nails, needles—all the many

436

things one simply could not buy in the South.

A ship also meant mail—letters from loved ones still not home from the war.

A wild boar brought down by Caesar's rifle would be roasted on a spit over a bonfire. The children would be allowed to stay up past their regular bedtimes.

"At least he didn't ask if his daddy would be on this boat," Calpurnia sighed as she served up a simple breakfast of biscuits and tea and honey. "Perhaps he has given up hope."

"Not a chance." Rumor replied. "He mentioned it last night as I was tucking him into bed." She chuckled. "I think he expects to see his father at the helm, in a pirate hat and flowing cloak, brandishing a glittering sword."

"It's that husband of mine who fills the boy with outlandish stories about pirates," Calpurnia grumbled.

Throughout the long, warm day, Rumor paused frequently in her chores to gaze down over the grassy slope toward the river. There was no real need to watch. A shipboard cannon would boom, when the prow came round the bend.

She tried not to hope that this boat would bring Aaron back to her and his child. He might not come by water at all, he'd said in his last letter, written last summer.

"Mrs. Washington has promised me a bay mare. I may stop at Mount Vernon and ride it home to Albemarle. Sending it by boat is too costly."

In addition, travel by land was dangerous these war years. Whole bands of robbers and vagrants terrorized both lone riders and those who came by carriage.

At dusk, after an early supper, Rumor retired to her bedroom to pore over the plantation bills and write some letters. Despite the fact that she had remarried, she kept up a correspondence with the Spenser cousins in England. While her remarriage deprived her of the Spenser inheritance, she was to be granted a small financial settlement. The money, however, would not be available until the war was well over.

One day, she hoped, she and Aaron would visit England. Jamaica, too. Though to tell the truth, Caesar and Calpurnia rarely spoke of their childhood home. She herself had almost forgotten the sunny isle where she had grown up and begun her stage career.

Liz Loring wrote several times a year. Her dearest friend had married the young officer she'd met in Philadelphia and maintained a house in New York. Her last letter had arrived in December.

> . . . The British are still here in the city. That idiot Clinton, with typical British arrogance, refuses to acknowledge that the war was lost at Yorktown in October. Your ex-stepmother has gone completely out of her mind, and has immured herself in Spenser House. Only one old servant has remained to care for her. Your generosity in deeding the house to the woman is commented on by many here.
>
> Your husband paid me a call last week. He bids me tell you he is well and may see you in early spring. General Washington cannot dispense with his services as yet . . .

Lifting her head from her cluttered desk, Rumor rose up and flung herself upon the bed. She suppressed the tiny surge of resentment within her. She would always come second best to George Washington in Aaron's heart.

It could be worse, she mused. Many men love their horses or even their hunting dogs more than their wives.

The spacious second floor end room was a pleasant, sunny place and Rumor spent many hours here. Her father had been born in it, though not on this bed.

The golden oak four-poster, along with the Chippendale desk, the damask-covered chaise, the tall bureau, and several colorful rag rugs had been shipped by river at Aaron's order from Golden Hill.

"By some miracle, my mother's bedroom furniture was spared in the fire that gutted the rest of the house," he had written. "The tenants moved out some furniture before the British arrived."

Rumor brooded often about where they would live when Aaron finally returned. His own plantation, Golden Hill, was close to his heart. True to his word, George Washington had managed to get it back for his favorite spy.

Would he ask her to leave Albemarle, after all the hard work she had done to restore it to a semblance of its former glory? Could she expect Calpurnia and Caesar to accompany her north to the banks of the Potomac? They both loved it here, had made friends with many of the workers on neighboring plantations. She would have to sell Albemarle or lease it to strangers. The very thought filled her with dread.

Or—and this was often her fondest wish—they would sell both plantations and emigrate to the Ohio Country. Several of the Pamunkey River families had done so. Congress had granted each man who had fought in the struggle for freedom a tract of wilderness land. Aaron had been awarded a thousand acres of land no hand had ever tilled.

She imagined the two of them and little George somewhere along the shiny banks of the great and beautiful Ohio. Aaron would build them a log cabin, like the one in Barren Hill where they had been so happy. (Little George could help him, he always talked of how he would help his daddy when he finally came home.)

Rumor put a hand on her brow, stroking away the beginnings of a headache. There were so many things to worry about.

She must have dozed, for she awoke in the dark to the noise of a booming cannon. The windows of the old house rattled, and a portrait of Aaron's mother fell right off the wall onto the carpet.

Her heart thudding, Rumor slid of the high bed and flew to the washbasin to splash water on her face. Bother that Calpurnia. She should have awakened her. This was no day to be lazily drowsing about.

Only one party frock hung in the swirled oak armoire. Rumor wore it when company was expected and for the rare social occasion such as a ship arrival. The others from the extensive wardrobe she had owned as Lady Spenser had been bartered away long ago.

Hurriedly, she donned the billowing turquoise watered silk, tying a scarlet ribbon around her narrow waist. She weighed ten pounds less than she had when Aaron had seen her last.

There was no time to loosen the thick chignon and run a comb through her long brown hair and tie ribbons in it. A lace-edged linen kerchief would have to do. After all, she was a matron now, and should look the part.

An hour later, Rumor stood on the wharf, chewing absently on a raisin cake. The feast was over, the children who were not sick from excitement and overeating were in bed. A weary Sue had carried an even more exhausted George David up to the house. The boy had struggled against weeping for disappointment that his father had not been on the boat.

"Next time," he said brightly as he kissed her good

440

night. "Don't cry, Mama."

Such a brave young man, she thought proudly. Even at three, the child could sense her own disappointment.

The older folks wandering off to bed, the younger ones lingered round the fire. Some of the seamen were spinning wild tales of their adventures.

Tomorrow, in the daylight, the unloading and loading would take place. That meant more excitement. Caesar was busy with the plowing, and she would have to take his place at the unloading, making sure that the goods they had ordered were in order.

The night was warm and fine with a southerly wind. The sky was clear, the moon was high. Someone at the fire was strumming a Spanish guitar and soon the marvelous sound of young voices resounded in popular tunes of the day. "Yankee Doodle went to town, a-riding on a pony . . ." and the ever haunting "Barbara Allen."

The boat rocked gently at its moorings. Its furled sails were ghostly in the moonlight. A sailor waved and called, "Best get in, ma'am, you'll catch your death."

Reluctantly, Rumor turned. The man was right. She could not afford to be sick. So much depended on her.

Her long nap this afternoon had left her wide awake. She might join the singers round the fire. She had a good, strong alto and a natural sense of harmony.

But as she neared the bonfire, the singing suddenly trailed off. Voices were raised in excitement. Someone called out gaily, "Mrs. Fleming, you have a visitor."

Aaron! Her heart stopped then began to race. Could it be? Dare she hope?

Tall as ever, and dressed in buckskin, he came down the road along the river. He was astride a large bay mare. Trailing behind him was what seemed at first a

441

herd of horses, but turned out to be two sturdy plow horses, a carriage mare, and a fetlocked pony.

The pony was for George David, he said as they went into the house. All were gifts of Martha Washington, whose husband was still in the North, endeavoring to chase the British from New York.

He had still not kissed her, severely disappointing the romantic group at the fire. He was too dirty, he said almost truculently, and much too hungry to do the thing properly.

"Especially with everyone gawking at us," he grinned.

After a hearty supper of roast boar and coffee in the kitchen, Aaron bathed in the river, lathering himself with the strong yellow soap she herself had boiled up in the outdoor kettle last August.

Finally, at midnight, they were alone, lying side by side in his mother's bed. Expecting to spend the rest of the night making love, Rumor had left off her muslin nightshift.

When he turned to take her in his arms, she held back teasingly. She would give him a dose of his own delaying medicine.

"Aaron, we've got to talk," she said. "I can't concentrate on anything until we settle where we are to live. Will it be here, or Golden Hill, or maybe the Ohio country?"

"Anywhere you like, sweet," he answered quietly. Then rising up on one elbow, he soberly regarded her by the light of the moon through the tall window. He did not touch her, nor did she dare reach out to him. It was almost as if they were afraid to touch each other. Perhaps it was all a dream, and there would be nothing there but vapor and illusions.

After a long time, he sighed. "Woman, you're far too skinny. There's hardly enough of you to fill a man's arms."

Boldly, as she used to do, she moved up and over to slide onto his long, sinewy body.

"Well, then," she giggled, "we'll have to do the best we can with what's here, won't we?"

Kissing him on the mouth with vigor, she spread her thighs wide apart to encompass his hard hips within her slender body.

Groaning mightily, he flung his arms round her and pressed her hard against him so that their bodies touched at every inch. His flesh was hard and firm, and hers responded wildly, every nerve and fiber tingling.

"No doubt about it," he muttered, "it's really you and me in the flesh."

The soldier had definitely come home from war.

Now you can get more of HEARTFIRE right at home and $ave.

Preview
Four Brand New
ZEBRA
Heartfire
Romance Novels...

FREE for 10 days.

No Obligation and No Strings Attached!

♥

Enjoy all of the passion and fiery romance as you soar back through history, right in the comfort of your own home.

Now that you have read a Zebra HEARTFIRE Romance novel, we're sure you'll agree that HEARTFIRE sets new standards of excellence for historical romantic fiction. Each Zebra HEARTFIRE novel is the ultimate blend of intimate romance and grand adventure and each takes place in the kinds of historical settings you want most...the American Revolution, the Old West, Civil War and more.

<u>FREE</u> Preview Each Month and $ave

Zebra has made arrangements for you to preview 4 brand new HEARTFIRE novels each month...FREE for 10 days. You'll get them as soon as they are published. If you are not delighted with any of them, just return them with no questions asked. But if you decide these are everything we said they are, you'll pay just $3.25 each—a total of $13.00 (a $15.00 value). **That's a $2.00 saving each month off the regular price.** Plus there is NO shipping or handling charge. These are delivered right to your door absolutely free! There is no obligation and there is no minimum number of books to buy.

TO GET YOUR FIRST MONTH'S PREVIEW... Mail the Coupon Below!